Sûr

The Tale of the Cycle

Murat Karagoz

DEDICATION

This book is dedicated to my dear grandmother, Zülfiye Karagöz, who has raised me since my childhood, guided me in many aspects, been an absolute source of inspiration, and played a significant role in the narrative of my story.

Her love and wisdom have touched every word in these pages, shaping the characters within. This book is not just a story; it is a reflection of my grandmother's life. Carrying her name adds depth and meaning to every word written in these pages.

With respect, love, and gratitude.

Murat Karagoz

CONTENTS

ACKNOWLEDGMENTS

As I stand at the brink of introducing "Sûr" to the world, my heart overflows with gratitude for the incredible individuals who have played a crucial role in shaping this journey. Writing this book has been a labour of love, and I am profoundly thankful for the unwavering support and encouragement that has accompanied me throughout.

First and foremost, my deepest appreciation goes to my family and friends. Your constant support has been my anchor through the highs and lows of the creative process. It is your encouragement that laid the foundation upon which the story of "Sûr" was constructed.

To all those who believed in the enchantment of storytelling, I extend my sincere thanks for being a part of this adventure. "Sûr" wouldn't be the same without your influence and unwavering support.

Last but certainly not least, I want to express my heartfelt gratitude to the readers. Your curiosity and willingness to embark on this literary journey mean the world to me.

Thank you all for being an integral part of this significant chapter in my life.

Murat Karagoz

CHAPTER 1

FORTUNE

Çarh, a man entrenched in the shadows of despair, sought solace in the bottom of a bottle, his refuge in the emptiness of life. The cruel twists of fate had worn him down, draining his energy and leaving him adrift in a sea of hopelessness. Lost in the perpetual haze of alcohol, he stumbled forward, memories of a forsaken past slipping away like grains of sand through his desperate fingers.

In the darkest depths of his life, Çarh found himself standing on the precipice, his strength depleted, and his spirit broken. Despair shrouded him, and the future seemed an abyss. Yet, a vision bloomed in that desperate moment. The sun, casting warm hues on a sandy beach, the salty embrace of the sea – a fantasy that became the fragile thread he clung to in the void of his existence.

That night, an insistent yearning propelled Çarh toward the beach, where the promise of a sunrise awaited. In his inebriated state, the journey became a disjointed dance of confusion. He staggered through the streets, each step uncertain on the uneven pavement. The night air carried a mix of salt and alcohol, a disorienting concoction that clouded his senses.

Lifting his head and following the distant glow of the sun, he turned left and right at random street corners. The city sprawled around him, a labyrinth of shadows and flickering streetlights. His feet moved with a mind of their own, guided by instinct more than conscious choice.

Amidst the aimless journey, internal turmoil churned within Çarh. Did he truly know where he was going, or was it a desperate attempt to escape the darkness that clung to him? The dissonance between his aimless steps and the purposeful yearning for the sunrise mirrored the conflicting forces battling within him.

Çarh, much like everyone else, cherished the warmth of the sun. Yet, for him, the sun held a special significance, a source of solace he desperately sought in the depths of darkness. Just a few months ago, he would descend from Sıraselviler and find respite in Sanatkârlar Park, bathed in the sun's radiant glow. The dazzling brightness, though blinding to others, was a pleasure beyond description for him.

In those sunlit moments, Çarh felt an inexplicable joy, as if the sun could momentarily dispel the shadows that haunted him. Unlike those who sought refuge in the shade, Çarh deliberately exposed himself to the sun's intense glare. There were days when its brilliance obscured his vision, causing him to stumble and fall, yet he revelled in the beauty of the sensation. And now, in the darkness, he yearned to experience that overwhelming brightness once more, a distant memory of a time when the sun held the promise of a brighter future.

Sûr

Now living in the realm of nights, Çarh completed his daytime chores in a state of quiet anticipation. Each passing hour felt like an eternity, and the seconds dragged on as if measured by the solemn ticking of an ancient pendulum wall clock that echoed through the house. In the long stretches of silence, he would mutter, almost in a whisper, 'What a life!' with a melancholic undertone, a phrase weighted with the heaviness of his existence.

Lately, he found himself navigating the silent streets of Istanbul during the nocturnal hours. His presence seemed to carry a silent protest against the city, as if he bore a grudge against its every alley and corner. His movements, akin to a horse running at full speed without a clear destination, mirrored a sense of helplessness and directionlessness that lingered in the night air.

The city, usually teeming with life, now stood silent and solitary in the embrace of darkness, a backdrop to Çarh's wandering contemplation.

As Çarh walked the streets, a sea of expressions mirrored the diverse emotions of those around him – tiredness, sadness, urgency. Yet, his own countenance seemed to cast a shadow, evoking a unique response. Some passersby attempted fleeting eye contact, while others deliberately averted their gaze. The depth of sorrow etched on his face, however, transcended the ordinary. It left an imprint on those who encountered him, sparking speculation about the source of his melancholy.

Observers speculated on the cause of Çarh's profound unhappiness. Some thought it might be rooted in a past loss, while others believed it was the weight of life's hardships bearing down on him. Amidst the sea of empathy and curiosity, Çarh, sensing the hunger within those gazes, chose a unique defence mechanism – he adorned himself with a mask of perpetual sadness. Convinced that every glance aimed his way harboured the hunger of unseen wolves, he embraced this facade, using it as a shield for his own security.

Behind the mask, Çarh navigated the streets, caught in a delicate dance between the authenticity of his emotions and the necessity of self-preservation.

The streets, a chaotic tapestry of disorder, elicited a dreadful feeling within Çarh. The narrow paths seemed to swallow him whole, leaving him adrift in the complexity of the labyrinthine streets. The disarray heightened his anxieties, casting a looming shadow over life's uncertainties. Each step through the seemingly endless maze brought forth dark thoughts, as if unexpected dangers lurked at every corner. Lost in this disordered chaos, Çarh felt unsafe and vulnerable, the streets becoming a metaphorical manifestation of his internal turmoil.

As he turned corners, the unpredictability of the streets unfolded before him. The darkness of the night further obscured the nature of his surroundings, intensifying the feeling of navigating an enigmatic landscape. At midnight, the streets echoed with a cacophony of rapid and incessant chatter. Men, women, children, and even street cats contributed to the symphony, their voices intertwining in a chaotic narrative that rendered everything incomprehensible. Each voice seemed to narrate its own story, leaving Çarh immersed in a world of shared but indecipherable thoughts.

Amidst the crowded group on the street, Çarh harboured a desire to listen to the conversations around him. However, the pervasive feeling of alienation weighed heavily on him, preventing him from recognizing his own value within the dynamic tapestry of voices. It was as if he couldn't comprehend their language, rendering him a stranger in the midst of a bustling street and inducing a deep sense of loneliness. The loud crowd, speaking in an unintelligible tongue, served only to distance him further from the shared human experience.

Undeterred, Çarh continued to walk with determined steps, each footfall a poignant reminder that he existed in the tangible world. As he moved forward, the impact of his feet meeting the ground served as a grounding force, reconnecting him with reality. The cacophony of people's conversations, the hum of vehicles, and the rhythmic breathing of the streets gradually became more pronounced. Each sound and smell became a reminder that, despite the initial sense of alienation, he was an integral part of this world too.

With each step, Çarh felt a burgeoning confidence, a quiet assurance that he could navigate the obstacles ahead. The anticipation of potential unpleasant surprises gradually dissolved the lingering fear within him. As his feet carried him forward, the oppressive impact of loneliness waned, replaced by a newfound sense of companionship born from the solace of self-talk.

Unfazed by the uncertainty lurking around each corner, Çarh found strength in the knowledge that he could handle whatever awaited him on his journey. His determined steps echoed not just in the physical world but also in the evolving landscape of his emotions. Talking to himself became a comforting ritual, creating a silent alliance against the solitude that once gripped him.

The unknown, instead of instilling trepidation, became a source of freedom, courage, and discovery. With unwavering determination, Çarh turned corners with an eagerness to confront whatever lay ahead. The feelings of liberation and the thrill of exploration became his companions, guiding him through the uncharted territories of his own journey.

Uncertain whether he was walking too slowly or if time itself had slowed down, Çarh felt the unrelenting weight of exhaustion settle with each step. The end of the street stretched endlessly, a constant ascent, either climbing a hill or ascending an unending staircase. Despite the desire to quicken his pace, he found himself trapped in a sluggish rhythm, the fatigue clinging to him like an oppressive weight. The destination remained elusive, but he pressed on, yearning to maintain some semblance of forward motion, if only to progress.

In the course of his continuing journey, the monotony was interrupted by a scene at a street corner. Two figures engaged in a heated argument, their voices escalating, making it challenging for Çarh to discern the topic of their dispute. Sharp glances and tension hung in the air, unsettling him. An instinctive unease prompted a desire to distance himself from the brewing conflict, yet without a clear direction to escape, he stood there, caught between the uncertainty of the argument and the ambiguity of his own path.

As Çarh continued his journey, he couldn't help but notice a hooded figure in the vicinity. The man, sensing Çarh's presence, seemed to be saying something, addressing him directly. However, the words were muffled, impossible to understand. In that moment, a creeping suspicion took root, prompting Çarh to take a cautious step back. The hooded man's intentions remained shrouded in uncertainty, his words unintelligible.

As doubt lingered, Çarh wrestled with conflicting thoughts. Was it a genuine attempt at communication, or just an illusion woven by the shadows? The unease settled in, urging him to quickly distance himself from the scene. Every detail heightened his awareness – the hood concealing the man's features, the indistinct murmurs that hinted at hidden intentions. With a sense of urgency, Çarh retraced his steps, leaving the enigma of the hooded man behind in the darkened streets.

"Please, can you help me?"

He momentarily hesitated at the hooded man's call, but to maintain his pace, he staggered forward, taking another step. When he turned back to see who the calling man was, the hood still concealed his face. The hooded man called out again, this time closer:

"Can you help me, please?"

Çarh asked cautiously, "Excuse me, did you call me?" As he turned back, the other man replied,

"No one's calling you. Mind your own business!"

Çarh, feeling a bit uneasy, took a step back. "I should mind my own business," he muttered to himself, then continued his internal turmoil. What was my business? What work was I doing? Why was I even here? The same voice echoed in his mind again.

"Please, help!"

Experiencing an internal struggle, Çarh, thought on one hand, "Don't get involved," while on the other hand, believed that intervening in the situation was the right thing to do. He believed in people helping each other, and therefore, he wanted to take action. However, he had to make this decision, and he wasn't sure what would happen afterward.

His mind was so muddled that his thoughts were tangled. Countless thoughts raced through his mind, and he wasn't in a state to do anything worthwhile. He decided it would be good to stop and gather his thoughts. He felt everything around him slowing down, as if time had come to a halt. But at the same time, the growing sense of unease within him was increasing. He needed to pull himself together, evaluate the situation, and take necessary steps.

He slowly raised his head and saw the sun shining in all its glory. Under the dazzling light that blinded his eyes, he felt as if he were losing himself. The energy of the sun flowed into his soul, giving him a sense of strength. He could feel something awakening within him. He felt reborn, overflowing with a sensation he had never experienced before. For a moment, he hesitated, but then gathering his courage, he stepped forward and intervened in the situation.

"Is there a problem?" he said, projecting his courage. The other man replied,

"Don't look for trouble; you're already drunk. You'll get what's coming to you, I'm telling you! Just leave."

No lies, he hesitated and took a step back. But the excitement within him couldn't be stopped, and he wanted to intervene in the situation as soon as possible. Approaching the man in front of him, he took two steps forward and grabbed the other man's arm. As the feeling of fear slowly gave way to courage, curiosity swelled within him. He wanted to ask, "Is there a problem?" but couldn't bring himself to speak. He struggled to understand the expression on the other man's face but waited to find out what was happening.

He thought the other man looked quite muscular and strong for his age. He was a middle-aged man with grey in his hair and beard, about Çarh's height. Although he couldn't see the hooded man clearly, he could sense how tall he was and guessed that his body was almost the same size as his own. The hooded man had a mysterious expression, perhaps the shadow on his face making him even more mysterious. But Çarh's feelings were so strong that he could no longer remain silent.

As he tried to understand the meaning of the hooded man's words, the situation became more complicated when the other man pushed him. Çarh, determined each time he rose, tried to keep the hooded man away from the other man. However, he struggled against the strong build of the other man. With each push, he moved further backward.

Each time Çarh fell, he saw the sun once again. With each rise, he became equally stronger. With determination, he ran towards the other man with all his might. He leaped onto him.

Çarh hit the ground with the impact. His head was spinning slightly, and although he felt the pain, he didn't give up. He slowly stood up and began to walk towards the other man. This time, he was more prepared. Step by step, he approached and swiftly kicked the other man's leg. The other man lost balance and fell to the ground.

At that moment, the hood of the hooded man opened, revealing a shadow in the darkness. The shadow caught Çarh's attention. Slowly approaching and examining the shadow, before he could say, "What's this..." he received a hefty punch from the other man.

When he woke up in the morning, he found himself lying on the ground. It was likely that someone had covered him during the night because there was a blanket on him. His head was pounding, and he didn't even want to open his eyes. He sat up and attempted to walk. His legs weren't cooperating; they were swaying. Thoughts of the hooded man and the other man crossed his mind. What had happened last night? Who had left him on the ground? Where would he go now? Questions piled up in his head. He took a deep breath and continued walking.

He tried to explore his surroundings carefully, looking around. His memory was slowly coming back. He tried to recall what had happened during the night. However, his mind was still foggy. At that moment, someone approached him, making eye contact. The person was slender, and their expression was curious.

The person asked, "Are you okay?"

"Yes, I'm fine. I just don't remember last night. What am I doing here, and what happened?"

"I think you had a bit too much fun last night. You were lying unconscious on the street. I brought you here. If you can't remember anything else, maybe you need more rest."

Çarh thanked him and continued walking around. He was trying to remember last night, but everything was fragmented. As he looked around more closely, he realised he was in Tarlabası. He added more confusion to his already complex thoughts. "When and how did I get here? What was I doing here?"

As he navigated through the lively street and sounds, he slowly began to recall last night. He was very drunk, and as he walked home from the bar, he confused the streets and found himself in Tarlabası.

Walking toward his home amidst the historic buildings of Tarlabası, the crowded surroundings helped him remember that he got involved in a fight last night. Although not very clear, he somehow knew he had participated in the brawl. There were a few blurry memories in his mind; a confrontation, shouting, punches, and maybe him falling. But he couldn't remember exactly what happened. When he found himself in the narrow streets of Tarlabası, his head was still fuzzy, and his body ached. Nevertheless, his resilient spirit prompted him to take action, and he began analysing the events of last night to figure out what had really happened.

After turning the corner, he suddenly collided with a hooded man. "Look where you're going, buddy, for goodness' sake!" He quickly apologised, but then a lightning bolt struck his mind, and he remembered that there was a hooded man among those involved in the fight last night. The image of the shadow he saw in the darkness and the punch that followed flashed in his mind. He paused for a moment, pondering what had happened that night.

Who was that person, he wondered. He tried to recall the strange appearance of the person he had fought with last night. As far as he could remember, they were of similar height, but there seemed to be something on top of their head, covered with a hood. He closed his eyes, attempting to remember, but the uncertainty gnawing at his mind prevented a conclusive recollection. "Anyway," he thought to himself, "overthinking this won't do any good." Accepting the ominous feeling, he continued walking.

As he passed through Taksim Square, he decided to grab a coffee at a corner to shake off some fatigue. The aroma of coffee filled the air as he approached Cihangir. There were many cafes and restaurants around, but he headed towards the small coffee shop on the corner, only in need of a coffee.

While waiting for the coffee to be ready, Çarh took out his phone and noticed no missed calls or messages. Unsurprised, as he wasn't in frequent contact with many people. Sitting at a table next to the shop, he went in and out of a few apps, not wanting to waste his time.

Browsing through his phone, Çarh observed the lives of people he followed. However, he also sought answers to the questions he directed at himself. Watching the lives of those, he wondered how genuinely happy they were. Yet, he couldn't be sure if they were truly happy because there was a high likelihood that what was shared on social media might not align with reality. Were the people he followed genuinely happy, or were they just living a fake life?

Engaging with these thoughts, Çarh was simultaneously reflecting on his own life. Was he truly happy? Was there something else he desired from this existence? He began delving deep into his emotions to find answers to these questions. He wasn't sure how accurately digital interactions on platforms like social media reflected the real lives of people. He often thought that individuals shared aspects of a life that weren't genuinely theirs, merely to present themselves in a positive light.

In the midst of these thoughts, the barista interrupted, asking,

"Would you like anything else?" Involuntarily, Çarh responded,

"Another life?"

The barista looked surprised and then smiled.

"We all think about that," she continued, looking into his eyes lost in the void, "But, in reality, we don't exactly know what we want, do we? Perhaps what we desire is already present in this life, and we're just not aware of it. Or maybe true happiness is found somewhere else, who knows."

These words somewhat dispersed Çarh's thoughts. The barista prepared his coffee and handed it to him. Çarh thanked her and continued walking through the streets of Cihangir. On the way, the barista's words lingered in his mind. Perhaps there truly was a place to search for happiness. Maybe this quest was a reminder of what truly mattered to him.

It was 10 minutes to 9 o'clock.

Çarh tasted his coffee and sighed. The place of coffee

20

in his morning routine was always special. Having a strong coffee before a sweet breakfast prepared him for the day, making him feel energised. The energy enveloping his entire body with the first sip motivated him. The aroma of his coffee was so enticing that with each sip, he felt like he was discovering a new flavour. As the warmth slowly spread across his palate, the clouds in his mind dissipated. These moments made him feel better throughout the rest of the day.

In the early hours of the morning, the bustling activity of so many people surprised him. Despite living in one of the busiest areas of Istanbul, this chaos always managed to astound him.

Just as he was about to turn the corner, he snapped back to reality with the harsh words of a man trying to pass by him. "Move, brother! What are you standing around for so early in the morning?" He continued walking without feeling unperturbed, but within himself, he pondered, "Why do people treat each other so rudely?"

As he turned the corner and continued walking towards his home, he observed the expressions on the faces of people he encountered. Some were happy, some sad, and some appeared hurried. There were many people lost in the complexities of life. These thoughts saddened him, and a sense of pessimism crept over him. He, however, approached his home undeterred.

It was 5 minutes to 9 o'clock.

The feeling of tranquillity he experienced when he reached the front of the apartment building embraced him. The white-painted walls of the building, the green garden, and the flowers together created a magnificent scene. The gentle breeze from the leaves of the trees gave him a sense of freshness. In this peaceful environment, even if only for a short while, he could clear his mind. The warm emotions helped him escape the stress he was under and dispersed the dark clouds in his mind. Therefore, being in front of the apartment always held a special meaning for him.

He tried to recall the events of the previous night, but all he could find in his mind was a strange void. Perhaps he had been overthinking throughout the night, and his mind was fatigued. However, the peculiar feeling within him suggested that something had changed. This feeling of being different might be a sign that he wasn't content with his life. He felt the need to do something new, to explore. He, however, didn't know what to do or how to do it. The strange feeling in his stomach was a reflection of this need, and it was giving him the courage to make a change.

As the apartment door creaked open, Çarh saw Aunt Zülfiye standing on the second floor, who always reminded him of his own grandmother, started descending the stairs with a bag in her hand. Whenever Çarh noticed her, the peculiar feeling inside him intensified. He greeted her with a smile, and for a brief moment, he paused and looked into her eyes, then he noticed a change in her gaze. A moment of silence followed, and then she smiled again, "Çarh, how are you, my dear?"

Noticing a hint of sadness and concern in her eyes, Çarh felt a sense of unease. "I'm good, Aunt Zülfiye, I hope you're well too."

As Aunt Zülfiye had taken a step behind Çarh, she turned round, lightly touched his shoulder, and then raised her hand to confirm that she was indeed doing well and continued walking.

Taking a relieved breath after Aunt Zülfiye confirmed her well-being, Çarh felt a mix of tranquillity and concern.

Çarh knew almost everyone living in the apartment, just

Sûr

like Aunt Zülfiye. The building was a classic 6-story art deco structure, reflecting the architectural style of Cihangir houses. The entrance door was wide, opening into a high-ceilinged hall that welcomed residents. The hall was dominated by the warm scents of coffee and fresh bread. On the right side, individually crafted mailboxes hung on the wall. Beneath the mailboxes, various pots of different sizes and types adorned the area. Directly across from the entrance, there was an old elevator in the middle of the spiral staircase. Although slow and antique, the apartment's elevator still served its purpose.

Aunt Zülfiye was one of the most orderly and meticulous among the residents of the building. She would check the mailboxes at least once a day and occasionally clean the accumulating dust. Every morning, she would start her day with a slight smile on her face, take her fresh tea and head towards the mailbox. She held a respectable place among the residents of the building. No one wanted to argue or fight with her. Moreover, she was one of the favourite persons among the children living in the building. She spent time with them, told stories, and played various games.

Çarh truly felt a deep affection for Aunt Zülfiye. Her warmth, sweet words, and cheerful demeanour had an impact. Most of the residents loved and respected her, and Çarh enjoyed chatting with her whenever possible. Having coffee at her house was a special pleasure. They would gather every day at 3 p.m. and discuss daily life. She shared memories from her past, and Çarh listened with admiration. Sipping their coffee and enjoying the conversation was a unique delight for Çarh.

As Çarh entered through the front door, he took in the atmosphere of the building, feeling a sense of tranquillity. While checking the mailbox, he was startled by the sweet voice of Aunt Hacer. After turning around and greeting her, he heard her request and used his key to open the mailbox. A letter came out, and he handed it to her. She thanked him, and closed her door, and Çarh began dusting off his mailbox with a smile. In that moment, he thought about Aunt Zülfiye and continued cleaning the mailboxes, "Aunt Zülfiye must have cleaned it for sure."

On the ground floor, a young couple lived with Aunt Hacer. She had lost her husband years ago and was a somewhat introverted person living alone with two children in her fifties. She mostly enjoyed spending time at home, rarely going out, and avoiding interactions with other residents. She, however, felt safe like other residents thanks to the peaceful and warm atmosphere of the building.

The arrival of the young couple had stirred excitement among the residents of the apartment. Since the majority of the residents were generally elderly, they had brought a sense of vitality. In the early days, the young couple didn't have much connection with the apartment; they would only salute and make eye contact. The man, a programmer, often worked from home, a detail not unnoticed by the residents. The woman worked at a school and usually came home late. As a couple immersed in their own world, they hadn't become particularly close to the other residents.

Çarh was surprised when he noticed that Aunt Zülfiye hadn't collected her electricity bill. Normally, she would retrieve it as soon as it arrived in the mailbox. Çarh took the bill and headed upstairs to attach it to her door.

It was 4 minutes to 9 o'clock.

The elderly couple living in the opposite apartment on the second floor were among Aunt Zülfiye's closest friends. Despite living in France, they visited Istanbul every summer and stayed in their apartment. Aunt Zülfiye always warmly welcomed them, prepared their favourite meals, and spent time with them.

As Çarh attached Aunt Zülfiye's electricity bill to the door, he felt a pleasant warmth. The memory she often shared instantly came to his mind. "She used to have a restaurant in Cihangir, and everyone called her 'sister'. The establishment was even known as 'Sister's Restaurant.'"

Before going up to the third floor, Çarh picked up the shoes in front of Aunt Zülfiye's door and placed them inside the shoe cabinet.

It was 3 minutes to 9 o'clock.

The third floor, where Melis and Zeynep lived, was quieter and calmer compared to the other floors. Melis, a lonely woman with an architecture degree, continued her life here. She didn't know many of the residents, but everyone respected her. Living a quiet and modest life, Melis's only companion was her cat. While she cultivated flowers in the apartment's balcony pots, her cat would sleep beside her, keeping her company.

Melis had noticed that Çarh was lonely and unhappy. That's why she always treated him kindly and understandingly. Whenever she saw him, she would show interest, inquire about his well-being, and try to uplift his spirits. Çarh appreciated Melis's attention in turn and felt understood.

On the other hand, Zeynep had a completely different character than Melis. She was energetic, talkative, and social. Using her home as an office created constant activity in the apartment. Zeynep's cats were also elements disrupting the silence of the building. However, Çarh enjoyed Zeynep's lively lifestyle, finding it different from other neighbours. Zeynep's move to the apartment had been a unique experience for Melis. Although Melis struggled to adapt to Zeynep's noisy and dynamic lifestyle, Zeynep's positive energy added some colour to Melis's life.

Passing by the third floor, Çarh, who usually felt more alive, noticed an increased restlessness within her as he passed in front of Melis's apartment this time.

It was 2 minutes to 9 o'clock.

On the fourth floor, Çarh and a different stranger stayed in the other apartment every day by renting through an application. The tenants changed constantly, and no one knew who would come and when. This situation created a kind of discomfort among the residents.

Once, one of the daily tenants had started disturbing the apartment residents by playing loud music late at night. Such issues rarely occurred in the building, so the other residents quickly alerted Çarh to the situation. Çarh promptly intervened, warning the tenant in the opposite apartment, and asking them to lower the volume.

It was 1 minute to 9 o'clock.

Aunt Fatma was one of the oldest residents of the neighbourhood and the building. She usually led a quiet life, but in the spring months, she would take care of flowers on her balcony and water the plants in the apartment garden. Before going for her morning walk, she never forgot to leave a handful of birdseed in front of her house.

On the fifth floor, her daughter Nihal lived along with Aunt Fatma. Nihal was a young woman who had gotten married two years ago. She frequently visited her mother and had coffee with her. Although Aunt Fatma didn't talk much about Nihal's husband, it was evident that she thought well of him.

On the sixth floor, Aunt Fatma's sons Kerim and Onur lived. Both had two sons each and were the only children in the building. They played ball continuously, sometimes causing discomfort to other residents. However, the joy of the children brought liveliness to the building and made other residents smile, including Aunt Fatma.

It was 9 o'clock.

Çarh turned the key and entered his home. It was quiet inside, and he wanted to start working as soon as possible. However, he found himself frozen at the entrance. He was thinking about the events of the night, grappling with myriad questions in his mind. Slowly, he entered his living room, feeling the warmth. He quickly sat at his computer, attempting to focus on his work, but his mind was still there. Before long, his phone rang.

"Good morning, Çarh," said a voice eager to get straight to the point.

"Are you coming to the meeting? We've started, and we're waiting for you."

Çarh replied, "Sorry, I'm coming," and hung up.

He quickly opened his computer and joined the meeting. Despite being present in the meeting, he couldn't shake off the influence of his thoughts. He wanted to understand who the hooded man he encountered last night was and why he was attacked. He was curious about what exactly happened that night. Throughout the meeting, Çarh listened to the discussions and occasionally responded, but he couldn't fully concentrate. His thoughts were occupied with figuring out the identity of that hooded man. When the meeting was finally over, Çarh got up from his computer in a huff.

He slumped into the chair, closing his eyes for a long while. The events of last night, the hooded man, and work stress had drained him. He took a deep breath and opened his eyes. To organize the chaos in his mind, he took a few more deep breaths and focused; however, the face of the hooded man still lingered vaguely in his mind. He shook his head, trying to rid himself of these thoughts, but there was an uneasiness within. Thinking that he needed some time to pull himself together, he leaned back in the chair, closing his eyes.

Walking through the dark streets of Tarlabası, Çarh glanced around anxiously. He was determined to find the hooded man, but he had no idea where he could be. As the discomfort and curiosity within him grew, he quickened his pace. His thoughts were jumbled, and his heart was beating fast. The streets were empty, everything was silent. Çarh only heard the sound of his own footsteps breaking the silence. The gentle breeze of the wind was swirling around him, accompanied by the rustle of leaves. Suddenly, he noticed something; a man walking on the street lowered his hood and looked directly at his face. His heart started beating rapidly. Even though the man's face was pitch black, Çarh thought he recognized him.

"Is it you?" he asked, and the man slowly nodded. A sense of relief washed over Çarh; he had finally found the hooded man. What could be the man's intention, what did he want? He wanted answers to the questions in his mind.

However, the man remained silent. Çarh took a step towards him, but he began to run away. He chased after him, but the man's speed was considerable. Eventually, Çarh gave up exhausted from the pursuit.

After a tiring chase, Çarh returned to the starting point. The dark streets continued to surround him with their silence and eerie atmosphere. Çarh then suddenly opened his eyes and looked around. Where was he? What was happening? He realised all the experiences that felt so real were actually just a dream.

Sûr

Çarh first shook his head to snap out of it. He rubbed his eyes, and when he opened them again, the thought that everything around him could be a dream dominated his mind. But at that moment, he felt his eyes, which were once deep blue, change suddenly. His pupils dilated, and his irises contracted. Çarh looked at himself in the mirror in astonishment. This change in eye colour was a sign that he was now a witch.

Taking a deep breath, he tried to pull himself together. The influence of the dream was still on him, and distinguishing between reality and the dream was proving difficult. He threw himself back into the chair and closed his eyes.

He tried to remember the face of the hooded man in his dream, but unfortunately, the face was blurry and unclear. At that moment, he wondered about the meaning of this dream he had just experienced. Why had he had such a realistic and detailed dream? Perhaps there was an unresolved issue or concern in his mind, and his dream was attempting to solve that problem. Trying to reassure himself, he took another deep breath and attempted to shake off the effects of the dream. Losing the perception of reality through the dream, Çarh began questioning the reality of his own existence. Were things around him still real? The events he experienced started to blur in his mind.

Doubts about whether everything around him was still real or not lingered in Çarh's mind as he questioned the reality of his own existence. To pull himself out of this situation, he looked around and saw many objects that seemed normal. However, the uncertainty in his mind was increasing simultaneously.

At that moment, he heard a voice saying, "Don't worry,

everything is real." Çarh suddenly turned around, but there was no one. Sensing the voice as if he had heard it, intensified his fear even more.

"What was that?" he muttered to himself, visibly frightened. He, however, felt that something had changed in his mind. He suddenly realised something; his eye colour had indeed changed. As he checked himself in the mirror, he noticed that instead of his deep blue eyes, a pair of green eyes were now watching him.

CHAPTER 2

DEVASTATED

Çarh had woken up early on a warm summer day. Despite the sun not having risen yet, he was already starting to sweat. The temperature would rise even more in a few hours. He decided to get ready and go outside. After a two-hour walk that left him feeling tired, he arrived at a park. The greenery and cool air of the park provided comfort to Çarh. He sat on a bench, took a few deep breaths, and began to look around.

There was no one in the park. Çarh had chosen this place because of its tranquillity and peace. Sitting on the bench, he felt a gentle breeze along with the warmth of the sun. He closed his eyes and took a deep breath, calming his mind like the waves hitting the shore.

Çarh suddenly sensed a presence, like a wave. As he opened his eyes, he noticed a woman sitting on the bench next to him. The woman, middle-aged, was wearing a simple yet elegant dress. He had never seen her before.

"Hi, I saw you in my dream. That's why I wanted to

meet you," said the woman with a smile.

Çarh looked at her in astonishment. Meeting someone in a dream was quite peculiar. The woman continued, "My name is Deka. Do you often come here?"

Çarh replied with a bewildered stare, "Yes, I spend time here frequently. My name is Çarh."

"A beautiful name. Are you seeking your own peace here?" said Deka.

Trying to ease his surprise with a smile, Çarh answered, "Yes, a bit. I find silence and peace here," he cleared his throat, "Your name is beautiful too."

"Thank you. I'm here for the same reason. I'm glad I saw you in my dream. Maybe we'll meet here again someday," said Deka and stood up with a smile.

As Çarh watched her leave, he was still in a state of bewilderment. What a strange experience it was. But Deka's smile and warmth had created a pleasant feeling in his heart.

He had thought about that woman all day. The woman who sat beside him in the park had given him a strange and unsettling feeling. Despite Deka having a beautiful face, Çarh felt that something was off. Perhaps it was just his paranoia, but he still felt uneasy. Deka's eyes, her voice, and the intriguing necklace she wore lingered in his mind.

He kept walking and thinking. Perhaps that strange feeling was an energy emitted by Deka, a moment where opposing emotions were in a delicate balance. Or was it just a product of his imagination? Çarh was lost in his thoughts, feeling trapped once again between reality and dream.

For the next few days, waking up early and going to the park became Çarh's new routine. Every time he opened his eyes, he thought of Deka and eagerly anticipated seeing her again.

Sûr

The park's tranquillity and peace helped him gather his thoughts. He searched the entire park step by step to find Deka. Throughout the day, he passed by perhaps hundreds of people, but none resembled Deka. A bit sad but not losing hope, he sat in the same place every day, believing that Deka might miraculously appear before him.

As days went by, Çarh didn't give up on going to the park and searching for Deka. Every morning, he went to the park, spending the entire day looking for any sign of Deka. Unfortunately, there was no trace of her each time.

Çarh decided to walk through the park one more time without succumbing to despair. He carefully examined his surroundings this time, and suddenly his eyes caught a dog behind the benches. The woman standing next to the dog was none other than Deka.

Çarh ran towards Deka and quickly introduced himself. However, the look of surprise on Deka's face heightened Çarh's concerns. What she said next shocked him.

"I'm very sorry; I couldn't recognise you," said Deka.

Çarh was in a mood of trying to understand, then asked, "What do you mean? You couldn't get me out?"

Deka replied, "Yes, unfortunately. I don't know you."

"How is that possible?" muttered Çarh, with a bewildered and confused stare.

Deka couldn't hear exactly what Çarh said. "Did you say something?"

"No, I'm sorry. Please excuse me. Have a good day," said Çarh and quickly walked away.

After the encounter with Deka, Çarh couldn't relax. The impact of that moment lingered in his mind, and he had no idea what to do. He slowed down a few times before going home, trying to stop and think, but couldn't come to a conclusion.

The next day, passing through the same area, he saw Deka again. This time, he didn't get as excited as before; he just passed by with a faint smile. However, after taking a few steps, he stopped and turned back to Deka.

"Hello, I'm Çarh. I apologise for yesterday; there was a misunderstanding. I wanted to apologise again," said Çarh.

The bewilderment on Deka's face indicated that she was so distant from the topic. "It's not a problem for us,"

Çarh suddenly confused, then asked, "When you say 'us'?"

"Sorry, I mean for me," said Deka and smiled. "See you later," she continued on her way.

Çarh stood there frozen. Were the events of yesterday, the days before, and today real, or just a dream? His confidence was shaken, and he couldn't fully comprehend what had happened. But his mind remained in the reality of those experiences, he wasn't sure if the events were still real. Lost in the crowd, he kept overthinking as he walked away. Perhaps all these experiences were a message from life. It was time for him to change some things in his life.

Çarh had walked all the way from Sanatkârlar Park to Taksim, passing by Galatasaray High School. When he reached Taksim Square, he got lost in the crowd. Walking among people, his thoughts continued to pull him. He was in an internal struggle, undecided about which direction to take. On one hand, he wanted to distance himself from these thoughts; on the other hand, lost in the crowd, he couldn't decide what to do.

These internal struggles had exhausted him. He was tired from walking; cramps had set into his feet. He sat on a bench in Taksim Square, his eyes scanning the surroundings.

Sûr

Lost amidst the crowded people, a sense of loneliness crept over him. He closed his eyes, attempting to calm himself with a deep breath. However, his thoughts still haunted him, questioning everything and eroding his self-confidence.

He sat there for a long time, listening to his thoughts. He observed the crowd around him, looking at the faces of people. Each had a different story, and he thought about his own. What was it? When did his story begin? How was it unfolding?

Çarh had accepted his loneliness and decided to isolate himself from the outside world. He enjoyed waking up as the sun rose, spending the rest of the day at home. He liked being alone, delving into thoughts, and dreaming.

Over time, this solitary life had further closed him off. He had become afraid of going out and talking to people. While sitting at home, he started thinking about past mistakes and missed opportunities. In times when he felt even lonelier, a depressive mood engulfed him.

One day, he startled when a friend called. The friend suggested going out and spending some time. Despite his initial reluctance, Çarh eventually yielded to the friend's insistence and went outside.

Spending time outside, feeling the warmth of the sun, talking to people, and laughing made Çarh very happy. The smiles and sincerity of people illuminated the darkness within him. That day, he realised something that had been inside him for a long time – how good it felt to talk to people, spend time outside, and meet new souls.

Compelled by his friend's persistent urging throughout the day, Çarh found himself in a bar by day's end. As he stood at the entrance, a sudden realization of his state washed over him, prompting him to question the reality of the situation.

Despite his reservations, pushed by his friend, he reluctantly entered the bar.

Upon entering the bar with his friend, he felt a sense of unease. Struggling to communicate with people due to his recent introverted life, the noisy atmosphere of the bar also made him uncomfortable. Despite this, he had decided to go along with his friend's insistence.

Sitting at the bar, sipping his drink, Çarh's eyes scanned the room in search of Deka. His thoughts continued to be consumed by her, but she was nowhere to be found. A tangible disappointment settled in as he fell into conversation with his friend, who was trying to fill the void inside him.

Just as things appeared to be falling back into place, Çarh spotted Deka once more. His emotions surged as he greeted her, only to be met with her lack of recognition. In astonishment, Çarh questioned why she didn't remember him, but Deka insisted they had never met. This situation deepened the void within Çarh, leaving him with a profound sense of being ignored, belittled, and out of place.

Overwhelmed by frustration, Çarh stormed out, seeking solace outside the confines of the bar. He took a deep breath and calmed down a bit. As he collected himself, he noticed the cooling weather, realising that his outfit consisted only of a thin jacket. Sensing the chill, Çarh decided to explore the surrounding streets, opting for a brisk walk.

The deserted streets enveloped in silence made Çarh's feeling of being lost even stronger. As he walked, the surprising reaction from Deka played on his mind. Why hadn't she recognized him? The possibility that Deka genuinely didn't know him started to emerge, raising questions about the validity of his feelings towards her. Perhaps, he considered, his emotions were founded on a delusion.

Sûr

Continuing his walk, Çarh eventually spotted a distant cafe. Desiring a refuge to escape his thoughts, he decided to enter, seeking solace in a drink. Seated alone in the cafe, he ordered a coffee. Despite the quiet ambiance outside, the cafe buzzed with some noise, accompanied by the background music playing softly.

Sipping his coffee and surveying the surroundings, a sudden wave of loneliness washed over Çarh. Without friends, loved ones, or familiar faces, he found himself accompanied only by his thoughts and the internal darkness. The weight of these thoughts started to consume him. It dawned on him that he needed to take action to liberate himself from these dark thoughts. However, there was a question in his mind: What could he possibly do?

The cafe door opened, and a woman entering called out, "Hello, Çarh. It's nice to see you here."

Çarh looked at the woman in astonishment. Could it truly be Deka? Or was it another illusion? Yet, the sincerity and familiarity in Deka's facial expression indicated that everything was real. Çarh stood up, extending his hand in a mixture of surprise and relief.

"Hello, Deka. Seeing you here makes me happy," he said.

Deka warmly held Çarh's hand and smiled. "Seeing you makes me happy too. Come, let's sit together," she said, gesturing to the empty chair next to her.

Çarh took a seat beside Deka and, feeling a bit embarrassed. He steeled himself, prepared to delve into the subject that had been gnawing at him, "The other day, I saw you in the park, and then approached you, but I think you didn't recognise me," he said and continued, "Even on the street the other day, and even tonight at the bar!"

Deka chuckled slightly. "Yes, that happened, didn't it?" she said, adjusting her hair with her hands. "But meeting again here is not a coincidence, I believe. Perhaps it has a meaning," she added with a thoughtful expression.

Deka's words helped Çarh to calm down a little more. Perhaps there was indeed some meaning to their meeting. But what could it be? Could Deka potentially have a place in his life? The questions were going round and round in Çarh's mind as he thought about the possibilities.

Çarh continued to talk with Deka with these thoughts. Deka's genuine and warm attitude somewhat alleviated the pessimism within Çarh. Perhaps he could make a new start in his life. However, Çarh found himself alone again, once Deka left and the pessimism within returned.

Consumed by these emotions, Çarh transformed into someone who visited the park and the bar daily in search for Deka. He occupied the same spots day after day, clinging to the hope of Deka's return. This quest had become the focal point of his existence, turning him into a person who rarely ventured outside the bars, was obsessed with Deka's elusive presence.

As days unfolded, Çarh's yearning for companionship intensified. The fear of being alone became an ever-present shadow, persistently haunting the corners of his mind. The echoes of solitude reverberated through his every step, and the weight of isolation became increasingly tangible.

During the moments when Deka was absent, Çarh felt a profound emptiness, a void that seemed to widen with each passing day. The once comforting solitude now transformed into a haunting loneliness that clung to him like a spectre. It was as if the world had become a vast, desolate landscape, and Çarh was the sole wanderer seeking connection.

Sûr

The bustling city of Istanbul, with its vibrant streets and lively markets, started to lose its charm in Çarh's eyes. The enchanting architecture and the mystical blend of tradition and modernity that once fascinated him now seemed to fade into the background. The city, once a lively tapestry, became a mere backdrop to the profound solitude Çarh grappled with.

In an attempt to escape the encroaching loneliness, Çarh sought refuge in the familiar haunts of the park and the bar. The faces around him changed, but the underlying ache persisted. He yearned for meaningful connections, a sense of belonging that transcended the fleeting encounters and ephemeral conversations.

It was during one of those solitary moments in the park that Çarh found himself reflecting on the dichotomy of his existence. The desire for companionship clashed with the fear of rejection, creating a turbulent inner struggle. The park, once a sanctuary, became a battleground where Çarh confronted his insecurities and yearnings.

Murat Karagoz

CHAPTER 3
CHANGE

Çarh stood up from the bed, a sense of bewilderment enveloping him, and he once again gazed into the mirror. The colour of his eyes had indeed changed, leaving him feeling quite uneasy. How could this be possible? Perhaps it had something to do with what happened last night.

Çarh entertained the initial possibility that he might have done something to himself, wondering if exposure to a chemical substance the cause of the change in eye colour could be. He also considered the idea that during the altercation, he might have suffered a serious blow leading to this alteration. However, deep down, a feeling within him suggested that this situation wasn't merely physical.

Çarh underwent a series of tests, and the results came back normal. Doctors suggested that the change in eye colour could have a psychological cause. To delve deeper into this mystery, he began delving into research, seeking answers to the alteration that seemed to transcend the physical realm.

As Çarh delved deeper into his research on "heterochromia", he discovered that the condition could be either genetic or acquired. Genetic heterochromia is often present from birth, while acquired heterochromia can result from various factors such as injury, inflammation, or certain medical conditions. Despite the intriguing information, Çarh couldn't find a clear explanation for the sudden and simultaneous change in both eye colours.

After spending a couple of hours in the library, Çarh eventually stumbled upon the subject of occultism. Occultism dealt with hidden sciences, esoteric teachings, and mystical practices. Many occultists believed that a change in eye colour had a supernatural cause.

Çarh considered that the change in his eye colour might be due to these supernatural reasons. Perhaps he had become aware of something, triggering the activation of the supernatural powers within him. Regardless, Çarh had to adapt to this new situation. He now had to live with his green eyes.

Judging by his actions and demeanour, he accepted the situation very quickly, and although he could not admit it to himself, he was excited by this change.

As Çarh embraced the change in eye colour, he began to believe that this might be a sign of something important in his life. Although he continued to anticipate change, he could not predict exactly what form it would take. Nevertheless, determined to remain open to the possibilities of his new reality, he embarked on a journey of self-discovery, ready to navigate any change in his life.

As Çarh walked towards his home, he noticed Aunt Zülfiye in a precarious situation. She was on the verge of falling as she descended the stairs, her foot slipping. In that critical moment, Çarh felt an extraordinary power surge within him. His eyes underwent another change, this time adopting a yellowish hue.

To prevent Aunt Zülfiye from falling, Çarh swiftly stepped forward and, caught her just in time with strong arms. She suddenly noticed the change in Çarh's eyes and looked at him in astonishment. Snapping out of the surprise of the moment, he immediately shifted his focus to assisting her, ensuring she regained her balance and safely descended the stairs.

In that moment, Çarh realised how much his life had changed. He saw with his own eyes that he now possessed a power and could use it to help people. Perhaps this was a part of his new life.

Çarh carefully carried Aunt Zülfiye to her home. Grateful for his assistance, she expressed her thanks and warmly invited him inside. Upon entering, Çarh couldn't help but notice the remarkable transformations throughout her living space. The furniture, pictures, and decorations had undergone a complete metamorphosis. Aunt Zülfiye explained that she had undertaken a thorough renovation, and the revitalized ambiance had a rejuvenating effect on her.

After conversing with Aunt Zülfiye, Çarh departed her house. Upon entering his own home and settling onto the couch, he pondered the significance of his yellowish eye colour. Whenever fear or anxiety gripped him, his eyes underwent a noticeable change in hue. Unsure of how to navigate these moments, he realised the pressing need to gain control over his emotions.

The following day, Çarh resolved to consult a doctor regarding the sudden alteration in eye colour. The doctor asked if he was aware of his "psychic powers". This question brought both surprise and relief to Çarh. Subsequently, he felt the pressing need to acquire methods for controlling this newfound ability.

Çarh began incorporating meditation and breathing exercises into his routine, following the doctor's recommendations. These practices enabled him to gain better control over himself and made him more adept at handling situations that triggered the change in eye colour.

Ever since Çarh started living with green eyes, numerous changes unfolded in his life. Initially, he grappled with discomfort over this transformation, but as time passed, He learned to embrace himself and adjust to his newfound existence.

Meditation and yoga became instrumental in fostering a profound sense of well-being, both mentally and physically. Delving into meditation, he discovered inner peace, while yoga bestowed strength upon his body. Emphasizing the significance of maintaining a healthy lifestyle, he initiated changes to his diet and exercise routine. This involved a shift towards a nutritionally rich diet, incorporating more vegetables and fruits, and a deliberate reduction in the consumption of fast food and snacks.

Thanks to these positive changes, Çarh now led a healthier, happier life. He felt more confident, made better decisions, and enjoyed life to the fullest.

One day at work, Çarh's boss appointed him as the leader of a special project – a significant opportunity that he embraced wholeheartedly. Determined to make the most of this chance, Çarh dedicated himself to the project, fostering strong teamwork and building positive relationships with his team members. As a result of their collective efforts, the project was successfully completed. Çarh's leadership skills and substantial contribution to the project left a lasting impression on his boss, who was highly impressed.

Çarh had firmly seized the reins of his life, accompanied by a newfound reservoir of self-assurance. In the quiet sanctuary of meditation and through purposeful exercises, he honed the skills to navigate the labyrinth of dark thoughts that once plagued his mind. As he ventured into a realm of increased social engagement, Çarh discovered the richness of a life adorned with new faces and experiences, embracing a spectrum of emotions that painted his existence with vibrant hues.

Çarh was cognizant of the shifts in his life, yet he gradually overlooked the transformation in his eyes. Presently, he traversed through life with an inner tranquillity, a heightened sense of contentment, and an overall serenity that enveloped him.

The transformation in Çarh became evident to those in his immediate surroundings. Neighbours in the apartment building and colleagues at work all remarked on the noticeable shift in his demeanour, noting how he had become more positive, energetic, and content. This positive change in his attitude translated into increased self-confidence, prompting him to actively participate in social activities and fostering a more vibrant social life.

Çarh visited the café nearly every day after work, eager to engage in social interactions. Upon arrival, he would habitually order a steaming cup of coffee and immerse himself in the latest daily newspapers. As he sipped his drink, he enjoyed warm conversations with those around him, occasionally sharing jokes with the amiable waiter. In these moments, he found true satisfaction, savouring the camaraderie and the simple pleasures of the café ambiance.

As Çarh immersed himself in the café atmosphere, he

gradually developed a familiarity with those in his surroundings, cultivating friendships along the way. He engaged in conversations, attentively lending an ear to the concerns of strangers, providing guidance when necessary, and occasionally revealing glimpses of his own life.

Çarh's hours spent in the café not only offered him new perspectives on life but also played a crucial role in his personal development. Occasionally, he would gather with the friends he had made at the café, engaging in various activities and leisurely strolling around the city.

One day, as Çarh sat in the café, he noticed a note lying on the adjacent table. The note, written in a woman's delicate handwriting, appeared to have slipped to the floor. Intrigued, Çarh picked up the note and began to read. It contained affectionate and longing sentences, evoking intense emotions within him.

Perhaps, like Çarh once did, the author of this note had experienced similar feelings. Maybe she, too, had undergone a significant change in her life, embarking on a new path. As Çarh read the note again, he couldn't help but contemplate who this woman might be.

Whether she frequented the café regularly or had merely coincidentally chosen it that day remained uncertain. As Çarh delved into the life story suggested by the note, he began to conjure images of the woman's daily existence.

The woman's story deeply moved Çarh, prompting him to ponder how he could positively impact her life. The weather, sunny and inviting, encouraged Çarh to take a leisurely walk to personally deliver the note to its owner. Eventually, he decided to take the note and leave the café.

Upon holding the note, Çarh immediately sensed the woman's energy. Gradually, he forged a connection with the potential location of her presence, recognizing the necessity of putting forth effort to locate her.

As Çarh walked, he relished the warmth of the sunny weather and grappled with a peculiar sensation. With every step toward the source of the woman's energy, his determination grew stronger.

Çarh was enveloped in the rich aroma of tea as it gently wafted through the air, immersing the street in its alluring fragrance. The beauty of the scent overwhelmed him, and his senses seemed to be awakening to a heightened state. Unbeknownst to him, a subtle transformation was taking place within. In harmony with the seductive aroma, he became aware of the moisture on his lips and embraced the soothing the warmth of the tea.

This realisation spurred Çarh into action. Contemplating the possibility that the note's author might be in a nearby café, drawn to the pervasive aroma of tea, he felt a surge of determination. Intrigued by the idea, he decided to follow the trail of the captivating fragrance, hoping it would lead him to the mysterious person behind the note.

Çarh embarked on a journey through the neighbouring cafés, exploring each one in search of the elusive figure. After a series of visits, he eventually arrived at a particular place. As he stepped inside, the robust fragrance of tea enveloped him, confirming his intuition. His eyes swiftly identified the object of his quest – a solitary woman, lost in her memories, cradling a cup of tea at her table.

Çarh extended the note towards the woman and gently uttered, "I believe this note belongs to you," The woman lifted her gaze to meet Çarh's, accepted the note, and as she delved into its contents, an overwhelming wave of emotion swept over her. Tears welled up in her eyes, and soon, sobs escaped from her, leaving her face flushed with grief. After a moment, she composed herself enough to share that the note was indeed hers. She had penned it in remembrance of her late husband, a soul departed from this world some time ago.

"My dear love,

I pen these lines to express the pain in my heart as we part ways. This moment of separation has become the most challenging and darkest period of my life. Even the mere thought of a life without you tears me apart.

With your departure, my world has undergone a profound transformation. Alongside you, my laughter, peace, and hope have also departed. You were the meaning of my life, and the prospect of living without you seems insurmountable.

I blame myself. Perhaps, I didn't love you enough, didn't spend sufficient time with you, or failed to create enough cherished memories with you. I couldn't make you happy enough or value you adequately. The fire of regret burns relentlessly inside me, and I am tormented by these self-imposed shortcomings.

Describing how much I love and miss you is an impossible task. You entered my life like the sun, connecting me to life, offering hope, and reminding me of life's beauties. Losing someone like you constitutes an immeasurable loss for me.

My love and longing for you will endure forever. I will never forget you, and you will always reside in my heart. Loving you and having the privilege of knowing a woman like you was an immense blessing for me.

Rest in peace, my love.

I love you."

Sûr

Having folded the note with care, the woman fixed her gaze on Çarh and inquired, "How did you find me?" Disbelief lingered in her eyes as she struggled to comprehend the seemingly improbable turn of events. The notion that a stranger could locate her through the note left her grappling with the mysterious and wondrous possibilities of fate.

As the woman shared the poignant backstory of the note, she revealed the depths of her grief and the pain she harboured for the loved one she had lost. She went on to explain her choice to leave the note not just anywhere in the city, but specifically at the café where she frequented for coffee. It was a symbolic gesture, a silent expression of hope that her departed loved one might return someday. Touched by her vulnerability, Çarh conveyed his understanding of her pain and offered his heartfelt support. In that moment, a connection formed between them, and they exchanged warm smiles, united in the shared understanding of loss and the solace that unexpected connections could bring.

To console the woman, whose eyes welled up with tears once again, Çarh instinctively opened his arms, offering a comforting embrace. The weary woman's body yielded to the warmth of the hug, her head finding solace against Çarh's chest. In that intimate connection, Çarh sensed a profound shift. As they held each other, it became evident that the woman carried an unwarranted burden of guilt for her husband's passing, despite her innocence in the matter. Çarh recognized the unnecessary self-blame consuming her, and in that shared moment of empathy, he vowed to offer not just physical comfort but emotional support to help alleviate the weight she carried.

Çarh's embrace, though unable to fully dispel the pain, offered a measure of solace to the woman grappling with her grief. She met Çarh's gaze with gratitude, and a moment of silence ensued. In the quietude, she mustered the courage to confess the heavy burden she bore — the belief that she bore responsibility for her husband's demise. "Perhaps I should have taken better care of him, maybe I should have acted differently," she murmured, voicing the self-blame that weighed heavily on her heart.

Listening to the woman's internal struggle, Çarh empathetically grasped the innocence she failed to recognize within herself. With a gentle touch, he sought to provide comfort, urging, "This is not about you," Çarh continued, his voice soft and reassuring, "Life often presents challenges beyond our control. You did your best, no matter the circumstances. There's no need to blame yourself," The woman lifted her gaze, absorbing Çarh's words, as a flicker of understanding and acceptance began to illuminate the shadows of self-reproach in her eyes.

Understanding the depth of the woman's anguish, Çarh felt a compelling need to help alleviate her burden. With a firm but compassionate tone, he urged the woman to confront the harsh reality. "It's not about you," he reiterated. "Facing the loss of a life is an incredibly challenging situation. However, there was nothing you could have done differently. Your husband is gone, and as difficult as it is, blaming yourself won't bring him back," Çarh's words, though poignant, carried a gentle reassurance aimed at guiding the woman toward acceptance and the gradual healing of her wounded soul.

The woman absorbed Çarh's words, nodding in agreement as she whispered, "Yes, you're right. There was nothing I could have done. I'm just wearing myself out," In response to her acknowledgment, Çarh offered a warm smile, continuing his efforts to provide reassurance and comfort to a soul burdened by grief. The exchange between them carried an unspoken understanding and the shared journey toward healing.

A contemplative silence enveloped them for a while, and then the woman, curious, inquired of Çarh how he stumbled upon her note. Çarh, with a calm demeanour, explained the serendipity of the discovery, leaving the woman incredulous. "How could you find my note?" she queried. Çarh responded, "Everything happens for a reason. Perhaps this note fell into my hands by chance. Maybe it's a sign that something is meant to change. Our paths crossed coincidentally, and perhaps we are here to help each other," His words carried a sense of destiny and the possibility of shared purpose in their unexpected encounter.

In the hushed ambiance of the café, a subtle understanding blossomed between Çarh and the woman. It felt as if the universe, in its enigmatic orchestration, had brought them together. The burdens they bore seemed to lighten, finding solace in the shared acknowledgment of each other's pain. In that quiet moment, a connection beyond words spoke of a profound empathy, offering a glimmer of healing and hope amidst the complexities of life.

Çarh delicately broke the silence, his words carrying a soothing cadence. "Life has its way of connecting people, sometimes in the most unexpected moments. We may not have all the answers, but perhaps we can find solace in the company of someone who understands, even if it's a stranger who stumbled upon a heartfelt note," His gentle reminder echoed in the quietude, emphasizing the power of shared understanding and the unexpected bonds that can emerge amidst life's intricate tapestry.

The woman, her eyes reflecting a blend of gratitude and

sadness, acknowledged Çarh's words. "You're right. It's strange how paths cross. Perhaps there's a reason for us to meet today," she mused. Pausing briefly, she added, "Thank you for being here, for listening." In that exchange of gratitude and acknowledgment, the cafe seemed to hold a space for shared healing and understanding, creating a moment of connection between two souls traversing the unpredictable journey of life.

Their conversation unfolded, gradually unravelling the threads of their own struggles, dreams, and the intricate tapestry of life. The café, once a haven of solitude for both, now resonated with shared stories and mutual understanding. The enchanting atmosphere of Istanbul outside the window seemed to permeate the café, transforming it into a sanctuary where two souls, each burdened by distinct sorrows, discovered a fleeting respite. Amidst the rich aroma of tea and the gentle hum of conversations, a connection blossomed, weaving a shared narrative of solace and companionship.

In this serendipitous connection, Çarh and the woman unearthed the potency of shared humanity – a poignant reminder that, amidst life's intricacies, compassion and understanding had the capacity to bridge the gaps between strangers. As they bid farewell, a lingering sense of warmth and hope enveloped them, a subtle transformation born from an unexpected encounter in the heart of Istanbul.

Sûr

CHAPTER 4
GONE

The incident at the café the previous week marked a turning point in Çarh's life. Since that day, he made a conscious decision to redirect his focus towards impacting the lives of those around him. Inspired by the possibility of helping numerous people, he embarked on a mission to make the world a better place, recognizing the transformative power of empathy and kindness in the intricate tapestry of human connections.

This newfound awareness had a profound impact on Çarh's life. Breaking away from the routine of visiting the same café daily, he ventured into different places, actively engaging with people, and extending his assistance. At times, he provided nourishment to those living on the streets, while on other occasions, he organized the provision of school supplies for children. The act of giving and making a positive impact became a guiding force, shaping his journey with a renewed sense of purpose and connection to the broader community.

Sûr

The shift in Çarh's life brought about a profound sense of happiness. By actively engaging with others and making a positive impact, he found fulfilment not only in his own journey but also in the lives of those he touched. Interactions with people evolved into one of the most valuable aspects of his life, becoming a source of joy, purpose, and a deeper connection to the shared human experience. In the tapestry of his transformed existence, the threads of compassion and meaningful connections became the vibrant colours that painted the canvas of his newfound happiness.

The adoption of this new lifestyle had a remarkable impact on Çarh's self-confidence. Feeling more useful and fostering a deeper love for himself, he experienced a profound shift in his self-perception. The connections forged through his acts of kindness had not only enriched the lives of others but had also resulted in the cultivation of numerous friendships. Discovering a purpose for himself added a new layer of excitement to each day, infusing his life with meaning and direction. Çarh, propelled by the positive changes he had initiated, found a newfound zest for life in the pursuit of his purpose.

Çarh held a belief that recognizing the beauties in life often required just a small shift in perspective. This conviction had its roots in a note from the past, a note that had transformed the woman who wrote it into one of the most significant factors in Çarh's life. Despite the inevitable ups and downs of life, everything seemed to be going well until the day Çarh confronted the death of Aunt Zülfiye.

The passing of Aunt Zülfiye plunged Çarh into profound sorrow. She held a significant place in his life, having been a familiar presence since childhood. Çarh deeply admired her lively and loving personality. The memories of the beautiful moments shared with Aunt Zülfiye, her infectious smile, and the warmth she radiated became indelible imprints on his heart, ensuring that she would never be forgotten.

At the funeral, Çarh found it impossible to restrain his tears. With a heart heavy with grief, he spoke about Aunt Zülfiye, who had played the role of a maternal figure in his life for many years. "Aunt Zülfiye, you were like a mother to me. You protected me, loved me, and inspired me. Every moment spent with you was very special and precious to me. In countless moments of my life, I had the privilege of your advice and support. The memories I shared with you will remain etched in my heart forever," Çarh expressed, his words a heartfelt tribute to a woman who had left an indelible mark on his life.

In the midst of mourning, Çarh poured out his emotions, expressing how Aunt Zülfiye had been a constant source of empowerment and inspiration. "You always gave me courage and encouraged me to face the challenges of life. I've never known a woman as strong as you. Through the battles of life, you stood tall. I've always looked up to you and learned so much from you," Çarh declared, highlighting Aunt Zülfiye's resilience and the profound impact she had on shaping his character and fortitude.

Expressing profound gratitude to Aunt Zülfiye, Çarh vowed, "In your absence, I will continue my life with the lessons you taught me and the strength you infused in me. I will never forget you, and your legacy will always be a guiding force in my journey."

Despite the presence of everyone in the building and close friends offering their support, the void left by Aunt Zülfiye's absence weighed heavily on Çarh. The funeral became a poignant gathering where memories of her life were shared, and heartfelt words spoken by everyone painted a beautiful tapestry of remembrance. In these moments, Çarh witnessed the depth of Aunt Zülfiye's impact and how profoundly she was loved by those who knew her. The collective expression of love and admiration for Aunt Zülfiye provided a bittersweet solace amid the grief.

The loss of Aunt Zülfiye delivered a profound blow to Çarh, prompting him to reflect on the brevity and preciousness of life. In that poignant moment, he recognized the profound importance of people and the significance of extending love, support, and understanding to one another. The memories of the unwavering support and love Aunt Zülfiye had bestowed upon him throughout her life remained etched in his heart. Vowing to keep her memory alive, Çarh acknowledged the enduring impact she had on his life, inspiring him to cherish the connections with others and to honour the love and support that make life meaningful.

Aunt Hacer, Çarh's neighbour residing on the ground floor, spoke consoling words, "Çarh, Zülfiye was not just a friend for you. She was like a mother to you. The beautiful moments you shared with her will forever be etched in your memory, and she will always hold a special place in your heart. While her passing deeply saddens you, remember that she will always love you and watch over you. I want you to know that even before this, you were like a son to me, and from now on, you can see me as your mother." Aunt Hacer's comforting words extended a maternal embrace to Çarh, offering solace and reassurance in the midst of his grief.

Çarh, somewhat comforted by his neighbour's words, experienced a slight alleviation in the intensity of his pain. Despite this, tears continued to flow uncontrollably. His neighbours stood by him, offering unwavering support until he could gather himself. In the collective presence of understanding and compassion, Çarh found solace, recognizing the strength that came from the communal bonds that surrounded him during this difficult time.

After the funeral, Çarh went to Aunt Zülfiye's house to immerse himself in her belongings and photographs. Methodically examining each item that held memories of her, he sought to preserve and honour her legacy. Aunt Zülfiye's warm smile and affectionate demeanour had become deeply significant in Çarh's life. True to the promise he made during the funeral, he took her photograph to his home, ensuring that her memory would remain a cherished presence in his life. The act of preserving her image became a tangible way for Çarh to hold onto the essence of Aunt Zülfiye and the indelible mark she left on his heart.

The photograph of Aunt Zülfiye became Çarh's most cherished possession. Every glance at it invoked a flood of memories, reminding him of the special woman she was and the invaluable advice she had given. Aunt Zülfiye had assumed the role of a mother figure in Çarh's life, and the moments shared with her served as a pivotal turning point. The photograph stood as a tangible link to the profound impact she had on Çarh, a constant source of guidance and a reservoir of cherished memories that continued to shape his journey.

Determined to preserve Aunt Zülfiye's memory, Çarh made a conscious commitment to embody the qualities she admired and follow her sage advice. Striving to become a better person, he resolved to carry her influence throughout his life. Despite her physical absence, Aunt Zülfiye's presence and memories would persist as among the most valuable and enduring aspects of Çarh's life, a source of inspiration that would continue to guide his actions and shape his character.

Sûr

As time marched on, Çarh gradually came to terms with Aunt Zülfiye's death. Yet, the void left by her absence would forever remain in the tapestry of his life. Her vibrant personality, the beautiful memories they shared, and the profound teachings she imparted had become an enduring legacy for Çarh. Determined to honour her memory, he committed to preserving the essence of Aunt Zülfiye, ensuring that her influence would endure, a guiding light shaping his life's journey forever.

Despite the passage of time, Aunt Zülfiye's loss remained a source of deep pain for Çarh. The photograph he carried with him wasn't merely a memory; it was a tangible reflection of her liveliness and warmth. Whenever Çarh gazed at that photo, it brought forth a feeling as if she were still present, the essence of her spirit captured in the image, offering a semblance of comfort and closeness even in her physical absence.

As Çarh returned home today, he was met with a surprising sight – the dining table was elegantly set. Unusually, he hadn't anticipated such preparations. A warm memory tied to Aunt Zülfiye touched his heart, creating a sensation as if she had paid him a visit. Taking a deep breath, Çarh seated himself at the table. To his astonishment, shortly thereafter, she emerged from the kitchen, holding a salad. Çarh was struck with disbelief, finding it hard to trust his own eyes. She was really there, a presence that seemed to transcend time and space.

As Çarh laid eyes on Aunt Zülfiye, an initial wave of confusion swept over him. What? Was she really here? However, a moment of realization followed, bringing with it the painful recollection that Aunt Zülfiye was no longer alive. He questioned whether what he saw was a dream. Yet, her genuine smile and the words, "Welcome, my child, I was expecting you," left Çarh both bewildered and deeply moved, as if the boundaries between reality and memory had momentarily blurred.

As Aunt Zülfiye, who had passed away, stood before him, Çarh felt his heart racing rapidly. The paradox of her presence left him momentarily frozen in shock. Despite the logical impossibility, she invited him to the table, and together they began to share a meal. The surreal experience unfolded, blurring the lines between reality and something that felt almost otherworldly. The moment held a mixture of astonishment and comfort, as if Aunt Zülfiye's spirit had returned to share a meal with Çarh, bridging the gap between the realms of the living and the departed.

The table was adorned with Aunt Zülfiye's favourite dishes. As Çarh indulged in the flavours of the food, his senses heightened by the familiar tastes, he found himself simultaneously captivated by watching her. The experience of sitting next to her brought a profound sense of comfort. In that moment, it felt as if they were seated side by side, akin to a mother and her son, sharing not just a meal but a precious connection that transcended the boundaries of time and space.

Çarh found himself immersed in one of the most beautiful moments of his life. The taste of the food was exquisite, and with each bite, Çarh couldn't help but be transported back to the beautiful memories he had shared with her. The experience was a blend of flavours and recollections, creating a tapestry of emotions that made this shared meal with Aunt Zülfiye an unforgettable and deeply cherished moment for Çarh.

After the meal, Aunt Zülfiye embraced Çarh and planted a kiss on his cheek. "I love you, my child. I am always with you," she whispered, and then, as mysteriously as she had appeared, she vanished. Çarh, caught between reality and a moment of profound happiness, couldn't be certain of the authenticity of the encounter. However, in that moment, he felt an overwhelming sense of joy. Tenderly, he kissed the photograph he had taken to preserve Aunt Zülfiye's memory and carefully placed it in a corner. Now, every time he looked at the photograph, the memories with her would spring to life, and he would feel an enduring closeness to her presence.

As Çarh awoke the next morning, he grappled with the reality of the events from the previous night. Had he truly witnessed the spirit of Aunt Zülfiye, or were those moments merely a product of his imagination? The uncertainty of it all unsettled him. Searching for answers, he turned his gaze to Aunt Zülfiye's photograph, silently wishing, "Please, let it be real." In that moment, the photograph held both the memories and the yearning for a connection that transcended the boundaries of the tangible and the ethereal.

As Çarh entered the kitchen to prepare his breakfast, he sensed once again the lingering presence of Aunt Zülfiye's spirit. Seated at the dining table, he began to eat. In the midst of his meal, a sudden recollection of her smiling face washed over him, and he silently addressed the unseen presence, thinking, "If you are truly here, please show me yourself," The quiet moments in the kitchen became a silent dialogue between the tangible world and the intangible realm, where the memory of Aunt Zülfiye lingered, leaving Çarh in contemplation.

Finishing his meal, Çarh turned his attention once again to Aunt Zülfiye's photograph. This time, he closed his eyes and, with a heart full of earnestness, pleaded, "If you are here, please give me a sign." In the quiet of the moment, his plea hung in the air, an expression of both longing and hope for a connection that surpassed the boundaries of the visible and the unseen.

After a brief moment, the sound of a bird outside the window caught Çarh's attention. Excitedly, he rushed to the window and witnessed a bird gracefully soaring in the sky. The significance of this event struck him deeply. Unbeknownst to Çarh, Aunt Zülfiye had left a note beside her photograph. As he moved away from the window, his gaze fell upon the note. It read, "I love you, Çarh. I am always with you." The presence of this note served as undeniable proof that the moments Çarh experienced were indeed real. Aunt Zülfiye, once a cherished memory, had transformed into a tangible presence, bringing a profound sense of comfort and reassurance to Çarh's heart.

Despite the beauty of the experiences, Çarh found it challenging to detach himself from the grip of reality. As captivating as the encounters with Aunt Zülfiye's spirit were, unanswered questions lingered, leaving him in a state of contemplation. Feeling powerless against the enigmatic events, numerous questions swirled in Çarh's mind: Did he genuinely witness Aunt Zülfiye's soul, or were these experiences a product of his imagination? If indeed her soul manifested before him, how was he able to perceive it? Recognizing the need for further exploration, Çarh understood that more time and introspection were required to unravel the mysteries and seek answers to these profound questions.

Preferring the solace of the outdoors to the confines of home, Çarh found comfort in the open air. It served as an escape, allowing him to navigate the impact of the recent peculiar events. As he wandered, the external surroundings appeared ordinary, yet the echoes of those strange encounters resonated within him. During his stroll, Çarh happened upon a small café nestled at a street corner. Seeking a moment of respite, he entered, ordered a coffee, and settled into a quiet corner. Lost in a contemplative gaze, his eyes wandered into emptiness, a plethora of thoughts swirling in his mind like leaves caught in a gentle breeze.

Unaware of the mysterious powers latent within himself, Çarh grappled with the sorrow stemming from the loss of Aunt Zülfiye. Alongside the grief, he couldn't shake the feeling that something fundamental had shifted. A distinct energy, unfamiliar and intense, now coursed through him, whispering messages and guidance. In a state of anxiety and uncertainty, it was as if he stood on the precipice of change, the knowledge lingering that everything in his life might transform suddenly and significantly. The mysterious forces within him seemed to propel him forward, urging him to navigate the uncharted territory that lay ahead.

After the loss of Aunt Zülfiye, Çarh experienced a profound shift, as if a veil had been lifted, revealing a different dimension to the meaningful events in his life. Initially, he became attuned to small occurrences, noticing the manifestation of his thoughts into reality. There were moments when he felt a loss of control over his emotions. Now, however, he recognized that his chakras were beginning to open. What was once elusive and without any apparent sign had become tangible. Çarh grappled with the realization that he was a witch, although uncertainty lingered. The power within him had led to the awakening of the witchcraft chakra, altering the course of his understanding of self and reality.

Lost in contemplation while staring at passersby, Çarh found himself once again immersed in thoughts. A recent memory surfaced – the note he had discovered in the café. Recalling how he had successfully found the woman connected to the note, a deeper realization dawned on him. Perhaps, the latent power within him had played a role in guiding him to that moment. Driven by a newfound curiosity, Çarh sought to unravel the mysteries within himself, eager to explore and understand the untapped potential that seemed to reside within his being.

As Çarh delved deeper into self-discovery, the once elusive aspects of his recent experiences began to crystallize. The distinctiveness he had sensed over the past few weeks, the supernatural powers, and the heightened sensations were, in fact, indicative of his latent identity as a witch. The death of Aunt Zülfiye seemed to have acted as a catalyst, compelling him to confront this newfound reality. The clarity that emerged unveiled a profound understanding of his true nature and the mystical capabilities that had long remained dormant within him.

Confronted with the reality of his witch powers, Çarh grappled with uncertainty about how to proceed. Faced with a lack of knowledge about witchcraft, he pondered whether to educate himself on the subject or attempt to suppress these newfound powers. Recognizing the need to learn how to control the witch powers within him, Çarh felt a pressing urgency to embark on this journey of self-discovery. However, the path forward remained unclear, leaving him with the challenge of navigating the uncharted territory of his own mystical abilities.

Çarh's mind swirled with turmoil as he grappled with the concept of witchcraft. Since childhood, he had internalized the widespread, incorrect, and often frightening perception that witches were inherently evil, bringing harm to people. However, his growing curiosity, intertwined with the powers awakening within him, nudged him towards a different perspective. The need to reconcile societal perceptions with the newfound understanding of his own abilities sparked a transformation in Çarh's beliefs, challenging the ingrained notions he had carried since youth.

As Çarh grappled with his newfound identity as a witch, he confronted a pivotal question: were witches limited to possessing powers used for malicious purposes, or was there a different, perhaps more nuanced aspect to their abilities? The multitude of questions swirling in his mind reflected a profound curiosity, a quest for understanding that propelled him towards seeking answers and unravelling the complexities surrounding witchcraft. With an open mind and a thirst for knowledge, Çarh embarked on a journey of self-discovery, determined to explore the diverse facets of his newfound identity and the powers that came with it.

Embracing the path of self-discovery as a witch proved to be a daunting challenge for Çarh. Fears of societal judgment and rejection loomed large, hindering his pursuit of knowledge. The prospect of accepting himself as a witch brought with it the unsettling belief that people might harbour hatred, exclusion, and judgment towards him. This fear, deeply rooted in the potential consequences of revealing his true identity, weighed heavily on Çarh, creating a formidable barrier to the open exploration of his newfound powers and the understanding of his own nature.

In addition to the external fears of societal judgment, Çarh grappled with internal concerns about the powers awakening within him. Questions about the responsibilities tied to this newfound power occupied his thoughts. Would he encounter situations where he couldn't control these abilities? Was there a risk of inadvertently causing harm to those around him? The internal struggle between the potential benefits and the potential risks of his newfound powers added another layer of complexity to Çarh's journey of self-discovery as he navigated the uncharted territories of being a witch.

Amidst the internal turmoil and conflicting thoughts, Çarh felt the call of witchcraft resonating within him. The urge to explore himself and embrace his newfound abilities tugged at his consciousness. Yet, gathering the courage to do so meant confronting his fears—fears of societal judgment and the potential perception of being seen as different by those around him. The internal struggle between the allure of self-discovery and the apprehension of societal scrutiny presented Çarh with a challenging crossroads, where the path forward required a delicate balance of courage and acceptance.

Despite the internal contradictions and the complexity of accepting this newfound identity, Çarh found himself unable to ignore the compelling call of the power within him. The internal conflict persisted, but the inexorable pull of witchcraft urged him forward. Recognizing that there was no turning back, Çarh steeled himself to confront witchcraft as an integral part of his identity. With a mix of trepidation and determination, he prepared to open the doors to an unknown world, embracing the journey of self-discovery that lay ahead.

As Çarh grappled with the uneasy historical context of witch hunts and the prevalent misunderstandings surrounding witchcraft, a series of intriguing questions swirled in his mind. Why was he a witch? When did this affinity for witchcraft begin? Was he inherently born as a witch, or did this transformation happen at a later point in his life? The enigma surrounding the origins of his witchcraft stirred a deep sense of curiosity, prompting Çarh to seek answers that could unravel the mysteries surrounding his newfound identity and the powers within him.

The weight of contemplation and the flood of

memories from the past began to take a toll on Çarh, leaving him with a persistent headache. The question lingered in his mind like a haunting refrain: "Why me?" The mysteries surrounding his identity as a witch and the origins of this power continued to sow confusion, prompting Çarh to grapple with the complexity of his own existence and the unique path that lay ahead.

While lost in contemplation at the café, Çarh had temporarily forgotten the memory of the hooded man. However, when he spotted the same mysterious figure passing by on the opposite sidewalk, a realization dawned upon him. It struck him that this very moment might have triggered the awakening of his witch powers. The enigmatic demeanour of the hooded man had always captured Çarh's attention, inducing a sense of anxiety and restlessness within him. Now, a multitude of questions swirled in his mind about the hooded man — who he was, why he kept appearing, and whether he played a role in the revelation of Çarh's witchcraft powers.

As the hooded man passed by, Çarh underwent a profound enlightenment. The questions that had lingered in his mind were now beginning to find clarity. A clandestine world, hidden from ordinary people, harboured ancient and secretive powers like witchcraft. Çarh recognized that he was intricately woven into the fabric of this mysterious realm. The enigmatic presence of the hooded man appeared to be a harbinger of significant influence on the course of Çarh's life, marking the beginning of a journey into the arcane and the unexplored.

As Çarh wrestled with his thoughts, a cafe worker approached him, breaking his reverie. Pulling himself together, Çarh finished his coffee, expressed gratitude, and left the cafe. He found himself contemplating a new aspect of his existence that he had never considered before. The awareness of his own witchcraft powers had dawned upon him, and now he grappled with uncertainty about what to do next. However, the realization that gaining control over these powers could usher in a significant change in his life lingered in his mind. These mystical abilities held the potential to open doors to new possibilities and reshape his entire existence.

As Çarh continued walking after leaving the cafe, a sudden transformation unfolded around him – the surroundings were enveloped in mist. Astonished, Çarh looked around, only to witness the mist gradually dissipating, revealing a park in its wake. As he gazed upward, the sun emerged on the horizon, casting its morning glow across the sky. The mystical experience left Çarh in awe, further emphasizing the extraordinary nature of the powers awakening within him.

Standing still for a moment, Çarh watched the sunrise, and as he observed the dawn, he felt the burgeoning power within him intensify. This newfound energy and vitality surged through him. Driven by a newfound determination, Çarh desired to gain control over this power. He intuited that once this force was harnessed under his command, it held the potential to bring about a profound and transformative change in his life. The sunrise became a symbol of both the awakening within him and the untapped possibilities awaiting his mastery.

As Çarh grappled with the swirling questions in his mind, he found it challenging to perceive the world around him. Having left the cafe in broad daylight, he now stood watching the sunrise – a situation he had never encountered before. The extent of his powers and how much control he could exert over them remained uncertain. With each surge in awareness, the energy within him intensified, leaving Çarh in a state of ambiguity. He had no clue how long this heightened state would last or what the ultimate outcome of this newfound power would be.

As the sun began its slow ascent in the sky, casting a faint red hue before unleashing its powerful rays, Çarh's gaze remained fixed on the sunrise. However, the questions that swirled in his mind persisted, lingering unanswered. The significance of the unfolding events, the potential applications of witchcraft powers, and the implications for his future remained shrouded in uncertainty. Çarh stood amidst the awe-inspiring sunrise, grappling with the profound mysteries of his newfound abilities and the uncharted path that lay ahead.

Facing the duality of the newfound power within him, Çarh turned inward and resolved, "I must now control this power." Recognizing the transformative potential that this power held, Çarh acknowledged that it could reshape his life and unveil unexplored opportunities. However, a silent fear lingered beneath the surface. He was aware of the inherent danger associated with this formidable force, and the realization of the responsibility that came with its control weighed heavily on him.

Seated on the bench, consumed by these contemplations, Çarh was startled as someone touched his shoulder. Holding his breath, he turned to see the person responsible for the contact. Before him stood a hooded man, the shadows concealing his eyes and veiling his face entirely.

"I was waiting for you too," the hooded man said calmly.

Çarh, taken aback, gazed at the hooded man who had surprisingly taken a seat beside him. Just as he readied himself to inquire about the reason behind the man's anticipation, the face concealed beneath the hood slowly became visible. A sudden recoil surged through Çarh as he recognized the person – it was the same individual he had encountered on that fateful night while inebriated.

"Me?" Çarh questioned, suspicion lacing his words.

The hooded man nodded slightly. "Yes, you. I've been observing you, and I needed to talk to you."

Çarh couldn't help but wonder why the hooded man had been observing him, but he hesitated to ask. The hooded man's tone was strangely soothing, but there was still a sense of unease within Çarh.

Despite knowing that the hooded man was the one involved in the fight on the night he was drunk, Çarh finally asked, "Who are you?"

The man's hood still concealed his face. "I am someone like you," the hooded man said.

Çarh didn't understand what this answer meant. "What do you mean?"

The hooded man slowly removed his hood, revealing a face that resembled Çarh's. "I am a witch too,"

Çarh was trying to comprehend what was being said. Could it be that the hooded man was also a witch? His mind, already confounded since discovering his powers, was now plunged into further confusion. The words spoken by the hooded man evoked both fear and curiosity within Çarh. The prospect of meeting another individual with similar abilities heightened his unease, yet a growing curiosity about the nature of the powers within him emerged.

The hooded man conveyed to Çarh that a pivotal decision lay ahead. Çarh faced a choice: to accept and embrace his newfound powers, allowing himself to be who he truly was, or to reject them, opting for the continuation of a normal, mundane existence.

Sûr

A profound internal conflict waged within Çarh. The desire to be authentic and embrace his powers clashed with the yearning for a simple, normal life. Yet, deep down, he sensed that life could no longer be the same as it was before. A significant choice loomed before him.

The internal voice within Çarh surged in strength, addressing him directly. A newfound sensation enveloped him, an exhilarating experience he had never before noticed. However, the excitement was tempered by the challenge of comprehending the significance of these powers. Despite his earnest efforts, Çarh found himself lacking sufficient information on this subject. As he continued to heed the voice within, he discerned the necessity for a structured approach and discipline. It became clear that he must master the control of these powers, shaping them into a tool at his command.

Finally, Çarh, driven by curiosity and a growing awareness of the powers within him, declared his readiness to embrace them. With this acceptance, he resolved to embark on a journey of self-discovery and unleash the latent potential within. Opting for a path away from a normal existence, he committed himself to the exploration of his abilities and the cultivation of control over these powers.

In the tranquil park, a discernible aura manifested around Çarh, signifying his acceptance of the powers within him. The people in proximity felt this aura, eliciting reactions ranging from astonishment to fear. Unaware of the impact he was having on those around him, Çarh delved into planning his exploration of these newfound powers.

Having embraced his powers and understanding the path ahead, Çarh realised that he was not alone in this transformative journey. The hooded man, standing before him, held valuable knowledge to impart. Armed with trust in himself, Çarh felt confident that he could navigate and control the powers within him. With this newfound confidence, he embarked on the journey to fully become himself.

As the hooded man rose from his seat, a sudden recollection surged in Çarh's mind. Vivid memories of the night shrouded in mist flooded back. The silhouette of the hooded man appeared distinct, sparking a realization in Çarh. An inkling crept in, suggesting that the man might be concealing something beneath the hood. It dawned on him that there might be more to the mysterious figure than he had previously noticed during that enigmatic night.

Çarh, driven by his persistent curiosity, decided to address the lingering question in his mind. With a hint of scepticism, he expressed, "I couldn't fully grasp it at the time, but it bothered me. The silhouette that night was very peculiar. Perhaps I thought it was due to being drunk, but later I realised it was different. You were different." Pausing for a moment to collect his thoughts, he took a deep breath and continued, "I'm curious. What was under the hood that night?"

The hooded man turned towards Çarh and, without uttering a word, simply responded with a mysterious smile.

As Çarh attempted to decipher the enigmatic smile of the hooded man, he found himself distracted by the sudden appearance of mist around him. The mist, like a subtle veil, enveloped the surroundings, creating an otherworldly ambiance. Intrigued and slightly disoriented, Çarh's attention shifted from the mysterious smile to the mysterious mist that now surrounded him.

As the mist dissipated, Çarh found himself standing in the midst of a dense forest. The transition from the mysterious mist to the vibrant forest left him in awe. The trees towered above, their branches interweaving to form a natural canopy. Sunlight filtered through the leaves, creating a play of shadows on the forest floor. Birds chirped in the background, and a gentle breeze carried the soothing scent of the woods.

Çarh was momentarily taken aback, trying to comprehend the sudden shift in his surroundings. The hooded man was no longer beside him, and Çarh felt a mix of curiosity and uncertainty about this enchanting forest.

As Çarh took in the serene beauty of the forest, he couldn't shake the feeling that something was missing. Despite the vibrant life surrounding him, a sense of quietude lingered. The absence of footsteps, the distant sounds of the city, or any sign of human presence left an eerie stillness in the air.

The forest seemed untouched, almost otherworldly, as if it existed in a realm of its own. Çarh wondered if he was alone in this mystical place or if there were unseen inhabitants within the depths of the woods. The mystery of the forest beckoned him to explore further.

As the voice of the hooded man resonated through the forest, Çarh felt a subtle vibration in the air. The unfamiliar words, "Tö'guarro¡," seemed to carry a mystical weight, echoing with a resonance that transcended the ordinary. It was as if the very essence of the forest responded to the incantation.

Curiosity and a touch of trepidation filled Çarh as he awaited the next moment in this enigmatic journey, uncertain of the secrets the forest held and the role the hooded man played in this mysterious unfolding.

Amidst the lingering questions and the mystical energy within him, Çarh surveyed his surroundings but found no one in sight. "Who's there?" he inquired, only to be met with a profound silence.

After a contemplative pause, he chose a direction and began walking, traversing through the forest for an extended period. Eventually, he reached a clearing, greeted by a breathtaking view. In the distance, the imposing silhouette of a massive mountain captivated his attention. On the other side of the forest, the vibrant hues of the sunset painted a captivating scene, adding to the surreal and otherworldly nature of his experience.

In the tranquil clearing, a butterfly gracefully alighted on Çarh's hand, capturing his attention with its wings adorned by black spots. Intrigued, Çarh began to examine the butterfly closely. To his astonishment, the butterfly underwent a sudden transformation – its colour shifted, and the black spots were replaced by peculiar symbols. These enigmatic symbols seemed to convey a message, leaving Çarh both fascinated and perplexed by the newfound form of communication unfolding before him.

Straining his eyes, Çarh attempted to decipher the symbols, which seemed to convey a message about the hooded man. However, the meaning eluded him, and he couldn't fully comprehend the information encoded in the intricate patterns. Abruptly, the butterfly fluttered lightly and took flight, disappearing into the surroundings, accompanied by the vanishing of the mysterious symbols. The encounter left Çarh with a sense of both wonder and frustration, as he grappled with the elusive secrets hinted at by the magical butterfly.

Driven by a fervent desire for answers, Çarh embarked on a pursuit of the elusive butterfly. The fleeting symbols and the potential insights into the mysteries surrounding the hooded man were too tantalizing to let slip away. Running with a singular focus, Çarh's thoughts were consumed by the singular goal of capturing the butterfly, as he raced through the landscape, determined not to let this opportunity escape his grasp.

With unwavering determination, Çarh continued his rapid pursuit of the butterfly, each step fuelled by the urgency of the questions swirling in his mind. The elusive creature fluttered swiftly, its flight becoming a challenging endeavour for Çarh to match. Despite his relentless effort, catching up with the butterfly grew increasingly difficult with each passing second, heightening the suspense and the stakes of the chase.

Breathless and consumed by his pursuit, Çarh pressed on, oblivious to the surroundings. In the intensity of his chase, he reached the edge of a cliff. The urgency to capture the butterfly had overshadowed his awareness of the perilous precipice before him. The danger went unnoticed as he remained singularly focused on the pursuit, the thrill of the chase blinding him to the potential risks that lay at the edge of the cliff.

Unaware of his proximity to the precipice, Çarh took a step, only to find his footing give way, plunging him into the void below. The rapid descent gripped his senses, and his heart raced as he felt the sudden acceleration of his fall. In that harrowing moment, his life seemed to flash before his eyes, the weight of the unexpected plunge etched into the fabric of his consciousness.

As Çarh descended, the fabric of reality seemed to stretch and warp around him, creating a surreal tableau. The once-vibrant dance of rustling leaves in the trees slowed to a haunting rhythm, each fluttering sound echoing with an eerie clarity in his ears. The rough texture of the rocks on the cliffside, typically overlooked, became a tactile symphony beneath his fingertips. In the midst of the freefall, the world unfolded in strange and heightened sensations, transforming the ordinary into an otherworldly experience.

While Çarh descended into the unknown, the butterfly that had guided him to the precipice continued its ethereal flight. Unfettered by the laws of gravity, its wings bore intricate patterns that glistened in the dimming sunlight. As it soared further away from Çarh, its otherworldly trail painted a mesmerizing path in the air, leaving behind a spectral imprint that contrasted with the impending darkness below.

As Çarh continued his descent, the atmosphere itself underwent a profound transformation. The air, rather than resisting, thickened around him, enveloping him in a weightless cocoon as he plummeted through the void. Time, typically a relentless force, now meandered, allowing Çarh to perceive the fleeting moments with an unprecedented level of detail. The descent became an exploration of the intricate nuances of existence, a surreal journey through a suspended reality where the boundaries of time and space blurred into a mesmerizing dance.

As the descent continued, the features of the landscape below gradually unveiled themselves with each passing second. A meandering river, its surface reflecting the hues of the setting sun, snaked through a lush valley. Trees, like silent sentinels, stood tall, casting long shadows that reached out to greet him. The unfolding scene below painted a tranquil yet surreal panorama, inviting Çarh into a world where the ordinary became extraordinary amidst the timeless descent.

In the midst of his free fall, Çarh's mind became a whirlwind of emotions. Fear, regret, and an overwhelming sense of the unknown intertwined with the exhilaration brought on by the swiftly changing scenery. It was a kaleidoscope of sensations, a surreal journey into the depths of his consciousness. Each passing moment heightened the intensity of his emotional landscape, creating a complex tapestry of feelings that mirrored the intricate patterns of his descent.

As the ground rapidly approached, transitioning from an abstract concept to an imminent reality, Çarh felt a profound connection to the earth he was about to embrace. In the fleeting moment before impact, the once-distant details of the landscape below merged into a mosaic of colours and textures. This vivid tapestry unfolded, creating a visual symphony that accompanied his final descent. The impending collision with the earth became a convergence of sensations, marking the culmination of his surreal journey through the suspended reality of the fall.

In a desperate attempt to delay the inevitable impact, Çarh instinctively reached out, grasping for the ephemeral elements surrounding him – the whispering leaves, the rugged cliffside – anything that could anchor him in this surreal descent. However, his efforts proved futile, as the intangible slipped through his fingers like elusive mist. The impending collision with the earth remained inevitable, and Çarh braced himself for the culmination of his free fall.

As the ground rushed up to meet him with an inexorable force, Çarh's senses heightened, capturing the vivid details of the world around him. The butterfly, the enigmatic guide of his fall, continued its dance – a delicate silhouette against the backdrop of the descending sun. The surreal beauty of the moment juxtaposed with the impending impact, creating a breathtaking scene that etched itself into the fabric of Çarh's consciousness.

In those final heartbeats, a surge of conflicting emotions coursed through Çarh. Fear, regret, and the tantalizing allure of the unknown collided within him. The landscape below, now a tapestry of colours and textures, painted itself onto his consciousness in the seconds before impact. The impending collision became an intricate dance between visceral emotions and the vivid canvas of the world rushing up to meet him.

As the ground loomed closer, the butterfly – a transient symbol of guidance – fluttered gracefully in front of Çarh's eyes. In that fleeting moment, a desire to pursue it briefly gripped him, but the laws of gravity had already sealed their separation. Çarh closed his eyes, surrendering to the inevitability of the fall. The impact, harsh and inevitable, jolted through every fibre of his being as he crashed onto the ground.

CHAPTER 5
TREASURE-TROVE

In the serene embrace of the mountains, distant from the hustle and bustle of the city, lay an isolated village. Surrounded by the awe-inspiring beauty of nature, the village was adorned with a spectrum of green hues. Its inhabitants found their livelihoods in agriculture and livestock. Rows of small houses, painted in pristine white, stood closely together. The tables of the villagers were graced with the bounty of vegetables and fruits cultivated in their gardens, while the neighbouring forests offered opportunities for hunting.

In the village square, vibrant pavilions and stalls were erected for a lively fair that drew everyone in attendance. The children of the village revelled in the joy of riding the spinning carousel and swings, their laughter echoing through the air. Meanwhile, the adults congregated, engaged in conversations, and shared laughter. Above them, the sky stretched in a cloudless shade of blue, and the sun cast its warm and radiant glow, enveloping the scene in a serene and inviting atmosphere.

The villagers savoured a happy and tranquil existence in

this picturesque setting. On a particular day, the village came alive with the organization of a fair. The air was filled with high spirits as the villagers sang songs, danced, and exchanged smiles. Children revelled in games in the village square, while adults engaged in animated conversations. Stalls adorned with handmade products added to the festive atmosphere, creating a vibrant celebration of the close-knit community's joys and shared moments.

Amidst the cheerful atmosphere, a little girl approached a small cotton candy vendor. Her face radiated the innocent laughter of childhood as she extended her hand towards the vendor and sweetly asked, "Could you please give me a cotton candy?" The vendor happily handed a fluffy creation to the girl, and she turned her joyful face toward the sun, savouring the moment as she slowly licked the sweet treat in her hand.

In that moment, Çarh opened his eyes to find himself on the edge of a cliff. The solitude enveloped him, and a sense of disorientation clouded his awareness. With hands trembling with fear, Çarh cautiously attempted to rise from the edge. Slowly pulling back, he sought to regain his alertness. Once on his feet, he surveyed his surroundings. Steep rocks flanked him on both sides, and in the distance, a village emerged on the horizon. The mystery of his whereabouts lingered as Çarh contemplated the unfamiliar landscape before him.

The sight of the village served as a stark reminder to Çarh that he was far from the familiarity of his home. Although the thought of returning home briefly crossed his mind, the allure of the distant village tugged at his curiosity. An eagerness to discover what was unfolding in that far-off community captured his imagination. Even as he chased butterflies, his thoughts were drawn in the direction of the intriguing village, sparking a sense of anticipation and a desire to unravel the mysteries that lay beyond.

Gathering his resolve, Çarh started the descent from the cliff, drawn toward the vibrant atmosphere of the village. A compelling curiosity fuelled his steps, eager to immerse himself in the festivities. Along the journey, he contemplated the lives of the villagers – their happiness and tranquillity stirred a sense of longing within him. Having grown up in the bustling city and faced numerous challenges, Çarh found an appealing contrast in the village, where people lived in harmony with nature, embracing a simpler and slower pace of life. As he approached, he observed the joyous scene of a fair unfolding in the village, with people dancing, eating, and revelling in the music.

The challenging journey took several hours, but Çarh persevered until he finally reached the village. Initially, the villagers were preoccupied with the peak of the festivity at the fair and paid little attention to the newcomer. However, as Çarh arrived at the entrance of the fair, his presence sparked surprise among the villagers. A stranger to everyone, he was met with warm welcomes and invitations to join in the festivities. Despite being unknown, the villagers embraced Çarh, extending their hospitality and inviting him to partake in the joyous celebration at the fair.

Embracing the warmth of the welcome, Çarh joined in the festivities with the villagers. Despite the joy surrounding him, his mind remained haunted by the terrifying moments on the cliff, leaving him uncertain about his next steps.

As Çarh wandered through the village, he stumbled upon the heartwarming scene of a little girl requesting a candy apple. The sheer joy radiating from the girl's face touched him deeply, offering a respite from his troubled thoughts. The infectious happiness of the villagers created a space for Çarh to momentarily escape his distress. Influenced by the buoyant atmosphere, he found solace in engaging with the crowd at the fair, striking up conversations, and sharing moments of laughter with the villagers.

The temporary respite of happiness was fleeting, and soon after, the haunting memory of falling from the cliff resurfaced in Çarh's mind. This time, the feeling of fear intensified, confronting him with the reality he had sought to escape. A realization dawned upon him – he couldn't evade the distressing situation; the only recourse was to confront it head-on. The juxtaposition of joy and fear underscored the complexity of Çarh's emotional journey, as he grappled with the unresolved challenges that lingered in the recesses of his mind.

Summoning courage from within, Çarh compelled himself to confront the fears that lurked in the recesses of his mind. He began to question the circumstances that led to his fall from the cliff, determined to unravel the mysteries that haunted him. Though the thoughts were unsettling and induced fear, Çarh recognized that evasion was not an option. With resolute determination, he steeled himself to explore the underlying reasons behind his plunge from the cliff, setting the stage for a journey of self-discovery and understanding.

Navigating the terrain with cautious steps, Çarh deviated from the path and ventured into the forest. Choosing not to flee from his fear, Çarh made the courageous decision to return to the scene of his fall. Guided by the enchanting presence of butterflies, he threaded through the branches, eventually arriving once more at the precipice. The initial fear that had gripped his mind gradually transformed into a mix of curiosity and excitement. With a newfound determination, Çarh prepared to scrutinize the surroundings more attentively this time, seeking a deeper understanding of the mysterious circumstances that led to his previous fall.

Drawing nearer to the cliff's edge, Çarh leaned forward and gazed downward. With a deep breath, he initiated his search for the elusive butterfly. Before too long, a small white butterfly came into view, and Çarh extended his hand to capture it gently. As he held the delicate creature, its wings adorned with vibrant spots captivated his attention, filling him with a sense of wonder and fascination.

In awe, Çarh observed as the butterfly's wings began to flutter, and the patterns on them became more defined, starting to shimmer. The colours adorning its delicate and graceful wings intensified, and for a fleeting moment, a radiant display of colourful lights enveloped the entire vicinity. Mesmerized by the spectacle, Çarh witnessed a beam of light emanating from the wings, and in a mysterious transformation, the butterfly underwent a complete metamorphosis before his eyes.

In the place of the butterfly stood a man, his hair gently swaying in the wind, exuding a powerful presence. A smile adorned his face as he advanced toward Çarh. The man's eyes bore a penetrating gaze, as if delving into the depths of Çarh's inner world. A moment of silence enveloped them before the man spoke, breaking the quiet with a simple, "Hello," accompanied by the offer of a robust handshake.

Çarh observed the man, now transformed from the butterfly, with a profound sense of astonishment. The man's visage carried the wisdom and age of an elder, and his penetrating gaze sent shivers down Çarh's spine.

The man's countenance bore the weight of wrinkles, yet his smile exuded youthfulness and cheerfulness. A cascade of long, white beard flowed down to his shoulders. Adorned in a robe that mirrored butterfly wings, the bright and harmonious colours of the wings seemed to dance gracefully across the fabric.

In the presence of the enigmatic man, Çarh found himself at a loss for words. The queries about the butterfly had slipped from his mind, replaced by the haunting memory of his fall from the cliff. In this mysterious figure, Çarh sensed the potential for answers and assistance.

"I... I tumbled from the cliff and found myself lost in this unfamiliar place. Can you lend me your assistance?" Çarh implored, extending his hand with eyes filled with hope.

The man responded with a gentle smile, observing Çarh's bewildered expression. "Your unexpected presence here has taken me by surprise, young man," he remarked, his voice carrying a subtle tremor. "Yet, I am cognizant of the forces that brought you to this place. I can sense that butterflies have summoned you here."

Çarh listened in astonishment to the man's revelation. "Butterflies?" he queried, seeking clarification.

The man nodded in affirmation. "Yes, butterflies. They wish to impart their messages to you. You have a task ahead, young man, and I am here to aid you in fulfilling it."

Locking eyes with the wise man, Çarh experienced an inexplicable sense of trust. He was certain that this knowledgeable figure would be his guide. The man nodded slightly and continued, "Regarding your current predicament, I can certainly assist you, but first, you must come with me. I will lead you onto the right path."

Accepting the man's offer, Çarh embarked on a journey with him. Along the way, he absorbed a wealth of knowledge and uncovered profound insights about himself.

Ultimately, the man guided him to the destination, and

Sûr

Çarh sensed that he was once again on the correct path. Although the initial questions about the butterfly had slipped from his mind, this journey bestowed upon him a more significant treasure: the chance to comprehend himself and the intricacies of his own life.

Still, as if attuned to Çarh's thoughts, the man smiled at him and revealed, "I am an Elf, and I will be your companion during this transitional period. Your curiosity and quest attracted me to you."

Çarh was taken aback. The notion of encountering an Elf had never crossed his mind, and while scepticism lingered, a peculiar sense of trust began to form within him.

Sensing Çarh's astonishment, the Elf approached him and spoke deliberately, "I am an Elf, and it was I who called you to this place, Çarh."

Intrigued, Çarh inquired, "Why did you summon me here? And where exactly is this place?"

The Elf explained to Çarh, "Pau was once infamous for its witch hunts, a place where witches and wizards faced imprisonment, torture, and execution. However, the tides have changed, and it has evolved into a village now governed by witches. I summoned you here to reveal the true prowess of witchcraft. The power and wisdom of witches persist in this place. There is something for you to learn here as well."

Çarh found himself caught between fear and curiosity. Despite the unsettling atmosphere, his desire to learn more about the witches and wizards of Pau prevailed. The enchanting spells cast by the witches, their adept use of medicinal herbs, and the mystical rituals held a captivating allure for him. In this mysterious world, Çarh felt a profound fascination taking root within him.

The Elf continued, "I sensed the quest in your heart,

and I wanted to help you."

Çarh was even more surprised by the Elf's words. "A quest in my heart? What do you mean?" he asked.

The Elf smiled reassuringly and carried on, "I perceive the quest within your heart, for I can connect with you. You seek a purpose in this world, feeling adrift. However, as you already understand, the answers are not external; you must delve within yourself."

Çarh absorbed the Elf's words and reflected. He admitted to feeling a void within and a yearning for purpose in his life. "Okay, but what is my purpose? What do I need to do?" he inquired.

The Elf responded, "I can be your guide, but you will chart your own course. You must undertake a journey to explore yourself and discover the power within. Yet, remember, you are not alone on this path; I will always be by your side."

Conquering his initial scepticism towards the Elf, Çarh questioned, "What kind of journey?"

The Elf listened in silence to Çarh's question, taking a deep breath before responding. "This journey will be a plunge into the depths of your soul," he articulated. "You will face unanswered questions, fears, and concerns within yourself with courage. Simultaneously, you will unearth the power within. This expedition promises to bring you freedom and happiness."

Çarh attentively absorbed the Elf's words and pondered for a moment. Then, he inquired, "Okay, where should I go?" The Elf responded, "Within yourself. You will embark on a journey of self-discovery into the depths of your soul."

Despite harbouring numerous questions about the Elf's cryptic guidance, Çarh made the decision to trust him. Sensing that a change was necessary within himself, he surmised that perhaps this journey was precisely what he needed. "Alright," he finally declared. "I'm ready."

The Elf responded, "Then let's begin," and struck the ground with his staff. In an instant, the surrounding landscape vanished, and Çarh found himself in an entirely different place.

Surveying his surroundings with a blend of fear and curiosity, Çarh beheld a scenery unlike anything he had ever seen. Before them stretched a sprawling forest, where trees interwove their branches as they ascended towards the sky. The air was thick with humidity, and, save for the occasional chirping of birds, an eerie silence enveloped the area.

The Elf detected Çarh's bewildered gaze and offered a reassuring smile. "Yes, you can think of it as teleportation," he explained. "Traveling to different places is one of the most crucial abilities of the Sögré[ii]. That's why I brought you here; together, we will explore this forest."

Çarh, still struggling to fully comprehend the Elf's words, asked curiously, "Sögré?"

The Elf responded with a smile, affirming Çarh's question. "Yes, Sögré. You are a witch."

This revelation filled Çarh's mind with more question marks. Could he truly be a witch? The idea had never crossed his mind before. In his family, among relatives, and even in his village, there was no mention of witches. Yet now, an Elf stood before him, claiming that he was a witch.

The Elf continued, seemingly attuned to Çarh's thoughts. "I will assist you in discovering yourself. Sögré are individuals with supernatural powers, capable of changing the world through these abilities. You will become one of them."

These words elicited a sense of fear within Çarh. Common beliefs about witches often included notions of possessing supernatural powers and the ability to alter the course of the world. Despite this apprehension, a compelling force within him insisted that he needed to undertake this journey.

"But I'm not a witch," Çarh protested. "Maybe I'm just dreaming."

The Elf smiled gently. "Actually, witchcraft is not a choice — at least not something humans can choose. Those chosen by Céwiaretza[iii] are born as witches and fulfil their duty based on the attribute assigned to them."

Already befuddled, Çarh, eager to make sense of the incomprehensible words, attempted to interrupt the Elf. "Céwiaretza? What is that? In which language are you speaking?"

Çarh was eager to decipher the meaning of the Elf's words. At this moment, one question dominated his thoughts: What did "Tö'guarro" mean? Was it the Elf who used this word, or was it someone else's voice? A troubling thought crossed his mind — perhaps he had hallucinated during the fall from the cliff, conjuring up this word himself. However, a lingering doubt persisted. Did the Elf assist him during the fall, or was he the cause of it?

Confused, Çarh looked at the Elf's face and asked, "What does 'Tö'guarro' mean?" The Elf, before explaining its meaning, took a moment of silence and drew a deep breath. Then, he replied, "Tö'guarro means 'I will save you' in the Ancient Language." However, the Elf had deceived Çarh, motivated by a desire to protect him. Through the Tö'guarro spell, the only magic that elves could cast against Sögré, the Elf had aimed to extract the witchcraft within Çarh. The ritual proved successful, and Çarh had now transformed into a Sögré.

Sûr

Çarh felt a sense of relief upon hearing the Elf's explanation, and some of his doubts began to dissipate. Nevertheless, suspicions about the Elf's true intentions lingered in his mind after this revelation.

Observing Çarh's confusion, the Elf understood that Çarh had not been raised as a witch and continued with a softer tone, "Forgive me for not providing details, thinking this would be as straightforward as the previous ones. Actually..."

Çarh felt ensnared in an unending cycle. What could this Céwiaretza be that the Elf mentioned? He had never encountered the term before. Perhaps it was something from previous cycles that he couldn't recall. The unsettling thought of an eternal loop loomed, threatening to imprison him forever.

Yet, within Çarh, a flicker of hope persisted. Perhaps this time could be different. Maybe he was indeed a witch, and with his newfound abilities, he could uncover a way to break free from this relentless cycle. It was this hope that kept him standing.

Once again, the Elf looked at him and stated, "Céwiaretza is shaped only by your choices. You are the sole determinant of the outcome of this journey."

Çarh grappled with the implications of these words. It appeared that destiny was asserted to be under his control, leaving him with a profound sense of responsibility. Whatever path he chose, the outcome would rest entirely on his shoulders.

Yet, hope within Çarh continued to burgeon. Perhaps this time could indeed be different, and he could wield the power to reshape his own fate.

Unbeknownst to Çarh, the Elf was attuned to his

thoughts. Consequently, the Elf continued, "In fact, there is much to discuss, as much as there is to learn. But ultimately, I know that you are a Sögré. The reason we came to this forest is for you to discover your natural powers. We can talk about the rest later; for now, we will perform magic together."

The Elf's words caught Çarh off guard. Despite his initial scepticism about magic, his burgeoning curiosity and thirst for discovery had started to overcome his doubts.

Lost in thought, Çarh snapped back to reality with the Elf's prompt. "Alright, but how will we do it?" he inquired.

The Elf swiftly raised his staff into the air, and the ritual commenced. It was as if he were dancing, feeling the air and energy around him.

Çarh watched the Elf's distinctive movements, his heart pounding rapidly. The intensity of the Elf's ritual was increasing, and the energy seemed to transform the very air around them. Symbols and shapes danced around Çarh, merging with brightly coloured lights that shimmered in the darkness, forming a magical circle. With each of the Elf's hand movements and the incantations uttered, the circle expanded and ascended.

Çarh was unprepared for the force of the spell. The enchantment overwhelmed him, unlocking all the dark thoughts within. Yet, even amid the darkness, he managed to maintain control, carefully observing the Elf's movements. He attuned himself to the flow of energy around him, building a resistance against the magic.

As Çarh sensed the magical power within him, a surge of excitement coursed through him. The allure of exploring the unknown powers within tugged at him, even as a longing for his old life persisted. Torn between two worlds, the conflicting emotions intensified.

However, as the ritual continued, a sudden realization struck Çarh. A power, previously dormant, had awakened within him. With this revelation, there was no turning back; a new chapter of his life had begun.

The Elf concluded the ritual, and the surrounding lights dimmed. Çarh was left with a newfound sensation of power, an experience unlike anything he had felt before. Everything had shifted, and he now stood on the brink of a new life as a witch. Excitement and anticipation welled up within him as he looked forward to discovering more about himself. Simultaneously, a sense of anxiety loomed, driven by the need to master and control these newfound powers.

With a reassuring smile, the Elf addressed him, "Now you know you're a Sögré. I will continue this journey with you, guiding you in learning how to harness your magical powers."

Çarh found himself taken aback by the Elf's words, yet a determination to ready himself for this new world began to set in. The prospect of embarking on a fresh journey with the Elf, delving into the discovery of himself and his magical powers, filled him with a thrilling sense of anticipation. However, he couldn't dismiss his lingering concerns.

The negative energy he had experienced during the ritual lingered in his mind, raising worries about the potential consequences of using magical powers. The fear of misuse loomed, adding another layer of complexity to his thoughts. Despite this confusion and the swirling thoughts in his mind, Çarh steeled himself to continue the journey with the Elf.

The Elf inquired of Çarh, "Did you feel anything different during the ritual?"

As Çarh pondered the Elf's question, he recollected a distinct sensation during the ritual. A surge of power had emerged within him, stirring excitement. Yet, simultaneously, there was something unfolding in his mind. The imagery he witnessed during the ritual seemed familiar, a glimpse from his past that he struggled to recall. Then, in a sudden flash of memory, he remembered the face of the hooded man who had spoken of a forgotten memory. This recollection prompted Çarh to delve into the enigma of his past.

The Elf listened to Çarh's account and remarked, "This means your powers are gradually emerging. And this journey is not just about magic; it's also a journey of self-discovery for you."

As Çarh absorbed the Elf's words, he found a ring of truth in them. He now possessed more magical powers, and he had taken a step towards exploring the depths of his own self. However, a sense of foreboding accompanied the Elf's words. Where would this journey lead him, and what unforeseen challenges might he encounter?

Breaking the silence, Çarh expressed his desire to return home. The Elf reassured him, "I brought you here, and it's my duty to take you home," waving his staff. In an instant, the surroundings changed, and Çarh found himself back in the familiar living room of his home.

With a final smile, the Elf said, "Until we meet again," and vanished. As Çarh sat in the living room chair, his mind remained in a state of confusion, struggling to fully grasp the events that had transpired. However, one thing was clear: his life had undergone a profound change. He was now a witch, and he needed to navigate the challenges that came with his newfound powers.

Sûr

CHAPTER 6
ACKNOWLEDGMENT

After the witchcraft ritual experience in Pau, Çarh returned to his normal life, but everything had transformed. Concepts like energy and magic held a deeper significance for him. He could now sense the subtle flow of energy around him and better comprehend the intricate forces of nature. The acceptance of the reality of witches and magic had opened numerous new perspectives for him. Over time, Çarh gradually integrated this newfound understanding into his daily life, forever changed by the magical journey that had unravelled before him.

For instance, Çarh began dedicating time to exploring the powers of plants and started incorporating natural remedies for health. He delved into understanding how his energy interacted with objects in his surroundings and learned how to influence them. Crafting his own spells, he continued to develop these newfound abilities. Çarh recognized that a profound change had occurred in his life, as he embarked on a new path of self-discovery and magical exploration.

As Çarh endeavoured to gradually adapt to his transformed life, he occasionally experienced a sense of strangeness. His mind continued to process the profound experiences he had during the ritual and the teachings the Elf had imparted. While concepts like magic and energy had taken on a deeper meaning, they couldn't entirely replace the significance of the people and events in his life. This sometimes left him feeling disconnected, struggling to align with the thoughts and lifestyles of those around him.

However, with the passage of time, Çarh began to accept himself more fully and integrate these differences into his life. In addition to exploring concepts like energy and magic, he also embraced the responsibilities of normal life, gradually adapting to the evolving balance between his newfound understanding and the realities of everyday existence.

Communicating with the people around him became challenging as Çarh felt like he existed in a different world. However, drawing strength from his transformative experiences, he gradually began to reshape his life. With newfound courage and confidence acquired through overcoming his fears, Çarh persevered through moments of feeling out of place. His commitment to practicing magic and energy work provided him with confidence and tapped into his inner strength.

As Çarh continued to explore these practices, he achieved things he couldn't have imagined before. His enhanced ability to sense and utilize energy became a source of empowerment. With growing courage and confidence, Çarh steered his life in a new direction. He expanded his social circles, pursued new hobbies, and seized fresh opportunities.

Freedom and courage emerged as significant aspects of his transformed life.

Due to the transformative changes, he had undergone, Çarh observed new doors opening up in his life. He found himself encountering diverse and interesting individuals, delving into new hobbies, and fostering a heightened openness to learning. Concepts and ideas that never crossed his mind in his old life now sparked his curiosity, motivating him to explore uncharted territories. Through these novel experiences, Çarh was enriching his life and developing himself.

Although initial fears and concerns had held him back, Çarh was now moving forward with newfound confidence and courage. His increased openness to innovations attracted new opportunities, and with each passing day, he found himself growing happier and more fulfilled.

On a seemingly normal day as Çarh returned from work, he unexpectedly encountered Aunt Fatma sitting in front of the apartment building. What used to be an ordinary encounter now carried a different weight. Aunt Fatma didn't feel as unfamiliar to him anymore. As they chatted, a sense of void lingered when Aunt Zülfiye was mentioned, and Çarh realised how much everything had changed. The days of missing Aunt Zülfiye became more poignant.

In that moment, tears welled up in Çarh's eyes, and Aunt Fatma tried to console him with a hug. However, the pain inside Çarh extended beyond the simple feeling of missing someone. The days spent with Aunt Zülfiye held a profound place in his life. She was not just a grandmother but also a friend, a guide, and a protector. The time shared with her had always been special to Çarh, and the reality that he could no longer be with her cut deeply into his heart.

Aunt Fatma, in an effort to console Çarh, began

recounting beautiful memories. She tried to evoke images of the sweets they made together, the laughter they shared, and the lessons Aunt Zülfiye imparted to him. These memories succeeded in bringing a fleeting smile to Çarh's face and helped dry the tears in his eyes.

Yet, the void within Çarh persisted. Longing and feelings of loss continued to disturb him. However, equipped with the strength he had gained from his experiences, Çarh was now ready to confront these emotions head-on.

Çarh's life was now interwoven with spells and elves, making it far from the normalcy it once held. Despite the fantastical elements, he had still experienced losses that were deeply precious to him, causing a lingering pain. Eventually, consoled by Aunt Fatma, he entered the apartment, aware that there was still something he needed to do to fill the void within him. The magical aspects of his life hadn't replaced the emotional weight of what he had lost.

Çarh found himself engulfed in a memory as he gazed at the mailbox at the entrance of the apartment building. In years past, Aunt Zülfiye used to check the mailbox every morning, finding joy in the letters she held in her hands. The memory of her excitement lingered as she opened the mailbox. Now, the mailbox was only filled with bills and advertisements. However, Çarh sensed that something had shifted. He now looked forward to checking the mailbox, hopeful that an important letter might one day arrive for him. The anticipation of potential surprises brought a new sense of meaning to this routine.

With a smile on his face, Çarh started walking towards his home, feeling a newfound sense of happiness. In his transformed world, even the smallest things held meaning, and his thoughts were brimming with new opportunities and adventures. As he approached his home, the idea of making himself a cup of hot tea and settling down with a book filled him with contentment.

However, as Çarh neared the door, he sensed something strange. His heart began to race, and his steps slowed. A feeling of unease settled in, as he realised that someone was inside his house. Fear and curiosity mingled as he opened the door and cautiously entered, eager to uncover the mystery of the unexpected presence.

The inside of the house remained quiet, and Çarh found himself in the hallway. His eyes darted to the doors of the rooms as he moved silently. With each step, his certainty grew – there was indeed a stranger in his house. Questions raced through his mind. Who could it be, and what was their purpose?

Eventually, Çarh reached the bedroom, and to his astonishment, Aunt Zülfiye stood before him. It was an unbelievable but undeniably true sight – she had returned. She greeted him with a warm smile, her arms open in welcome.

Overwhelmed with joy, Çarh's heart raced. He hugged her tightly, tears streaming down his face. Aunt Zülfiye spoke, "Hello Çarh, I've missed you so much," as she took Çarh's hand, filling the room with a sense of reunion and warmth.

Çarh's eyes widened, and tears streamed down his face. "Aunt Zülfiye, you are here! I've missed you so much!" he exclaimed.

Overwhelmed with emotions, Çarh wondered why Aunt Zülfiye was there and asked, "Aunt Zülfiye, what are you doing here? How did you come?" She replied with a warm smile, "I came to visit you. It's been a long time, hasn't it?"

Still grappling with disbelief, Çarh couldn't fathom the reality before him. Aunt Zülfiye, one of his favourite people, had passed away long ago. Yet, here she was, standing before him, and Çarh couldn't find words to express the immense happiness welling up inside him.

Aunt Zülfiye gently pulled him inside and said, "Come on, I invite you to have tea." Still in a state of astonishment, Çarh followed her. It felt like an unreal dream, but he acknowledged that sometimes realities in life could be otherworldly. The recent experiences he had encountered had sparked a deeper interest in the mysteries of life. Instead of dwelling on why he saw her, Çarh chose to savour the moment.

Believing that everything in life held a meaning, he considered the appearance of Aunt Zülfiye as a significant occurrence. Çarh saw that moment as a secret feeding his curiosity, and with this newfound perspective, he continued on with his life.

After the unexpected encounter with Aunt Zülfiye, Çarh found himself unable to shake off the lingering questions in his mind. Nevertheless, a sense of excitement accompanied this mysterious event. Viewing it as a secret that fed his curiosity, Çarh continued with his daily life.

The following day, he worked tirelessly at a hectic pace in the office. By the evening, exhaustion weighed heavily on him. However, the mystery lingered within him. Was Aunt Zülfiye truly there, or was it just his imagination? Despite the ambiguous questions in his mind, Çarh chose to savour the thrilling feeling that this unexplained event had brought into his life.

On the next day, as Çarh was leaving home for work, he noticed an envelope in the mailbox. Recognizing the address on it, his heart skipped a beat – it was Aunt Zülfiye's address. For a moment, his eyes froze, and then he eagerly opened the envelope. Inside, he found a note and a small gift. In her heartfelt note, Aunt Zülfiye expressed how much she missed him, conveyed her desire to surprise him, and mentioned that she would come to visit him soon.

Excitement bubbled within Çarh as he read the note repeatedly, his curiosity intensifying with each word. The mysterious events in his life seemed to be unfolding in unexpected and magical ways.

The hours at the workplace that day proved to be a bit more challenging for Çarh. His mind was preoccupied with dreams of Aunt Zülfiye's upcoming visit. Upon returning home, he immediately set about cleaning and making preparations for her arrival. He even rehearsed a few sentences to greet her. When the doorbell finally rang, Çarh eagerly and happily opened the door.

However, as soon as he opened the door, the excitement within him quickly turned to disappointment. His astonishment was so evident that he couldn't conceal it until the Elf spoke. The Elf entered, gesturing for Çarh to follow. Filled with doubts, Çarh hesitantly followed the Elf. Inside, he was perturbed to find that everything in his house resembled Aunt Zülfiye. Slowly, he followed the Elf, and with each step, his discomfort heightened.

The Elf asked, "Do you remember me?" Çarh affirmed that he did but expressed his confusion about the Elf's unexpected visit. In response, the Elf stated, "I want to show you something. Follow me," and guided Çarh to Pau, the village.

As Çarh followed the Elf to Pau, he observed that everything remained unchanged. The witch village stood as it always had, with no discernible alterations. The Elf inquired, "How do you feel now?" Çarh replied, "I feel very strange, like I've been here before."

Sûr

The Elf explained, "Yes, here lies your past. Now it's time to confront it," and with a gesture, the Elf disappeared, leaving Çarh to grapple with the unfolding revelations.

Çarh looked around in astonishment, attempting to comprehend the connection between himself and Pau, and the resurfacing memories and emotions from his past. The Elf's words seemed to be a guide for the growing power within him, aiding him in accepting his own truth.

Upon the Elf's return, he held two mirrors in his hands, both mysteriously glowing. The enchantment of the images reflected in the mirrors captivated Çarh. Although the mirrors didn't exactly resemble each other, when brought together, they formed a complete cycle, creating a sense of unity and completion.

The Elf brought the mirrors close to the back of Çarh's neck, revealing the reflected image. To Çarh's surprise, his tattoo appeared in the mirrors. Examining the tattoo with astonishment, Çarh knew it was impossible to have such a tattoo. In bewilderment, he focused on the mirrors in the Elf's hands, appreciating their beauty and trying to grasp the significance of what Elf wanted to show him.

The power of the mirrors amazed Çarh. The Elf had promised to reveal something, and indeed, he had accomplished something extraordinary. The mirrors unveiled a mysterious piece of Çarh's life, prompting him to wonder about the other secrets these powerful objects might uncover.

Çarh, with a curious gaze, inquired about the story behind the tattoo. The Elf responded with a smile to Çarh's question, saying, "The story is very ancient and long, but I can express it like this: in your world, it's not possible for people to have tattoos. Tattoos can only belong to the Sögré. This tattoo signifies that you are a Sögré and, at the same time, is a symbol of the witch ancestry. Unlike many Sögrés, your tattoo is hidden but can be seen by the einéx mirrors – that is, these twin mirrors."

Breathless, Çarh asked, "Witch ancestry? Were there other witches in my ancestry aside from me?"

The Elf continued to explain, "It doesn't work exactly like that. Being a Sögré is not something inherited from the family. Sögrés are chosen by Céwiaretza. Céwiaretza selects Sögrés who have certain powers to maintain the balance of nature. Anyone can be born as a Sögré under suitable conditions and shapes their life accordingly. But, unlike you, of course, you weren't born as a Sögré."

Çarh struggled to comprehend the Elf's words. He had initially believed that Céwiaretza was a being responsible for maintaining the balance of nature. However, the revelation about Sögré choices surprised him. Since being a Sögré wasn't something inherited from family, he wondered how these powers were determined. The Elf continued to clarify, saying, "You have earned your tattoo. Céwiaretza has chosen you. Before listening to its words, you saw yourself as just a regular human. But now, you are different. You are a tool for the balance of nature."

Faced with this revelation, Çarh gazed at the Elf in astonishment. He had never considered himself as possessing anything powerful. However, with the Elf's words, a realization began to dawn within him about the latent powers he held. He now grasped more clearly the uniqueness that set him apart.

Taking the mirror into his hands once more, Çarh inquired of Elf about the meaning of the tattoo. As he listened to Elf's explanations, Çarh found it initially difficult to believe. A depiction of a trumpet? The trumpet that Israfil[iv] would blow? How could this be possible? The notion crossed his mind that the Elf might be mocking him. However, upon scrutinizing the Elf's expression, Çarh realised that the Elf genuinely believed in what he was saying.

Çarh peered at the mirrors in the Elf's hands with curiosity, searching for his tattoo, but to his surprise, he saw nothing. Was this something the mirrors failed to reflect, or perhaps the Elf was truly joking, attempting to deceive Çarh? The mystery lingered, leaving Çarh perplexed.

The Elf sensed a bit of discomfort in Çarh's reaction. He felt obliged to tell the truth, even though he was certain Çarh might find it hard to believe. Nevertheless, the meaning of the tattoo was crucial, and Çarh needed to comprehend it. The Elf patiently continued to speak, making an effort to explain.

"The tattoo is the symbol of Sögré. The trumpet that Israfil will blow represents our special connection. This symbol embodies the power of a Sögré who maintains the balance of nature. It is a part of the Sögré ancestry, which includes you as well."

Çarh remained unconvinced, unable to discern a trumpet in the tattoo, and the Elf empathized with his scepticism. In the Elf's world, Sögré and elves were real, but for humans, comprehending such concepts proved challenging. The Elf acknowledged Çarh's reaction, stating, "It was a bit early to learn the truth," and they resumed their journey, collecting their mirrors.

As they walked towards the town centre of Pau, Çarh's curiosity reignited. "So, why do we keep coming here?" he inquired.

The Elf explained that Pau served not only as a hub for witches but also as a pivotal location for maintaining the balance of nature. In this place, the presence of Céwiaretza was most profoundly felt, drawing Sögré together to pool their powers. Furthermore, during the annual grand witch assembly held in Pau, decisions regarding the balance of nature were made, and witches collaborated. The Elf proposed to Çarh that he attend these meetings, but Çarh felt he wasn't yet prepared for such an endeavour.

Hearing the name Céwiaretza repeatedly, Çarh inquired about its meaning. The Elf took a moment to explain Céwiaretza. "Céwiaretza is the source of life. You can envision it as a colossal tree situated at the centre of the world, especially in the cold land. The entire world, with its branches and roots, exists within this tree. Witches harness the powers of the tree to maintain the balance of nature."

Çarh was astonished; he had never encountered such concepts before. However, the idea sparked something within him. It made him feel like a part of something greater.

As Çarh and the Elf continued walking, a voice called out from a distance. The Elf recognized the voice and smiled. As they approached, they saw a group of people gathered around a flickering fire. In the centre of the group sat a woman. Çarh asked the Elf who the leader of the group was, and the Elf mentioned that the woman's name was Kelly.

Mab warmly welcomed the Elf upon seeing him and invited him to join her. As the Elf approached her, the Mab uttered a phrase that Çarh couldn't comprehend: "Wöviaséenger de Marr Halte Napréséenger[v]," then the Elf responded, "Tiaxöpra de Sreimtai il Cuae Mab Pémadruiren[vi],"

Mab smiled and said, "It's delightful to see you, my old friend," continuing with curiosity, "I see you've found yourself a new companion."

The Elf replied, "Yes, this young man is Çarh; he is

teigretexen[vii],"

Mab's eyes widened, as if they were about to pop out of their sockets. She couldn't believe what she had heard. Encountering a teigretexen was beyond her expectations. "Really?" she asked in disbelief.

Çarh, interjecting the conversation, said, "I don't know if you're aware, but I'm here. I didn't understand what you were talking about at all. What does teigretexen mean?"

Mab replied, "It's not important. I apologize; let me offer you something warm." Çarh appreciated Mab's friendly gestures but remained curious about the mysterious term, teigretexen. Instead of providing an immediate answer, Mab brought a cup of hot tea and placed it on the small table beside him. "We make this tea from the plants grown here. It has a delightful taste and is quite warming," she said with a smile. Çarh took the tea and sensed a sweet flavour with the first sip. However, he didn't hesitate to inquire again, "Why did you interrupt talking about teigretexen?"

Mab fell silent for a moment. Then she responded, "Teigretexen means backup witch in an ancient language called Heikwounnéls[viii]. It is used only among us witches. Since the topics we discuss are sensitive, we usually prefer using this language for privacy. It is not only for secrecy but also crucial to prevent misunderstandings about witchcraft-related information."

Çarh attempted to comprehend Mab's explanation but still struggled to fully grasp it. Did witches indeed have a special language? He yearned to learn more about this topic. However, Mab's serious expression suggested it was a private matter. "Okay, I understand," he conceded. "I'm still new, and I respect your secrets. Even if you explain, I won't understand anyway."

Mab appreciated Çarh's maturity and felt somewhat more at ease. "You are our guest; don't hesitate to ask anything. A teigretexen's questions are always welcomed and answered gladly," she assured him.

Çarh sipped his hot tea, still surprised by being referred to as a teigretexen. He continued chatting with Mab and the other witches, taking another step into the mysterious world of Pau, eagerly anticipating where this adventure would lead.

Listening intently to the conversations among Mab and the others, Çarh heard them discussing their powers, and he couldn't help but wonder about his own. The Elf, sensing Çarh's thoughts, explained to him how the powers worked. He mentioned that Sögré had natural powers that could be developed and controlled over time. The Elf also emphasized that each Sögré possessed a unique power. However, he stressed the importance of using these powers wisely. Hearing this, Çarh felt the excitement of discovering his own power. Still, he thought it was too early to embark on the journey of exploring that power.

The Elf turned to Çarh, saying, "You're not ready to discover your power yet. You need time to know yourself, understand your powers, and learn to control them. This journey won't be easy, but I'm here to guide you through it."

Mab shared her power, stating, "My ability is to shape time. I can temporarily stop time, change events. Also, because I manipulate time, I appear younger. In reality, I'm 55 years old," revealing a surprising truth. Çarh was astonished because Mab didn't look anywhere near 55.

Another Sögré added, "My power is to travel in the world of dreams. I can see people's dreams, guide them, and even alter them."

Yet another Sögré explained, "My power is to record

memories. I can see, possess, and memorize all the memories of anyone I come into contact with."

As Çarh listened in awe to the powers of the other Sögré, he wondered how he could possess such remarkable abilities. Mab, seemingly reading his thoughts, spoke, "You will discover your power when the time comes. Each Sögré's power is different and emerges at the right moment. You need to be patient to discover what your power is."

Curiosity and a hint of fear in his eyes, Çarh turned to the Elf and asked, "What will my power be?"

The Elf smiled and replied, "We will see in time. Now, we must go."

Mab slowly moved her hands, and a light shimmered in the air. Then, she gently placed the light in her palm. Çarh watched in wide-eyed amazement as Mab performed the enchantment. Nothing was moving; time had stopped. Mab turned to Çarh, saying, "As you saw, my power is to stop time. But using this power requires great caution. If misused, the consequences can be disastrous," she warned.

Çarh gazed at Mab in admiration. The ability to perform such a potent spell was truly incredible. Yet, he couldn't help but ponder the challenges that came with wielding such immense power. Mab set time in motion again, and everything returned to normal.

Meanwhile, the Elf, who had been looking around in bewilderment when time froze, initially didn't comprehend what had happened. However, as he perceived Mab's extraordinary power, he regarded Mab with astonishment and admonished, "Mab! Time should not be tampered with." Undeterred, Mab insisted, "But he needed to see."

Çarh expressed, "I feel very fortunate to have witnessed such a remarkable moment." Despite a tinge of sadness, he bid farewell, eager to explore the answers to the myriad questions swirling in his mind about the dormant power within him, as he departed Pau with the Elf.

Three months had passed since Çarh's experience in Pau. Lately, he had been constantly suffering from headaches. There were days when he lay in bed, unable to do anything. Doctors couldn't identify the reason for his discomfort. Some suggested that something might be forming inside his head, but a precise diagnosis remained elusive.

The pains that Çarh experienced were slowly driving him to madness. Everything seemed to mix up in his mind, reaching even into his dreams in a way that he couldn't comprehend. One night, the pain in his head was so intense that he woke up, and the Elf was right beside him. "What's happening?" Çarh asked. Holding his head, he said, "Something is happening, but I don't know what." The Elf expressed his willingness to help. Slowly lifting him up, he cradled Çarh's head in his hands, and they sat motionless in the darkness for a long time. The Elf was murmuring something in a language Çarh couldn't understand.

As Çarh started to feel better, he decided to speak. "Why do I feel like this, Elf? Why won't these pains leave me in peace?" he asked.

The Elf responded, "Perhaps your magical power is emerging. Sometimes, when your magical power emerges, physical discomforts occur. The energy needs to rebalance."

Çarh contemplated the Elf's words and grappled with the idea of his magical power emerging. He resolved to focus on understanding his own power and pondered what he needed to do to balance it. Simultaneously, he wondered about the nature of his magical abilities. The image of the tattoo he had glimpsed through the mirrors in Pau flashed in his mind.

Sûr

Recalling the story, the Elf had shared about Israfil's Trumpet, a notion he hadn't taken seriously at the time, now lingered in his thoughts. Could such a thing be real?

Reading Çarh's thoughts, the Elf said, "It's time to fully accept it, Çarh. I think it's time for you to tell you about your magical power, because you'll learn about it very soon. You need to hear this from me."

Çarh was overcome with curiosity. What could it be, he wondered. Eager for the Elf to explain, he looked into the Elf's eyes. The Elf said, "We need to go somewhere, and you are ready for it now. I need to tell you beforehand. The place we're going to is very special," he continued, "If you're ready, let's hit the road."

Çarh looked at the Elf in astonishment. Where could they be going that was so special? Yet, he was also intrigued. The Elf's journeys had always been interesting, and this one was bound to be different. Saying he was ready, Çarh began to follow the Elf.

On the way, the Elf began to explain to Çarh where they were headed. The place was called Céwiaretza, where the Tree of Life, believed to possess magical powers and of great importance to the entire world, was located. This place, shrouded in great mystery, could only be visited by the chosen among the Sögrés.

Çarh listened in admiration to the Elf's narration, finding the prospect of visiting such a powerful place exhilarating. Fortunately, this time, he had a guide he could trust.

Various thoughts circulated in Çarh's mind. Being a witch himself, the significance of performing rituals here for the further development of his powers was substantial. When they arrived at the place the Elf had described, Çarh was

surprised. It was a place he had been to before and knew well –
Göbeklitepe. Çarh asked the Elf, "Is this it?" the Elf replied,
"Yes, this is a bridge to Céwiaretza."

With the discovery of Göbeklitepe, archaeologists had
uncovered its historical importance and its connection to
magic. However, it was not only seen as a historical relic but
also as a centre where witches could perform their rituals.

The colossal stones at the centre of Göbeklitepe
exceeded Çarh's expectations, appearing even more impressive
than he had envisioned in his mind. He held the belief that the
rituals conducted in this sacred space would amplify the
witches' powers. Guided by the Elf amidst the stones, Çarh
couldn't help but be captivated by the natural beauty that
enveloped him. The steppe vegetation, the birds gracefully
soaring in the sky, and the gentle breeze all contributed to the
enchanting atmosphere of the place.

Upon reaching Göbeklitepe, Çarh experienced a
profound sense of belonging. He sensed that the rituals he was
about to undertake in this sacred site would play a significant
role in enhancing his powers. Immersed in the energy of
Göbeklitepe, he felt a stirring within the Sögré power within
him. No longer just a historical relic, this place transformed
into more than that; it became a potent witch centre where he
truly felt he belonged.

In response to a movement the Elf made with his staff,
Çarh abruptly discerned a transformation in his surroundings.
Instead of Göbeklitepe, he found himself standing before a
colossal tree. This tree was none other than the Tree of Life,
Céwiaretza, and Çarh had never experienced such potent
energy in his life. The branches, leaves, and roots of the tree
exuded an overwhelming force, enveloping every cell in Çarh's
body. A profound sense of peace and empowerment washed

over him.

Observing Çarh's astonishment, the Elf offered an explanation, "This is Céwiaretza, the Tree of Life. Here, you can communicate with the tree and harness its energy. However, you must exercise caution, for this is a potent place, and its energy has the capacity to transform you."

Heeding the Elf's warning, Çarh began to move around the tree. The energy emanating from it worked to rejuvenate his body, infusing him with a strength he had never known. Yet, under the influence of this powerful force, he also gained a deeper understanding of his own inherent power. As a witch, he realised that mastering the correct use of the energy within him could lead to even greater potency.

The Elf explained to Çarh that the potent energy wasn't confined to Céwiaretza alone; such energies existed throughout nature, empowering the Sögré. However, the Elf underscored the importance of using this power responsibly, reminding Çarh, "Power requires responsibility, and you are powerful enough to bear that responsibility."

Although the Elf's request for Çarh to touch the tree unsettled him, his curiosity as a witch prevailed, and he chose to comply. Upon contact, an explosion of energy surged through his body, simultaneously frightening, and astonishing him. Subsequently, the Elf took a small piece from the tree and placed it on Çarh's forehead, transferring the tree's power to him. The seed was planted. Çarh abruptly lost consciousness. Upon awakening, he sensed a different energy coursing within himself.

Upon regaining consciousness, Çarh found himself in a world that felt foreign, one he struggled to recognize as his own. The sights before him evoked both fear and curiosity, a paradoxical blend of the unknown and enchantment. It was a realm unlike anything he had ever known, with stars dancing in the sky as if engaged in a celestial competition. A power emanating from the ground enveloped and elevated him, signalling a profound shift that left him grappling with the realization that everything had changed.

The Elf proclaimed the completion of the ritual, declaring that Israfil had now passed into Çarh. These words left Çarh in deep astonishment. Israfil? Passed into him? The notion of such a powerful presence both excited and frightened him. Despite lingering doubts about the Elf's reliability, Çarh could not deny the palpable transformation within himself. As he attempted to comprehend the events that had unfolded, his curiosity was piqued by the mention of the trumpet the Elf had alluded to.

The Elf clarified that the seed planted in Çarh was intended to empower him to wield more potent magic. With the seed, Çarh had transformed into a stronger and more effective Sögré, capable of tapping into greater mystical energies.

Standing beside Çarh, the Elf offered a gentle smile to reassure him. "This is normal," the Elf explained. "A tremendous energy has been transferred to you. You are now a different being. Israfil has awakened within you."

While Çarh struggled to fully comprehend the Elf's words, he recognized the gravity of the situation. He was no longer a mere human; this newfound power within him held the potential for a significant purpose.

Writhing in pain and holding his head, Çarh felt the agony, paradoxically strengthening him, signalling the awakening of Israfil – a crucial part of his destiny.

Everything had changed. Çarh's life had now become a struggle to grapple with these extraordinary powers. Yet, he

Sûr

understood that mastering these powers could empower him to change the world.

CHAPTER 7
METAMORPHOSIS

Çarh returned home with a mind swirling with the information bestowed upon him by the Elf. Overwhelmed with a mix of fatigue and astonishment, he quickly succumbed to sleep, finding solace on his bed. His slumber was deep and serene, ushering him into a dream where he wandered through a magical forest, surrounded by the enchanting power of the surrounding trees.

Upon awakening, Çarh felt remarkably rested. The earlier headache had vanished, and his body radiated with a newfound freshness. Seated in his room, he reflected on the Elf's explanations – the ritual at Göbeklitepe, the energy from the tree, the planting of the seed on his forehead, and the presence of Israfil now residing within him. It all felt surreal, as if he were still caught in a dream.

Yet, Çarh acknowledged that he needed time to contemplate and make sense of it all. His focus now shifted towards understanding the extent of his powers and navigating the complexities of controlling the presence of Israfil within him.

Despite the passing days, Çarh found himself making little progress in understanding the significance of Israfil within him. Each morning, the lingering question of why Israfil was planted within him persisted, creating a sense of unease. Though he sensed a change within himself, the exact nature of that change eluded him. Filled with these thoughts, he sought refuge in the library, delving into the spell books provided by the Elf and other witches he had encountered months ago.

Hours passed as he read and researched, yet the answers remained elusive. Israfil, it seemed, had no openly stated purpose for anyone. Different witches offered varying interpretations – some believed Israfil represented different powers, while others asserted it played a role in determining the destiny of its bearer. However, Çarh's paramount concern was understanding why Israfil had been planted within him.

After prolonged contemplation, Çarh awoke with a new perspective. Perhaps Israfil had been bestowed upon him to grant him a purpose. It occurred to him that there might be a task awaiting him, and Israfil had equipped him with the power necessary to fulfil that task.

Yet, Çarh couldn't shake the feeling that something crucial was missing, prompting him to yearn for more information about Israfil. Driven by curiosity, he found himself frequenting a library meticulously crafted by witches on an almost daily basis.

Each day, building on the knowledge acquired the day before, he delved deeper into his research. Lost among the books, he sensed that he had merely scratched the surface of the information bestowed upon him. However, surrendering to the challenge was not an option. With unwavering determination, he returned to the library daily, driven by the quest to uncover something new. Gradually, as he unearthed more about the secrets of Israfil, he became increasingly attuned to the power that had been planted within him.

In the hours spent within the library, Çarh delved into the mysterious history of the magical world, immersing himself in the tales of past adventures of witches. Slowly but steadily, he advanced toward unlocking the secrets of Israfil. However, despite his efforts, some questions lingered unanswered in his research. Why was Israfil carried by a human? And, most significantly, why had Israfil been planted within him? These questions demanded a more exhaustive inquiry.

Days turned into weeks, yet Çarh persisted in his research within the library. As he grew more attuned to the power bestowed upon him, his dedication intensified. Attempting to unravel the mysteries of the magical world, he found himself grappling with an ever-expanding labyrinth of knowledge. The deeper he delved, the more he felt entwined in a complex and endless web of secrets.

Çarh's quest for understanding led him to the oldest books in the library, where he meticulously examined each page. He immersed himself in ancient religions, mythologies, and legends, seeking to unravel the story of Israfil. Every page he turned revealed a different narrative – some depicted Israfil as the angel closest to the creator, while others painted him as the harbinger of the world's end.

Lost in the hours of reading, Çarh remained in the library until late at night, tirelessly continuing his research. His dedication was unwavering as he sought to learn every detail about Israfil. In this pursuit, he hoped to uncover not only the mysteries surrounding Israfil but also gain a deeper understanding of himself.

In the darkest corner of the library, Çarh stumbled upon an ancient book that told a distinctive tale about Israfil. According to this account, the angel descended to the earth with a mission to touch the hearts of humans, correcting, healing, and guiding them. This narrative struck Çarh as unique among the varied stories he had encountered. While it revealed that Israfil had a mission on earth, the specifics of that mission remained elusive.

Undeterred, Çarh persisted in gathering information about Israfil from diverse religious sources. The angel featured prominently in Islam, Judaism, and Christianity. In Islamic belief, Israfil was designated as one of the angels tasked with blowing the trumpet on the Day of Judgment by Allah's command. In Judaism, Israfil was more prevalent, portrayed as an angel contributing to the implementation of God's judgment. In Christianity, Israfil played a role in the events of the last days, with some traditions considering him an angel heralding the return of the Messiah.

As Çarh gathered information about Israfil, he began to forge connections within himself. Was the power residing within him akin to Israfil's judgment and the force he wielded in the last days? When he sensed this power coursing through him, had Israfil's energy been transferred into him?

With each piece of information he uncovered, Çarh's excitement grew. His excitement grew with each piece of information he encountered. Çarh delved into different stories about Israfil, discovering that this archangel played a significant role across various religious traditions. In Islam, Israfil was depicted as a celestial being assigned the crucial task of heralding the apocalypse. By blowing the trumpet on the last day, Israfil signalled the end of the world, a momentous event associated with the Islamic concept of the Day of Judgment.

In Christian theology, Israfil assumed a different yet equally impactful role. Here, he was envisioned as an angel entrusted with the solemn duty of judging humanity in the final days. The trumpet associated with Israfil resonated with the Christian eschatological belief in the sounding of the Last Trumpet, linked to the resurrection of the dead and the commencement of divine judgment.

Judaism, too, presented a distinct perspective on Israfil. Within Jewish traditions, Israfil was characterized as an angel who would wield the shofar on the last day. The shofar, a sacred musical instrument made from a ram's horn, held profound significance in Jewish religious ceremonies, particularly during Rosh Hashanah and Yom Kippur. Israfil's role as the one who sounds the shofar aligned with the belief in the resurrection of the dead, emphasizing a shared motif with both Islamic and Christian narratives surrounding the archangel.

As Çarh delved deeper into these stories, he experienced a growing resonance with the power within himself. It seemed as if the diverse aspects of Israfil's roles in various religions mirrored the multifaceted nature of the energy now coursing through him.

Taking meticulous note of both the similarities and differences in these narratives, Çarh discerned that each religion assigned a distinct meaning to Israfil. His keen awareness led him to contemplate the reasons behind these varied interpretations, fostering a broader understanding of the complexities intertwined with the entity now residing within him.

Through his extensive research, Çarh uncovered that

Sûr

Israfil is an angel who, under God's command, will bring about the end of the world. Recognizing himself as a vessel implied that Israfil might determine the fate of the world through him. However, these thoughts didn't instil fear in him; on the contrary, they heightened his curiosity and excitement. Being the bearer of Israfil entailed a significant responsibility, but it also bestowed upon him a tremendous honour. Filled with these thoughts, he continued his daily research, diligently preparing himself to answer Israfil's call.

As Çarh gathered information about being infused with Israfil and chosen as his bearer, his respect for religious values deepened. To him, this event carried profound spirituality, signifying the purpose of being used as a conduit. The more he learned, the deeper his curiosity grew, and he started to feel a sense of excitement about when Israfil would choose to utilize him. Within him, there was a sensation as if he were in a sacred space where the voice of Israfil echoed. This feeling infused him with hope and further solidified his determination to fulfil the task bestowed upon him by Céwiaretza.

While engrossed in his books, Çarh is interrupted by a stuttering woman who inquiries about his search. Upon explaining his focus on the stories of Israfil and Sûr, Çarh sparks the woman's interest. He introduces himself as only Çarh, in return she shares a lengthy name in the Heikwounnéls language, "Anixöpra de Sreihn Wövia Pelin Alluixeutzeren," She quickly suggests that Çarh can call her Pelin for short. Intrigued, Pelin queries Çarh about his identity as a witch. Çarh, hesitant to provide a straightforward answer, discloses that he is a teigretexen. Pelin cannot conceal her astonishment at this revelation.

Çarh, driven by a newfound awareness of being a teigretexen, had harboured an eagerness to delve deeper into understanding himself. However, the information gleaned from books proved insufficient. Recognizing Çarh's interest, Pelin, sensing an opportunity to assist, stepped forward. She revealed that she had dedicated many years to researching teigretexens and possessed extensive knowledge about them. Pelin clarified that teigretexens were beings capable of harnessing natural powers, akin to witches, but with the distinction that they evolve into witches later in their journey.

Çarh's bewildered expression, lacking any comprehension of the subject, raised suspicions for Pelin. Undeterred, she continued, revealing that, to her knowledge, there was only one teigretexen, and that individual belonged to the Cépfiarexen ancestry. Intrigued, Pelin questioned Çarh, "Are you a Cépfiarexen? Where is Sûr, then?" Confused and failing to grasp the meaning behind her words, Çarh was unable to respond. Frustrated and suspecting deception, Pelin abruptly left. Left feeling foolish, Çarh began his journey home, his mind clouded with confusion.

On the road, the questions Pelin posed lingered in Çarh's mind, creating a swirl of confusion. What is Cépfiarexen? Who or what is Sûr, and why is it elusive? What does it truly mean to be a teigretexen? His thoughts were a jumbled mess, and anxiety gripped him.

Upon reaching home, Çarh sought solace in his books and immediately dove into research. Fuelled by an insatiable curiosity, Çarh continued his research late into the night. The words on the pages became a conduit for understanding, and he absorbed every piece of information with a thirst for knowledge. Hours turned into a blur as he grappled with the complex stories of these mystical beings.

Eventually, fatigue claimed him, and he fell asleep amidst his books. In the realm of dreams, Çarh found himself standing at the intersection of ancient myths and present realities. Israfil's angelic wings stretched wide, casting shadows over the landscape. Sûr, a dark and elusive figure, lurked at the edges of his vision.

The dream unfolded like a surreal tapestry, weaving together threads of uncertainty and revelation. As Çarh slumbered, the enigmatic forces that guided his destiny continued to intertwine with the secrets hidden within the pages of his books.

The next day, as Çarh opened his eyes, he was greeted by a branch extending towards his face, with a flower at the end pushing towards his forehead. The sight immediately triggered a recollection of Israfil, causing panic to surge within him. However, the woman's words from the previous day echoed in his mind, suggesting that this branch might aid Israfil's emergence.

Despite fear gripping him, Çarh closed his eyes and took a deep breath. His heart raced in rhythm with his anxiety, but curiosity also fuelled his courage. Intrigued by the mystery of Israfil's presence within him and the purpose behind its planting, he braced himself for the potential pain that the branch might bring.

Çarh immersed himself in the power of the tree, sensing the presence of Israfil. A warmth enveloped his heart, radiating throughout his body. As the branch moved towards his forehead, he initially experienced pain, but the movements soon became gentler and more soothing.

After a few minutes, Çarh perceived that the branch had ceased its movements. Slowly opening his eyes, he noticed the pressure on his forehead had dissipated. The branch was no longer there, yet Çarh sensed a profound change within himself. He realised that he had become a part of Israfil, forging a stronger connection with the enigmatic force within him.

Relieved, Çarh took a deep breath when he realised that it was just a dream. He recalled waking up at that moment and instinctively checked for any pain on his forehead. Finding none, the reassurance that the pain wasn't real comforted him.

Reflecting on Israfil and Sûr's story that manifested in Çarh's dream, the Elf remarked, "Perhaps what you were truly seeking was hidden in this dream." Although Çarh still lacked a clear idea of what he was searching for, he acknowledged that dreams could sometimes carry important messages, prompting him to remain vigilant for the insights they might offer.

Çarh, sensing that his dream held a message, considered that he might need to approach his research from a different perspective. The Elf's words lingered in his mind, prompting him to return to the library and continue his quest for understanding.

While perusing the shelves, a black-covered book, previously unnoticed, caught his eye. The cover bore no inscription, yet an inexplicable intuition led Çarh to believe that this might be the book he was seeking. As he opened it, the word "teigretexen" jumped out at him, instantly capturing his attention, and focusing his efforts on unravelling the meaning behind this mysterious term.

According to the writings in the book, the Cépfiarexen ancestry is entrusted with the responsibility of carrying Israfil. Unlike other witch lineages, only one witch from this ancestry can bear Israfil, and every 12 years, Cépfiar witches born during that time are designated as Teigretexens. These Teigretexens are safeguarded and trained by other members of the Cépfiarexen ancestry, as well as by Elf, the representative of the witch lineage. While Teigretexens inherently possess magical powers, they are unable to fully utilize this potential unless they commit to the task of carrying Israfil.

However, once chosen as the carrier of Israfil, Teigretexens undergo specialized training, enhancing, and refining their magical abilities during this process. The book shed light on the unique and pivotal role Teigretexens played within the Cépfiarexen ancestry and the intricate connection between their powers and the enigmatic entity, Israfil.

Israfil is recognized as the angel who, at the end of the world, will sound his trumpet, Sûr, ushering in the resurrection of humanity. Given the significance of this event, the task of witches carrying Israfil is of paramount importance. The primary duty of Teigretexens is to stand ready to assume the task if the witch currently bearing Israfil cannot fulfil it.

The unique power inherent in Cépfiar witches is specific to the individual carrying Israfil and cannot be replicated by another witch. In the event that the current carrier of Israfil cannot fulfil the task until the end of their life, they are obligated to transfer Israfil to another Teigretexen. To ensure the safety and appropriate transition of Israfil, the witch carrying it develops a special spell during the task, safeguarding against harmful effects from other witches. This precaution ensures that the transfer occurs only at the right time and to the right individual, guaranteeing the safety and continuity of Israfil's protection.

Çarh was astonished by the profound importance of the task of carrying Israfil, a duty reserved for individuals from a specific witch ancestry. The revelation that Teigretexen witches did not possess magical powers at birth and could only acquire them through undertaking the responsibility of carrying Israfil added another layer of surprise.

As Çarh continued to peruse the pages of the black-covered book, he encountered more information about the Cépfiarexen ancestry. Unlike other witch lineages, it was written that members of this ancestry possessed the ability to see and control souls. This newfound knowledge shed light on the reason behind his ability to perceive and interact with Aunt Zülfiye's soul. The revelations within the book deepened Çarh's understanding of his lineage and the intricate connections between his powers and the responsibilities tied to carrying Israfil.

As Çarh turned the pages of the black-covered book, he came across a drawing that depicted a male figure with something resembling a horn on his head. Accompanying the drawing was a statement: "Sûr has been planted, has grown successfully, and is ready to be blown." Intrigued and determined to understand the meaning behind these words, Çarh continued to read the pages with care.

Exiting the library, Çarh found his thoughts consumed by mixed and anxious emotions, his gaze still fixed on the drawing of the horned figure. The prospect of something like that emerging from within him sent shivers down his spine. The question of when this transformation would occur lingered in his mind, casting a cloud of uncertainty.

As Çarh stepped onto the street, greeted by a gentle breeze and the warmth of the sun, the dark clouds within him refused to disperse. Contemplation loomed over him, forcing him to grapple with the meaning of the change within him, the significance of the horn, and the path he needed to navigate moving forward.

Çarh walked towards home from the library, his mind consumed by thoughts of the emerging horn and the enigmatic information about the planting of Sûr. Desperately wanting to unravel the meaning behind the horn that would soon manifest from within him, he found himself at a loss for understanding. Reluctant to share his fears and concerns with others, he avoided delving into the topic altogether, leaving his emotions in turmoil.

As he neared home, his curiosity and anxiety intensified, leaving him feeling lost and unsure of what steps to take. Upon reaching home, Çarh headed straight to bed, his mind deep in contemplation. Simultaneously, he attempted to recall other pieces of information from the book, hoping to find solutions that could disperse the dark clouds overshadowing his thoughts. In the quietude of his room, Çarh continued his quest for answers, seeking a way to navigate the uncertainties within him.

Amidst contemplations about the responsibilities tied to the Cépfiarexen ancestry, an idea crossed Çarh's mind – the possibility of transferring Israfil to another Cépfiar witch. Seeking guidance, he thought of the Elf and promptly summoned him.

The Elf appeared, willing to address Çarh's questions, but the responses fell short of satisfying him. "What you say is true, such a thing is possible, but there was only one teigretexen, and that was you. Therefore, transferring it to someone else doesn't seem possible. I'm sorry, Çarh. With the manifestation of Sûr and becoming a true Cépfiar witch, a new teigretexen will be designated. Only then might it be possible. I wouldn't want you to get your hopes up because this could take years. It's best for you to accept this and live with it."

The Elf's words conveyed a sense of inevitability, urging Çarh to accept the circumstances and continue living with the responsibilities and changes that Israfil's presence brought to his life.

Upon realizing the seeming hopelessness of his

situation, Çarh felt as though he had descended into a void. However, in embracing the notion that he couldn't fully control the trajectory of his life, he found a form of liberation. Surrendering to the flow of life and remaining open to its unexpected turns, rather than attempting to dictate the outcome, became a source of comfort for him. In this acceptance, he discovered a sense of serenity.

Choosing to accept himself as he was and being prepared to adapt to the changing circumstances that Israfil's presence brought seemed to be the right path for Çarh. This newfound perspective allowed him to find peace amidst the uncertainties.

The next day, when Çarh awoke, he sensed something akin to a mark on his forehead. Rushing to the mirror and scrutinizing himself closely, he realised it wasn't a mark like a scar but the emergence of the horn – Sûr. Çarh stared at the mirror in astonishment, observing Sûr slowly growing. This situation instilled fear within him, but he comprehended that it was an inevitable process he could no longer halt. The enchantment cast upon him would unfold, and he would have to bear the consequences.

Fear and anxiety permeated Çarh's inner self. Unease lingered as he pondered on how those around him would perceive him during this transformation. The emergence of Sûr brought pains that the Elf had to use magic to suppress, intensifying Çarh's sense of terror and uncertainty.

The growth of Sûr became increasingly evident, and soon, a horn-like protrusion appeared in the middle of Çarh's forehead. Bewildered by this transformation, he grappled with the question of how he would conceal it. Concerns, fears, and uncertainties overwhelmed Çarh, leaving him in a state of utter bewilderment. The solitude of his predicament prevented him from seeking guidance or sharing his situation with anyone, intensifying his sense of isolation.

As days passed, Çarh found himself retreating further into his room. The fear of public perception and the physical changes wrought by Sûr began to encroach upon his normal life. Everyday activities such as eating, sleeping, and even reading a book became increasingly challenging. Feeling the weight of this internal struggle, Çarh knew he needed to find a way out of the isolation and distress that had enveloped him.

After the Elf was convinced that Sûr had grown enough, he made the decision to assist Çarh, accompanied by a confession. "Çarh, I'm sorry I couldn't help you before. I couldn't risk Sûr because it needed to grow. But now, I can help you. I assure you; I have your well-being in mind. I know what it feels like to be ostracized, to be marginalized. That's why I will help you. It is possible to conceal Sûr."

The Elf's confession took Çarh by surprise. Learning that it was feasible to conceal Sûr filled him with hope and, simultaneously, relieved the loneliness that had enveloped him. The sincerity in the Elf's words further calmed Çarh, who understood the challenges of being ostracized from society. The assurance that the Elf would lend a hand made him feel less isolated.

Deciding to distance himself from the city, Çarh initiated the necessary preparations. He acknowledged that the fears and concerns within him still lingered, but with the Elf's assistance and the prospect of concealing Sûr, he found motivation.

Çarh streamlined his belongings, discarding unnecessary items and retaining only the essentials. Equipped with a small tent, a sleeping bag, and a supply of food and drinks, he and the Elf embarked on a journey with their destination known only to them.

The following day marked the commencement of their departure from the city. Throughout the journey, the Elf gathered the required materials for the impending magical procedure. Çarh moved forward with determination, the once-dominant dark clouds within him gradually diminishing, leaving room for a glimmer of hope to shine through.

Their journey spanned several days, culminating in their arrival at the forest where the Elf began gathering the materials required for the magical procedure. However, the Elf remarked that something crucial was missing and that they had to venture to a perilous place to acquire it.

Listening to the Elf's words, Çarh couldn't help but feel anxious about what they were seeking in such a dangerous location. The Elf elaborated on the necessity of gathering the final piece: a rare plant found in the dark caves, vital for the successful execution of the magic.

Acknowledging the Elf's courage, Çarh couldn't shake the uncertainty surrounding the potential dangers awaiting them in the dark caves. Nevertheless, understanding the importance of taking this risk to conceal Israfil, Çarh approached the Elf and resolutely said, "Let's do it."

Following Çarh, the Elf embarked on the journey. Along the way, the Elf provided Çarh with information about the caves, cautioning, "Dangerous creatures inhabit the caves. Some of these creatures can be quite aggressive, and we might need to flee if we encounter them."

Taking the Elf's words to heart, Çarh treaded more cautiously. Contemplating the potential dangers ahead, he found himself entertaining the thought of staying behind. The only disruption to the prevailing silence was the sound of their footsteps touching the ground. While walking, a sudden roar echoed in the distance, sending shivers down their spines. However, they quickly discerned that it wasn't the furious bellow of a bull but the roar of an unknown creature.

The Elf cautioned, "Be prepared; besides creatures, there might be hidden traps here." They continued their journey, proceeding with deliberate and cautious steps, keenly aware of their surroundings. Encountering a few traps along the way reinforced the importance of their vigilance. However, they didn't encounter any creatures during this stretch.

As they advanced, they discovered footprints and stumbled upon a campsite marked by half-eaten meals, indicating that two individuals had been there previously. The Elf opted to trace the footprints, with Çarh following suit. As they followed the tracks, the duo made their way toward a cave.

Approaching the cave, the Elf halted Çarh with one hand and used the other to push aside the bushes. To their surprise, they discovered a roasting chicken over a fire inside the cave. The Elf remarked, "This chicken isn't ours, but it indicates that someone has been here. Let's be careful."

The Elf ventured into the cave, wielding his staff, and Çarh followed suit. Upon entering, they were suddenly attacked by a creature. Çarh instinctively stepped back to evade the creature's claws. It was the first time he had encountered such a being, shaking the foundations of his beliefs. He questioned whether creatures were real or merely confined to the realm of fairy tales.

Just before the monster lunged at them, Çarh caught sight of a gigantic creature with red eyes and sharp claws, illuminating the cave's interior. The terrifying screams and menacing claws of the creature confronted Çarh, freezing him in fear. His eyes widened, breath caught in his throat. The monster's movements were unpredictable and swift, forcing Çarh to retreat helplessly in an attempt to escape. The creature's hissing breath and flickering eyes tracked his every move.

The monstrous creature, adorned with gleaming feathers, massive claws, and sharp teeth, emitted a bone-chilling roar. Its sheer size and power left Çarh trembling in fear. The Elf, however, quickly moved to defend against the creature's attack, standing firm in the face of the monstrous threat.

Observing Çarh's panic, the Elf approached him reassuringly. "Don't worry, creatures are real, but we can deal with them," he said, his calm voice serving to comfort Çarh and bolster his confidence.

The Elf acted quickly, using his staff to neutralize the creature, leaving both of them breathless. Anxious, Çarh questioned, "What was that?" the Elf responded, "It was one of the creatures that live in these caves. Encountering them is quite common. We need to be prepared." The encounter served as a stark reminder of the dangers they faced in their quest.

Çarh examined the creature's lifeless form, taking in the details of its formidable features. The tough feathers felt like steel armour, and its sharp teeth and claws highlighted the creature's predatory nature. Stepping away, Çarh approached the Elf with a sense of unease.

"Where should we go to find the plant?" Çarh inquired. The Elf consulted the map and responded, "We must continue our path. The plant is a few hours away from here." Together, they resumed their journey, proceeding with increased caution to avoid potential encounters with other cave-dwelling creatures.

Sûr

Upon reaching the supposed location of the plant, the Elf expressed astonishment, stating, "The plant is not here." The unexpected turn of events added an element of uncertainty to their mission.

Determined to find an alternative solution, Çarh turned to Elf with anxiety and questioned, "What do we do now?" the Elf took a moment, considering their options, and then revealed, "If the plant is not here, we only have one option left, and it's a more difficult task. Only one person can help us."

The prospect of a more challenging task left Çarh uneasy. He couldn't help but wonder who this person was and why seeking their help was necessary. Looking into the Elf's eyes, Çarh sought answers, asking with curiosity, "Who is this person? Why do we need them?" the Elf took a deep breath before responding, "He is a famous witch. But at the same time, he is very dangerous. He won't care about us, and he might even harm us. But we have no other choice to find the plant."

With a determined expression, Çarh nodded and said, "Okay, when do we set out?" the Elf smiled with satisfaction and replied, "As soon as possible." Together, they embarked on a journey, aware that ahead of them lay a long and challenging road, fraught with uncertainty and potential danger.

Murat Karagoz

CHAPTER 8
EXCHANGE

The sudden and mysterious disappearance of Çarh from his apartment left everyone bewildered. Aunt Fatma, while inclined to believe Çarh's explanations, couldn't shake the nagging feeling that something was awry. His colleagues, on the other hand, found his explanations inconsistent, unaware of the truth that eluded them.

Meanwhile, Çarh was in the process of constructing a new life for himself, driven by the magical abilities bestowed upon him and a newfound purpose. Yet, leaving the past behind proved to be a formidable challenge, a journey marked by complexities and uncertainties.

Çarh grappled with the difficulty of fully abandoning his past life. Despite the magical abilities bestowed upon him, he found himself treading a different path than before. While he was aware of his identity and purpose, he couldn't be open with those close to him, recognizing the societal reluctance to accept magical powers. Internally conflicted, he struggled to find a way to erase the traces of his previous existence.

The prospect of embarking on a journey with the Elf filled Çarh with excitement. This adventure not only promised the exploration of a new world but also the opportunity to wield magic that could reshape his life. However, his paramount motivation was to conceal Sûr and regain access to his former life. In a city teeming with hundreds of people who shared his daily existence, Çarh was apprehensive about being perceived as strange and foreign. Past unpleasant experiences had instilled in him a fear of societal ostracism. Consequently, the ability to conceal Sûr became crucial for him to reconnect with the people who had once been integral to his life.

As Çarh walked alongside the Elf, he found himself immersed in contemplation. Was the monster in the cave a tangible reality? He was certain that the entity saving them from the attack was real, but grappling with the existence of such a colossal creature posed a profound question. Could it truly exist, or were they perhaps entangled in the surreal tendrils of a nightmare unfolding in the dark cavern?

The Elf walked in silence beside him, but the quiet presence did little to stem Çarh's thoughts. The idea of seeking clarification from the Elf crossed his mind, yet the fear of appearing insane held him back. How could he broach such an otherworldly topic without sounding irrational in the Elf's eyes?

After a stretch of silence, the Elf came to a halt and turned around. "What's on your mind?" he inquired.

Çarh looked up, meeting the Elf's gaze. "Was the monster in the cave real?" he asked.

The Elf's brows furrowed in surprise. "Certainly, it was real," he affirmed. "A creature of that magnitude can't be dismissed as a mere nightmare. Moreover, it was the very thing that saved our lives."

The Elf's response brought a sense of relief to Çarh. "You're right," he acknowledged. "However, the idea of monsters lurking in dark caves still unsettles me."

Smiling, the Elf reassured him, "Don't worry, I'll assist you. I'm always by your side. Come, let me share the story of that monster."

In the mystical heart of the enchanted forest, a young witch, with her last remaining resources, entrusted a small plant to a creature known as Huarstedegröda, dwelling in the city of Erzurum in the eastern region of Türkiye.

Çarh inquired, "Are we in Erzurum?" the Elf nodded in confirmation.

This creature, identified as "Kurt Baba" (Wolf Father), bore a resemblance to a wolf. Legends spoke of Kurt Baba being significantly larger than an ordinary wolf, with striking bright red eyes.

Facing an insurmountable challenge in safeguarding a vital plant, one of the essential elements in the life of witches, the young witch dedicated her best efforts. However, as powerful hunters displayed a keen interest in the plant, she concluded that entrusting it to Kurt Baba was the only means to ensure its survival.

Residing in the cave of Çifte Minareli Medrese in Erzurum for centuries, Kurt Baba cultivated an ecosystem where various plants thrived in harmony. Recognized as a guardian, he had protected the plants within his cave for years.

Upon the young witch's entrustment of the plant to Kurt Baba, hunters targeted it for their own purposes. Embracing his role as a guardian, Kurt Baba swiftly took action. A hunter ventured into the cave, seeking the plant, but Kurt Baba fiercely battled and defeated him, asserting his commitment to protect the precious life within his sanctuary.

Following the victorious battle, Kurt Baba pledged to safeguard the plant indefinitely. Collaborating with the other plants in the cave, he played an active role in nurturing and fostering the growth of the plant entrusted by the young witch. Assured of its safety and optimal conditions for thriving, the young witch found solace in Kurt Baba's unwavering protection, offering a beacon of hope for the preservation of crucial elements in the lives of witches.

As Çarh absorbed the Elf's narrative, thoughts of tales from Tarsus surfaced in his mind. Rumours circulated about Sahmaran, a mythical creature, half-woman and half-snake, residing in the underground world. Could such stories be true? Were there similar mythological beings in other cities? These questions began to gnaw at Çarh's thoughts.

Observing Çarh's contemplation, the Elf turned to him and remarked, "Many legends and stories carry a grain of truth, but some may be entirely fabricated. Sometimes, finding the truth requires putting ourselves in danger." He issued a warning, adding, "Speaking of Sahmaran, stay far away from her. She is undoubtedly one of the most dangerous monsters that have ever existed."

Çarh acknowledged the Elf's caution. Determining the boundary between reality and myth proved challenging. The Elf's words momentarily painted Sahmaran as a true threat. However, fuelled by curiosity and courage, Çarh resolved to venture into this realm, seeking to unravel the mysteries. Throughout his journey, he would engage with the people, listen to their stories, and investigate the reality behind the myths.

When Çarh inquired about the missing plant that should have been in the cave, the Elf responded with a contemplative expression. "The plant should have been here, but evidently, someone took it," The shock and concern mirrored on Çarh's face reflected the Elf's own feelings. The significance of this plant for their spell made its disappearance a substantial problem. After pondering a few ideas, the Elf turned to Çarh and declared, "The only option here is to set out to retrieve the lost plant and reclaim it from the person who took it."

Çarh voiced his concern, "But we don't even know who took it. How will we retrieve it?"

The Elf responded with a worried expression, "I don't know, but there's only one person who can help. He is a very powerful and dangerous witch named Nail. Unfortunately, Nail tends to act according to the person. However, it seems we have no other option to retrieve the plant."

The revelation that Nail was a powerful witch sparked a glimmer of hope within Çarh. Perhaps with Nail's assistance, they could recover the plant. However, the notion that Nail's actions were influenced by the person concerned Çarh. Seeking clarification, he asked, "Where is Nail then?"

When the Elf mentioned Istanbul, it reignited a longing within Çarh. Despite having adapted to a life immersed in nature, away from the chaos of city life, Istanbul's magnetic allure had always tugged at him. The city's energy, its organized chaos, and its inherent beauty had held an enduring fascination for him. Therefore, learning that Nail was in Istanbul filled him with excitement.

Acknowledging the challenges ahead, Çarh recognized that this journey wouldn't be easy. Navigating the complex and perilous streets of Istanbul, heading towards an uncertain destination, facing potential encounters with thieves and even monsters – Çarh was well aware of the difficulty of this mission. Nonetheless, he was prepared to undertake anything to retrieve the plant.

Curious about teleportation, Çarh inquired of the Elf, who was preparing for the process, "When can I teleport?" He looked at the Elf, eagerly anticipating the response. The Elf explained, "Teleportation is only possible at certain points, so we need to identify a specific location there before we can teleport to our destination." Çarh hadn't realised that the process was so intricate.

The Elf further clarified, "Unfortunately, it's not that simple. Teleportation is a challenging process and carries many risks. Moreover, it's not possible to take you anywhere. Everything is subject to specific rules and conditions." Expressing his interest in learning more, Çarh was promised a detailed training session on teleportation later by the Elf. With a smile, the Elf suggested, "If you're ready, we can teleport right away." Excitedly, Çarh nodded, confirming his readiness to teleport.

The Elf focused, striking the ground with his staff, and shortly after, the two transformed into a white beam of light. This beam advanced swiftly towards Istanbul, obliterating everything in its path. After a few seconds, the teleportation slowed down, and they found themselves at the Maiden's Tower.

Çarh, though tired, looked around with happiness. The historical structures, the lively streets, and the bustling atmosphere of Istanbul enchanted him. The Elf, with a sense of purpose, informed Çarh, "I know where to find Nail," and gestured for him to follow. "First, we need to go to the Galata Tower."

Çarh followed the Elf through the vibrant streets of Istanbul, and upon reaching the Galata Tower, they entered a shop the Elf had pointed out. Inquiring about Nail, they spoke to the shop owner, Çarh's heart pounding with anticipation. Was Nail here? The shop owner informed them that Nail was at one of the largest markets in the city. Without hesitation, they headed to the market, eager to find Nail.

Excited about the prospect of exploring the shops in Istanbul, Çarh delved into researching information about Nail and the shops he owned. He meticulously examined old maps, engaged in conversations with locals, and immersed himself in the tourist spots to connect with the community. Eventually, he discovered that Nail's shop was located in the Grand Bazaar.

The bustling and lively atmosphere of the Grand Bazaar immediately filled Çarh's thoughts. Although he hadn't visited the bazaar in a long time, memories of numerous antique shops and the historical texture of the place fascinated him. Eager to find Nail's shop among the antiques, he began his search. However, the challenge lay in not knowing the name of the shop, a detail even the Elf couldn't provide. Undeterred, Çarh resolved to conduct further research to pinpoint the location of Nail's elusive shop.

Approaching the Grand Bazaar, Çarh found himself engulfed in a sea of people and the accompanying noise. Wandering through its narrow streets adorned with traditional Ottoman architecture, he directed his steps toward the antique shops. Each establishment showcased a variety of antiques, historical items, and antique jewellery, each item telling a unique story.

As Çarh navigated the labyrinthine streets of the Grand Bazaar, he became lost in the bustling crowd. Many of the shops, each filled with historical artifacts, added to the charm of the bazaar. Once at the heart of the Ottoman Empire's trade with the world, the Grand Bazaar retained numerous historical structures.

In the midst of his stroll, Çarh abruptly halted in front of an enchanting shop. The window displayed impressive artworks, antique clocks, and a myriad of historical items. The shop's door bore the inscription "Nail Antiques." With anticipation, Çarh maneuvered through the crowd and entered the captivating shop.

Çarh delved into the exploration of Nail's shop, encountering a myriad of intriguing antique items that seemed to narrate the tales of history and the past. As he perused the shop, an old clock triggered memories of a similar one that adorned his family's home. A porcelain vase stirred recollections of a similar item from a neighbour's house during his childhood. Each artifact seemed to evoke a memory, enveloping Çarh in a world rich with historical narratives. In this moment, he felt a growing confidence that finding what he sought was not only possible but imminent in this place.

As Çarh continued navigating through the shop, a sense of déjà vu overcame him. Everything felt strangely familiar, as if he had encountered this place before. The streets he passed on the way to the shop also seemed oddly recognizable. Although most of the antique items around him were of an age he shouldn't have encountered before, there lingered an unexplainable sense of familiarity in everything.

Caught off guard by the approach of an employee, Çarh, deeply engrossed in his exploration of the shop and preoccupied with the strange feelings within him, had momentarily lost awareness of the employee's presence. The sudden question jolted him back to reality.

"Sorry," Çarh apologized. "I was just looking around. A friend told me he has a shop here. His name is Nail. I'd like to talk to him."

The employee responded, "Of course, I can call him. Where can I direct you?"

"No, thanks. I'll wait," replied Çarh, declining the employee's suggestion.

Çarh's attention was drawn to a locked box. Intrigued, he expressed his desire to open it to one of Nail's employees. However, the employee declined, "Unfortunately, there's no key for this box; it's kept locked at the boss's request." Çarh felt a twinge of disappointment, wondering if the item he sought could be inside that box.

When the Elf joined Çarh, he too began scrutinizing the surroundings, examining everything just as he had done earlier. Initially thinking the strange feeling was unique to him, Çarh realised that the Elf's behaviour indicated they both shared a similar sensation.

As Nail approached Çarh and the Elf, he greeted them with a smile and inquired, "How may I help you?" Çarh explained that they came in search of a missing plant and needed Nail's assistance.

Nail retorted, "Are you aware of what kind of shop this is? What plant?"

Before Çarh could respond, the Elf interjected, speaking in a language that Çarh couldn't understand, reminiscent of the Heikwounnéls language from their previous encounters. "Neirkwöpia, Jahnaxöpra de Sröllia Nail Gualluiçen,"

Nail responded, saying, "Neirkwöpia[ix]. You're an Elf. It's been a long time since I've seen an Elf in my shop."

The Elf explained, "We wouldn't have come if we didn't need something. We need that plant for a spell."

Nail repeated, "A spell? I'm an antique dealer; I don't sell plants. Maybe you can find it somewhere else."

The Elf insisted, "But we need this. We came here because we need your power to locate the plant."

Nail replied, "It seems there's nothing I can do to help," and then walked away to assist another customer.

Frustrated, the Elf exclaimed, "Nail, you're really being absurd. You have no connection to that plant. The reason we came here is to use your power to find it."

Nail turned to Çarh and asked, "My power? Well, do you know how it works?"

Çarh, caught off guard and lost in thought, was startled by the sudden question. "No, I don't know," he admitted.

The Elf interjected, saying, "Tell us what you want in exchange." The mention of an "exchange" left Çarh astonished. This was unexpected. What kind of exchange?

Nail, appearing bewildered and clearly disturbed, then sharply asked, "What do you Elves want?"

The Elf responded, "We have a task, and you need to help us."

Nail retorted, "There's nothing I can help you with here."

The Elf insisted, "That's proof right there that you need to work with us somehow. Otherwise, everyone loses."

Intrigued, Nail responded, "Things are getting more interesting than I thought. Well, what plant are you so eager about? Why do you want this plant?"

The Elf simply stated, "It's a plant that is important to us, that's all. Tell us what you want in exchange."

Çarh struggled to understand the conversation. What was happening here? What exchange were they talking about? His head was spinning.

Nail, not enthusiastic about the Elf's suggestion, sought more information before committing to any assistance. Before delving into why he should help them, he wanted to understand more about the plant and the type of spell they intended to perform. He approached the exchange offer with scepticism, aware of the complexity of their situation. Çarh, too, listened with curiosity, attempting to comprehend the unfolding situation.

Nail persisted, "Why do you want that plant?"

The Elf appeared reluctant to answer Nail's question, but Çarh stepped in to clarify the situation. Removing his hat, he revealed the grown Sûr on his forehead and explained that they needed the plant to conceal his horn.

Astonished, Nail observed Çarh's horn closely and then gazed at it with great admiration. "Since you are from the Cépfiarexen ancestry," Nail remarked, "I might need to assist you. You should take good care of your horn. So, what is that plant?" he inquired.

The Elf responded, "Fritillaria ehrhartii. It's a rare species, found only in a few places worldwide. It forms the raw material for many elixirs. It should also be in the cave of Çifte Minareli Medrese in the city of Erzurum. Someone must have taken it."

After a moment of thought, Nail agreed to help, but he made it clear that he expected something in exchange. The Elf, straightforward, urged, "Just tell us what you want for the exchange."

Nail then revealed, "There's a necklace I desire greatly. It's almost impossible to obtain from its current owner. But if this young man can get that necklace, I can find the plant."

Upon hearing Nail's request, a tremor went through Çarh's mind. For a moment, his thoughts became entangled. While he had been listening reluctantly until then, suddenly, he started paying closer attention. When asked about the necklace's whereabouts, Nail mentioned that it belonged to a woman living in the Cihangir district. However, as soon as he revealed her name was Deka, something stirred within Çarh. Yet, this disturbance wasn't merely excitement; it was a stirring that reopened a wound. As Nail continued, disclosing that her name was Deka and the necklace was in her possession, Çarh's heart seemed to stop for a moment. Hearing the name Deka had deeply affected him, reopening a wound in his life.

Upon hearing the name Deka, Çarh felt as if he were getting lost in a sea of memories. Months ago, a challenging event had deeply affected him because of Deka. Since that moment, Çarh's inner world had started to tremble, haunted by painful memories of his past. However, in recent times, the weight of the experiences he had lived through had caused him to forget. Now, upon hearing the name Deka, all these painful memories rushed back.

Attempting once again to rein in his emotions, Çarh said, "Okay, I'll try to handle it." However, the unease and worry within him were unsettling. He wasn't ready to face Deka, but he knew he had to. Despite the turmoil within, Çarh did everything he could to calm the chaos. Taking a deep breath to gather his courage amid the confusion, he turned to the Elf, asking, "Are you ready?"

The Elf's mind was entangled with Nail's request, suspecting that the necklace meant more than just a piece of jewellery. He wondered about the hidden implications and questioned whether Nail had another purpose in mind. Was there a different plan to obtain the necklace, one that could lead them on a dangerous journey?

Despite his suspicions, the Elf kept his thoughts to himself, respecting Nail's and Çarh's plans and acknowledging Çarh's right to make decisions. Drawing from his own experiences, the Elf recalled times when he needed the help of others and had to fit into their plans.

Silently deciding to wait and patiently observe what would unfold, an underlying worry persisted within the Elf, causing discomfort. Turning to Çarh, he said, "I'm ready; we can go."

Murat Karagoz

CHAPTER 9
FACE OFF

As Çarh contemplated broaching the subject with the Elf regarding the impending journey to fulfil Nail's unusual request, a maelstrom of emotions and uncertainties churned within him. The mere thought of confronting Deka once more added an intricate layer to his already conflicted feelings. He found himself unprepared to face the emotions evoked by their prior encounters and the perplexity surrounding Deka's apparent lack of recognition.

The Elf, taken aback by Çarh's sudden focus, diverted his attention from his own thoughts and inquired, "No, I was just pondering Nail's request. Why do you ask?"

After a momentary pause, Çarh responded, "I sense that something is amiss. I don't believe Nail would go to such lengths for just a simple necklace. Aren't you aware of it too?"

The Elf was surprised by Çarh's words. Nail's request did indeed strike him as peculiar, and he grappled with understanding the underlying reasons. "Yes, it did seem a bit strange, but I don't exactly know what's going on," he admitted.

Çarh revealed, "I need to tell you something. When I first heard the name Deka, I wasn't certain, but upon noticing a particular detail later, I'm now convinced that I might know Deka."

The Elf, taken aback, listened in surprise to Çarh's revelation. The impact that the name Deka had on Çarh was evident, but the possibility of a personal connection left the Elf even more astonished.

"Really?" the Elf inquired with curiosity.

Çarh nodded slightly. "Yes, but I'm not entirely sure. There's someone I knew with the name Deka, but they were very unstable. Part of me hopes it's that person, and another part hopes it's not."

Observing Çarh's expression, the Elf comprehended his concern. "Perhaps you're mistaken," he suggested. "It's plausible for people to encounter others with the same name."

Çarh concurred with the Elf, yet the lingering worry within him persisted. "Yes, maybe, but when I heard the name Deka, it feels impossible not to remember that person," he replied.

The Elf, empathetic to Çarh's concerns, sought to offer support. "What do you plan to do?" he asked.

After a moment of contemplation, Çarh resolved, "We need to get the necklace. Deka might not be that person, but I want to be sure," he declared.

The Elf expressed his respect for Çarh's decision and conveyed his readiness to assist. The two set out, preparing to confront Deka after securing the necklace.

Walking together from the Grand Bazaar to Karaköy and then towards Cihangir, the Elf began to share his experiences. "You might not remember, but I've been in this Buenuta[x] for a very long time, witnessing its most beautiful years," he recounted. Çarh listened in astonishment. Many things still seemed strange, but what he heard filled him with great excitement. The more he learned, the more he wanted to know.

Çarh interjected, "Actually, I don't know much about you. I'd like to hear your story sometime," he said.

The Elf replied, "Of course, the more information you have, the better for you," and continued, "By the way, I need to go handle something."

When the Elf mentioned he had to leave to take care of something, Çarh felt the exhaustion. They parted ways with a promise to meet again tomorrow.

Çarh continued his journey toward home through the narrow streets of Cihangir. The past few weeks had been intense, and the decision to resume his adventure by leaving home brought a surge of emotions. However, as he approached the apartment building, a lingering sadness clung to him. Climbing the entrance stairs, memories of Aunt Zülfiye flooded his mind. Her loss, just a few months ago, had forced him to confront the uncertainty of life and the inevitability of death. Grief still lingered; the suddenness of everything weighed heavily on him.

Checking the mailbox at the entrance, he noticed several letters. Some were from friends, while others were advertisements. But the most intriguing one was a handwrit-ten letter. He didn't know who it was from, but his curiosity led him to open it. As he read the letter, his sadness deepened. The letter had come from Ali and Sevgi, who spent most of his time in France, and lived across the hall from Aunt Zülfiye. They had written in response to Aunt Zülfiye's passing.

Reading the letter, Çarh felt a significant void in his heart.

Each step he took seemed to draw him closer to Aunt Zülfiye, and the profound wound of her absence resonated within him. Reflecting on the recent weeks, the act of climbing the stairs paled in comparison. However, as he ascended the final step, a subtle sense of relief enveloped him, as if he had found a momentary solace.

Just as he was about to enter his home, he encountered Aunt Fatma. She had assumed the role of a second mother for Çarh after Aunt Zülfiye. She embraced him as if they hadn't seen each other in years, asking about why he wore a hat and inquiring about what he had been up to. Çarh chatted with her for a while and eventually said goodbye to go home.

Upon reaching his doorstep, a glimmer of hope had sprouted within him. Entering, he half-expected Aunt Zülfiye to greet him, just like in the old days. However, as soon as he opened the door, a silence enveloped the room. The atmosphere inside felt different. Çarh missed her immensely – her compassionate, understanding, and loving gaze. Perhaps, upon entering, he thought, he might find something that would remind him of her.

Çarh began to roam around, eventually reaching the bedroom. There, a photo frame on the bedside table caught his attention. In the photo, Aunt Zülfiye was captured with a beautiful smile from her youth. He took the photo, settled into a chair, and with teary eyes, gazed at the picture. Her radiant smile, frozen in time, brought a momentary warmth to Çarh's heart.

However, even this poignant memory couldn't fully alleviate the pain. With sorrowful thoughts lingering, Çarh stood up and continued to wander through the house. A weight rested heavily on his mind, a mixture of grappling with the shock of what he had learned about Deka and trying to cope with the profound sadness of losing Aunt Zülfiye. The conflicting emotions tugged at his heart, creating a complex and challenging internal landscape.

Being alone at home during those moments was comforting, providing a space to gather his thoughts. He sat for a while, embracing the silence. Then, he stood up and walked towards the kitchen. Perhaps a cup of tea could offer solace. Upon entering the kitchen, his eyes caught sight of something unusual – a note on the kitchen table. Intrigued, he read the note.

As Çarh absorbed the words, his heart lightened momentarily. Aunt Zülfiye's words felt like a bridge of communication, as if they were connected once again. As his eyes traversed the note, he reminisced about her distinctive handwriting. Though only a few words were written in bold letters, their significance was profound. The note conveyed her longing for him, her concerns, and a presence that could fill the emptiness, bringing a momentary joy to Çarh.

However, amidst this emotional connection, he couldn't escape the stark reality. Aunt Zülfiye had truly departed. Despite the expression of missing him in the note, it served as a stark reminder of an irreversible separation. With these poignant thoughts, he carefully folded the note and placed it back on the table.

Çarh grew tired of confining himself within the walls of his house, and so, he made the decision to step outside. Perhaps a walk and the open air could provide some solace. He headed to the café he frequented and ordered a hot coffee. Seated at a table, quietly sipping his coffee, Çarh was suddenly startled by a voice. When he turned his head, he saw Deka. Confusion washed over him. What was Deka doing there?

Initially bewildered, Çarh's concern then began to surface.

Approaching Çarh, Deka started the conversation, "It's really nice to see you again."

Çarh attempted to respond, trying to gather himself. However, a palpable tension lingered within him. While being with Deka was pleasant, Çarh was not prepared for this conversation. He hadn't fully comprehended his feelings about her. "It's nice to see you too, Deka," he managed to reply. Nevertheless, seeing Deka brought happiness to Çarh, and the emotions he harboured for her remained fresh.

Deka took a seat beside him and turned to Çarh. "What's going on? I wanted to talk to you," she said. Çarh hesitated for a moment, uncertain about what to say. The direction of the conversation eluded him. However, Deka's sincere demeanor reassured him. "Tell me what's happening with you," Çarh responded, somewhat nervously.

"I don't know if you remember, but after our first meeting, I saw you a few times and greeted you. You ignored me. In our last encounter, you continued talking without addressing this issue. Now, you're saying 'it's nice to see you' again. I really don't understand you, Deka," he added, expressing his confusion and concerns.

Deka explained, "You're right, I couldn't express myself properly. Actually, it wasn't me who ignored you, at least not consciously."

Çarh asked, "Not you? What, do you have a twin or something?"

Deka smiled gently and expressed her desire to continue the conversation in a calmer place.

Sensing an opportunity to clarify matters and retrieve the necklace around Deka's neck, Çarh agreed. They left the café and headed to a quiet park. During their walk, they remained silent, each lost in their own thoughts. However, when they reached the park, Deka started to speak. "Çarh, I'm really curious about you. I want to know what you're thinking, what you're feeling, and what you want to do," she said, opening the door to a deeper conversation.

Çarh remained silent for a moment, then looked into Deka's eyes and began to pour out his feelings. "Deka, everything is so complicated for me. I've been through tough times, and I still don't exactly know what to do. The day I met you, many things changed for me. Initially, this change was positive, but due to your inconsistent behaviour, I closed myself off, living a life from one bar to another every day. Then I lost someone close to me, and my life turned upside down. Long story short, I don't know how to unravel this confusion."

Deka felt saddened by Çarh's words but tried to understand him. "I understand, Çarh. You've been through tough times, and you're still trying to recover. I assume you're expecting an explanation related to me, and you're absolutely right."

Deka couldn't quite figure out how to broach the subject. Admitting she was a Sögré wasn't an easy task, but what Deka didn't know was that Çarh had recently become a Sögré as well. As they exchanged glances, Çarh's attention was drawn to Deka's necklace. Its beauty and value were apparent, sparking various scenarios in his mind about its origin and how he might acquire it. Should he inquire politely or consider a more forceful approach? These thoughts were pushed aside as he pondered why Nail couldn't claim the necklace. "The necklace... it's quite intriguing. An heirloom from your family, perhaps?" he inquired.

The silver of the necklace sparkled with the reflection

of lights, its delicate chain attached to an elegant staff-shaped pendant. Hanging downward from this staff was a small crystal, within which something was discernible, though a closer look was required to identify it.

Deka explained, "Yes, it's actually a family heirloom passed down to me from my mother. It contains an apple tree seed. I know it's not something very special, but it gives me a unique power."

Surprised, Çarh remarked, "An apple seed?" Expressing his desire to examine the necklace more closely, Deka regretfully mentioned that she couldn't take it off. "Please don't be surprised; I can't remove the necklace. And while we're on the topic of the necklace, I want to share something about myself,"

Upon realizing that Deka couldn't remove the necklace, Çarh pondered on how he could acquire it. Magic crossed his mind, but he wasn't proficient in that aspect yet.

"What do you know about witches?" Deka asked. Caught off guard and quite astonished, Çarh repeated, "Witches? Why are we talking about witches?"

Deka explained, "I was just curious. Because when I tell the story about myself, I want you to believe me."

Çarh listened attentively, becoming intrigued. "Really?" he asked. "I would love to hear what you have to say."

Deka continued, "I am a Sögré, which means I am a witch. Another thing you need to know about me is that I have many identical appearances, or tömté[xi], that look exactly like me."

Çarh couldn't believe what he had heard. Was Deka a Sögré? What did she mean by doppelganger that closely resembled her? Many questions raced through his mind. He remained silent after Deka's revelation. In an attempt to break the silence, Deka continued to explain, "Tömté is a being that looks exactly like me but possesses a completely different soul." Çarh started to grasp the concept a bit. "On the first day we met, you truly encountered me. I was the one who saw you in my dream, the one who talked to you. However, the people you saw in the following days were actually my tömté."

"So, that's why they didn't remember me?" Çarh asked.

"Yes," Deka replied, her expression somewhat saddened, and continued, "Whenever I tried to explain this situation, no one understood me. However, sensing something different in you, I felt compelled to reveal this truth."

Çarh found himself torn between disclosing the truth about himself or not. As he reminded himself that his primary goal was to obtain the necklace, a question surfaced in his mind. Did Nail know about this truth regarding Deka? The answer came swiftly without much contemplation. "Of course, he knew. He was aware of how difficult it was to obtain the necklace; that's why he tasked me with it, as if I could accomplish such a feat."

Deka, perceiving the pain etched on Çarh's face, asked, "Are you okay?"

In reality, Çarh was far from okay. Shaken by the revelation of Deka's true identity and the striking resemblance of the images, he found himself grappling with the complexity of Nail's request for Deka's necklace and her Sögré status. The awareness of his own vulnerability and the impracticality of his pursuit weighed heavily on him, leaving him lost in a sea of self-doubt. Nevertheless, he acknowledged that escaping this situation without obtaining the necklace was not an option.

Çarh felt utterly drained after his conversation with Deka. Fatigue compounded as he exited the café. Searching for a polite excuse, he murmured, "I've realised I'm quite tired; I'd like to go home." Deka understandingly bid him farewell, wishing him a good night.

As Çarh made his way home, he pondered the unfolding events. The revelation of Deka's true identity had left him profoundly surprised. Furthermore, the task assigned by Nail to obtain the necklace loomed as a worrisome challenge. The difficulty of the mission and the fear of failure cast a shadow over him. The Elf, still oblivious to these recent developments, remained uninformed. Çarh wondered what the Elf's reaction would be to all of this. On the journey home, he decided it was time to formulate a new plan.

The next day, Çarh awoke to find the Elf patiently waiting at the head of the bed, a routine that never failed to startle him. He scolded the Elf for this habit, expressing his discomfort. In a cheerful manner, the Elf responded,

"Do you realise I am not human anymore, at least not now?"

Çarh, choosing not to engage with the Elf's words, simply smiled in silence. "When you say, 'at least not now,' were you previously human?" he inquired.

Just as the Elf was about to answer, Çarh interjected, "You know what? Don't bother answering because I don't care anymore; whatever happens to me is already a result of curiosity."

The Elf, now intrigued, asked about the events of the previous night. Çarh began to explain, "We delved into the question of whether the Deka I know is the same person or someone else. Last night, I met with Deka. She is undoubtedly the same Deka I know. What's more, Deka is a Sögré. Can you believe it? Nail deceived us," he revealed. Having already risen from bed, Çarh made his way to the kitchen. As he opened the fridge to prepare breakfast, he noticed its meagre contents.

Such small details served as a stark reminder of how much his lifestyle had changed, tormenting him with the weight of the recent revelations.

The Elf asked, "Did you ever suspect?" Çarh continued to explain, "Deka told me interesting things about herself. She has images resembling a tömté or something. I've encountered a few of them before, greeted them, but they didn't remember me. Turns out that's why,"

The Elf's eyes widened. "Wait, you said tömté?"

Çarh, taken aback, asked, "Yes, what's wrong?" anticipating an unsettling answer.

The Elf inquired sharply, "Did she definitely say they were tömté?" Çarh, hesitatingly, affirmed. The Elf was bewildered. Had he witnessed the existence of a witch belonging to the witch ancestry, a mystery even in his own world? The reality of the situation seemed almost unbelievable. He urged Çarh to recount every detail of what happened previous night, and Çarh obliged, with the Elf listening in awe.

After Çarh finished explaining everything in the finest detail, a moment of silence hung in the air. Breaking this silence, he asked, "Elf, are you hiding something from me? What do you know about Deka?"

The Elf, taking a deep breath, began to explain. He described tömtés as entities with images exactly like Deka, a feature exclusive to a single witch ancestry. Additionally, he mentioned that the Sögré belonging to this witch ancestry was shrouded in mystery. Çarh listened in amazement, finding Deka's reality intriguing. He had pointed out that the Sögré of this particular witch ancestry was not documented, yet, based on his recollection, it should be the representative of the Quordéen witch ancestry.

At some point, Çarh, feeling his head spinning, asked,

"What do you mean? Do we have a powerful and mysterious Sögré in front of us, and you don't exactly know what it is? And are we trying to obtain its necklace?" When the Elf suggested that the situation could be even more complicated, Çarh grew even more uneasy. Could the situation be that intricate? Various scenarios played out in his mind as he listened to the Elf. Despite Deka appearing quite ordinary, the Elf's description painted her as complex and mysterious. What made her so special? Was she truly as enigmatic a Sögré as the Elf described? The looming revelation that he, too, was a Sögré added another layer of complexity. How would he react to this truth? Most importantly, how would he secure the necklace?

The Elf, intuitively sensing Çarh's thoughts, said, "Tell me about the necklace." Çarh proceeded to explain the significance of the silver necklace adorned by Deka. At its end hung a wand, and at the wand's tip, a crystal held an apple seed. The Elf found this arrangement intriguing and remarked that he couldn't fathom why Nail desired the necklace. If Nail was aware of Deka's power, the Elf speculated that he might aim to create a tömté. However, the Elf added that the power of each Sögré was unique; in other words, one Sögré's abilities couldn't be harnessed by another. Confessing his lack of understanding regarding Nail's true purpose, the Elf expressed the need for time to investigate the matter.

Çarh listened attentively to the Elf's words. He recognized the necessity of uncovering Nail's true motive and marvelled at the necklace's importance. The revelation of Deka being a Sögré had initially unsettled him, but a growing sense of trust had developed towards her.

While Çarh contemplated how to plan the retrieval of the necklace, the Elf offered a suggestion. "Perhaps you should take your relationship with Deka to the next level to better understand and obtain the necklace."

Çarh was taken aback by the Elf's suggestion and felt a bit uneasy. While there was no romantic relationship between him and Deka, he harboured such desires. However, he was reluctant to exploit her just to obtain the necklace. Understanding Çarh's concerns by reading his thoughts, the Elf offered reassurance: "Certainly, you don't want to use Deka for your own interests, but perhaps if you build a closer bond with her, you can tap into her power. Besides, Deka might be willing to give you the necklace, but she might want to establish a closer connection with you first."

Çarh remained sceptical about the Elf's idea, but he acknowledged that spending more time with Deka and forming a closer bond might prove beneficial. "Alright," he said, "Maybe what you're saying is right. I'll spend more time with Deka and establish a connection with her. But that doesn't mean using her just to get the necklace, does it?"

The Elf smiled and replied, "Of course not. Don't forget that Deka is still human. Establishing a genuine relationship with her is more important than obtaining the necklace. Perhaps through this, you can discover new ways to benefit from Deka's power."

Murat Karagoz

CHAPTER 10
CONFESSION

Çarh woke up, feeling the familiar ache in his head. As he looked in the mirror, he was surprised to notice the growing Sûr, now starting to cover his hair. Realizing that his hair concealed the Sûr, Çarh decided to let them grow. The hat became his indispensable accessory as he felt different from humans now, fearing potential ostracization. This fear fuelled his desire for Deka's necklace. Regardless of everything, he needed a plant to perform the growth spell, and for that plant, he had to obtain the necklace Nail desired.

Reflecting on the conversations with the Elf from the day before, Çarh found himself puzzled by the revelation of Deka's powerful and mysterious witch ancestry, especially considering the Elf's lack of knowledge. Questions swirled in his mind. How many witch ancestries existed, and perhaps elves were not familiar with every lineage? Despite attempting to console himself with such thoughts, Çarh was acutely aware of the gravity of the situation. He couldn't help but contemplate Deka's tömtés.

As Çarh grappled with understanding the purpose and existence of Deka's tömtés, his mind was in turmoil. The initial notion that they might have been created to control Deka's power didn't satisfy him. The question of how tömtés could control Deka and why they needed to do so remained unclear.

Concerns about how to handle Deka's tömtés troubled Çarh. If the tömtés had truly surpassed Deka's control, he had no idea what to do. Perhaps seeking Deka's assistance in this matter was a consideration, although he wasn't even sure if she would be willing to help.

While these thoughts swirled in Çarh's mind, he continued to focus on his own transformation. Eager to rid himself of the Sûr he saw in the mirror, he put on his hat and left home to meet Deka, determined not to waste any time.

Çarh began to scrutinize every moment spent with Deka, making an effort to understand her thought processes. He paid close attention to her actions, words, and emotions, working diligently to strengthen the bond between them. As their connection grew stronger, Çarh delved into learning more about Deka's tömtés.

Deka explained to Çarh that the tömtés were not distinct entities but rather a kind of reflection. Their purpose was to evenly distribute Deka's power to ensure her protection. Çarh wondered about the nature of the power that allowed her to create reflections for protection. Deka revealed that while she had control, it wasn't absolute. "They don't recognize you because they don't act with my consciousness, but they are, in fact, me. I know it's quite complicated. I apologize for bombarding you with these topics," she explained. Çarh responded, "Not at all; on the contrary, I want to learn more."

Çarh endeavoured to comprehend the challenges Deka faced, sharing in her struggles, and seeking solutions together, thereby fortifying the bond between them.

As Çarh delved into a better understanding of Deka, he inched closer to unravelling the secrets of her powers and abilities. Throughout this process, Çarh devoted his best efforts to helping Deka harness her powers more effectively. This reciprocal exchange contributed to Deka placing greater trust in Çarh, prompting her to open up about herself.

Now possessing a deep mutual trust and respect, Çarh and Deka collaborated more effectively, with Deka's enhanced control over her powers improving the efficacy of Çarh's plans.

The relationship between Çarh and Deka played a pivotal role in achieving his goals. Empowered by Deka's abilities, Çarh made progress toward objectives that would have been unattainable before.

Choosing to walk alongside Deka, Çarh decided to inquire about the necklace. His curiosity stemmed from wanting to learn more about Deka's story, hoping it might provide some clues. As they walked in silence, Çarh gazed at Deka's face and asked, "What is the story behind the necklace?"

Deka paused for a moment and then nodded slightly, saying, "The necklace was a gift from my family. The wand was one of the holiest objects in our family, and the crystal symbolized that my family was a powerful Sögré. The apple seed carried the memory of the previous generations of my family."

Çarh attentively listened to Deka's account, realizing the profound significance of the necklace. Discovering that Deka possessed the wand, one of her family's holiest objects, intrigued him. "I didn't know Sögré had wands," he remarked.

Deka explained, "Yes, nowadays Sögrés don't use wands; instead, they are born with magical abilities. In the past, wands were used, but when Céwiaretza created the 2nd generation of witch ancestries, they introduced the ability to perform magic with tattoos instead of wands."

As Çarh listened, he understood that Deka's ancestry traced back to the 1st generation of witch ancestry, revealing the deep roots of her Sögré heritage. However, the concept of magic through tattoos intrigued him, and he sought clarification. "Performing magic with tattoos instead of wands?"

Deka explained, "You may have noticed; when you try to get a tattoo, your body rejects it. That's because tattoos can only be on Sögré, specifically marked naturally by Céwiaretza. Each Sögré has a tattoo on the back of their neck. Theoretically, by looking at these tattoos, you can determine if someone is a Sögré and to which ancestry they belong."

Çarh, feeling a slight anxiety, recalled his own tattoo. Deka wasn't supposed to see it, as the Elf didn't want her to know he carried Sûr. Considering Sûr's rapid growth, he needed to act quickly and secure the necklace without Deka noticing. "Very interesting," Çarh said. "So, do tömtés have tattoos?"

Deka, impressed by Çarh's intellect, hesitated to reveal this truth. "Yes, tömtés have tattoos because they are my reflections," she explained, adding a slight smile to her face.

Çarh was taken aback by Deka's response. The idea that tömtés would have tattoos had never crossed his mind, offering a different perspective that intrigued him. He admired the depth of knowledge in Deka's mind and once again realised the value of the time he spent with her.

"What about the necklace?" Çarh inquired.

Sûr

For a moment, Deka felt uncomfortable with these questions, suspecting that Çarh's real intention was not to get to know her. Nevertheless, she chose not to dampen the energy of the atmosphere and responded somewhat ambiguously, "Like a tattoo."

Çarh sensed that Deka might be hiding something from her response. Perhaps the story of the necklace held a special meaning for her, leading her to avoid a detailed explanation. Without insisting to gain Deka's trust, Çarh decided to change the subject. "Are we hungry? If you want, we can go to my place. I'd like to cook for you." Remembering her hunger, Deka accepted the offer, and they walked home together.

During the walk, Çarh noticed inconsistencies in Deka's answers, sensing a mismatch between her words and actions. He felt that Deka was not being entirely honest, which concerned him. Çarh recognized the need to make more effort to understand Deka's true intentions.

Upon arriving at the apartment building, Çarh invited Deka inside. As they entered the building, Çarh gestured towards the door and said, "Please, come in." Deka experienced an interesting energy upon entering, which was evident from her expression. Çarh noticed her surprise and inquired, "Did something happen to you?"

After a moment of thought, Deka replied, "I felt an energy when entering the house. It was something different. I don't usually feel such things."

Çarh contemplated asking if she sensed Aunt Zülfiye's energy but refrained, as doing so would mean revealing the truth about himself. Instead, he chose to remain silent and playfully brushed it off, saying, "I haven't visited home for a long time. Did you smell something bad?"

Deka, smiling lightly, said, "No, of course, I just felt

something that shouldn't be here," and continued, "Anyway, you mentioned food. What are we having?"

"Well, I can make a vegetable dish using vegetables that shouldn't be here, and with your help, we can make it even more delicious," he said. Deka, laughing at his joke, accepted his suggestion, and they began cooking together. While preparing the meal, they chatted, and their bond grew stronger. After finishing the meal, they sat at the table and enjoyed their food. Çarh expressed, "Deka, the time I spend with you is truly precious. I'm so happy to know you," and smiled at Deka. Feeling his sincerity, Deka smiled back, saying, "I'm also really glad to have met you, Çarh. I really care about you." Both nurtured sincere feelings for each other, and with the strengthening of these emotions, their bond deepened.

As Deka headed to the kitchen to get some water, she noticed a woman in the kitchen. In momentary shock, she dropped the glass. Hearing the sound of the glass breaking, Çarh immediately got up and went to Deka. Looking at the surprise on her face, Çarh tried to understand what was happening. "What happened?" he asked.

Deka, still feeling shocked, replied, "There was a woman here."

Çarh repeated with astonishment, "Aunt Zülfiye?" Deka nodded in confirmation. "Is it the recently deceased aunt? But how can it be? She's dead," she added, expressing her thoughts.

Çarh paused for a moment before answering Deka's question. Then he said, "You know, Aunt Zülfiye passed away a few months ago." Deka was surprised. "Yes, but she felt like she was here. It's strange," she replied.

Çarh explained, "Maybe her spirit is still lingering here. This sometimes happens." Although Deka didn't quite believe in this explanation, she accepted that there was a reality without a clear explanation.

Then Çarh added, "You already have energy sensitivity. Maybe you felt her too." Deka hesitated for a moment upon hearing Çarh's words. Energy sensitivity was something she didn't talk much about, and it was surprising to learn that Çarh had knowledge about it.

As Deka began to return to the meal, Çarh picked up the broken glass from the floor. However, Deka noticed something else from the corner of her eye — a small tattoo on the back of Çarh's neck. This sudden realization distracted her attention, and the possibility that Çarh was lying came to her mind. She had never considered that Çarh could be a Sögré. The trust she had in him was now shaken.

Çarh, sensing Deka's gaze, slowly turned his head and looked at her. When he saw the expression on Deka's face, he understood what was going on. "What happened? Did you see something that worries you?" he asked.

Deka pointed to the tattoo on the back of Çarh's neck and asked, "What is this?"

Çarh froze for a moment. "I... I am a Sögré," he confessed. "I wanted to tell you, but I'm even ashamed of my condition. I didn't want you to run away, so I didn't say anything."

Deka wanted to believe what Çarh said, but she still felt uneasy. "What condition?" she asked.

Despite Deka's bewildered looks, Çarh tried to stay calm. Being a Sûr carrier had been a great burden for him. That's why he hadn't wanted to tell anyone. But now it was time to share the truth with Deka.

Çarh slowly took off his hat, explaining, "One day, I woke up, and this Sûr was here. Since that day, I've been carrying it. But like you, I don't know why it's on me."

Deka was surprised by what Çarh revealed. Being a Sûr carrier was a highly unique condition, according to Deka's beliefs. Throughout the history of Israfil, Sûr had been a protective and powerful source. Sûr carriers were rare Sögrés who could control the energies of Sûr.

"Being a Sûr carrier is a very special condition," Deka responded, "But at the same time, it can be very dangerous. Everyone around you may want your power and energy. That's why they can harm you."

Çarh agreed with what Deka said. Being a Sûr carrier had been a burden for him. However, as Deka pointed out, this situation was very special for him.

Deka added, "Also, being able to see and communicate with spirits because you're a Sûr carrier is quite normal."

Çarh was attentive to Deka's words. He could infer some things from her words, and that disturbed him. What Deka knew were things not even known by the Elf. Was it an ability she somehow learned, or was it something innate? Was there a secret involved?

While Çarh continued to contemplate Deka's words, he also persisted in asking her questions. Despite Deka sincerely answering, Çarh sensed an inconsistency in her responses. Was Deka hiding the truth, or were the thoughts in Çarh's mind incorrect?

Despite Deka's revelations about herself, Çarh still wondered about her true power. He knew she wasn't an ordinary human, descended from an unknown lineage, possessing supernatural abilities. However, he couldn't accurately gauge how powerful she truly was.

Deka responded to Çarh's question with a smile. "My real power isn't my supernatural abilities. It lies in the knowledge and understanding I possess. Every day, I strive to develop a deep understanding of the meaning of life and the human soul. Using this knowledge, I do my best to help people."

As Çarh admired Deka's words, she continued, "Moreover, like many ancestries, our lineage has some supernatural abilities. However, these powers can only be used up to a certain level, and abusing them is not right. Therefore, my true power is more based on knowledge and understanding."

Çarh pondered Deka's words, realizing that her true power wasn't solely in her supernatural abilities but also in her knowledge and understanding. He was eager to learn more about Deka's lineage.

As he listened to Deka's narrative, Çarh became more intrigued. Deka's powers had impressed him, but he still couldn't comprehend why she created tömté. Understanding the nature of tömté and why they formed required mental effort. He realised that knowing the extent of Deka's power didn't necessarily mean understanding her. Deka's power was a force originating from all the energies existing in the universe. She could penetrate the source of the paradoxes causing tömté to form and control them.

Çarh turned to Deka and asked, "But why do you create tömté? What impact do they have on your power?" Deka smiled and replied, "Tömté result from paradoxes. My power lies within the paradoxes themselves. Tömté are a physical manifestation of these paradoxes. My duty is to solve these paradoxes and ensure the proper functioning of the universe. The existence of tömté creates an imbalance in the universe, and my task is to rectify this imbalance."

Çarh struggled to comprehend Deka's words. Her

power was the source of everything in the universe, enabling her to overcome paradoxes. However, he couldn't fully understand the nature of the paradoxes that led to the formation of tömté.

Deka began by explaining that there were different types of paradoxes. Some involved logical inconsistencies, while others were considered thought experiments. However, the most intriguing paradoxes were deep contradictions within the human mind. For instance, individuals who valued their freedom might simultaneously seek authority to limit that freedom. These contradictions, rooted in the essence of human existence, were the deepest paradoxes and could occasionally result in tömté.

After listening to Deka's explanations, Çarh was amazed once again at the complexity of the human mind.

Deka, looking at Çarh, whose mind was now thoroughly perplexed, said, "Long story short, my power is to bring forth and resolve the paradoxes within the depths of the human mind." She wanted to provide an example. "Let me tell you the story of Kathre Beauthönt. When Céwiaretza created the Ist generation of witch ancestries, the most powerful witch was Kathre. However, Céwiaretza wanted to create another witch ancestry to reclaim the power she had bestowed upon Kathre. This new Sögré had the ability to travel through time. Nevertheless, the act of time travel by this Sögré could create a time paradox – a logical contradiction. For instance, when you alter the past by time traveling, you change your future-self. In this case, the Sögré time traveling would create a future where she didn't exist but would still come back from the future to correct it. This creates a paradox. At this point, I intervene and create a copy of myself, known as tömté. Tömté is a reflection of the power I use to mend the cracks in time. Through tömté, the ruptures in the Buenuta heal, and the paradox is prevented."

Çarh gazed at Deka with admiration after her revelation. Her extraordinary ability to resolve paradoxes in the human mind through her power impressed him deeply. Despite carrying a Sûr, he couldn't help but feel dwarfed by the simplicity of his own abilities in comparison to Deka's capacity to handle intricate thoughts.

Deka's narrative continued to reverberate in Çarh's thoughts. The emergence of another witch ancestry by Céwiaretza to reclaim the power bestowed upon Kathre left numerous questions swirling in his mind. The power of Sögré, capable of manipulating time, and the potential paradoxes it introduced challenged Çarh's comprehension. It underscored the immense value in Deka's words.

What Deka had shared about tömté now took on a new significance in Çarh's understanding. Tömté, crucial for preventing time paradoxes by repairing temporal cracks, became a focal point. Deka's story was reshaping Çarh's thoughts, emphasizing the extraordinary nature of her power in resolving complex paradoxes and mending the ruptures caused by time travel. His respect for her abilities grew.

Contemplating the timeline of Deka's story, Çarh speculated about the possibility of Deka being the Sögré who traversed through time. He questioned whether she might be the one creating her own tömté, recalling her mentioning it while narrating her story. He also considered the alternative that, if she wasn't time traveling, she must be older than he initially assumed. Intrigued by Deka's age, he found her enduring thousands of years astonishing, especially since she didn't appear old. Deka, once again, expressed admiration for Çarh's intelligence.

Çarh observed Deka and decided to voice the questions swirling in his mind. "Deka, how old are you?"

In response to Çarh's question, Deka smiled. "My age surpasses the lifespan of ordinary humans," she replied. "Over time, I've managed to endure by harnessing my power. My life has unfolded across far more years than you can fathom."

Deka's revelation startled Çarh. While her narrative had already been impressive, the revelation of her age being much older left him even more astounded. The realization that Deka's life spanned well beyond the ordinary made him eager to delve deeper into her story and the extent of her powers. For now, though, Çarh remained focused on learning more about the intricate facets of Deka's extraordinary journey.

Sûr

CHAPTER 11
PARADOX

The following day, as the Elf entered the house, he immediately discerned the expression on Çarh's face and endeavoured to grasp what had transpired. Çarh initially remained silent before recounting the events of the preceding night to the Elf. Due to his prior research on Quordéen witches, the Elf wasn't overly surprised by Çarh's revelations. Unlike other witch communities, the Quordéen witches maintained a veil of secrecy.

The Elf speculated that Quordéen witches might adhere to special rules governing their powers, potentially explaining why Deka never removed her necklace. Çarh concurred with the Elf's conjecture. In addition to Deka's extraordinary abilities, the enigma surrounding her seemingly eternal life intrigued Çarh. He mused on the possibility that Quordéen witches possessed a method to slow down aging and, driven by curiosity, inquired, "Are Sögrés immortal?"

The Elf, clarifying that Sögrés were mortal with no

existence of immortal ones, observed a discrepancy between Deka's account and his own response. When Çarh sought confirmation, the Elf reminded him of his elven nature, stating, "We always know more than a Sögré." For the Elf, Deka's belonging to a mysterious witch ancestry did not alter their hierarchical status in the Duete[xii] world, where elves were considered superior beings to Sögré.

Çarh found himself astounded by the Elf's revelations. The revelation that Sögrés were mortal defied his expectations. Nevertheless, the thoughts taking shape in his mind led him to a conclusion. He postulated that Deka's power emanated from her necklace, a notion supported by the Elf.

Upon requesting the Elf's assistance in gathering information about acquiring the necklace, Çarh made a conscious decision to strengthen his bond with Deka. Recognizing that relying solely on physical strength wouldn't suffice, he aimed to intensify his dedication and love for Deka. Seizing every opportunity to spend more time with her, better understand her, and promptly fulfil her needs.

As Çarh and Deka shared their lives, they created beautiful memories together – strolling, reading books, and exploring new places. Each moment spent with her brought him a profound sense of peace.

Over several days, Çarh devoted significant time to Deka, engaging in shared activities and opening up to her. These experiences, such as leisurely walks, shared reading sessions, and exploration of new places, fostered a growing trust and affection from Deka's end.

While Çarh focused on building a deeper connection, the Elf diligently acquired more knowledge about Quordéen witches and the necklace's properties. Through his research, the Elf discovered that the necklace was indeed instrumental in creating tömtés. However, the crucial revelation was that Deka had to willingly remove it herself. The necklace symbolized Deka's power, intricately integrated with her being.

Elf, deeply rooted in the belief of maintaining the balance of nature, chose to withhold the information about the integration of the necklace with Deka's power. The delicate nature of attempting to take the necklace from Deka posed a potential disruption to the balance of nature. Advising Çarh, the Elf suggested that he should spend more time with Deka without openly discussing the necklace, emphasizing the need for their relationship to strengthen further. Despite his concern about the necklace's potential danger, the Elf felt the imperative to conduct more research on the matter.

As Çarh increased his love and dedication to Deka, he and the Elf began planning how to safely remove the necklace. Due to the perceived danger to Deka's life, they recognized the necessity for extreme caution in their plans.

Over the passing days, the bond between Çarh and Deka deepened. They created beautiful memories together, and Deka realised the sincerity of Çarh's love for her. Trusting that he could take Deka's necklace, Çarh sought updates from the Elf. Uneasiness crept over Çarh when the Elf remained silent.

Inquiring about any new developments, Çarh asked, "What happened? Did you learn anything?" the Elf shook his head slightly and replied, "I haven't learned anything yet. However, I continue my research. This matter is quite complex and requires a thorough investigation." Despite wanting to believe the Elf's words, a sense of worry gnawed at Çarh. He felt that time was running out to acquire Deka's necklace.

Each day, Çarh experimented with various methods to conceal the growing Sûr. From different hairstyles to various hats, he attempted to diminish its visibility. However, as the

Sûr continued to grow, it became increasingly noticeable. Although Çarh wasn't pleased with the situation, Deka held a different perspective. She insisted that Çarh's outward appearance was perfect and encouraged him to take pride in it. Deka emphasized that focusing solely on external appearance was misguided and urged Çarh to pay more attention to his inner world.

Çarh harboured a belief that the monstrous presence within him intensified each time he faced his reflection in the mirror. He was convinced that this internal monster would eventually consume him. Despite Deka's persistent efforts to reveal his inherent beauty, Çarh found it challenging to dispel these self-deprecating thoughts. Constant self-criticism and the listing of perceived flaws became a daily ritual, gradually eroding his self-confidence. One day, as he glanced into the mirror, he was horrified to see a monstrous visage staring back at him, devoid of any resemblance to himself.

On another occasion, as he faced the mirror again, Deka approached him, sharing the reflection. "You are truly beautiful, Çarh," she insisted. "Your face carries only your story, and this story defines who you are."

Initially resistant to Deka's words, Çarh gradually accepted them. She asserted, "Your outward appearance is a reflection of your strong, brave, and loving soul. It defines you, Çarh." Deka's words served as a beacon, dispelling the darkness within Çarh, and fostering self-acceptance. Now, when he looked in the mirror, he saw only the beautiful story etched on his face.

The bond between Çarh and Deka deepened further, prompting Çarh to consider taking the necklace. However, he grappled with concerns about the potential harm it might cause to Deka. The necklace held the power to ensure her survival and eternal youth, making its loss a significant risk. Çarh recognized that Deka's immortality and strength were tied to the necklace. Before acting, he decided to consult the Elf one last time.

Çarh reached out to the Elf for guidance, initiating a detailed discussion about his plan, weighing potential risks and benefits. Çarh expressed his decision to take the necklace but voiced apprehensions about the potential harm to Deka. The Elf emphasized the importance of maintaining the balance of nature and advised Çarh to carefully consider and plan thoroughly. Taking the Elf's advice into account, Çarh resolved to proceed more prepared, with a comprehensive plan in place to take the necklace.

The following day, Çarh arrived at the designated meeting place to find Deka in her usual cheerful and energetic state. Despite his reluctance to dampen Deka's spirits, Çarh remained steadfast in his determination to acquire the necklace.

Engaging in a friendly conversation with Deka, Çarh subtly sought a fitting opportunity to implement his plan. Employing humour and ensuring an enjoyable atmosphere, he skilfully diverted her attention. Seizing the moment when Deka adjusted her necklace, Çarh initiated his plan, expressing admiration, "The necklace is so beautiful; can I take a closer look?"

Deka hesitated, choosing to downplay the significance of the necklace, dismissing it as ordinary. Unfazed, Çarh had anticipated this reaction and continued to execute his plan step by step.

Upon returning home, Deka's necklace still adorned her neck. During their conversation, Çarh shifted the focus, inviting Deka to dinner. At the dining table, he shared his desire to give her a special gift — a box containing a necklace he believed she would adore. Deka's surprise was evident when she saw the necklace. Observing her reaction, Çarh made his next move, standing up to put the necklace on. He politely asked Deka to remove her current necklace, expressing his wish to adorn her with the new one.

Perceiving Deka's astonishment, Çarh decided to explain, "This necklace will complement you perfectly and enhance your beauty. I also consider it a gift to express my love for you." Grateful for the gesture, Deka conveyed her thanks but mentioned she couldn't remove her own necklace. Suggesting that Çarh could place the new one over it, Çarh responded with slight disappointment, saying, "As you wish." Sensing Çarh's disappointment, Deka felt the need to explain, but the words stuck in her throat. Unsure of what to say, she managed a simple "Thank you."

As Çarh silently continued his meal, a sudden knock on the door startled him. Upon opening the door, he was confronted by a figure identical to Deka. Initially, he considered the possibility of her having a twin, only to later realise that it was Deka's reflection, known as tömté. His surprise was evident as tömté requested permission to enter. With the arrival of the real Deka, Çarh grappled with the peculiar situation, and Deka attempted to make sense of tömté's existence. Addressing Çarh, Deka said, "You know the story." Çarh began to reflect on Deka's words, acknowledging his awareness of the power of the necklace that allowed Deka to create reflections. However, this situation also raised concerns about the balance of nature. Tömté's presence added complexity to Çarh's emotions, prompting questions about her nature and whether her existence could provide a solution to maintaining balance.

As these questions swirled in Çarh's mind, Deka turned to tömté and affirmed, "Çarh knows our story." Tömté entered and got straight to the point. Deka's face displayed signs of concern, and Çarh listened intently. Tömté stated, "A paradox is occurring, and urgent intervention is needed." In response to Deka's inquiry about the nature of the paradox, tömté explained, "There was a traffic accident. A culprit attempted to escape the police by swerving through traffic. Another driver intervened to stop the culprit, resulting in the culprit's vehicle flipping and dragging for 1 or 2 kilometres,"

Deka looked at tömté with concern, while Çarh remained silent. Tömté continued, "The culprit died at the scene. The driver, initially a passerby, became the hero due to the action taken to stop the culprit. This contradiction has created a paradox, affecting the future. Urgent action is required."

While Deka attempted to comprehend tömté's message, Çarh quietly immersed himself in his thoughts. Tömté's explanation seemed complex to Çarh, but Deka's silence heightened his concern. Çarh finally spoke, "How can we resolve this situation?" Tömté took the floor, explaining, "It appears possible to resolve this paradox. Yes, there are risks, but for the sake of maintaining balance, it must be done."

Taking a step closer, Deka held her own necklace with her right hand and tömté's necklace with the other. Intrigued, Çarh watched as Deka held tömté's necklace, attempting to grasp the connection between tömté's words and Deka's actions. Deka elucidated, "My necklace is a duplicate of tömté's necklace. Together, these similar yet opposing pieces can be utilized to resolve a paradox."

Curious, Çarh sought more information on the matter. Deka continued, "To resolve the paradox, tömté must travel back in time and choose a different path instead of intervening with the driver. However, this would erase the heroic situation. Here, my necklace can reverse the wheel of time, restoring balance by resolving the paradox."

Uniting the necklaces, Deka created a beam. After tömté left with gratitude, Çarh looked at Deka's actions in admiration and remarked, "You truly are a sorceress." Deka smiled and replied, "Just a master of time." When Çarh inquired if she could travel through time, Deka clarified that it wasn't time travel but a manipulation of perspectives, altering the choices available to those living. Although Çarh didn't fully grasp this explanation, he continued to admire Deka's abilities.

Deka directed her meaningful gaze at Çarh and commented, "Now you have a clearer understanding of how paradoxes form," Acknowledging his confusion, Çarh confessed that his mind was still in a state of bewilderment. Patiently, Deka began to explain, "Paradoxes arise from contradictions in the chain of events, influencing each other and leading to conflicting outcomes. These contradictions usually stem from a single cause. In this case, the culprit was simultaneously punished for guilt and rewarded for heroism, creating a disruption in the events, and resulting in a paradox on the timeline."

Listening attentively, Çarh tried to comprehend Deka's explanation. "So, can the contradictions caused by paradoxes be somehow rectified?" he asked.

Deka replied, "Yes, through specific alternative solutions, we can prevent the emergence of paradoxes or resolve existing ones," she explained. "However, these solutions often come with significant risks and consequences. Therefore, it is crucial to be careful and meticulous."

Çarh understood the gravity of Deka's words and took a deep breath. "How do you do this?" he asked. Deka smiled, saying, "You've seen how I did it with the necklace. In fact, this is my magical power. It's an inherited trait from my witch ancestry. As a Quordéen witch, I control the paradoxes in the Buenuta."

Having contemplated the responsibility brought by carrying Sûr for a long time, and considering the idea that his death would break the cycle, creating a paradox, Çarh wanted to ask about it now that the topic had arisen. Deka, responding to Çarh's question, answered thoughtfully, "Yes, it could create a paradox. However, remember that a paradox doesn't always encompass every possibility. Perhaps Sûr finds a way not to disappear with you, or your death doesn't eliminate the existence of Sûr; it just alters your role. A paradox doesn't always point to a definite outcome. That's why we should always seek alternative solutions."

As Çarh attentively listened to Deka's words, her explanation provided him with a new perspective. Now, he understood that paradoxes not only posed problems but also harboured opportunities.

A few hours later, Deka's phone rang, and the caller was the messenger who had come to the door, "Everything is under control." After Deka hung up the phone, she took a sigh of relief, and a faint smile appeared on her face. She whispered to Çarh, "Everything is fine." Deka was relieved. Her worries were erased, and now she wanted to sleep.

She lay on her bed and closed her eyes. After a long day, her body had become weary. Slowly, she drifted into sleep, with traces of the day's events still lingering in her mind. However, Deka forced herself to relax and eventually succumbed to a deep slumber.

Sûr

While Deka's body slept peacefully, only the necklace occupied Çarh's mind. He couldn't resist the power of the necklace and had wanted to take it. However, once he had it, he was undecided about what to do next. Should he run away immediately after taking the necklace? Or should he spend more time planning? The questions were driving him crazy, and he couldn't make up his mind. The confusion within him was growing. Çarh found himself in an emotional turmoil that was never foreign to him. However, now, he couldn't control the indecision and anxiety within. Taking a step, thinking this opportunity might not come again, he tried to grab the necklace. But Deka's unexpected disappearance while attempting to take the necklace had left Çarh bewildered. Without understanding where she went, he was left with only the necklace in his hand.

Murat Karagoz

CHAPTER 12
DISCOVERY

Unable to resist the allure of the necklace, Çarh succumbed to its power and impulsively decided to take it. This rash choice, however, resulted in unexpected consequences. Deka's sudden disappearance left Çarh bewildered, wondering how such a thing could happen. Blaming himself, he hastily pocketed the necklace, eager to escape the confusion that surrounded him. Despite his attempt to flee, questions about Deka's vanishing lingered in his mind. Would they ever see her again, or was her departure permanent? The situation had become a tangled mess, and Çarh found himself unable to determine the best course of action.

Alone in the room, Çarh examined the necklace, marvelling at its intricate engravings. Yet, an uneasy feeling gnawed at him, knowing the power it possessed. Uncertainty about Deka's whereabouts weighed heavily on his conscience. Did taking the necklace cause her disappearance? Guilt began to creep in, and the thought of never seeing Deka again tightened his heart. Despite his confusion, Çarh couldn't pinpoint the exact reason for her departure. The lingering sense of guilt prevented him from finding peace.

Taking some time to clear his mind, Çarh heard a voice when he approached the door. Turning around, he found Deka standing in front of him. The two exchanged a silent gaze, Çarh still clutching the necklace. Breaking the silence, Deka inquired, "Çarh, what are you doing?" Çarh's eyes welled with tears as he lowered his head in shame. "I took the necklace, I'm sorry," he murmured. Deka, sensing Çarh's sincere remorse, approached him with trust.

"You couldn't resist its allure, could you?" Deka asked. Çarh nodded. "Yes, I couldn't resist the power of the necklace," he confessed. Deka understood him with compassion and said, "Don't do such a thing again."

Çarh, relieved by Deka's sincere attitude, explained, "I apologize; I not only fell for the charm of the necklace but also wanted to take it from you." Curious, Deka wanted to hear the story behind Çarh's actions. "Because there is a spell to conceal Sûr, and the necessary plant for that spell is missing. Finding the plant depends on fulfilling a request from a Sögré. If I can deliver your necklace to him, he promised to help me," he said.

Deka was shaken. "Could that Sögré be Nail?" she asked. Çarh, surprised, confirmed that it was Nail and asked how she knew. "Nail has been playing these kinds of games for years, trying to take my necklace. But taking the necklace from me is impossible," she said, continuing, "Are you aware of what you just did? By taking the necklace from me, what kind of paradox did you create?"

Çarh heard what was being said, but understanding required more effort. "What do you mean?" he asked. Deka explained, "By taking my necklace, you created a paradox. The necklace represents my power. When you took it, there wouldn't have been the Quordéen witch ancestry, meaning me. Since there was no such witch ancestry, there shouldn't have been the necklace either. So, you shouldn't have been able to take the necklace. This loop created a paradox, but you can think of it as a defence spell because it occurred with me."

Deka took her own necklace from under her blouse and showed it to Çarh. "I leave a fake necklace behind to protect both the necklace and me," she explained. Çarh placed the necklace in his hand on the table. "This is fake," he repeated. Deka said, "Yes, there is no way to take the necklace from me," and added, "I wish you had told me; it didn't have to be this way."

Çarh comprehended what Deka was conveying. The weight Sûr had placed on his shoulders left him feeling helpless. The only way to save himself was to take the necklace and perform the magic to conceal Sûr. However, Deka's explanation opened Çarh's eyes to the immense responsibility and consequences that came with the power of the necklace. His actions in the panic of helplessness had blinded him.

Understanding Çarh's predicament, Deka wanted to find a way to help him. Without the necklace, Nail wouldn't assist Çarh, and without help, Çarh couldn't perform the magic to conceal Sûr. Therefore, she proposed taking the fake necklace to Nail. Çarh was initially surprised, but then he realised that Deka's plan could work. This way, the authenticity of the necklace wouldn't be noticed, and Çarh could save himself by giving the fake necklace to Nail.

Though Deka thought the plan would be successful, she never imagined that Nail, who had been attempting and failing for years, would casually accept something he couldn't achieve. When Çarh handed over the necklace, Nail would likely test its authenticity. Deka turned to Çarh and explained, "Although the necklace looks like the real one, it is not enchanted. When you take the necklace to Nail, he will test it. We can't afford any loopholes in this regard." Çarh was shaken. He thought the fake necklace would work, and everything would be resolved. "How do we enchant the necklace?" he asked.

Deka responded thoughtfully to Çarh's question. "To enchant the necklace, we need a certain power. Obtaining this power, however, is not easy." When Çarh asked how this power could be obtained, Deka thought for a moment and then replied, "This power can only be obtained by completing a special ritual. But this ritual is quite risky."

Çarh listened attentively to what Deka said. He knew there was risk and danger involved, but he was willing to do anything to lighten the burden on his shoulders. "What do we need to do?" he asked.

Deka took a silent breath. "Firstly, we need a source of power to enchant the necklace. This source could be a soul. Souls are entities trapped between this world and the afterlife, seeking peace. You might not fully realise it yet, but you come from the Cépfiarexen ancestry, a rare ancestry capable of soul passage," she explained. Çarh, still trying to fully grasp what Deka meant by soul passage, wasn't aware that being able to see Aunt Zülfiye was evidence of this ability. Deka continued, "Do you remember the day I came to your house? I felt something strange in your home, and later in the room, I saw Aunt Zülfiye's spirit. You told me it was her soul."

Confirming Deka's words, Çarh attempted to connect the two stories in his mind. "Your ability to see Aunt Zülfiye's soul is actually your power. Moreover, you can facilitate the passage of any soul with your power, including Aunt Zülfiye's, into anything," Deka continued, observing Çarh's astonishment. "Yes, thanks to your power, you can not only see souls but also control them. By using your power, we can enchant the necklace. This will be possible by placing Aunt Zülfiye's soul into the necklace." Çarh still found it difficult to believe he could possess such a great power. However, Deka's explanation was logical and convincing. Now, the only thing left to do was to enchant the necklace and deliver it to Nail.

Listening to Deka's words, Çarh contemplated. He wanted to release Aunt Zülfiye's soul and set her free. But how could he do that? How would he harness this power? Deka advised, "The crucial thing is to know the right time. You'll do it when you feel ready." Taking Deka's advice to heart, Çarh decided to try to control the power within him. Together, they set off towards Çarh's apartment.

Upon Deka's words, Çarh took a deep breath, attempting to control the power within him. He didn't believe he would succeed, but there was no harm in trying. Deka accompanied and supported him as they approached the door of the apartment.

Çarh felt his heart racing as they approached the door. Deka inspired confidence in him, but activating the power within him was still intimidating. When he felt the right moment, he closed his eyes and took a deep breath. Focusing the power within him, he placed his hands on the door of the apartment. Suddenly, the door began to tremble, as if the hands holding it had entered his fingertips. He sensed an energy wave around him. When Çarh, with fear, opened his eyes, there were no hands on the door, but he saw that the door had opened. Deka smiled at him, and they entered the apartment together.

Inside, as they approached Çarh's home, Çarh felt the power within him again. He wanted to release Aunt Zülfiye's soul, and he felt that he could do it. Deka nodded at him and offered support. Çarh unleashed his power and felt Aunt Zülfiye's soul. The soul appeared in the middle of the room as a white light and stood in front of Çarh.

For the first time, Çarh could clearly see Aunt Zülfiye's soul. It manifested in the middle of the room as a luminous white light, standing before him. The two were in a silent communion. Aunt Zülfiye, with a melancholic expression, gazed at Çarh and then smiled. Approaching her, they locked eyes. Though Çarh's heart raced, a profound sense of peace enveloped him. After a silent nod from Aunt Zülfiye, she slowly faded away, leaving Çarh astonished. This marked the first time he established such a clear and powerful connection. Deka smiled, congratulating Çarh, "You did an amazing job. You're truly something special." Çarh beamed happily, having gained control of the power within him, ready to enchant the fake necklace.

As Çarh took command of the power, a newfound self-confidence surged within him. Believing he could enchant the fake necklace, Deka stood by, providing assurance. Çarh held the necklace, closed his eyes, and activated his power once more. Sensing energy coursing through the necklace, he opened his eyes to witness a radiant glow. The necklace was now enchanted.

This moment marked a crucial step for Çarh. As he harnessed his inner power, he realised its transformative potential. He resolved to go to Nail and deliver the necklace, ensuring this time it would be genuinely enchanted, meeting Nail's expectations.

Çarh took the fake necklace in his hand, activating his

power. Vibrations surged through the necklace, indicating its enchantment. With a powerful aura indistinguishable from the real one, he could now give it to Nail with peace of mind. Yet, a lingering unease persisted. How sustainable was it to create such a powerful charm? Would this newfound power be a protective force or pose a threat?

Deka smiled, acknowledging Çarh's effective control of his power. Grateful for Deka's guidance, Çarh had not only discovered his power but also enchanted the fake necklace. This empowering experience instilled confidence, fortifying him to face future challenges.

This transformative experience led Çarh to a deeper understanding of his identity and inner world. Taking control of his power not only brought confidence but also unveiled latent abilities, providing a profound journey of self-discovery.

Deka bid farewell with a smile, leaving Çarh alone at home, filled with words and experiences. He felt secure, having taken control of the power within him, understanding his ability to wield it responsibly. A voice whispered that he could transfer his power, much like Aunt Zülfiye.

Listening to the inner voice, Çarh contemplated the ability to transfer his power to other things, acknowledging the potential risks. Deka's teachings emphasized the importance of maintaining control, a lesson Çarh kept in mind.

Excited and frightened, Çarh began exploring the limits of his power. Having resolved the issue with the fake necklace, he eagerly anticipated the next step. The Elf entered and joined him, and they discussed recent events. Çarh explained how he had enchanted the fake necklace, freeing Aunt Zülfiye's spirit with Deka's help. The Elf, expressing surprise, filled Çarh with pride.

The Elf's words strengthened Çarh's power, presenting

a challenge in controlling it. The concept of spirit transference intrigued him, prompting Çarh to ask the Elf for clarification. The Elf explained, "Spirit transference is the transfer of one being's soul to another. The being can be living or lifeless. With your power, both are possible."

Astonished, Çarh pondered his newfound capabilities. The Elf continued, "Let me address the question in your mind. Yes, you can transfer your own soul to another being. However, it won't make you immortal. Each transference diminishes your magical power. Transferring your own soul depletes it entirely. At that point, you won't be a Sögré anymore. All your magical power will be gone."

Troubled by this revelation, Çarh understood that this option should only be a last resort. The Elf's explanation highlighted the finite nature of magical power, emphasizing the importance of using it judiciously.

The Elf's curious gaze indicated that Çarh had something to ask. Çarh inquired with internal fear, "Do you think Nail will realise the necklace is fake?" Eagerly awaiting the Elf's response, Çarh found reassurance in the Elf's attempt to allay his concerns. "If you make Nail believe the necklace is real, he won't realise it's fake because it's enchanted. However, remember, magic is a powerful weapon, and its proper use is crucial."

Paying close attention to the Elf's words, Çarh fell into deep thought. Proper use, proper timing, and controlled use – all of these were crucial aspects of wielding his power. However, the Elf's words didn't entirely convince him, and he remained anxious about Nail discovering the deception. He also pondered what Nail might do if he realised the necklace was fake.

Despite the Elf's assurances, Çarh found himself in

contemplation about the possibility of Nail detecting the necklace's true nature. The persistent fear lingered within him. What if Nail, with his keen observation, discerned the deception? Çarh considered the enchantment he had woven into the necklace, hoping it would suffice to conceal the truth.

Engaged in these thoughts, Çarh entertained a counter-narrative, suggesting that perhaps Nail wouldn't notice the intricacies of the enchantment. Yet, beneath this optimistic notion, an unsettling fear lingered. What if Nail not only recognized the counterfeit nature of the necklace but also unveiled the magic Çarh had woven into it? The potential repercussions weighed heavily on Çarh's mind, casting shadows of doubt over his confidence.

Expressing these anxieties to the Elf, Çarh sought reassurance. In a supportive tone, the Elf tried to allay Çarh's fears. "Don't worry; your power is much greater. If needed, you can use it." Relying on the Elf's encouragement, Çarh managed to restore a measure of confidence within himself. However, the trepidation regarding the potential consequences of Nail discovering the truth still lingered, creating a complex tapestry of emotions within Çarh's mind.

The Elf asked, "Do you know what you need to do?" Çarh shook his head, indicating his uncertainty. The Elf explained, "You need to get a deep sleep. Tomorrow is a big day; you'll take the necklace to Nail. Resting is essential."

Following the Elf's advice, Çarh lay down on his bed. After pondering for a long time, fatigue eventually enveloped him, and he fell asleep. In his dreams, he saw Nail noticing the fake necklace, and everything was ruined. Yet, even in his dream, he felt a sense that the power within him could save him.

Murat Karagoz

CHAPTER 13
THE TRIPLE GODDESS

In the quiet weeks that followed without a word from Çarh, Nail's unease steadily grew. A sense of apprehension took root as he pondered the possibilities: Had Çarh faced obstacles in securing the imitation necklace, or perhaps, had he considered Nail nothing more than a dispensable pawn now? Such uncertainties swirled in Nail's mind, casting shadows of doubt and discomfort.

On one hand, Nail focused on his work, and on the other, he made intense efforts to trace the necklace. However, his patience towards incoming customers was decreasing. One day, a customer at his workplace asked him a question. Nail responded sharply, "We're here to answer our customers' questions. However, I have a very important matter to attend to right now. Please leave me alone," he said.

Though the customer seemed a bit surprised, they didn't respond to Nail's harsh reply and quietly left. Later, Nail realised how rude his behaviour was and found himself in a moment of conscience. The stress and uncertainty brought by not hearing from Çarh had begun to take control of him. Besides chasing the necklace, he now had to manage these feelings of anger and ambition within him.

Feeling trapped, Nail's concerns gradually transformed into feelings of ambition and determination. As long as he couldn't hear from Çarh, he never gave up his determination to find the necklace. Yet, during this process, his concerns had led him into a deadlock. As days passed, these concerns gave way to feelings of ambition and determination. Now, he would not only trace the necklace but also try to control the anger and ambition within himself.

Nail started to act with a power he had never experienced before. The anger he felt from Çarh's betrayal, and the disappearance of the necklace's trail, made him even more powerful. Filled with self-confidence, Nail felt no doubt that he would find the necklace. Therefore, despite being harsh to customers at his workplace, the feelings of ambition and determination within him inspired him.

Perhaps Çarh's betrayal was a truth he never wanted to face. However, with determination to find the necklace, Nail dedicated himself to overcoming this uncertainty.

Lost in his concerns, Nail found himself talking to himself at times, thinking, "Could Çarh really have taken the necklace? Even if he did, would he bring it to me?" His doubts increased, and with time, he was falling into despair. In moments when he thought the necklace would not come back, he felt trapped and sensed his own powerlessness behind his despair.

Despite hours passing in the Grand Bazaar without any news from Çarh, Nail had now lost hope. Every passing minute further diminished his chance of finding the necklace.

Sûr

Meanwhile, Çarh was enjoying a peaceful morning in Cihangir. Sipping his coffee at the beginning of a sunny day, he pondered the fake necklace he had created the night before. While happy to deliver it to Nail, he couldn't help but wonder if Nail would realise its authenticity, given the magical enchantment he had woven into it. Despite being disturbed by these thoughts, he felt peaceful knowing he had completed the task.

Swiftly setting off with the necklace in hand, Çarh chose to walk towards the Grand Bazaar, relishing the weather and scenery. Moving through the streets, he immersed himself in the bustling crowd of the city. The hurried steps of people and the noise of vehicles composed the rhythm of the city, something Çarh always enjoyed getting lost in. Despite the beauty of the city, he was in a hurry to deliver the necklace, walking along the street, greeting passersby, and continuing without any worries. As he approached the Grand Bazaar, his excitement grew.

Pausing for a moment on the Galata Bridge, Çarh was affected by the pleasant conversations of people fishing and the serene gazes of those immersed in the view. The sunlight playing on the bridge created a wonderful natural tableau, bringing a smile to Çarh's face. However, the reality of delivering the necklace heightened his excitement. The crowd, sounds, and colours of the Grand Bazaar further elevated Çarh's enthusiasm.

As Çarh stepped into the Grand Bazaar, he became lost among the people. The crowd pressed him from one side while energizing him from the other. With every shop he looked at, his excitement and curiosity increased. In the midst of the colourful market, the sounds and smells enchanted Çarh even more. In this chaotic and lively atmosphere, the idea of delivering the necklace to Nail had become a purpose for him, and he was ready to do anything to achieve this goal.

Walking through the lively crowd in the Grand Bazaar, Çarh approached Nail's shop. The excitement on his face grew step by step, and the idea of delivering the necklace had transformed into a passion. Passing through the bustling streets, he paid close attention to everything around him — people, shops, stalls, colours, smells — as everything served the purpose of delivering the necklace.

The energetic activity within the Grand Bazaar heightened Çarh's excitement. Moving through the crowd, he had to slow down to avoid bumping into some people, but the only thing that mattered to him was reaching Nail's shop. With each step, the dream of delivering the necklace expanded.

Upon arriving at Nail's shop, Çarh navigated through the crowd and entered. Nail was waiting for him. Silent greetings were exchanged as Çarh took off the necklace and handed it to Nail. The joy inside Nail reflected outward as he accepted the necklace, and both of them smiled.

Observing Çarh, Nail felt all his worries vanish. "I thought you might not come for a moment," he admitted, then added, "I guess getting the necklace was more challenging than I expected." Çarh smiled and replied, "Yes, I struggled a bit, but I managed in the end."

Çarh couldn't hide his astonishment when Nail invited him to the back room. Greeted by a standing cuckoo clock, he felt like he had stepped into a place where time moved backward. Separated from the rest of the shop, filled with various handmade and rare items, Nail's office brought silence to the chaos.

Carefully examining the necklace, Nail tried to determine its authenticity. The idea that the necklace should possess magical powers created a question mark in his mind. In his inner world, he imagined many scenarios about the features and powers of the necklace. Meanwhile, when Çarh asked where he got the necklace, Nail pondered the difficulties related to Deka. However, when Çarh confidently stated that he obtained the necklace, Nail's suspicions eased a bit.

"Thank you for bringing the necklace. Now, as I promised, I can help you," Nail said and continued, "I can find that plant you want. You can summon your Elf; we need to discuss the details."

Nail's words surprised Çarh. The realization that someone could now help him brought both happiness and unease. "My Elf? I don't know how to summon. Just I don't know," he admitted.

Observing Çarh's lack of knowledge about elves, Nail decided to assist. "Yes, to summon," he replied. "I'm here to help you. I can show you how to summon an Elf."

Çarh felt a moment of astonishment at Nail's offer. Acknowledging that he didn't know how to summon his Elf embarrassed him. He wondered why he knew so little about the Elf he had been with for months. Perhaps he had always been the one summoning the Elf, neglecting what it wanted or felt.

Contemplating these thoughts, Çarh began to question why the Elf had kept this information hidden. Maybe the Elf had done something to disrupt Çarh and didn't want to lose him. Or perhaps the Elf had a specific reason for keeping Çarh in the dark. This curiosity created a concern within Çarh.

Nail explained, "Actually, it's a very simple spell. You repeat the magical words "saurta qua shého céng" by reaching into your inner power, and the Elf comes right beside you."

Excited at the prospect, Çarh eagerly embraced the

chance to try it out. Summoning the Elf for the first time, he spoke the magical words, feeling a palpable change in the aura around him. Everything momentarily froze, and then the Elf emerged from within a cloud of smoke. Çarh was breathless with excitement.

The Elf greeted him, "Hello Çarh, you summoned me." Proudly, Çarh explained, "Yes, I summoned you using magic. I delivered the necklace to Nail; he will help us find the plant we're looking for, and you need to be part of it." The Elf's gaze suggested reluctance to discuss this here. Getting straight to the point, he said, "Yes, Nail. With the necklace in hand, use your magical power to help us find the plant we're looking for."

Nail said, "Describe the plant you're looking for; I need to visualize it in my mind." The Elf explained, "Fritillaria ehrhartii, a rare plant species growing in the Eastern Anatolia region, particularly in the cave of Çifte Minareli Medrese in Erzurum. Another name for this plant is 'Erzurum velvet flower,' and it only grows in a few places worldwide. It is a bulbous plant. Its stem grows thin and erect, with green leaves bearing striped patterns. The flowers are bell-shaped and pale purple in colour."

Nail closed his eyes and concentrated. The pupils moving from under his eyelids entered a search mode for a target. Utilizing all his knowledge and memory, his mind worked to find the plant the Elf described. Silence dominated the room as all his attention focused on locating the plant. After a long time, he opened his eyes and excitedly announced that he had found the plant. Çarh was in awe of Nail's ability.

Nail said, "I need an object to perform the exchange. I'll be right back," and went inside. Çarh and the Elf were left alone in the room. As Çarh was about to express his thoughts on summoning him, the Elf interjected, suggesting that it might be better to discuss it later. Çarh didn't insist, thinking that the Elf must have a reason. However, Nail's explanation had left him puzzled, and he wondered what Nail meant by exchange.

In Nail's absence, the Elf shared some information about him. "Nail is a representative of the Gualluiçen ancestry. The Gualluiçen ancestry holds a significant position within the Sögré community. Unlike other types of Sögrés, they have the power of exchange, the ability to swap one thing for another. They can obtain what they want by using these powers. However, some special magical objects cannot be acquired through exchange. Deka's necklace was one such object," the Elf explained.

Çarh realised how interesting and extraordinary a Sögré Nail was from the Elf's narrative. He genuinely wondered if Nail could trade anything and everything. While he couldn't exchange magical objects, he pondered where the boundary started and ended for other matters. All this curiosity drew Çarh more towards Nail. He noticed that he wanted to learn more about him but was aware that Nail's personality was filled with secrets, as Sögrés typically hesitated to disclose their abilities. Perhaps in the future, Çarh could learn more about Nail's powers.

When Nail returned to the room with a photo frame, it caught Çarh's attention. Çarh examined the photo frame Nail brought, recognizing it as an old and beautiful one. Eagerly inspecting the photo, he revealed a young man and a woman. The woman wore Ottoman-style clothing with a smile on her face, and the man wore a military uniform. There was a handwritten note in Ottoman Turkish on the back of the photo, but its content was indecipherable.

Nail explained, "This photo belonged to a former customer. It belonged to his grandfather and grandmother. It was one of his most valuable heirlooms. It was the only harmonious item in the entire shop."

Captivated, Çarh watched Nail's magic. Holding the photo frame in his right hand and opening his left hand, Nail awaited something. He repeated the magic words. Instantly, the photo frame disappeared from his right hand, and in its place, the plant they desired appeared in his left hand.

In astonishment, Çarh asked, "Is this real?" Nail smiled and replied, "Yes, it's real. The exchange power of the Gualluiçen is truly incredible."

Nail extended the plant to Çarh. "Now, the rest is up to you. You can use this plant to conceal the Sûr," he said. Overwhelmed with excitement, Çarh could only express gratitude. Nail reminded him, "Remember, this is a trade," implying he was waiting for something. Despite being surprised, Çarh happily received the plant, and with the Elf, they left the shop.

Delighted to have the plant, Çarh considered the acquisition of a plant he had never seen before crucial. As they left the shop, he examined the plant in his hand, inhaling its scent. Although unfamiliar, with each breath, he could feel the power of the plant.

The Elf noticed Çarh's excitement and curiosity about how to use the plant. To satisfy his curiosity, the Elf provided more information about the plant's characteristics. As they discussed all the details about how to use the plant, they left the shop and continued on their way.

Eager to learn more about the power of the plant, Çarh asked the Elf with curiosity. The Elf provided explanations about the characteristics of the plant. From the Elf's descriptions, Çarh understood that the plant indeed possessed significant power, leaving him impressed. He considered the plant to be truly special and sought more information about its capabilities. Çarh inquired, "How does the power of this plant work? How do witches become more powerful?" the Elf explained, "This plant enhances witches' magical powers by increasing their energy. Witches who have lost their powers can regain them by using this plant." Çarh was astonished by this information, realizing once again how valuable the plant was.

After a long and tiring walk, Çarh and the Elf finally reached home. Excitedly turning to the Elf, Çarh asked, "So, what do we do now?" After a brief silence, the Elf responded, "The spell involves one of the most fundamental practices of witchcraft: the Triple Goddess and the elements! To perform this spell, we need two more Sögrés."

Çarh wondered about the Triple Goddess. He never expected to need two more Sögrés to perform this spell. Even if he wanted to collaborate with other Sögrés, he hardly knew any. Whom could he call? He wasn't sure. Deka was the only one that came to mind, but he felt embarrassed after recent events.

The Elf continued, "Don't worry; I've already taken care of the other two Sögrés. You represent the air element, and the other two will represent earth and water. Since I knew we would get the plant today, I made all the arrangements in advance. They'll be here shortly."

Çarh breathed a sigh of relief. Feeling relieved of the burden, he slumped into the chair. After a while, exhausted and succumbing to sleepiness, Çarh fell asleep, and in his dreams, he shaped a life without Sûr.

In Çarh's dream, the imagery of a life without Sûr

unfolded in his mind. He imagined himself running amidst lush green forests, surrounded by wildflowers. The sky was blue, and the clouds were white. The air was so clean that it filled his lungs to the brim. Away from Sûr, he felt immersed in silence, with only the beauty of nature around. Suddenly, a passing butterfly caught his attention. The colour of the butterfly was so vivid that it dazzled his eyes. The butterfly, passing by his side, suddenly transformed into a giant bird, and soared into the sky. Çarh chased after it, and after a while, he found himself flying alongside the bird. The wind hitting his face, his hair swirling around, gave him a sense of freedom. Çarh thought about how wonderful it would be to experience such freedom in a life without Sûr and sighed deeply.

Çarh abruptly woke up as the unexpected visitors rang the doorbell, the sound echoing in the room. He got up and walked towards the door. Upon opening it, he saw the other two Sögrés. Utku and Kera were both smiling, holding small gifts in their hands. Çarh invited them inside, and they started chatting. Meanwhile, Çarh was curious about their gifts but chose to wait instead of asking directly.

Utku came from a witch ancestry that controlled sleep. He could put anyone to sleep for as long as he wanted, whenever he wanted. Additionally, the intensity of dreams or nightmares people experienced during sleep varied based on his mood. Çarh found all this fascinating. Kera, on the other hand, came from a witch ancestry that could communicate with animals. When Çarh asked what it felt like to talk to animals, Kera expressed that it was actually quite unsettling. She explained that animals didn't think like humans and spoke in a very disorganized manner. Despite not finding the power exactly as expected, Çarh still thought that talking to animals was an intriguing magical ability. Kera added that the best part of talking to animals was that they kept her informed about everything. Çarh couldn't believe what he was hearing.

With the arrival of Utku and Kera, Çarh sensed that their gathering was something special. Each of them hailed from different regions as Sögré, and this coming together presented a fantastic opportunity to explore one another's cultures, skills, and perspectives. The happiness evident on Utku and Kera's faces showcased their open-mindedness. Being around people like them offered Çarh a unique perspective on how people from diverse parts of the world understood and interpreted each other. Therefore, as Çarh engaged in conversation with Utku and Kera, he found himself becoming more receptive to a broader worldview.

Upon the Elf's entrance, he spotted Utku and Kera, and a smile illuminated his face. Greeting them, he said, "Welcome! Now that you're here, we can proceed with the spell to conceal the Sûr," Utku and Kera responded with joyful smiles. The Elf gathered everyone around the table, the designated spot for the impending spell, and began preparing the necessary materials.

Curious about the process, Çarh listened as the Elf explained the steps. "First, draw some power from the plant. Utku and Kera will assist you, and the magic will flow through them to avoid exposing you to excessive magical power. If the transferred power becomes too overwhelming, they'll break the ring to end the ritual. Is everything clear up to this point?" Concerned about the potential dangers, Çarh asked, "Is it dangerous?" the Elf acknowledged the inherent risks in any magic but emphasized the added danger due to drawing power from a source. However, he reassured Çarh that there was no need to worry; Utku and Kera were there for that reason.

The Elf's warning instilled a sense of caution in Çarh,

making him grasp the seriousness of the upcoming magic. As the Elf continued with instructions, Utku and Kera prepared themselves, collecting materials and harnessing their powers. This spell required not only a potent source but also impeccable coordination. While Çarh absorbed the Elf's guidance, he observed the meticulous preparations made by the others, contemplating the potential consequences if things did not go as planned.

As the Elf's words resonated with magical energy, Çarh and the others anxiously focused on the changes in the plant. Squinting their eyes and holding their breath, they waited. After a while, an energy wave emanated from the plant, first reaching Utku and then extending towards Kera. Çarh observed this extraordinary experience with astonishment. When the waves enveloped his body, the sensation was indescribable. Suddenly, the weight he had carried for years disappeared, and his body felt lighter. The Elf smiled with joy with shining eyes, recognizing that the magical power of the plant had worked. Their powers had increased, and they were now ready to achieve greater feats.

As the Elf explained that they had reached the final stage of the spell, excitement filled the air. The Elf instructed Çarh to prepare himself and recite the magical words. Eagerly, Çarh started chanting,

"Sûr qué bégteo!"

With the echo of these words, the energy waves in the room intensified. The Elf assisted Çarh, while the other Sögrés did their best to ensure the success of the spell.

After the Elf completed the ritual, Çarh felt a slight shake and lost his balance. Utku and Kera held him, guiding him to a chair. The Elf announced the success of the ritual, prompting Çarh to quickly check the mirror. He was shocked to see that Sûr was still visible. However, the Elf had already explained that the spell was only effective for humans; now, humans wouldn't be able to see Sûr. Therefore, it was normal for Sûr to still be visible to Çarh. This revelation brought great relief to him. Assured that the spell had worked, Utku and Kera wished Çarh success in his new life and departed.

Alone in the room after Utku and Kera left, Çarh sat on the chair and gazed into the mirror. Sûr was still there, and it saddened him. This face, which had been with him for years, had become a part of him. The Elf's explanation, however, reassured him. Perhaps the fact that humans would no longer see Sûr was more important. Speaking to himself with these thoughts, he occasionally glanced into the mirror. Despite his desire to free himself from the current situation, he couldn't help but gaze at Sûr. Finally, he accepted that the spell had succeeded and somewhat alleviated the sadness within him.

Murat Karagoz

CHAPTER 14
COVEN

Çarh began to feel a sense of normalcy once again. The spell that concealed Sûr had not only hidden him successfully but also granted him newfound self-confidence. With this assurance, he seamlessly resumed his normal life, in harmony with himself. His interactions with others flourished, and the fear of societal ostracism dissipated. The only distinction lay in the fact that only those with magical powers could perceive his true form, a matter of little consequence to him. In stark contrast to the loneliness, he once felt due to prejudice, Çarh now cherished genuine friendships that bolstered his self-esteem and allowed him to express his true self. He embraced and accepted who he was, feeling liberated from the shadows of the past. Rather than dwelling on dark memories, he now accumulated positive experiences that provided comfort and balance in his life. As he contemplated the future, Çarh left the past behind.

Since Çarh began spending more time with Utku and

Kera, their bond had deepened, offering him a sense of security. The days of hiding and marginalization were now a distant memory as he revelled in the joy of being with friends and prepared to re-enter the life he missed.

Yet, the painful echoes of his past experiences lingered, often pulling him into moments of reflection. With the unwavering support of Utku and Kera, Çarh learned to shed the weight of the past and focus on the future. Their shared magical practices strengthened their bond, deepening their loyalty to one another. Çarh, recognizing the significance of this connection, treated his friends with increased sensitivity and respect, offering unwavering support when needed.

Utku and Kera observed Çarh's growing self-confidence and reciprocated with their own support. Through magic, their understanding of each other deepened, enriching Çarh's life with a profound and invaluable bond.

Çarh's immersion in the company of Utku and Kera unveiled a profound realization that being a Sögré transcended the mere practice of magic and spells. In their companionship, he found acceptance and safety, understanding that being a Sögré meant belonging for those who felt estranged from society. This newfound insight not only fostered a deeper understanding of himself but also cultivated a positive perspective towards those who, like him, were different. Recognizing the value of diversity, Çarh came to believe that these differences complemented one another.

Externally, Çarh presented as an ordinary individual, concealing the unique personality that defined him as a Sögré. However, as he embraced his inner confidence and courage, he gradually revealed his true self. The anonymity surrounding his true identity became a source of relief, providing a sense of liberation. The lessons learned in the world of Sögré began to weave into his daily life, allowing him to find joy in incorporating magic into mundane tasks. Whether handling household chores, cooking, cleaning, or gardening, Çarh seamlessly integrated magic, completing tasks swiftly and with ease. Engaging in magic served as a therapeutic escape, momentarily transporting him to a realm of enchantment, free from the troubles of the world.

Contemplating a return to the business world, Çarh acknowledged that true happiness lay in practicing magic. With this realization, he sought opportunities in fields where he could seamlessly merge business and magic. One such option was applying to the Sögrétza[xiii], the Coven at Topkapı Palace, a suggestion put forth by Kera.

Enthusiastically embracing Kera's proposal, Çarh envisioned the prospect of working within the Coven. Such a role would allow him to align his work with his desires while advancing his magical abilities through collaboration with other witches. The intrigue surrounding the existence of the Coven at Topkapı Palace excited him, given his personal involvement with magic. However, lingering doubts surfaced about whether the general populace was aware of this secretive enclave, speculating that it might be veiled through magical means.

As Çarh made his way towards Topkapı Palace, he pondered on the perceptions people held. Did even his fellow Sögré know about the existence of the Coven, or was it a sanctuary reserved for a select few? These musings accompanied him on his journey, a path that, surprisingly, seemed to go unnoticed by those around him.

Walking towards Topkapı Palace, Çarh experienced a profound sense of relief as the indifferent gazes of passersby allowed him to blend seamlessly into the crowd. The fear of standing out, which had once fuelled a strong sense of exclusion, had now dissipated, granting him the freedom to traverse the streets with ease. His anticipation grew, fuelled by the excitement of returning to his professional life through the practice of magic. However, lingering concerns about societal prejudices against magic cast a shadow over his enthusiasm. How would he be received at the Coven in Topkapı Palace? Would acceptance be readily extended to him? These questions weighed on his mind.

Despite these reservations, the empowering aura of magic further invigorated him, solidifying his determination to prove his worth to the Coven and delve deeper into the mysteries of magic within its confines.

Upon arriving at the palace, Çarh once again surveyed his surroundings. Amidst the imposing walls of Topkapı Palace and the bustling masses, locating the elusive secret passage mentioned by Kera proved to be a challenging task. With no concrete evidence of the Coven's gathering place for the Sögré, there were no discernible doors or signs to guide him. Following Kera's directions, Çarh meticulously examined corners and irregular stones around the palace until he uncovered a subtle clue hinting at the passage's possible location. Passing through the door known as the Gate of the Shawl[xiv], Çarh embarked on a journey through history, named after the Ottoman Empire era, when sultans used this gate to connect the Harem[xv], with the common people. While one could turn left to proceed to the Harem section, a Sögré who had the strength to pass through the door, would find the path curving to the right, leading straight to the Coven.

As Çarh passed through the door, the air in the historical palace enveloped him, and he couldn't help but be awed by the grandeur and history that lingered within its walls.

In that moment, he envisioned himself as one of countless witches who had traversed this passage throughout the years. The dark corridors he navigated heightened his excitement and curiosity, leading him to the door that marked the entrance to the Coven.

Upon swinging open the door, Çarh found himself stepping into a mystical world. The Coven chamber, bathed in light, boasted a ceiling adorned with intricate paintings. Tables were laden with spell books and magical components, and the witches present engaged in hushed conversations, their eyes gleaming with the magic that surrounded them.

Following a welcoming witch into the room, Çarh encountered a woman of middle age, her warm smile extending an invitation to the enchanting realm. Returning the gesture, Çarh accepted her outstretched hand, feeling the warmth and noticing the age-marked wrinkles on the witch's skin.

Taking a moment to survey the room, Çarh was drawn to an open book on a large wooden table at the centre. The pages, influenced by an unseen breeze, curled gently, revealing dazzling magical symbols.

As Çarh approached the table to examine the book, a cautionary voice reached him from a few steps away. The woman warned, "Do not touch that book. It contains a very powerful spell and can only be used by skilled witches." Heeding the advice, Çarh stepped away and turned to the woman, inquiring, "I came here to work; what can I do?"

The woman smiled at Çarh and responded, "You can contribute in various ways here." Her gaze focused on Çarh's head. "I can tell by the Sûr on your head that you are a Cépfiarexen. The ability to perform soul transitions is your main strength, and witches like you, rare Sögré, are always needed," she added.

Expressing gratitude to the Sögré by his side, Çarh said, "It's a quite new situation for me; I only learned a few months ago that I am a Sögré." The woman, surprised, asked, "Are you a teigretexen?" Çarh hesitated before answering, but in reality, he had already given the woman his response.

The Elf had previously provided information about teigretexen, but Çarh hadn't understood why it was considered so peculiar by other Sögré. To satisfy his curiosity, he asked the woman, "Why were you so surprised when you learned that I am a teigretexen?"

The woman explained, "Teigretexen refers to those who are born as wizards, Duetex, and later become Sögré, known as witches. Teigretexen are more powerful than Sögré because they can establish a connection with ancient Sögré, thus combining their powers." Çarh was astonished at what he heard. Connecting with the previous Sögrés? How would that be possible? he wondered. Thanking her for the information, Çarh decided to leave the Coven, promising to return the next day. The woman bid him farewell, saying they would meet again. However, she could sense Çarh's anxiety.

Exiting through the Gate of the Shawl, Çarh found himself in the midst of a crowd. However, the fact that he couldn't conceal his witch abilities was an undeniable reality. So much so that a child had noticed him emerging from the wall. The child, unable to believe his eyes, called out to his mother. Çarh smiled silently at the child and brought his index finger to his lips, saying, "Don't tell anyone." The child, still in shock, only nodded and walked away with his mother.

Çarh had been avoiding getting close to Deka since discovering his witch abilities. However, on his way home, he ran into Deka, and this time, he was embarrassed. With Deka's help, they had enchanted the fake necklace to deceive Nail.

They had been able to perform the concealment spell for the Sûr. Now, he felt a debt of gratitude towards her.

Deka noticed Çarh's embarrassed state and asked what had happened. Çarh explained that Nail couldn't tell if the necklace was fake, delivered the plant, and they performed the concealment spell for the Sûr. Deka was relieved to hear this. She was glad to contribute to Çarh leading a normal life. Çarh took a deep breath and asked, "Do you know about the Coven?" Deka responded, "Of course, why do you ask?" Çarh wanted to share his experience, spend time with Deka like before, and seek her advice. Deka suggested having a coffee, turning Çarh's thoughts into reality.

As they sat in the café, Çarh excitedly recounted his experience from today. Deka was surprised that Çarh had discovered Sögrétza, known as the Coven, so quickly. She wondered if he had mentioned the Elf. Towards the end of his narration, Çarh added, "Just as I was leaving the Coven, a child noticed me passing through the wall. If you could have seen the expression on the child's face, Deka, you would burst into laughter. Fortunately, I approached him sympathetically and told him it was an optical illusion." Deka warned, "You should be careful with such incidents." Çarh nodded, acknowledging the advice.

As Çarh and Deka sipped their coffees, silence prevailed. Apart from the conversations of other people around them and the music playing in the bar, there was no sound. Breaking the silence, Çarh looked at Deka, who had helped him, and said, "I've missed you." These words brought an even broader smile to Deka's face. Both sat quietly for a long time, content with each other's presence.

This time, Deka broke the silence. "So, tell me. Are you going to the Coven tomorrow?" In response to Deka's question, Çarh sipped his coffee with a thoughtful expression. Going to the Coven was still a new and exciting experience for him. When it came to what he wanted to do there, he hadn't fully decided yet. Perhaps he just wanted to meet and observe other witches, learn about their different abilities, and improve himself. Additionally, he knew there were various ways to use the power of the Coven to improve people's lives. He, however, didn't have a clear idea of what he could do yet. With mixed thoughts, he replied, "I haven't decided completely yet, but maybe I just want to meet and observe for now."

When Deka suggested that Çarh should go to the Coven, it raised numerous questions in his mind. He had no idea what he would do, what he would learn, and how long it would take. Deka's words sparked a light in his mind. Everything he learned there could guide him and boost his self-confidence.

Çarh thanked Deka with a smile. "Yes, I'll go to the Coven tomorrow. I'll send greetings to Seda," he said. He didn't know who Seda was, as Deka had mentioned her, but maybe he would meet her at the Coven.

After finishing their coffees, Çarh and Deka left the café. Accepting Çarh's offer, Deka started walking towards home. Çarh felt excited but also anxious for tomorrow. He wondered what would happen and what he would learn at the Coven. Deka's reassuring words, however, had given him courage.

Çarh and Deka walked the streets for a while, deciding to do some shopping. They entered one of the city's famous markets and began exploring the colourful stalls. While Deka gathered fresh vegetables and spices, Çarh selected meats. They communicated not with words but with silent gestures. Later, they went home and started cooking in the kitchen. Both enjoyed the process of preparing a meal. After the preparations were complete, they had a delightful dinner and relaxed by watching a movie.

With the growing intimacy between Çarh and Deka, Çarh found himself feeling happier. He had never experienced such closeness with a woman before, and he struggled to define these feelings. Deka also seemed pleased with Çarh's interest in her. As they grew closer, the chemistry between them intensified. However, they hadn't decided yet where these new emotional connections would lead. They decided to enjoy the moments they spent together. Every moment they shared became increasingly valuable.

As the doorbell rang, Çarh's heart began to race. After the intimate moments he shared with Deka, such a visit made him uneasy. When he opened the door, he saw someone who looked exactly like Deka. He couldn't believe his eyes and didn't know what to do. Paradox cases were not unfamiliar to Çarh, but each time he encountered one, he couldn't help but be astonished. What he saw was Deka's tömté.

Deka apologized and said she needed to leave. Allowing her to go, Çarh wanted to be alone for a while. He continued to soak in the warm atmosphere Deka left behind, taking a deep breath. Suddenly, he realised something: Deka's energy still lingered in the house. Çarh thought it might be related to Sögré powers. Perhaps Deka's energy would stay with him, connecting them over time. With these thoughts, he spent his evening happily.

When Çarh woke up, he noticed he had dozed off on the couch. His sleep was disrupted, and he had a slight headache. Gathering himself quickly, he got ready and set out for the Coven. Passing through the familiar paths, he arrived at the location of the Coven. Entering the secret passage, he stepped into the Coven within the palace. A woman approached him right at the entrance. "Hello, I'm Seda," she said. Çarh replied, "You must be the Seda, Deka mentioned. Hello, I'm Çarh." Smiling, Seda welcomed Çarh, expressing her willingness to help Deka's friend. When Çarh mentioned that he wanted to work here and learn more, Seda preferred to give him a tour of the Coven and inform him about its history first.

While guiding Çarh through the Coven, Seda provided information about the history of witchcraft. The history of the Coven in the Topkapı Palace dates back to Sultan Selim II[xvi]. But it has reached the present day. During the Ottoman Empire, influenced by the witch hunts in Europe, Sultan Selim II initiated campaigns against witchcraft with a decree in 1573, imposing harsh measures against accusations of witchcraft. The decree outlined the capture, trial, and punishment of those accused of witchcraft. The Sögrés in the palace enchanted the corridors where the current Coven is located to find a secret place to protect themselves. Thus, this place, unnoticed by those without magical powers, gradually became a space where magic was discussed and governed.

After Sultan Selim II, Sultan Murat IV[xvii], in the 1630s, enacted laws for even stricter measures against accusations of witchcraft. Similarly, Sultan Mehmed IV[xviii], in the 1680s, emphasized witch hunts and the fight against witchcraft with a law.

The period influenced by the Ryöschaett[xix] ideology that started in the 1500s in Europe led to the formation of centres for witches in each region. These centres were tasked with protecting misunderstood Sögrés and maintaining balance in the Buenuta. The first centre was Kapalitza[xx], a place where many Sögrés were imprisoned. Over time, the number of these centres increased, reaching the present day. In Türkiye, the central hub of the Coven is located in Topkapı Palace.

When Çarh stepped into the Coven, he embarked on a journey into the depths of the magical world. He learned many things about the period when witches were influenced by the Ryöschaett ideology, things he had never heard of before. Discovering that the centres were tasked with protecting the lives of Sögrés and maintaining balance in the Buenuta, he also found out that Kapalitza was a place where many Sögré were imprisoned, and similar places had multiplied until today. The central hub in Türkiye was this Coven in Topkapı Palace. He realised that this information was just the beginning. The magical world was an infinite treasure trove of knowledge, and he considered his own understanding to be just a grain of sand in the ocean. He couldn't shake off his astonishment and was eager to learn more.

As Çarh explored the Coven, he met different wizards and witches in each room, listened to their stories, and gained knowledge about various magical techniques. Time seemed to slip away unnoticed, and when he realised it was evening, he sighed with regret. He had learned so much that he didn't want to leave. The Coven was not merely a magical adventure for him; it was a world with endless exploration. Saying his goodbyes, he immersed himself in the crowd and headed towards Deka. When he saw her, a slight smile appeared on his face. Deka also welcomed him with the same sincerity. They both knew they had a lot to share with each other. Çarh began telling Deka about what he had seen and learned in the Coven, and Deka listened with interest. They spent a long time engrossed in conversation.

Meanwhile, Deka observed Çarh's recent changes. After

joining the Coven, she noticed a gleam in Çarh's eyes. The previous hopelessness had given way to curiosity and a desire to explore. Deka witnessed Çarh's increasing knowledge about the magical world and shared his excitement. Both supported each other on this journey of discovery and worked together to explore the magical world. Deka felt great pride in Çarh's eagerness to learn, and she considered herself lucky to be by his side.

Sûr

CHAPTER 15
LIBRARY

Nail found himself alone in the shop after the departure of Çarh and the Elf. Sensing the power of the necklace in his hand, he pondered how Çarh had come to possess it. Perhaps he acquired it from Deka in some way, he thought. However, as someone well aware that everything had a price, Nail was certain that this necklace too came with its own cost. The power within demanded great responsibility. Nail had to wield it correctly and be conscious of its potency. Thoughtfully, he gazed at the necklace, contemplating what the future might hold.

Although Nail knew of the necklace's power, uncertainties lingered about how to activate it. To explore its potential, he began to roam around, considering that some members of the Coven might possess information on the matter. Thinking it might be a good idea to visit the Coven, he set out on the journey.

As Nail researched how to activate the necklace's

power, he felt concerned about the lack of trust among the witches in the Coven. The place was always rife with gossip and conflicts, making Nail realise how careful he needed to be before utilizing the necklace's power. However, he needed to find a way to activate it, as it could potentially alter Nail's entire destiny. Until he found someone in the Coven he could trust, he wouldn't fully comprehend how to use the power of the necklace.

Walking towards the Coven, Nail contemplated different scenarios of using the necklace's power. Upon arriving at the door, a pair of Sögré stopped him, asking, "What business do you have here?" Nail replied, "I need to speak with some members of the Coven." One of the Sögré said, "You are not welcome here." Simmering with anger, Nail was ready to protect himself. Maintaining his firm stance against their condescending words, he sharply retorted, "You're lucky it's not you I'm looking for; now get out of my way!" His assertive response surprised the arrogant Sögré, but Nail's resolute demeanour made them step back.

Walking through the halls of the Coven, Nail noticed the surrounding silence. It was usually vibrant and lively, but now it resembled a ghost town with its haunting quietness. The walls of the corridors looked pale due to the absence of energy within. However, Nail could sense this silence and unknown. He had a goal, and he possessed the power required to reach it. That power could pierce through even this silence.

Upon entering the grand hall, Nail was immediately greeted by an old friend, Buse, who enveloped him in a warm hug. Buse's sincerity lessened Nail's fear of the unknown. Inquiring about Nail's purpose, Buse offered to guide him as Nail explained his need to speak with some Coven members and seek answers.

Nail revealed he possessed a necklace with potent energy but lacked knowledge on activating its power. Buse suggested consulting the Coven members to learn about the necklace's origin. However, Nail expressed reservations about finding trustworthy individuals within the Coven. Assuring Nail, Buse pledged to help him and introduce him to reliable members. Intrigued, Nail and Buse explored the Coven together. While Buse had a few names in mind, certainty eluded her.

Upon hearing that Buse knew Sögré who could assist, Nail felt a glimmer of hope, wondering which Sögré might hold information about the necklace. Understanding Nail's thoughts, Buse smiled, and they set out to find the most suitable Sögré.

Buse mentioned having excellent communication among the Sögré and suggested a particular Sögré with unique abilities might have information about the necklace. Nail eagerly awaited Buse's choice, a spark of hope igniting within him. A new path unfolded, offering the opportunity to unravel the necklace's secret and fully harness its power.

Buse nodded thoughtfully. "Perhaps Lena, Gara, or Kira?" she suggested. Contemplating the names, Nail thought, "Lena might be the best option." Lena's knowledge and foreseeing abilities made her a promising choice. Buse, seemingly understanding Nail's thoughts, approved of Lena, and they continued exploring the Coven to find her.

As they wandered, Buse, curious about Lena's powers, got lost in thought. The ability to foresee was indeed formidable. Wondering how Lena's abilities worked, she turned to Nail and asked, "How does Lena's ability to foresee work?" Nail responded thoughtfully, "Foreseeing is the ability to see the future beyond time. Lena receives visions or intuitions through this ability, allowing her to anticipate significant events in the future." Buse, listening attentively, couldn't resist asking how Lena could see such important events. Nail explained with a smile, "Lena's connection goes deep with the roots of magic, particularly through her own Elf, linking her to Céwiaretza. This provides her with great intuition and understanding. However, foreseeing has its limits, and to fully comprehend how it works, you'll need to speak with Lena." Buse grew even more curious about Lena and eagerly anticipated meeting her.

Lena, renowned as one of the most talented witches for her prophecies, was spotted a little further ahead by Buse. Eager to inquire about Lena's abilities, Buse approached her. Lena shared that her prophecies often came through images, sounds, and intuitions. Some arrived as symbols in her dreams, requiring a separate skill to interpret their meanings. Buse, curious about the reality of the prophecies, questioned Lena, who assured her that most of her predictions came true.

As Buse's curiosity grew, questions about the chances of Lena's prophecies coming true and the potential consequences of a specific prophecy filled her mind. Simultaneously, she pondered the secrets Lena might be keeping about her own destiny.

Upon hearing a particular prophecy involving Nail causing her death, Buse recoiled in shock and asked, "What do you mean? How could Nail cause my death?"

Lena replied calmly, "It's just a prophecy; maybe it won't come true. Prophecies are not always certain, only possibilities." Despite Lena's reassurance, Buse remained worried, contemplating various scenarios.

Nail, struggling to understand the situation, reflected on how he hadn't done anything to cause harm to Buse. While contemplating how to prevent the prophecy from coming true, Lena's words echoed in his mind. Perhaps it was just a possibility, and the prophecy might not unfold.

Despite Lena's reassurances, Buse remained anxious about the possibility of the prophecy coming true. Nail, feeling helpless, believed there was nothing more he could do than be there for his friend. They sat in silence, lost in contemplation.

Attempting to shift the focus, Nail showed Lena the necklace he held in his hand. Lena's attention was immediately drawn to it. Placing her hand on the necklace to feel the power within, she fell silent for a moment before whispering, "This necklace is connected to the source of dark powers. Once activated, it will enable you to perform powerful spells, but it will also put you in danger," revealing her prophecy about the necklace. However, Lena felt uneasy because she couldn't fully comprehend the power within. Still, Nail assured her that he would do everything to control it.

Observing Lena's worried expression, Buse suggested, "Maybe Nail should never activate the power within this necklace." However, Nail believed that the necklace would provide him with a significant advantage and expressed that he didn't want to leave without finding the key to using it.

Despite Lena's warnings about the dangerous power of the necklace, she couldn't change Nail's decision. He had found someone to help him, and he didn't want to miss this opportunity.

Nail listened attentively to Lena's insights about touching the necklace, considering her knowledge crucial in understanding the power within. Curious about Lena's experience, he inquired, "What did you feel exactly when you touched the necklace?" Lena closed her eyes, attempting to relive the moment. She vividly recalled the coldness and gloominess of the necklace and the images from the other side. "The coldness and gloominess of that place frightened me," she said. "But at the same time, I saw fragments of something. A primal power, perhaps the power of an Elf." Though curious about the nature of the power within, Nail found Lena's account thought-provoking. "A primal power?" he thought to himself. "What does that mean?"

After Lena responded to Nail's question, she took the necklace into her hand once again. This time, she examined it for a longer duration and concentrated, feeling various images and sensations. However, interpreting them proved challenging. "The power within this necklace is very ancient and primal," Lena said. "But I haven't fully understood where it comes from. The images resemble an underground cave, but I can't pinpoint its location. And controlling it seems quite challenging as well."

As Nail listened, a concerned expression appeared on his face. Eager to know how to control the necklace's power, he remembered there were other Sögré who might possess knowledge about it. "What about others who might know about this necklace?" Nail asked. "Are there any other Sögré who can help me?"

Lena, recognizing the value of the magical world's library, suggested it as a valuable resource. Throughout history, it housed works by wizards, witches, and other beings. Nail and Buse accepted Lena's suggestion, and she determined the location of the library and suitable books for their research. However, she reminded them of the need for special permission to access it.

Deciding to complete the formalities required for library access, Nail and Buse understood that accessing the information within could help them unravel the secret of this dangerous power.

Nail considered Lena's words, recognizing the importance of consulting the library's wisdom. However, he was aware that entering the library was a risky endeavour. Despite the risks, he acknowledged the necessity of taking this step to control the power within the necklace.

"As you said, Lena," Nail said seriously. "The wisdom of the library is crucial for me. I need to explore the library to understand and control the power within the necklace. But I will be careful while doing so. I will think through every step."

Lena looked at Nail with understanding, sensing his determination and the power within him. They were prepared to move forward together. Nail decided to take the necessary steps to access the library, and Lena would assist him in the process. A strong bond had formed between them, and they were ready to embark on this mysterious journey together.

The Beyazıt State Library was no ordinary library. For centuries, it held a significant place in the magical world, boasting numerous books and documents, making it one of the most comprehensive sources of information about the history, culture, magic, and rituals of the Sögrés.

Situated in Beyazıt, a historic area of Istanbul, the library was one of the oldest, with a captivating atmosphere owing to its historical texture. Its significance for the Sögré lay in housing secret pieces of information about the world of magic — magical books, ritual materials, and other items that helped Sögrés gain a deeper understanding of magic.

However, gaining access to the library was no simple task. It was open only to a specific group, and strict rules governed it. A specific procedure had to be followed, with guardians closely monitoring entrants. Despite the challenges, gaining access to the library was a great honour and privilege for the Sögré.

Inside the library, enchantment awaited. Hundreds of bookshelves, cabinets containing magical materials, glass showcases displaying ancient objects, and a spacious workspace filled the space.

Upon entering, Sögré would reach the cistern through a magical passage after undergoing a few procedures – the heart of the library where everything they sought could be found.

The path to the cistern extended into the depths of the library, following a magical stone staircase adorned with symbols. As Sögré walked these stairs emitting light in the dark, they approached the legendary cistern. It was a place where the highest level of magical abilities was required to access the books and objects within.

Nail, Buse, and Lena wandered through the quiet corridors of the library, surrounded by bookshelves exuding the scent of history. With each step, they encountered traces of the past. Their true destination, however, lay in the section within the cistern where the most valuable works of the Sögrés were hidden.

To enter the library, Nail, Buse, and Lena had to go through various procedures. First, they had to explain their reason for entry. The library administrators enforced strict control to protect its secrets. The most stringent rule was the suppression of magical power. Using magic inside the library was forbidden, and everyone entering had to be purged of magical influence. Despite the difficulty of accepting this rule, Nail, Buse, and Lena entered the library, suppressing their magical powers.

When they opened the door to the cistern, the stairs beneath their feet transformed into a dark journey, accompanied by an eerie silence. Stepping into the cistern, they felt as if the spirit of an ancient witch enveloped them. In the dim candlelight, dark waters reflected mysterious symbols on the walls, concealing the secrets of the Sögrés.

As Nail, Buse, and Lena ventured deeper into the cistern, they sensed themselves lost in the depths of history. With each step, they confronted the wisdom and power of past witches, hoping to find answers to unlock the secrets of the necklace.

Wandering among the shelves, their eyes navigated the dusty pages of ancient books filled with prophecies and magical formulas carefully penned by Sögrés. The trio carefully examined each page, searching for information to unravel the necklace's secret. However, comprehending the meaning of these ancient works proved challenging, requiring deep insight and attention due to centuries of accumulated knowledge and magic.

In the cistern of the Beyazıt State Library, they embarked on a journey into the secrets of the magical world. In every page, in every symbol, a clue about the future and the true power of the necklace lay hidden. Their research continued in the dark, turning pages filled with wisdom, filled with hope.

As hours passed and they delved into the lower floor of the library, despair loomed over Lena. Nail insisted on continuing their research, and Buse sat silently, surveying the surroundings. Suddenly, she spotted the symbol of the necklace between the pages of a book.

Quickly opening the book, she flipped through its pages and found an explanation of the necklace's power. It belonged to the Quordéen ancestry. While Nail comprehended the significance, Lena and Buse were uncertain. Although the purpose of the necklace was not fully explained, information on each page indicated that only a Quordéen witch could wield it.

A disappointment appeared on Nail's face, and he angrily threw the necklace against the wall. The necklace hit with force, echoing in the library. An accumulation of anger and disappointment surged within Nail. He had hoped the necklace would bring him power and a solution, but now it had become useless. This sudden reaction momentarily disrupted the library's silence, reflecting Nail's emotional turmoil with its echoing sound.

Nail's frustration and anger reached a boiling point as he realised that Çarh had deceived him. Thoughts raced through his mind, questioning how he could make such a mistake, having trusted, and helped Çarh find the plant they sought, only to receive a fake necklace in return. Enveloped in profound disappointment, he felt his efforts to obtain the necklace's power had gone in vain.

Buse sympathized with Nail's anger, attempting to calm him down. "Calm down, maybe this fake necklace can be used to replace the real one," she suggested. Lena added, "The energy I felt when touching the necklace was different. I'm not sure, but the necklace might not be fake. It could be suppressed. Maybe the power of the necklace is still within you. I can try to transform the fake necklace into the real one using that power."

Nail's shocked expression shifted into a glimmer of hope as Lena's words resonated. Buse remained silent, absorbing her friends' thoughts.

Nail handed the necklace to Lena, who concentrated, attempting to feel its power. However, nothing happened. Since performing magic inside the library was not possible, they quickly left. Lena decided to release the power of the necklace by reciting magic words in her mind.

As Nail and Buse watched in amazement, Lena's body was enveloped in light. The necklace's power held her in a captivating light halo, with lightning flashing around, and the wind blowing rapidly. After a few minutes, everything returned to normal, and Lena descended slowly. Her friends rushed towards her, embracing and rejoicing.

Lena, wide-eyed with astonishment, revealed the discovery of an old lady's soul inside the necklace. "This necklace must be enchanted with her soul. It's definitely a fake necklace."

Nail, astonished, sought an explanation. "How is that possible? How can this necklace be enchanted with a soul?" Lena answered thoughtfully, "I don't know, Nail. But in the world of magic, sometimes extraordinary things happen," adding, "Someone must have communicated with souls."

Agreeing with Lena, Nail contemplated deeply. "Yes, it could be true. And that person must be Çarh. He must have the knowledge and ability to perform such magic."

Buse interjected with a worried expression. "Well, what could Çarh's purpose be? Why did he try to deceive you with this fake necklace?" Lena's eyes gleamed with determination. "Maybe Çarh doesn't want you to find the real necklace. Or perhaps, he wants to test you in some way. You need to be more careful to disrupt his game."

Nail, feeling the anger rising within him, decided it was time to confront Çarh. He acknowledged Çarh's game and wondered how he had been deceived, but Nail didn't lose faith in himself and his friends. Turning confidently to Lena and Buse, he looked them in the eye with strength and determination. "We won't play this game according to his rules anymore," he declared with an unwavering tone. "We hold the cards, and we will confront him by transforming this fake necklace into real power."

Lena and Buse felt Nail's determination, and hope began to sprout within them again. They would join forces to disrupt Çarh's plans, find the real necklace, and restore the balance of the magical world. Nail, as their leader, was determined to overcome the obstacles ahead.

Leaving the Beyazıt State Library, they navigated the complex labyrinths of the magical world. The path would be challenging and dangerous, but they moved forward with brave steps. They aimed to disrupt Çarh's order, find the real necklace, and bring back the balance of the magical world.

Nail, fuelled by hope, quickened his steps with his friends. Now, he was more determined than ever. He was no longer a part of Çarh's game; he was a player changing the game and determining its end.

Although Buse and Lena might not fully understand Nail's true purpose, they were willing to help him. Nail assured them that he would handle the rest on his own and walked away from them.

Nail hoped to use the necklace to survive. In the event of Israfil's trumpet being blown, death was inevitable. Nail believed that by using the power of the necklace against Sûr's force, he could protect himself. But now, realizing he had a fake necklace, his hopes were shattered.

Blinded by his belief that Çarh and Deka played a game together, he thought the real necklace was with Deka.

Nail was aware that finding Çarh and Deka in Istanbul wouldn't be an easy task. He couldn't rely on conventional means, as their locations were likely concealed using magical means. Nail decided to tap into his network of magical connections and seek guidance from mystical sources.

As he delved deeper into the magical realm, he consulted with other Sögrés who possessed the ability to sense magical energies and locate individuals. Through these interactions, he gathered information about the unique magical signatures associated with Çarh and Deka.

Nail's quest for information led him to an ancient Sögré, a wise being with knowledge of mystical energies and hidden realms. The Sögré, residing in a secluded part of the magical world, provided Nail with guidance. Through a series of rituals and consultations, the Sögré helped Nail attune himself to the magical frequencies associated with Çarh and Deka.

With newfound insights and a heightened sense of magical perception, Nail set out for Cihangir. As he navigated the streets, he relied on his honed magical senses to detect the distinctive energy signatures of Çarh and Deka. The magical resonance, like an ethereal trail, guided Nail through the winding alleys and hidden corners of Cihangir.

He was making plans in his mind, walking with determined steps towards the Cihangir district. He wanted to disrupt the game Çarh and Deka had set up together.

Cihangir's streets were narrow and winding. Nail felt like he was in a labyrinth filled with traces of the past. The mystical aura that Sögrés had felt when they came here was still lingering. It was as if it were a world lost in time.

Eventually, Nail reached his destination. He admired the atmosphere of the café. The pleasant conversations and comfort of the people turned the café into a magical world. Even extraordinary beings like Sögrés could feel normal here. The café's garden was filled with flowers, and spending time here was refreshing for the soul.

In the café, there were interesting people. Some were

sipping their coffees, some reading their books, and others chatting with friends.

Çarh and Deka were sitting in the garden of the café, chatting pleasantly. Nail quietly approached and observed them. From their words, he concluded that the necklace was indeed with Deka. However, he was still indecisive about how to take it. Capturing both Sögrés at once could be risky.

Nail, making plans in his head, began to evaluate possible scenarios. While he wanted to capture both Çarh and Deka, this situation could be risky. Nail finally decided to make a smart move. He approached them as if nothing had happened, intending to greet Çarh. However, this was only one part of his plan. To truly convince Çarh and take the necklace, he needed a deeper strategy.

Gathering himself, Nail approached Çarh and Deka. Çarh seemed momentarily surprised to see him but then smiled and said,

"Hello Nail, it's great to see you here!"

Deka raised her head, smiled at Nail, and greeted him. Despite their warm welcome, Nail tried to hide his anger.

"Hi," he said in a short tone. "Can I join you for something to drink?"

Murat Karagoz

CHAPTER 16
EXPRESSION

Çarh couldn't hide his surprise when Nail appeared in front of him. He hadn't seen him much since the day he gave him the necklace. At that moment, Çarh wondered about Nail's intentions. Perhaps he wanted to ask him something, or maybe he was there for another purpose. Çarh observed him carefully to understand Nail's intentions.

Nail approached them with a warm smile, and there was no threatening look in Çarh's eyes. Çarh decided to engage in a short conversation with him.

"Hello, Nail! It's a surprise to see you here. What's up?" Çarh said.

Nail, maintaining his smile, replied, "Just wandering around, and running into you was a surprise."

Çarh felt comfortable with Nail being there, but he wasn't sure how Deka would react to Nail's presence.

Çarh noticed from the corner of his eye that Deka was uneasy. He understood that she wanted to leave because Nail's sudden appearance had muddled her thoughts. However, at Deka's request, Çarh turned to Nail and said politely, "We were just about to leave. See you."

Although Nail was a bit disappointed, he nodded understandingly. "Of course, I understand. Have a good day," he said.

Çarh thanked Nail and smiled at him, then walked toward her. Deka looked at Çarh with a worried expression, and they nodded silently. The two of them moved away from the café's garden together.

When Nail found himself alone, he immersed himself in his thoughts. Filled with the sadness of not achieving the desired outcome, he was determined not to give up. Perhaps he could find another way. He resolved to put more effort into figuring out how to obtain the real necklace and achieve his goal.

Çarh was worried because he noticed Deka's uneasiness. The tension and hesitation in her eyes disturbed Çarh. He was grappling with an internal conflict. Turning to Deka, he asked quietly, "Are you okay?"

After a brief moment of thought, Deka smiled gently. "Yes, I'm fine," she said. However, Çarh was trying to understand how Deka truly felt. The mysterious gleam in her eyes unsettled him. Simultaneously, he pondered about what he could do to help her.

Çarh stood silently beside Deka, and with a deep sense from the depths of his heart, he turned to her. "If something is bothering you, you can tell me," he said gently. "I want to help you."

Feeling Çarh's sincerity, Deka found some comfort. As she thanked him, she attempted to conceal a faint pain in her eyes. "I know," she said in a soft tone. "I have some thoughts, but I'm unsure for now. Nail was wearing the necklace we gave him, but the enchantment had disappeared." Çarh, with great seriousness, inquired, "What does that mean?" Deka responded, "He probably realised that the necklace was fake."

Çarh was stunned by this revelation. He had assumed Nail was merely greeting them after a chance encounter. Witnessing the worry on Çarh's face, Deka approached him in a calming manner. "Don't worry, maybe I'm mistaken. But still, we should be careful."

Çarh agreed with Deka's words, and they continued walking together thoughtfully. He mulled over Nail's peculiar behaviour and whether the fake necklace had been noticed. Deka, understanding Çarh's concerns, acknowledged them. It was evident she was also curious about Nail's reaction and possible retaliation. After a thoughtful silence, she remarked, "Nail seems clever and ambitious. Perhaps he could make a move against us. However, we must be prepared. We should act with a strong strategy and leverage our own power."

Çarh concurred with Deka's sentiments. He, too, harboured concerns about Nail's magical abilities. Moving together and supporting each other was crucial. "Yes, you're right. Together we are strong, and we won't let Nail defeat us. We should devise a solid plan and be cautious."

Deka smiled with determination. "Okay, Çarh. We will do our best to deal with Nail. We must trust each other and know that nothing can intimidate us."

With Deka's reassuring words, Çarh felt a bit more at ease. They would collaborate to prepare for Nail's potential moves. Their strength and determination would guide them through this challenging struggle.

Çarh couldn't shake the feeling that Nail's appearance and the need to confront him would cast their lives into a gloomy turn once again. He pondered silently, complex emotions stirring within him. Having led a peaceful and calm life before, Çarh now felt trapped in the complexity and uncertainty of the magical world.

As he walked alongside Deka, he tried to suppress his internal conflicts. Thoughts and worries weighed heavily on him as he considered how to confront Nail and deal with his power. The uncertainty and danger in the struggle between them dragged Çarh into despair.

Feeling Çarh's inner turmoil, Deka turned to him and spoke in a calm tone, "Çarh, don't worry. Yes, we are at a difficult crossroad, and there is a great challenge ahead. But we can overcome these challenges by moving together and combining our strength. Let's not lose our confidence in ourselves."

Gratefully, Çarh looked at Deka for her reassuring words. Her determination and courage illuminated the despair within Çarh. Putting aside his internal thoughts for a moment, he endeavoured to gather his motivation again. Aware that not everything would go smoothly, he chose not to give up but instead confront the difficulties they faced.

Pushing aside the pessimism within, Çarh turned to Deka and smiled. "You're right, Deka. Instead of giving up, we must be strong and overcome every obstacle in our way. Our task is to face difficulties together and rediscover our strength. No matter how powerful Nail may be, he won't intimidate us."

Deka nodded with a smile. They decided to leave pessimism behind and focus on their future struggles, trusting each other. Together, they resolved to stand strong and resolute against Nail's threats.

However, Nail found it odd that Çarh and Deka hastily

left. Their sudden behaviour raised suspicions that they were planning something. Thinking to himself, "There's something going on," Nail decided to act immediately. He chose to follow Çarh and Deka, needing to catch up quickly. This was his last chance to seize the real necklace, and he had to plan rapidly and effectively, grappling with his own uncertainties.

As Nail tried to gather his thoughts, countless scenarios played in his mind. Which path should he follow to deceive Çarh and Deka? And what would be the best timing to seize the necklace? Combining all these thoughts, he made his decision. Moving with determined steps, he would first act to seize the necklace and then devise a strategy to deceive Çarh and Deka. While making these plans, one question lingered in his mind: "Will everything go according to plan?"

As questions continued to swirl in Nail's mind, his anxieties heightened. Nevertheless, he retained confidence in his abilities and intelligence, assured that he had chosen the right people to work with. While considering seeking help from Buse and Lena, concerns about their safety led Nail to a firm decision to handle everything on his own.

Navigating through numerous possibilities for his next steps proved challenging for Nail. Seeking to untangle the confusion in his mind, he focused on preparing his plan with utmost precision.

Upon arriving home, Çarh felt exhausted, with Nail's words lingering in his mind throughout the day. Finding Deka resting with closed eyes, Çarh decided to prepare a meal. Engaging in the soothing act of cooking, he felt as if all his troubles were transforming into a deliciously erased meal. As Çarh cooked, he drifted into silent contemplation.

The sound of the pot boiling brought Çarh back to the present, yet Nail's words echoed in his mind. Stirring the meal,

Çarh's unanswered questions lingered. Resolving to let Deka rest after eating, Çarh moved only to call the Elf.

The Elf responded promptly, sitting across from Çarh at the dining table. Çarh shared the encounter with Nail and the realization that Nail had discovered the necklace was fake. Feeling cornered, Çarh poured out his concerns. The Elf listened silently and then spoke with a thoughtful expression.

The Elf listened attentively to Çarh's words and responded soothingly, "There's no point in worrying in this situation, Çarh. Nothing you did was wrong. Nail realizing the necklace was fake was just a possibility, and you guided him in the best way. Now, what you need to do is ensure that Nail won't do anything to you or Deka. You need to have confidence in yourself and your actions."

Contemplating the Elf's words, Çarh consumed his meal slowly. As fatigue settled in after finishing his food, he decided to rest. Setting aside his worries, he lay down on his bed and closed his eyes.

Falling asleep proved challenging, as thoughts about Nail's situation persisted. Çarh wondered if Nail had truly noticed the fake necklace and what actions would follow. The Elf's advice echoed in his mind, urging him to approach the situation from a different perspective. Eventually, fatigue prevailed, and Çarh drifted into sleep. However, nightmares plagued him, intertwining Nail's plans with his own mistakes, preventing true rest.

Observing Çarh's unrest, Deka, aware of Çarh's recent stress and the added worries from the fake necklace, approached him to offer comfort. "Don't worry, everything will fall into place," he reassured. Despite Deka's words, Çarh struggled to shake off the dark thoughts and find rest.

Deka, understanding what to do, gently guided Çarh

from the bed and embraced him. "Don't worry," he said, "I'll take you somewhere." Çarh, silently following, found himself at Deka's home after a short walk. Deka, revealing the enchanting garden, tended to each plant individually, creating a magical atmosphere. Çarh felt at peace, the garden helping him forget the world's troubles. Deka, aware of Çarh's emotions, explained, "Many people see the garden only as a flowerbed. But you, you see the garden as a living space. We live together with plants, trees, and animals. It's a very special place for us."

Çarh continued to breathe in the magical air of Deka's garden. At that moment, a shooting star streaked across the sky, prompting Çarh to make a wish. Reaching towards the sky, hope began to sprout within him once again. Deka stood by Çarh's side and said, "Always look at the sky, full of hope. Because in the sky, there is infinite hope."

Feeling a sense of peace and hope washing over him, Çarh found sanctuary in Deka's garden. Despite life's challenges, solace awaited him here, where he realised that life's beauties and pains coexisted. Most importantly, there was hope in this garden.

Closing his eyes, Çarh sat in the garden, immersed in his inner world. Suddenly, his mind opened as if a door had been unlocked. Out of nowhere, he vividly imagined people and places he had never seen or known before. Initially considering these images as mere dreams, the realism made him understand it was something more.

With his eyes closed, Çarh saw a woman standing on the summit of a mountain – exceptionally beautiful, with long black hair, an innocent face, and a powerful stance. Wondering about her identity, he realised he didn't know her name. When he opened his eyes and looked at the garden, everything seemed normal, but the vivid images remained in his mind.

Meanwhile, Nail was surprised to see Buse and Lena waiting in front of the shop. Wondering why they were there, he approached them and inquired about the situation. Buse and Lena explained that they were curious and wanted to support Nail's return. Entering together, Nail looked uneasy, but the strong support from his friends reassured him. Buse and Lena pledged to do their best and reminded him that they were always there for him.

Noticing something in Nail's expression, Buse approached him and started asking questions. "Nail, what happened? Why do you look like that?" she inquired. Initially puzzled, Nail quietly confessed, "I ran into Çarh and Deka in Cihangir. They were sitting in a cafe, and I approached them, pretending as if nothing had happened. However, they must have understood the situation because they wanted to leave suddenly," he revealed.

Listening to Nail's story, Buse and Lena looked at him in astonishment, their minds filled with swirling questions. What would Çarh and Deka do? Was Nail's action the right thing? Was pretending as if nothing had happened a good strategy to corner them? Buse wished she had been there to witness the events, while Lena silently disagreed with Nail's move, feeling it wasn't the right approach. Both chose to remain silent, leaving their questions unanswered.

Breaking the silence, Lena asked, "What are we going to do now?" Buse expressed uncertainty, saying, "It's hard to guess what Çarh will think." Nail remained silent, prompting Lena to suggest, "Maybe he will talk to us, maybe not. But if we're going to do something, what we need to do is talk to them." Nail sharply retorted, "Absolutely not, the two of you stay out of this."

Nail's words saddened Buse and Lena. The uneasiness

Nail felt after realizing the necklace was fake also concerned them. "But as your friends, we don't want to leave you alone," Buse said. "Yes, we can act together with you. Besides, maybe you need our support," Lena added.

Nail nodded. "Thank you, but this is my problem, and I want to handle it alone," he replied. Buse and Lena remained silent for a while, and then Buse said, "Well, we're here to support you. Let us know whenever you need us,"

Moved by the sincerity of his friends, Nail expressed his gratitude. "Thank you," he said. "I love you both, and having friends like you is essential to me." After a tight hug, Buse and Lena bid him farewell and left the shop.

Alone in the silence he created by being by himself, Nail meticulously formulated his plan. He planned every step he would take and every word he would say in advance, and took all necessary precautions to ensure no one would be harmed. He intended to use the Witch Trap known as Sögrédehöben to stop Deka, but since each Sögré was connected to different elements, he first needed to learn which element Deka was linked to. Therefore, the first step of his plan was to observe Deka and discover which element she was connected to.

Silently tracking the streets, Nail followed Deka. After visiting a few shops, Deka headed towards the gathering place of the main Sögrés. As Nail approached the vicinity of the gathering place, he maneuvered through the crowd and approached Deka. He took her arm to greet her, but Deka couldn't help but startle. Nail apologized and expressed his desire to talk. Uncertain of his intentions, Deka declined, saying she didn't want to talk, and began to step back. Nail, making a move, grabbed the necklace around her neck. With the necklace in his hand, Nail watched as Deka transformed into a small whirlwind and disappeared. At that moment, he understood that Deka was connected to the air element. Holding the fake necklace in his hand, he remained stuck in the midst of the crowd.

While attempting to comprehend the situation at home, Deka carried a persistent sense of worry in her heart. The surrounding silence only heightened her anxiety. Suddenly, Çarh came to her mind, prompting her to call him.

Deka retrieved her phone and swiftly dialled his number. The button sounds on the phone played like a pleasant melody to Deka's ears. The call was answered a few seconds later, and Çarh's voice came through.

"Deka, what happened?" Çarh asked.

Deka began narrating the events that had unfolded. Initially dismissing them, she later realised that something terrible had occurred. Çarh listened to Deka's account with a worried expression. Finally, she recounted how she had pulled Nail's necklace. Çarh expressed confusion about why Nail would do such a thing.

"What should we do?" Deka asked.

In an attempt to calm Deka, Çarh reassured her, "Nothing will happen to you. Don't worry; I will protect you. Now, what you need to do is stay at home to ensure you're safe. I'll come to you shortly, and we'll discuss what to do."

Drawing strength from Çarh's calm demeanour, Deka replied, "Okay. Thank you, Çarh. I love you."

When Çarh heard the easing tone of concern in Deka's voice, he said, "I love you too, Deka. Nothing can harm you. I promise," and hung up the phone.

Çarh prepared to go to Deka to ensure her safety. Before that, he pondered why Nail had taken such action. Although he had promised to protect Deka, his mind grappled with why Nail had set a trap for her in the midst of the crowd. Accepting this was difficult, but, on the other hand, he did not want to believe that Nail was capable of such a thing. But, to prevent harm to Deka, he had to confront Nail.

Çarh had been questioning the reality of the recent dreams he had been having. The events and faces he saw had begun to disturb some corner of his mind. His dreams included memories of experiences and people he had not encountered in real life. Though they frightened him, they also granted him a certain power. With each passing day, he remembered more things, and the mysteries of his past began to unfold.

While this situation made Çarh uneasy, it also provided him with a sense of purpose. He wanted to explore the power within him and unravel the mysteries of his past. Therefore, he took action to find out why Nail had attacked Deka. Feeling a newfound strength, he was simultaneously anxious about the unknown. Struggling with these conflicting emotions, he headed towards Nail's shop.

As Çarh walked the streets, every sight triggered a different memory. Some were beautiful moments from the past, while others were filled with dark memories. However, all of them were vague and tangled in Çarh's mind. He couldn't understand their origin or why he remembered them. On one hand, he questioned whether these memories were real or just illusions. This situation scared him, yet the power he felt was as intense as his fear. Perhaps, he thought, these memories came to teach him something. To comprehend, he first needed to find the source of these memories.

He had a notion about the origin of these memories – a connection to Israfil and Sûr residing within him. The fear of teetering on the brink of madness gripped him, intensified by the inability to confide in anyone about the distress these emotions stirred. A sense of loneliness and helplessness settled in.

With these tumultuous thoughts, Çarh pressed on with his journey. Seeking distraction, he surveyed his surroundings. Yet, every sight triggered a different recollection – the leaves of a tree, a child's innocent smile, the fragrance of a wildflower – each encapsulating him in a relentless cycle of memories.

Çarh was convinced that these dreams originated from Sûr. The magical influence wielded by Sûr toyed with the fabric of his recollections, convincing him that he was a mistake in his own reality. The presence of Israfil heightened his trepidation. The looming fear of losing control to the burgeoning entity within him fuelled his growing anxiety.

Çarh desired solitude to grapple with his thoughts, resolving to keep them confined within. Slowly, he pressed forward, intent on finding a solution for himself.

Approaching Nail's shop, an inexplicable chill enveloped Çarh. Unprecedented dark thoughts surfaced, drawing him with an irresistible force. Realization struck – he had been in this place before, yet those memories had not troubled him until now. Their resurgence left him feeling like a different person, almost as if he inhabited someone else's body. Despite the overwhelming terror, he composed himself, took a deep breath, and entered Nail's shop.

Nail, seated at his table, was startled by the creaking door. His gaze met Çarh's determined entrance. Çarh's unexpected presence caught him off guard; he needed more time, more preparation. The anticipated events were accelerating, unfolding before he was ready.

Çarh fixed Nail with a stern look, demanding an explanation. "Why did you do this?" Nail, maintaining a calm demeanour, met Çarh's gaze and replied, "I don't understand what you're talking about." Çarh found the response inadequate but determined not to leave without understanding Nail's intentions.

On one hand, Çarh grappled with the desire to question Nail about his intentions toward Deka while desperately trying to preserve the trust he once had in him. "I'm talking about Deka. Why are you following her? Wasn't the necklace I gave you enough? Were you after her from the beginning? What do you want now?" Çarh demanded answers. Nail, unwilling to expose the revelation that the necklace was fake, responded, "There must have been a misunderstanding. I just wanted to say hello. Deka disappeared all of a sudden, and I don't understand what happened." Though Çarh found the explanation unsatisfactory, he instructed Nail not to interfere and exited the shop. Tension lingered in the air as Çarh navigated the darkened streets, his mind swirling with unanswered questions, the narrow alleys closing in, and the distant sounds of the city echoing around him.

It was already dark as Çarh approached Deka's house. From the opposite direction, a hooded man emerged, triggering an old memory. Though the man's face remained obscured, Çarh sensed a significant connection to his past. The passing hooded man briefly brought recent memories to mind, including an encounter with someone in the neighbourhood that marked a turning point in his life. Despite the unclear recollection of the man's face, Çarh felt a chilling certainty that he knew him. This realization frightened him, though the reason remained elusive. Doubt crept in – was he the person from his dreams? However, Çarh dismissed the idea, attributing it to his mind playing tricks. Suppressing his fear, he continued towards home.

Çarh's walk grew increasingly arduous. With each step, the throbbing pain in his head intensified, making the simple act of walking a formidable challenge. The chaotic and overwhelming nature of the memories played havoc with his mental faculties, leaving him mentally drained. The unexpected appearance of a hooded man approaching from the opposite direction, reminiscent of someone he might not have seen for a hundred years, added another layer of surprise. Though the man was unfamiliar, the tangled memories insisted that Çarh knew him.

The echoing pain in Çarh's head seemed unbearable. In a particular memory, he realised that the voice pleading for help belonged to himself. But how could that be possible in the present when the memory was from months ago? Everything became jumbled, creating a sense of insolvability in his mind. The pain persisted, making even the act of walking excruciating. The influence of Sûr was becoming increasingly apparent, instilling a fear of losing complete control.

Struggling with a severe headache, Çarh attempted to retrieve the memory of the hooded man seeking help. Months prior, in a drunken stupor, he had witnessed an argument on the street and heard a man pleading for assistance. Responding to the plea, he had intervened, but the memory blanked out after the incident. Now, he conjectured that the hooded man might be him – someone who had asked for help. This idea relentlessly spun in his head, exacerbating the headache, and further weakening him.

Çarh, grappling with an unrelenting tightness within, pressed on with his walk. The throbbing headache impeded his steps, making it difficult for him to move properly. In a fleeting moment, he closed his eyes, attempting to piece together the events. The hooded man's plea for help flashed in his mind, and he vividly remembered rushing to assist. Yet, the perplexing question lingered – why was he now re-living that memory? What accounted for the unbearable intensity of the headache?

In that moment, Çarh succumbed to the unbearable pressure and let out a scream, a visceral expression of the tightness within him. The scream echoed with such power that even Deka, who was some distance away, heard it, and the people nearby witnessed the manifestation of Çarh's Sûr. The protective veil concealing Sûr had dissipated, exposing it to the world. What heightened Çarh's headache was the simultaneous loss of control over Israfil within him. With his secret now laid bare, Çarh felt a level of fear unlike any he had experienced before. Deka rushed to him, attempting to offer support, but Çarh found himself slipping away amidst the astonished gazes of onlookers. Everything had transformed, and Çarh was now confronted with a multitude of problems.

Within the chaos of his unravelling reality, Çarh's inner voice screamed louder than his outward cry. It was a symphony of fear, confusion, and regret. "How did it come to this?" he wondered, the echoes of his thoughts drowned out by the relentless pounding in his head.

The revelation of Sûr to the world marked a point of no return. Çarh felt the weight of the stares, the judgment of those around him, and the exposure of a secret he had desperately tried to conceal. Israfil's unrestrained influence within him only fuelled the anguish. "I've lost control," Çarh admitted to himself, a realization that struck with the force of a hurricane.

Çarh grappled with the consequences of his actions and the fear of the unknown that now lay ahead. "What have I become?" he questioned, a tremor in his inner voice mirroring the tremors that shook his very being.

The once familiar streets now seemed alien, and Çarh felt like a stranger in his own existence. The tightening grip of the headache refused to let go, mirroring the tightening grip of fate around him. "Can I regain control?" he desperately pondered, a plea within his inner voice that echoed into the uncertain abyss that stretched before him.

CHAPTER 17
AWAKENING

Deka's panic intensified as the onlookers, spurred by Çarh's piercing scream, bore witness to the manifestation of Sûr. She felt a profound sense of distress watching Çarh struggle to conceal the entity on the ground. Acting swiftly, they called upon the Elf to facilitate their return home through teleportation. Lying in bed, Çarh continued to endure the persistent throbbing in his head, the aftermath of the chaotic events outside.

Despite Deka's efforts to provide comfort by gently stroking his head, Çarh's thoughts remained ensnared by the recent tumult. The image of people discovering Sûr heightened Çarh's fears, and this singular concern eclipsed all other thoughts in her mind. The memories from the past and the enigmatic figure of the hooded man intertwined, creating a whirlwind of confusion and chaos within Çarh's mind.

Amidst this mental storm, Deka, with a soothing tone, endeavoured to bring solace and clarity. She spoke words of reassurance, attempting to untangle the knot of anxieties that gripped Çarh's thoughts. In the quiet of their home, where the echoes of the outside world were muted, Deka sought to be a pillar of support for Çarh amid the tempest of his inner turmoil.

Observing the distress in Çarh's eyes, Deka approached with a compassionate understanding. Gently stroking Çarh's head, she sought to alleviate the turmoil. In a calm voice, Deka expressed her willingness to help, asking, "Can you tell me what happened?" Çarh, sensing the tranquillity in Deka's words, took a deep breath. He rested his head on the pillow and closed his eyes, and Deka stood by his side in silent support, patiently waiting for him to share.

With Deka's reassuring presence, Çarh began to recount the chaotic memories of that night. The image of the hooded man and the events leading to the manifestation of Sûr spilled forth as Çarh attempted to gather the fragments of the disarrayed narrative. In the quiet intimacy of their home, Deka remained a comforting presence, providing the space for Çarh to release the weight of her troubled thoughts.

In the hushed confines of their home, Çarh began to unveil the fragments of the haunting memory that had seized her mind. "That night, as I walked down the street, I witnessed two people embroiled in an argument. The hooded man sought my help, and I willingly intervened," Çarh continued, his voice carrying the weight of the unresolved events. "After that, there's only a vague recollection of taking a punch, and the next thing I knew, I woke up on the street the following morning. But the details elude me. Instead, there's just this lingering feeling, an unshakable anxiety."

Çarh's gaze, clouded with the fear of Sûr being exposed, reflected the internal struggle. "My dread of others seeing Sûr is escalating, and that's precisely why," he admitted, the words laden with vulnerability. "What if someone witnessed my Sûr? Or worse, what repercussions might unfold if someone does see it?" The uncertainty in Çarh's voice echoed the profound concerns that haunted him, leaving the air heavy with the weight of unspoken fears.

Listening attentively to Çarh's concerns, Deka attempted to offer reassurance. "Perhaps not everyone witnessed your Sûr," she suggested gently, hoping to ease Çarh's apprehensions. The words provided some relief to Çarh, yet an undercurrent of worry lingered.

As Deka continued to lend a supportive ear and offer comfort, she noticed the subtle signs of magical disturbance. Objects around Çarh began to tremble, a manifestation of the turmoil within. Swiftly, Deka cast a shielding spell, enveloping the house in a protective barrier. Turning to Çarh, she spoke with a soothing confidence, "Stay calm, don't lose control. Everything will be fine." The weight of Deka's words aimed to be a source of stability amid the magical upheaval, reassuring Çarh that, despite the chaos, there was a sanctuary within their shared space.

Despite Deka's reassuring words, Çarh found it challenging to quell the rising tide of anxiety. Taking a deep breath, he endeavoured to compose himself, but the persistent thought that everyone at the scene had witnessed his Sûr continued to torment his mind, intensifying his fears.

Deka, sensing Çarh's internal struggle, responded with a calm and comforting tone, "Don't worry too much, Çarh. No one saw your Sûr. It's just your fears playing tricks on you. Everything is fine; I will protect you." Deka's unwavering support and assurance aimed to create a sanctuary of calm amid Çarh's tumultuous thoughts, emphasizing the importance of trust and the sanctuary they had created together.

The words of reassurance provided a measure of comfort to Çarh, and with the easing of his headache, he gradually rose from the bed. Embracing Deka, he expressed his gratitude, "Thank you. You mean a lot to me."

Deka reciprocated the hug, her smile radiating warmth, and she replied, "You're important to me too, Çarh. I'm always here for you."

As time passed, Çarh succumbed to the gentle embrace of sleep. Deka, tenderly covering him, silently left the room. A quiet resolve settled on her face as she made her way to seek counsel from the Elf, her trusted confidant, about the lingering questions and concerns that continued to weigh on her mind.

In the silent exchange between Deka and Elf, the weight of the situation hung heavily in the air. While Deka's suggestion held merit, the magnitude of its implementation appeared nearly insurmountable. Altering the memories of individuals, a consequence of Çarh's manifestation of Sûr, presented a challenge that transcended the boundaries of conventional tasks. Rectifying these memories required a meticulous approach, with each person needing to be located individually, and the correct information delicately reintroduced to their consciousness.

However, the complexity of the situation was daunting, and time seemed to slip away with every passing moment. The urgency of the task and the intricate nature of memory manipulation added layers of complication, creating a palpable sense of tension in the room. The impending challenges loomed large, casting a shadow over the room as Deka and the Elf grappled with the realization that the path ahead was laden with difficulties and uncertainties.

The Elf, sensing Deka's inner turmoil, reached out and

gently touched her shoulder, a gesture of solace. Speaking in a quiet tone, he offered, "Maybe with time, people will forget, or they won't want to remember." Deka, lost in her thoughts, lifted her head to meet the Elf's gaze, contemplating the wisdom embedded in his words.

It was a subtle realization that altering the fabric of people's memories might not be the only path forward. Instead of forcibly changing the past, allowing time and the natural progression of people's lives to shape their memories could be a more prudent and compassionate choice. Deka, absorbing the Elf's perspective, found a measure of relief in the possibility that, with time, the impact of Çarh's manifestation of Sûr might fade into the recesses of memory, becoming a distant echo rather than an intrusive presence. The weight of their shared dilemma began to lift as they considered the potential for healing through the passage of time.

Deka's thoughts remained clouded and uncertain, with the persistent fear of people witnessing Sûr lingering within her. Yet, the Elf's idea introduced a glimmer of relief. The notion that time might possess a healing power, gradually easing the impact of Çarh's manifestation of Sûr, sparked a sense of hope within her. While the fear still resided somewhere in the depths of her consciousness, the prospect of a return to normalcy through the passage of time offered a reassuring possibility. In the quiet contemplation of their shared space, Deka found solace in the belief that, with time, the scars of the recent events might fade, and a sense of equilibrium could be restored.

In the early morning light, a knock on the door stirred Çarh from his drowsy state. With sleepy eyes, he approached the door and discovered their neighbour, Aunt Fatma, waiting outside. As Çarh opened the door, he closed his eyes momentarily, welcoming the gentle touch of sunlight on his face. He took a deep breath, allowing the fresh morning breeze to invigorate his tired body.

Aunt Fatma, casting a curious glance at Çarh, sensed that something might be amiss. Learning about Çarh's troubled night, concern etched her features. Çarh's somewhat hooded demeanour as he opened the door hinted at an underlying issue. Aunt Fatma's worries eased when Çarh, fatigued and exhausted, expressed his desire to rest.

Despite Çarh's reassurance, Aunt Fatma, still curious, insisted on asking questions. The recent events with the hooded man and the revelation of Sûr lingered in Çarh's mind, making the prospect of sharing his troubles with someone else feel daunting. Aunt Fatma inquired about how she could help him relax, and Çarh, grateful for her concern, expressed a need for solitude. As he closed the door, Aunt Fatma, lingering with lingering concern, wondered about the cause of Çarh's distress. Respecting his wish for privacy, she left the house quietly, leaving Çarh to grapple with the weight of recent events in the solace of his own thoughts.

As Çarh closed the door, a heavy sigh escaped him, and a rebellion brewed within his thoughts. "I can't live like this," he pondered, a yearning for the familiarity of his old life washing over him. The desire for safety and the longing to revert to a time before the manifestation of Sûr weighed heavily on his mind. While the notion of casting a spell to conceal Sûr once more held a certain allure, Çarh recognized that the real problem ran deeper.

The true challenge lay in overcoming the fears that gripped him from within and adapting to the complexities of this new reality. It wasn't merely about concealing the external manifestations but addressing the internal turmoil. As Çarh grappled with these thoughts, he knew that embracing this altered existence required a resilience that transcended magical concealment. It entailed confronting the fears head-on and finding a way to coexist with the changes that had unfolded, ultimately sculpting a new sense of normalcy in the wake of the unexpected events.

In a moment of reflection, Çarh came to a sobering realization – his past life, the one where Sûr remained hidden and his existence unaffected, was no longer attainable. The temporary solutions of concealing Sûr once more, altering people's memories, or even erasing his own recollections were only superficial remedies. The fundamental truth lingered: Sûr had been exposed, witnessed by all, and this revelation marked an irreversible change in Çarh's life.

Acceptance of this newfound reality became a crucial step for Çarh. The awareness that attempting to revert to the past was futile compelled him to confront the altered course of his existence. The challenge now lay in navigating this changed landscape, finding a way to coexist with the consequences of Sûr's revelation, and sculpting a new path forward in a world where the unknown had become known.

Acknowledging the challenges ahead, Çarh, Deka, and the Elf united in a shared quest to navigate the complexities of this altered reality. The collective effort aimed not just at finding a solution but at fostering understanding and acceptance of Sûr among the people they encountered. The prospect of working together buoyed Çarh's spirits, instilling a sense of encouragement.

Understanding that feeling safe again required confronting and overcoming his own fears, Çarh embraced this necessary step on the journey ahead. The willingness to face the unknown and make peace with the changes in his life marked a pivotal moment. Prepared to turn a new leaf, Çarh stood ready to embark on a fresh start, eager to chart a new path forward alongside Deka and the Elf.

The unexpected words tumbled out of Çarh's mouth, surprising even himself. "I actually turned into that hooded man I saw," he admitted. The revelation unsettled him, casting a shadow of doubt on his own identity and shaking the foundations of his confidence.

Caught in contemplation, Çarh grappled with the realization that, much like the peculiarity he had observed in the hooded man before, he had transformed into that very figure. A wave of uncertainty washed over him as he considered the possibility that others might also notice this change in him. Deka's suggestion of openness, letting Sûr be known, crept into his thoughts. The idea that people needed to confront the reality of Sûr and that he, in turn, would have to face his fears, seemed like a plausible path. However, the prospect frightened him, and a yearning to return to the familiarity of his old life lingered within him. The dichotomy between facing the truth and clinging to the past created a turbulent inner struggle for Çarh.

Observing Çarh's inner turmoil, Deka sensed the weight of his internal conflict and approached him with understanding. Placing a comforting hand on Çarh's shoulder, she offered her support. "Çarh," she spoke gently, "Perhaps facing this change could be a way to discover your true self. You must accept the power within and deal with your fears."

Çarh, enveloped in his thoughts, pondered Deka's words. The internal battle between the familiarity of the past and the daunting prospect of embracing the unknown waged within him. Accepting that the world he once knew had changed proved to be a challenging hurdle, yet a glimmer of truth resonated in Deka's counsel. The path forward demanded a confrontation with the essence of who he had become, a journey towards self-discovery, and an acknowledgment of the power that resided within. As Çarh grappled with these profound considerations, the echoes of change reverberated, hinting at the transformative potential that lay ahead.

In a moment of determination, Çarh turned to Deka with gratitude and drew a deep breath. "Yes," he declared with resolve, "I am ready to accept myself and embrace the new reality that comes with change. I will take steps to discover the power within me and confront my fears." Deka, beaming with support, smiled at Çarh's commitment. A journey of internal transformation and self-discovery lay ahead for them.

Deka's smile became a beacon of hope and encouragement for Çarh as they ventured into this path of change. The presence of Nail still loomed outside, a persistent threat disrupting their peace. Acknowledging this reality, they both recognized the need to further empower themselves in order to face the challenges ahead.

United in purpose, Çarh and Deka set forth on a journey of self-acceptance, embracing the transformations that awaited them. The interconnected threads of their internal transformation and the looming presence of Nail hinted at a narrative yet to unfold, where strength, resilience, and self-discovery would be their guiding lights.

United in purpose, Çarh and Deka devised a plan to track Nail and unravel the mysteries of his intentions. Recognizing the significance of their internal transformations, they committed to simultaneously focusing on overcoming their fears and uncertainties, finding the strength needed to confront Nail.

Embarking on their pursuit of Nail, they walked the streets together, following the trail left by this lingering threat. The openness of Sûr marked them in the eyes of the public, drawing glances from those around them. Some onlookers expressed surprise, while others observed with curiosity. Undeterred by the attention, Çarh and Deka pressed forward, resolute in their purpose.

Amidst the gaze of curious bystanders, Çarh and Deka forged ahead, unwavering in their determination to face both external threats and the internal challenges of transformation.

As Çarh and Deka traced Nail's elusive trail, their journey took them to various places, each locale serving as a backdrop for events that prompted them to delve into deeper contemplation. This pursuit of Nail proved to be more than a mere external quest; it became an opportunity for them to explore the intricate landscapes of their inner worlds. As they faced challenges along the way, Çarh and Deka endeavoured to push their limits, their experiences serving as catalysts for personal growth.

While following the traces left by Nail, they uncovered numerous clues that hinted at his true intentions. A hidden connection seemed to intertwine their paths, and both Çarh and Deka were convinced that Nail was intricately linked to past events.

In their relentless pursuit, Çarh and Deka grew more convinced that Nail held a profound connection to past events. A breakthrough occurred for Çarh as he began to unravel the mysteries within his own mind. The realization that the hooded man from his memories was, in fact, himself brought a newfound clarity. Memories unfolded like a tapestry, revealing the truth as Çarh replayed the moment he was attacked. It became evident that Nail was one of those hooded figures involved in the past.

This revelation triggered a seismic shift in Çarh's inner world. Confronting his hidden identity proved to be a challenging and transformative process. The events of that fateful day now existed as fragmented pieces in his mind. On one side, he grappled with the recollection of the hooded man's attack, while on the other, he pondered the mysterious presence of Nail. Unravelling the intricate connection between these two aspects became imperative for Çarh to uncover the complete truth that lay concealed within the depths of his past.

Recognizing Çarh's internal struggle, Deka approached him with empathy. Placing her hand warmly on Çarh's, she spoke in a calm tone, "Çarh, we can overcome this. Accepting the truth within you will unleash your strength. Discovering who Nail is, is part of this journey. Together, we can succeed."

Çarh found solace in Deka's reassuring words. United in purpose, they pressed on in their pursuit of Nail, each step bringing them closer to the darkness within Çarh. The encounter with Nail held the potential not only for relief but also to illuminate the shadows shrouding past events. Trusting in their shared strength and determination, Çarh and Deka faced the challenges of their journey with resilience, prepared to confront the truths that awaited them in the depths of their shared history.

As Çarh delved deeper into the puzzle of past events, the pieces slowly started to come together. Motivated by the power and determination within him, he sought to comprehend the reasons and purpose behind Nail's attack. Dark connections and enigmatic motives began to surface, creating a puzzle that demanded solving.

Gradually, clarity emerged. Çarh started to grasp the motivations and intentions behind Nail's assault. Deka contributed to this understanding by revealing that Nail was a collector, specifically gathering Sûrs. A memory stirred in Çarh's mind, recalling an encounter with Nail in his mysterious shop. While he had initially felt a sense of familiarity, he realised that the sensation was not from his own memories but from the presence of other Sûrs within Nail's collection. The revelation brought them one step closer to unravelling the mysteries that surrounded Nail and the shared history of Sûrs.

The memory of Nail's mysterious shop became more vivid in Çarh's mind. It was no ordinary establishment; instead, it was a repository of artifacts collected from the depths of Sûr. Objects resonating with powerful energies intrigued visitors, and Çarh recalled the dark atmosphere that pervaded the moment. Now, an opportunity presented itself to unravel the secrets concealed within that enigmatic shop.

With a shared resolve, Çarh and Deka proceeded toward Nail's mysterious establishment. Along the way, they observed that people still held a keen interest in Çarh's transformation, their curiosity undiminished. Rather than being deterred by the attention, this situation served to strengthen Çarh's determination.

As Çarh and Deka stepped into Nail's shop, the atmosphere underwent a sudden and dramatic transformation. Drawn into a dark vortex, they found themselves surrounded by artifacts that seemed to reflect energies from different dimensions. The Sûr within Çarh stirred, awakening in connection with the mysterious aura of the shop.

Amidst the unsettling ambiance, Çarh began to piece together the significance of Nail's collection. It dawned on him that this assortment of artifacts was not a random assembly but part of a larger plan. Nail's intention was clear – to accumulate and control the power of Sûrs. By gathering potent artifacts, Nail served his dark ambitions, seeking to harness the energy emanating from the Sûrs.

In a moment of revelation, Çarh understood that Nail was a collector of Sûrs, attempting to control and manipulate their energy through the accumulation of powerful artifacts. This realization fuelled a renewed determination within Çarh. His resolve solidified as he vowed to thwart Nail's sinister purpose and safeguard the delicate balance of Sûr from being exploited for dark ambitions.

As the revelations unfolded in Nail's mysterious shop, Deka experienced a revelation of her own. She now better understood the significance of the necklace Nail coveted. This precious ornament held ties to Deka's past and harboured a special power within. Nail's interest in the necklace was driven by a desire to access and harness Deka's unique abilities. However, hesitant to divulge this truth to Çarh, Deka grappled with the weight of this secret.

Amidst the artifacts and revelations, Nail's men quietly approached Çarh and Deka. The tension in the air escalated as Nail, scrutinizing them with his piercing gaze, inquired, "Whom were you looking at?" Despite the rising tension, both Çarh and Deka chose to remain silent. Avoiding direct eye contact, they calmly started moving away from Nail's men, navigating the precarious situation with a shared determination to keep their secrets guarded. The air hung heavy with unspoken truths and the imminent threat that loomed within Nail's enigmatic domain.

While on their way home, Çarh and Deka found their minds swirling with different thoughts. Çarh harboured concerns that Nail's men might have grown suspicious, fearing that Nail himself could be watching and setting traps. A pervasive sense of danger lingered, and Çarh felt they were not safe; a threat could emerge at any moment.

In contrast, Deka was engrossed in her internal musings. Recognizing the need for more information to unravel Nail's intentions and thwart his plans, she pondered how her own unique power could stand against Nail's malicious designs.

Despite the divergence in their thoughts, both Çarh and Deka converged on one crucial point: they needed to act together to halt Nail's machinations. Nail's insatiable desire to control power posed a significant threat to the delicate balance of Sûr. By exposing Nail's true purpose and fortifying themselves, they believed they could resist this imminent threat and safeguard the equilibrium of Sûr. The path ahead was fraught with challenges, but their shared determination bound them together in a quest to confront the impending dangers and unveil the mysteries that surrounded Nail's dark ambitions.

As Çarh and Deka approached their home, a palpable silence enveloped their surroundings. The weight of their shared mission hung in the air, intensifying their focus. Upon entering their dwelling, Çarh and Deka gathered in a dimly lit room, their determination casting a glow that surpassed the subdued lighting.

In the quietude, Çarh gently approached Deka, holding her hand with warmth. Speaking in a calm voice, he addressed her, "Deka, Nail's men looked at us suspiciously. I know Nail and his men are closely watching. We must be more careful from now on," conveying a shared understanding of the heightened danger that surrounded them. The dimly illuminated room bore witness to their shared commitment and the resolve to navigate the impending challenges with

Sûr

caution and unity.

Upon Nail's arrival at the shop, his men promptly informed him of Çarh and Deka's presence. Furious that his men hadn't reported earlier, Nail angrily questioned them, "Why didn't you tell me earlier? How did you let them escape?" The fear-filled eyes of Nail's men darted between each other, and trembling in the face of Nail's anger, they remained silent. An oppressive silence hung in the air, exacerbating Nail's frustration as he seemed infuriated by his men's perceived incompetence.

"How could you not follow them?" Nail shouted. "Go after them immediately and find out where they went. We must not lose their trail!" With Nail's command, his men hastily exited the shop, determined to pursue Çarh and Deka. Left alone in the shop, Nail struggled to restrain his anger, his mind abuzz with complex thoughts and plans.

A heavy silence settled over the shop once again. While his men were in pursuit of Çarh and Deka, Nail remained still, resolute in his decision to wait for them to execute his dark intentions. Following the duo would not only advance Nail's plans but also aid in eliminating any obstacles that dared to stand in their path. The air was thick with tension as Nail bided his time, driven by a malevolent determination to see his sinister designs through.

As Nail surveyed the old Sûrs in the shop, he felt the rise of power within him. The significance of these artifacts for controlling his power and directing the energy of Sûr was immense. Nail's intention was clear – to seize control of Sûr with the help of these potent artifacts and achieve his nefarious purpose. However, one crucial object still eluded him – the necklace, a missing piece essential for his dark designs to come to fruition. The quest for this elusive object added a layer of urgency and anticipation to Nail's already ominous intentions.

Nail's men executed their duties with meticulous precision. Concealed strategically in the vicinity of houses, they observed every move of Çarh and Deka. Whenever the duo left their residence, Nail's men shadowed their every step, ensuring to report their movements back to Nail promptly.

Slinking silently among the shadows, the men took care to record every detail, ensuring they never lost sight of their targets. Their mission was to be vigilant and unyielding, tracking Çarh and Deka relentlessly to provide unwavering support for Nail's unfolding plans.

Regularly reporting developments to Nail, his men documented intricate details – ranging from the locations visited by Çarh and Deka to the individuals they conversed with. This information, conveyed to Nail, became the foundation upon which he laid out his calculated and malevolent next steps. The seamless coordination of Nail's men added an extra layer of menace to the unfolding events, as they served as the watchful eyes feeding crucial information to their dark and determined master.

Çarh couldn't shake the internal awareness that he was being watched. A lingering sense that his every step was shadowed had settled within him, prompting him to adopt a facade of normalcy with careful precision. In his attempts to appear unaffected, Çarh meticulously calculated each move, almost staging a performance to conceal his internal concerns.

Acknowledging the constant surveillance behind his eyes, Çarh approached each day with heightened caution. Engaging in routine tasks, he portrayed an image of an ordinary day, attempting to suppress his inner anxieties. Developing coping mechanisms to endure the pervasive feeling of being watched, Çarh transformed into a meticulous observer of his surroundings. The persistent sense of scrutiny compelled him to scrutinize people and events more attentively, delicately balancing his words and actions to conceal his true feelings. This internal struggle manifested as a delicate dance between authenticity and concealment, as Çarh grappled with the weight of the constant gaze upon him.

The persistent reality of being silently watched created a profound unease in Çarh's soul. The awareness of constant scrutiny cast him into a metaphorical spotlight, and the weight of potential consequences for any misstep loomed over him. Consequently, Çarh meticulously controlled every detail of his existence, from his outward appearance to the nuances of his facial expressions, diligently avoiding actions that might attract unwanted attention.

Yet, as Çarh turned the corner of the street, he was confronted with an unforeseen tableau. Nail's men stood directly in his path. A sudden pause gripped Çarh as uncertainty loomed. The men, too, appeared taken aback, perhaps anticipating Çarh's escape or surrender. However, propelled by unexpected determination, Çarh swiftly attempted to flee, and the men, equally resolute, gave chase in pursuit of their elusive target. The unexpected encounter plunged Çarh into a tense and precarious situation, where the delicate balance of control he had strived to maintain was now hanging by a thread.

As Çarh navigated through several streets, the realization struck him that the path he had chosen was a dead-end. Turning back with a quickened pace and a panting breath, he found Nail's men standing resolutely in his way. A surge of fear engulfed him, but within that fear, a dormant inner strength began to awaken. In a sudden revelation, Çarh recognized the latent power residing within him and made the conscious decision to harness it.

With a voice still trembling from fear, Çarh confronted the looming threat, asking, "What do you want from me?" The men, maintaining an unsettling silence, continued to advance towards him. As the fear inside Çarh intensified, he briefly succumbed to despair. However, driven by instinct, he instinctively triggered the power within him.

A surge of energy emanated from Çarh, unfolding like a shockwave radiating from his body. The force propelled the men backward, causing a resounding impact as they crumpled to the ground. The air resonated with the echoes of their agonizing groans. In that critical moment, Çarh had tapped into his inner strength, wielding it as a shield to protect himself from the encroaching danger. The unexpected display of power marked a transformative juncture for Çarh, revealing the untapped potential that lay within him.

The unexpected revelation of his own power left Çarh himself in a state of surprise. This marked the first time he truly experienced the intensity of his latent potential. The realization of the power and energy coursing through his body elicited a complex blend of fear and newfound self-confidence.

As Çarh observed the motionless bodies of the men on the ground, an unusual and perplexing scene unfolded. Their forms appeared frozen, as if they had transitioned into a vegetative state. His gaze lingered in astonishment, and then, to his bewilderment, a cat and a mouse approached the incapacitated men, engaging in what seemed to be a form of communication. It was a surreal and inexplicable tableau, leaving Çarh grappling with the incomprehensible nature of the events transpiring before him.

In the aftermath of the peculiar events, the Elf materialized, his curiosity piqued by the unfolding scenario.

Inquisitive about the unexpected turn of events, the Elf queried Çarh, who, in turn, explained that he had used his inner strength to render the men powerless but remained uncertain about the nature of the occurrence. The Elf provided an explanation that left Çarh both intrigued and bewildered. According to the Elf, Çarh possessed the extraordinary ability to perform soul transitions, allowing him to transfer the souls of living beings. In this instance, Çarh had unwittingly transferred the souls of the two men to the nearest living creatures – the cat and the mouse.

The revelation of these newfound powers sent Çarh into a deep shock. Coming to terms with these extraordinary abilities presented a challenging process, forcing him to confront the reality of his own identity and purpose. The existence of capabilities like soul transitions and soul transfers raised profound questions about Çarh's place in the intricate tapestry of existence.

The Elf, after restoring Nail's men to their original state on the ground and manipulating the memories of those who witnessed the incident, turned toward Çarh, reassuring him with the words, "No need to worry. I've taken care of everything." While Çarh exchanged a look of understanding with the Elf, a captivating expression of intrigue lingered on his face.

Recognizing Çarh's astonishment, the Elf responded with empathy, acknowledging that these newfound discoveries could be overwhelming. He explained that Çarh's inner journey would now deepen even further, delving into uncharted territories of fear, uncertainty, curiosity, and the desire to explore his inner power and potential.

The awakening of Çarh's inner power instilled in him a profound sense of strength. The abilities of soul transition and soul transfer positioned him as a potent force within the vast expanse of the universe. This revelation pushed the boundaries of Çarh's perceived limitations, unlocking doors to possibilities that were previously unimaginable.

CHAPTER 18
TRUTH

Çarh hurriedly shared the recent events with Deka upon returning home. He described how Nail's men had their souls transferred to other beings, emphasizing the impact it had on him. Deka, acknowledging Çarh's potent witch abilities, couldn't conceal her astonishment at the sudden surge of power displayed in this incident.

Listening to Çarh's account, Deka found herself in a state of shock and amazement. Though she had always been aware of Çarh's magical prowess during their time together, witnessing the raw potency and consequential effects of his power left her genuinely taken aback. The explosive manifestation of Çarh's abilities, particularly his capacity to transfer the souls of other beings, raised a multitude of questions in Deka's mind.

Approaching Çarh, Deka expressed her sincere willingness to understand. She conveyed her desire to jointly unravel the mystery and comprehend Çarh's powers. With genuine concern, she advised him to exercise caution and learn to control his abilities. Despite Deka's attempts to console and alleviate his concerns, Çarh could discern the lingering worry in her eyes. It was in that moment that he vividly realised the truly frightening potential of his actions.

Though grateful for Deka's words of hope, Çarh managed a smile, yet the persistent fear within him endured. As he embarked on this new path, Çarh acknowledged the significant responsibility he bore – one that could profoundly impact both himself and those around him. Deka's concerns, though appreciated, didn't entirely quell Çarh's internal turmoil and anxiety.

At this pivotal juncture, Çarh grasped the paramount importance of striving to further develop himself and master control over his powers. Determined to confront his internal darkness, he acknowledged the need for careful and conscientious use of his abilities. With unwavering resolve, he committed to facing and overcoming his own fears.

In an effort to alleviate Çarh's internal distress and shift the atmosphere, Deka changed the subject. "So, Nail's men followed you, huh?" she remarked. Çarh, grateful for her understanding, expressed his thanks and took a deep breath. He seized this opportunity to temporarily set aside the intense thoughts swirling in his mind.

As Deka spoke about Nail's men, it raised questions in Çarh's mind. He pondered, "Why are they following me? What could Nail have planned for me beyond what I already know?" Suddenly, Çarh felt a renewed sense of insecurity, as the exact intentions of Nail's men remained unclear.

Deka continued, seemingly attuned to Çarh's thoughts, aiming to alleviate his concerns. "Perhaps Nail just wants to observe you. Maybe he has some suspicions about you." Çarh listened carefully to Deka's words, finding the theory plausible. The idea that Nail might seek to gather more information about him opened a new window in Çarh's mind.

However, Çarh couldn't dismiss the possibility that this situation posed a threat to him. It was impossible for him to relax without understanding Nail's intentions. Çarh told Deka that he wanted to ponder this further and formulate a plan to lose the trail of Nail's men.

With a concerned expression, Deka looked at Çarh and said, "Yes, you're right. It's important for Nail to follow us, and we need to understand his intentions. We should act together and combine our powers."

Curiously, Çarh asked Deka what they could do, hoping to discover a new path or ability. Thoughtfully turning to him, Deka paused for a moment before sharing a revelation, "In my past lives, I know that Sögrés, belonging to the Cépfiarexen witch ancestry, could freely travel by transferring their souls to the living beings they desired."

Surprise appeared on Çarh's face as this information offered him a completely new perspective.

Deka continued, "For example, you can fly by entering the body of a bird or wander in the body of a cat. These abilities stem from the Sögrés connection to nature and, along with soul transfer, bring a new experience and freedom." Çarh listened with admiration to Deka's words. This newly discovered information opened the doors to a magical world for him.

While listening carefully to Deka's explanations, Çarh felt a mix of excitement and uncertainty. The ability of soul transfer was both liberating and a power that required responsibility. However, using this ability to escape the surveillance of Nail's men and uncover the truth could give

Çarh strength and an advantage.

Çarh felt a surge of excitement within. The thrill of this new knowledge made him feel like he could soar into the skies. He instantly wanted to try this ability; he could feel the excitement of the unexplored power within him.

Expressing his excitement through his eyes, Çarh turned to Deka and said, "I should try this ability without further delay." Deka, sharing his enthusiasm with a smile, readily approved, and they swiftly began the necessary preparations. Together, they entered a room quietly. Standing at the centre, they tuned into the energy surrounding them. Çarh honed his focus on locating the source of his power and took a deep breath. Calming his mind, he began to sense the vibrations of his soul.

In the role of a researcher navigating his inner world, Çarh endeavoured to control and direct the energy. Extending his hands, he felt a moment of transcendence, as if surpassing the confines of his body. His soul spread outward, enveloping, and surrounding everything in its ethereal embrace.

Closing his eyes slightly, Çarh cantered his focus on the form of a bird. Drawing a deep breath to immerse himself within the avian essence, he fortified the longing to transcend. Within his mind's eye, he vividly painted the tapestry of a bird's freedom – the majestic power of wings slicing through the air and the gentle caress of the wind against feathers.

Çarh noticed a bird perched just above the apartment and felt an irresistible pull towards it. When he opened his eyes again, he was astonished to find himself within the body of that very bird. Instantly, he stretched his wings, eager to take flight. However, grappling with the unfamiliarity of the avian form, he soon realised the challenge of controlling this newfound body. Determinedly, he made a concerted effort to decipher the intricacies of wing movements, striving to understand which actions would propel him into the air.

Peering down from the apartment, he experienced a twinge of anxiety stemming from the height below. Having never taken flight before, this entirely new experience overwhelmed him. Yet, observing the graceful freedom of other birds soaring through the skies bolstered his courage. Gathering his resolve, he tentatively began to flap his wings, determined to embrace the uncharted realm of flight.

Initially, he grappled with the challenge of controlling his wings, but with unwavering determination and a meticulous balance of movements, he started to adapt to the rhythm of his newfound appendages. Synchronizing with the natural ebb and flow of his wings, assisted by a gentle breeze, he began to ascend gradually. Gliding with ease into the open sky, a profound sensation of freedom enveloped him, marking the triumphant culmination of his efforts.

Basking in the newfound sense of freedom and weightlessness that the avian experience bestowed upon him, Çarh observed the world from an entirely different perspective. The view from above served as a poignant reminder of the enchantment inherent in nature, underscoring his role as a minuscule component within the vast expanse of the universe. The gentle symphony of the wind echoed in his ears as he gracefully traversed through the clouds, venturing towards the infinite horizon.

Beyond confining himself to the transformation into the body of a bird, Çarh sensed an untapped reservoir of power within him and boldly pushed against the boundaries of the known world. This transformative experience heightened his awareness of untapped potential residing within, intensifying his insatiable hunger for future discoveries.

Deka stood alongside Çarh, observing him with profound admiration. A smile of excitement adorned her face as she witnessed the transformation of her friend who had unearthed a latent ability. Together, they had ventured into the uncharted territories of this new world, taking a collective step towards unravelling its hidden secrets.

As Çarh emerged from the avian experience, he gradually reconnected with the reality of the room. Opening his eyes, a radiant smile of immense joy adorned his face, signifying the embrace of profound change and discovery within himself. With the unlocking of a new door on his inner journey, he now wielded the strength required to confront Nail's men.

Observing the happiness on Çarh's face, Deka approached him with genuine joy. "It was an incredible experience!" he exclaimed excitedly. "This ability grants you immense power and freedom."

Approaching Deka, Çarh placed a friendly hand on her shoulder. "Indeed, Deka, it was a truly incredible experience. Now, I possess greater strength against Nail's men, and together, we can shape our own destiny."

Watching Çarh's exhilarating experience of flying as a bird, Deka was filled with genuine joy. His success planted a seed of hope in her heart. Aware that time was swiftly slipping away, and the threat of Nail loomed larger with each passing moment, she recognized the critical importance of hastening the process of returning to her true self.

Çarh retained the vivid memory of the bird's perspective in his mind. The excitement of that moment and the lingering sense of freedom continued to circulate within him. The weightless sensation of soaring in the sky as a bird had granted him a unique perspective on the world.

Sûr

This experience served as a poignant reminder to Çarh that he possessed the potential to transcend the confines of an ordinary human. It hinted at the possibility of pushing the limits of the powers inherited from his witch ancestry and undergoing transformative changes. For Çarh, this profound experience stood as compelling evidence that he held the power to reshape reality itself.

The tranquillity of the moment was abruptly shattered by the ringing of the phone, compelling Deka to abruptly depart. Çarh felt a twinge of unease at Deka's sudden exit, as she had always been a steadfast life companion. Contemplating how to navigate these newfound powers without her support, Çarh recognized the necessity of her hasty departure due to the urgent phone call. Reluctantly, he accepted that being alone was the only option at the moment.

Despite Deka's warnings, Çarh found himself unable to suppress the yearning for freedom and transformation within. As he retreated to the bedroom to rest his fatigued body, the sensation of being in the bird's body replayed repeatedly in his mind. Closing his eyes, he could vividly feel the powerful flapping of wings, the embrace of the wind enveloping his body, and the exhilarating sensation of soaring high above.

As Çarh soared through the skies like a bird, he experienced a profound detachment from the real world. Gazing down from above, houses, streets, and people appeared as mere tiny dots. The pervasive sensation of weightlessness, brought by gliding through the sky, reverberated in Çarh's inner world. Thoughts inundated his mind, suggesting the possibility of surpassing his own limits and evolving into a being beyond the realms of imagination.

Yet, as Çarh continued to relive these experiences repeatedly, the cautions from Deka appeared to fade into the background. Even before succumbing to sleep, he found solace in the lingering sensation of soaring as a bird, even while lying in bed. As he surrendered to the embrace of sleep, he envisioned himself flying as a bird in the realms of his dreams.

The passion burning within Çarh, coupled with the exhilaration of soaring freely like a bird, proved too potent to be suppressed. Now, he drifted into sleep with a liberated spirit, unburdened by thoughts of the struggles and responsibilities that tomorrow might unveil.

Deka returned home earlier than expected, her work not taking as long as she had anticipated. Despite feeling a bit tired, she entered with a sense of excitement. Discovering Çarh deeply asleep, she observed him silently for a while. Her attention then shifted to the Elf in the living room, who seemed to be patiently waiting for her.

Deka approached the Elf, engaging in a discussion about Çarh's experiences with him. Both recognized the profound significance of this journey for Çarh and acknowledged the remarkable progress he had achieved. Deka conveyed her pride in witnessing the rapid and impressive transformation within Çarh. The Elf, in turn, expressed his belief that Çarh was now fully prepared for what lay ahead.

As the conversation unfolded, a smile graced Deka's face. She felt a profound sense of pride in Çarh's courage and newfound strength. Now, they stood side by side on the precipice of a great mission. The Elf, drawing upon his wisdom and experience, reassured Deka that he would guide Çarh and steadfastly be there for him.

In response to Deka's inquiry about revealing the truth to Çarh, the Elf responded with careful consideration. The Elf noted that Çarh's internal transformation process had not reached completion, and there remained more information to impart. He emphasized the necessity for Çarh to fully comprehend and wield his power. The Elf also highlighted the importance of taking additional time to uncover Nail's true intentions. He added that Çarh would learn the details when the timing was deemed right.

Deka comprehended the Elf's words, yet a sense of concern and indecision welled up within her. Her conviction that Çarh needed to be acquainted with the truth stemmed from her past experiences; she was determined to shield him from a similar fate. However, the Elf's wise counsel, particularly his insistence on the importance of timing, left Deka grappling with a dilemma.

Turning to the Elf, Deka shared her thoughts. "Maybe you're right," she began. "But I believe Çarh needs to be aware of this truth. He has to learn to control the power within him and find harmony with it. If we don't guide him at the right time and in the right way, there's a risk he might veer onto the wrong paths on his own."

The Elf listened attentively and nodded thoughtfully. "You know I understand," the Elf replied, "but it might be risky for now. Çarh needs time and guidance to fully control his powers. Let's allow Sûr to grow without restraint and protection."

Though Deka still harboured concerns, she acknowledged and appreciated the Elf's logical and sensible approach. Contemplating Çarh's future, she opted to remain silent for the time being, placing her trust in the concept of the right time. Deka believed that Çarh would learn the truth when he was truly ready.

The Elf's words had a profound impact on Deka. She found herself once again contemplating the immense potential within Çarh's power. Coupled with the Elf's warning, her concerns intensified. The prospect of Çarh learning the truth loomed, and with it, the realization that he would confront an uncontrollable power. They were on the precipice of facing the reality of an irreversible path.

The Elf's words sent a shiver down Deka's spine. The potential danger posed by Çarh and the escalating power of Sûr painted a frightening reality for both of them. The worry etched on Deka's face deepened.

The Elf continued in silence, "When he confronts the truth, Çarh's power will be unleashed. And if he fails to control this power, it could lead to disastrous consequences. At that point, once set in motion, it becomes unstoppable."

The Elf took a deep breath and began recounting the details of the incident in Beirut to Deka. "Three years ago, on August 4, 2020, a dreadful event unfolded when Sögré, the previous representative of the witch ancestry, discovered the truth," the Elf continued solemnly. "Unable to control her power, Sögré triggered a catastrophic disaster. The souls of all living beings within a 1.5-2-kilometer radius of Beirut were transferred."

Deka listened to the Elf's account with astonishment. The scale and effects of the incident horrified her. While she recalled the event, she was unaware that it had been caused by a Sögré. The realization that no one would want a repetition of such a tragedy weighed heavily on her.

The Elf continued, his tone grave, "When dealing with powers of such magnitude, the importance of control cannot be overstated. If Çarh progresses without fully comprehending the power within him and learning to control it, we risk facing a similar event to the horrific incident in the past."

A blend of worry and determination etched itself onto Deka's face. "That's why," she said, "it is crucial to patiently await Çarh's understanding of the truth and teach him the correct usage of his power. We must guide him, explaining the potential dangers when the time is right. But for now, we must allow him the freedom to explore and experience the full extent of his newfound abilities."

Deka found herself in a state of inner turmoil. While she yearned to support Çarh's burgeoning potential and facilitate his understanding of his newfound power, she couldn't ignore the warnings voiced by the Elf. The echoes of past tragedies resonated vividly in her memories, and the fear of Çarh suffering a similar fate weighed heavily on her heart.

A moment of contemplative silence enveloped them. Finally, Deka reached a decision and turned to the Elf, expressing, "Perhaps Çarh needs more time to grasp the truth. Let's persist in guiding him, aiding his understanding of his power. We'll patiently wait for the opportune moment as Sûr grows within him."

The Elf, understandingly acknowledging Deka's words, responded, "You are doing the right thing. Let's persist in guiding Çarh to harness and control his power. The truth can be revealed at the appropriate time. Nevertheless, we must exercise caution and tread carefully in every step of this process."

In silent contemplation, Deka weighed a myriad of questions swirling in her mind. Could Çarh bear the weighty responsibility accompanying this immense power? Might it spark power struggles and conflicts among people? The Elf's concerns echoed, resonating with a note of validity. Still, Deka held firm to the belief that a complete understanding of Çarh would only emerge once he grasped the truth — a fundamental element defining his identity and potential.

The Elf's warning intensified the complex emotions

within Deka. Caught between the conflicting desires to protect and conceal Çarh, and the impulse to reveal the truth and offer support, she found herself in a delicate balance. Recognizing that both paths required careful consideration, they concluded that more time was needed to determine the right moment and approach for the revelation.

Çarh, freshly awakened and making his way from his room to the living room, observed Deka and the Elf engrossed in a serious conversation. The gravity of their tones and the intensity of their facial expressions hinted at the discussion's importance. Intrigued, he approached with quiet steps, silently joining them to discreetly overhear their conversation.

Deka's voice resonated clearly, "I believe Çarh needs to know the truth. As this power continues to grow, controlling it will become increasingly challenging. To prevent a repetition of past disasters, we must disclose the truth to him."

The Elf's response hinted at deep contemplation. "Yes, but the timing is crucial. If Çarh learns the truth before comprehending and mastering the control of his power, we might set him on an irreversible path. It could lead to potentially dangerous consequences."

Filled with complex emotions upon hearing this, Çarh experienced a mixture of curiosity and anxiety. Despite his yearning to uncover the truth, the gravity and caution in Elf's words prompted him to ponder the potential consequences. Choosing to remain silent for the moment, he continued moving towards the living room, absorbing the weight of the unfolding discussion.

However, the fire of curiosity within him did not wane. Çarh sensed that his desire to learn the truth about his journey and power was intensifying. He had unlocked the doors to a world brimming with uncertainty and mystery, and the urge to step through that door proved too compelling for him to stand still.

Approaching the living room with silent steps, Çarh harboured a mixture of excitement and anticipation in his heart. Eager to uncover the topic of Deka and the Elf's conversation, he couldn't shake the awareness of the potential dangers he carried within himself.

As Çarh entered the room, he found Deka and the Elf turning towards him with smiles. The expressions on their faces bore traces of the secrets and weighty conversations they had engaged in. Çarh sensed that the opportune moment for revelation had not arrived, and in response, he offered a smile, attempting to conceal his inner curiosity.

As Çarh approached Deka and the Elf, he spoke with great calmness and determination. "So, what do we do now? How do we confront Nail?" he inquired, his eyes reflecting a mixture of resolve and uncertainty.

Deka took a deep breath and spoke thoughtfully, "To stand against Nail, we must adopt a strategic approach. Initially, we need to gain a complete understanding of our power and master its control. This will afford us greater flexibility and capability. Subsequently, we must closely observe Nail's movements, identifying his weaknesses. Our goal is to devise a comprehensive plan capable of overcoming his formidable power."

The Elf listened silently, gathering his thoughts. "Yes, Deka is right. Strength is essential, but wisdom in our actions is equally crucial. We require time to decipher Nail's plans and gain a strategic advantage over him. As we unravel the mysteries of our own power, we should aim to surprise Nail, placing him in a situation he is not accustomed to."

As Çarh attentively listened to Deka and the Elf, he

discerned a recurring theme in their words: waiting. Intrigued, he couldn't help but wonder what exactly they were waiting for. This emphasis on patience echoed in their previous conversations as well. "There is a constant emphasis on waiting," he mused. Amid these thoughts, he began to realise the existence of something unknown to him. What could it be?

Within Çarh, curiosity and excitement intertwined. The sense of power and freedom derived from past experiences compelled him to take action. Nevertheless, Deka and the Elf consistently emphasized the importance of patience, urging him to wait until he fully understood the truth and had complete control over his newfound abilities. The question persisted: Why this insistence on waiting? He yearned to unravel the mysteries of their impending encounters and comprehend the significance of time in this enigmatic journey.

Çarh, attempting to subdue the flames of curiosity within him, managed to regain his composure. He earnestly hoped that Deka and the Elf would provide explanations. Perhaps, under their guidance, this uncertainty could find clarification. In the quietude saturated with these contemplations, he persevered in his patient wait.

Breaking the silence, Deka gazed at Çarh with determination. "Çarh, you will learn everything when the time is right. Acting without a complete understanding of the uncertainties we face now can lead us into dangers. We must utilize this time to strengthen ourselves and become strategic in our fight against Nail."

The Elf, in agreement with Deka, chimed in, "Çarh, your power is immense, and your potential is limitless. Nevertheless, advancing without full control of this power can leave us vulnerable. Waiting is essential to grow stronger and devise a strategic plan."

Sûr

Çarh listened attentively to both, making an effort to suppress the curiosity within him. Perhaps this waiting was necessary to assert a stronger stance against Nail and minimize risks. With this realization, he began to appreciate the importance of time even more.

While grappling with impatience, Çarh placed his trust in Deka and the Elf. He believed in their experience and wisdom, understanding that waiting now meant taking essential steps toward future success. Therefore, he chose patience, recognizing it as a key to fully understanding the power of the unknown and developing a strategic approach against Nail.

After a while, observing that Çarh had regained his composure, the Elf departed from the house, followed by Deka, who had to leave abruptly to address an emerging paradox. Alone in the house, Çarh's curiosity and excitement surged once more. With Deka and the Elf gone, he felt a newfound ease and decided to attempt changing his form again. Gazing out of the window, he spotted a seagull perched on the roof of the opposite building. A desire welled within him, and he endeavoured to enter the seagull. Swiftly, he felt himself transforming into the body of the seagull. Now, he was a seagull, soaring freely through the skies.

Soaring above Istanbul, Çarh encountered a magnificent sight. Amidst the bustle of the city's streets, buildings, and crowds, he gained a fresh perspective on the world. As he flew over the Grand Bazaar, thoughts of Nail occupied his mind. Descending, he landed on top of Nail's shop, attempting to listen quietly. Perhaps, in the hushed conversations below, he could glean a clue about Nail's intentions.

Silently, Çarh waited within the seagull's body, striving to capture the sounds emanating from Nail's shop. The murmur of people, the tactile shuffle of products on the counter, and the ambient noise from the bustling crowd filled his ears. He listened intently to every nuance, concentrating all his attention on deciphering Nail's words. However, as he strained to extract information, his focus was diverted by an unexpected source. A group of pigeons descended near the shop, engaging in their own amusement. Amidst their cooing, the clarity of Nail's conversations eluded him.

Çarh lingered a little longer in the form of a seagull but failed to intercept Nail's conversations. Perhaps there were limitations to this experience that he was yet to comprehend, or maybe he needed to position himself more strategically at the opportune moment. With a sense of realization, he departed the seagull's body and returned to his own.

Reflecting on his experience, Çarh found his curiosity and determination intensifying. He recognized the necessity of gathering more information about Nail's plans to take effective action against him. Sensing the power of shapeshifting once again, he believed that time would serve as his guide, helping him determine the next steps in this intricate pursuit.

In a bid to chart a new course for his future actions, Çarh resolved to seek a different perspective. Contemplating the idea of embodying a smaller creature, his attention was drawn to a buzzing fly nearby. Filled with excitement at the prospect, he swiftly shifted into the body of the fly. Now, he could perceive the world through the compound eyes of this tiny insect.

As Çarh assumed the body of the fly, his experience took a dramatic turn. The diminutiveness and lightness of the fly's body altered his perception of the world significantly. The small eyes of the fly demanded increased movement to survey a wider area. Colours seemed more muted, and distinguishing details became slightly more challenging. Yet, the fly's small and agile body enabled him to explore his surroundings rapidly.

In the body of the fly, Çarh discerned scents in the environment with heightened clarity. Various scents served as indicators, guiding him to the location of foods and signalling the presence of entities in the surroundings. This intensified sensory experience was facilitated by the fly's sensitive antennae. Simultaneously, he felt the subtle airflow through the tiny hairs on the fly's body, granting him a keen sense of balance and direction as he maneuvered through his surroundings.

In the guise of a fly, Çarh leveraged the advantages of its diminutive size. A fly, often overlooked by other creatures, granted him increased privacy and numerous opportunities for observation.

As he approached Nail's shop, silently navigating the interior in the fly's body proved to be a significant advantage, allowing him to move surreptitiously, observe events, and gather information.

Squeezing through a small gap to gain entry, he landed on a shelf, from where he could quietly observe Nail. With the fly's sensitive sensations, he immersed himself in the atmosphere, smells, and sounds of the shop, closely watching as Nail perused the books and listened attentively to the surroundings.

As Çarh observed Nail moving to the back, his curiosity intensified. Intrigued by the object resembling a twig in Nail's hand, he yearned for a closer look. When Nail inquired about the sacrifice made to obtain the mysterious item, Çarh's curiosity reached its peak. Squinting his eyes, he listened intently to the man, eagerly awaiting Nail's response.

Nail, holding the mysterious object, paused briefly before quietly stating, "This is a part of Céwiaretza," Çarh was immediately struck with shock. Céwiaretza was the Tree of Life, the fount of magical power. As Çarh grappled with the profound implications of this revelation, he sensed the doors to an unknown world creaking open. Questions about the nature of the sacrifice made to obtain a part of Céwiaretza filled his mind, but Nail's words remained shrouded in mystery, leaving Çarh yearning for answers he was not yet ready to share.

Upon learning of this mysterious event, a potent mix of determination and restlessness stirred within Çarh. The atmosphere in the shop, charged with the presence of the mysterious object, heightened the flames of curiosity within him. Suddenly compelled to distance himself from the shop, he swiftly exited through the door and promptly returned to his own body.

Seated at home, lost in thought, Çarh pondered the enigma of how Nail had severed a branch from Céwiaretza. His quest to comprehend the nature of the mysterious object and Nail's intentions consumed him. Straining his imagination, he considered various scenarios. Could this branch hold supernatural abilities under Nail's control? Or perhaps it served as a gateway, opening doors to unknown possibilities? The mysteries surrounding the Tree of Life fuelled Çarh's curiosity, propelling him into a realm of speculation.

As Çarh's thoughts swirled, he suddenly became aware of Deka's presence. Silently entering, Deka stood waiting in the corner of the room. A sense of discomfort gripped Çarh upon Deka's arrival. It became evident that the time for uncovering the truth had arrived.

Sensing Çarh's hesitation, Deka approached and sat in

silence. Meeting Çarh's gaze, Deka finally acknowledged the necessity of revealing everything. Çarh's heart quickened, sensing that an unexpected truth was on the verge of being unveiled.

As Çarh recounted the events in the shop, a mix of excitement and concern enveloped him. Every detail about the mysterious twig in Nail's hand spilled out as he vividly described the atmosphere upon entering the shop, Nail's behaviours, every step, conversation, and movement.

Interrupting Çarh's narration, Deka eagerly asked, "What kind of twig?" Curiosity and concern coloured his voice. Çarh paused briefly, taking a deep breath before answering, "A piece from Céwiaretza," his voice carrying a noticeable tremor of both excitement and awe. Deka's question held profound implications, and Çarh sensed that this revelation had swung open doors to an unknown world.

Rising swiftly from his seat, Deka approached Çarh with a mingling of concern and determination etched on his face. The flickering light in his eyes betrayed the gravity of Çarh's revelation, yet she sought further assurance. "Are you sure?" she inquired, her voice marked by meticulousness. Though aware of the answer, Deka wanted Çarh to confess sincerely, underscoring the significance of the revelation.

Çarh grasped the weight of Deka's question, and a look of indecision painted his face. The uncertainty in his eyes mirrored the complex emotions within. "Yes, I'm sure," he responded, his voice carrying a blend of confidence and unease. In response, Deka squinted her eyes for a moment, lost in thought. She recognized the truth in Çarh's words, understanding that this reality was setting the stage for a significant journey ahead.

Curiously turning to Çarh, Deka inquired, "Was he

drawing something on the ground with that twig?" Çarh, momentarily taken aback, looked at her with surprise, pondering the question. Initially, he didn't recall paying attention to that detail. However, as he reflected on the moment after leaving the shop, he remembered noticing something. The recollection made everything clearer.

Turning toward Deka to respond, Çarh said, "Actually, no, he wasn't drawing," with a hint of hesitation. Almost immediately, a moment from his memory surfaced, and his expression changed. "But now I remember; as I was leaving the shop, I noticed a drawing on the ground," he added. After uttering those words, his eyes drifted into the distance as he attempted to relive the memory.

Reconstructing the mental image, Çarh focused on the memory. In his mind's eye, a glowing drawing materialized on the floor – an intricate composition featuring a circle and a triangle adorned with strange letters. Though the drawing hadn't seized his attention initially, recalling the memory now illuminated its meaning.

Deka, observant of the change in Çarh's expression, continued to listen attentively. "What kind of drawing was it?" she asked, her curiosity intensifying. Çarh turned his eyes to Deka and explained, "There was a triangle inside a circle on the ground, with strange letters written around it," his excitement evident in his voice.

Attempting to contain her rising excitement, Deka approached Çarh with a determined expression. "Then we know what we need to do," she declared, determination resonating in her voice.

"Are you ready to learn the truth?"

Sûr

CHAPTER 19
SÛR

Two days ago, Çarh confronted Nail's men, channelling a potent energy that transferred their souls into the nearest cat and mouse. The sudden transformation of these animals left chaos and astonishment in its wake. Unexpectedly, the Elf intervened swiftly to restore balance, returning the souls of the animals, which had lost control, to their original bodies. Despite the Elf's timely intervention, some eyewitnesses observed the event, and this information reached Nail's ears.

Nail gained a deeper understanding of Çarh's power and potential through the recent incident. Recognizing the need for caution, Nail realised that Çarh must learn to control his formidable abilities. The incident highlighted the potential dangers of unbridled power, posing a significant threat not only to Çarh himself but also to his surroundings. This newfound awareness prompted Nail to consider the importance of guiding Çarh in harnessing and mastering his extraordinary capabilities.

Sûr

As Çarh's power continued to expand, Nail found himself increasingly disturbed by his inability to obtain Deka's necklace. The significance of this necklace weighed heavily on Nail, prompting relentless efforts to acquire it. Despite his persistent attempts, Nail remained unsuccessful in obtaining the cherished item. Çarh, noticing Nail's frustration and recognizing the necklace's importance, became intrigued. This realization ignited Çarh's determination to intensify his own power, driven by the mysterious allure of the necklace and its connection to Nail's growing unease.

Nail immersed himself in dedicated research within the confines of the library, determined to unearth a solution to his predicament. His focus extended to perusing ancient tomes, exploring the realms of spells and rituals in an attempt to rediscover long-forgotten secrets. As he delved deeper into the esoteric knowledge of the past, the concept of the Witch's Snare, also known as Sögrédehöbem, emerged as a final recourse in his mind. Recognizing the potential potency of this elusive trap, Nail saw it as the last glimmer of hope to wrest the coveted necklace from Deka's possession.

The casting of the Witch's Snare proved to be a formidable challenge. Its execution required a complex and intricate process, involving precise drawings and meticulous activation in a designated location. Faced with limited options and driven by an unyielding determination to secure the necklace, Nail concluded that he had no other choice. Acknowledging the inherent risks, he resolved to take this daring step, recognizing the necessity of the Witch's Snare to achieve his goal.

Executing the Witch's Snare demanded considerable effort from Nail, unfolding in a meticulous two-stage process. The initial stage necessitated obtaining a branch severed from

Céwiaretza, a symbolic object imbued with the essence of nature's energy. Armed with this potent branch, Nail aimed to harness its power to craft and activate the elusive Witch's Snare. The intricate nature of this ritual reflected Nail's commitment to employing every available resource in his quest for the coveted necklace.

Yet, the branch alone proved insufficient. The second stage demanded the enchantment of the branch with the elemental force tethered to the witch, coupled with the intricate task of inscribing a precise pattern onto the ground. The success of the ritual hinged on effectively trapping the witch's energy and power. The correct placement of symbols corresponding to each element was of paramount importance, as the functionality of the Witch's Snare depended on the meticulous alignment of these symbols. Each element, with its unique symbol and characteristics, added a layer of complexity to the enchantment process, underscoring the critical nature of Nail's attention to detail.

In the preceding days, Nail confronted Deka to discern the elemental force to which she was connected. This pivotal information held the key to the successful execution of the second stage of the Witch's Snare. Now armed with the knowledge he sought, Nail turned his attention to the next step – acquiring the branch severed from Céwiaretza. Employing his unique ability to facilitate exchanges, Nail prepared to invest significant effort in obtaining this crucial component for the intricate ritual ahead.

Endowed with the ability to exchange objects, Nail had a unique power that enabled him to manipulate and acquire various items. This exceptional capability opened up numerous opportunities for him. Leveraging this power to locate the branch essential for crafting the Witch's Snare bestowed a substantial advantage upon Nail. However, the pivotal challenge lay in determining the current possessor of this vital component, a mystery that would need unravelling before Nail could proceed with his quest for the elusive branch.

Leaving the confines of the library, Nail meticulously surveyed his surroundings, attuning himself to the energies that enveloped him. He engaged in a discerning analysis of the energies emanating from both people and objects in close proximity, diligently homing in on the distinct energy signature of the sought-after branch. Operating in seamless harmony with his instincts and the unique capabilities of his exchange ability, Nail initiated a thorough search for clues that could lead him to the person or location holding the crucial piece.

Empowered by his distinctive ability, Nail skilfully traced the trail of the item he intended to exchange. Utilizing this extraordinary skill, he could physically touch an object, tapping into its past information, and glean insights into its users and previous owners. This particular capability endowed him with the means to effortlessly discern the present possessor of the branch severed from Céwiaretza, facilitating his quest to locate the crucial component with precision and efficiency.

Following an extensive search, Nail successfully tracked the trail of the item he aimed to exchange. Methodically touching various objects, he meticulously analysed their energies, delving into the histories embedded within them. Sensing the unique energies emanating from each object, he sought vital clues that could unravel the mystery of the branch's current possessor. Through this intricate process of feeling and interpreting energies, Nail endeavoured to pinpoint the individual currently in possession of the branch separated from Céwiaretza.

At long last, Nail unravelled the mystery of the branch's current possessor. His unique exchange ability, unveiling the intricate web of previous users and owners of the item, provided the necessary insights. Armed with this invaluable information, Nail successfully identified the individual presently holding the crucial piece in his quest for the branch.

Over a substantial period, the branch had consistently changed hands among various Sögré, each harbouring distinct intentions. Some sought to acquire it for the specific purpose of drawing the Witch's Snare, while others regarded it as a prized collector's item. Each successive owner had employed or safeguarded the branch in alignment with their individual objectives. Yuka, the current possessor, had utilized the branch to ensnare a witch, and presently, it held a prominent place in his collection, showcasing the diverse and multifaceted history of the coveted item.

Fully cognizant of the branch's significance and potent capabilities, Yuka handled it with meticulous care. To him, the piece transcended mere objecthood; it stood as a symbol of considerable importance. By prominently displaying it alongside other items in his collection, Yuka underscored its unique value to all who observed. The branch became a source of pride for him, an emblem that captured the attention of onlookers. In showcasing this object, Yuka sought not only to highlight its individual importance but also to draw admiration and attention from those who recognized the rare and powerful nature of the branch.

Discovering that Yuka retained the branch in his collection presented a significant advantage for Nail. Armed with this knowledge, Nail recognized the opportunity to negotiate a trade and effortlessly obtain this valuable item using his exchange ability. The information about the branch's location within Yuka's collection paved the way for a strategic and potentially successful exchange, aligning with Nail's quest to secure the crucial component for the creation of the Witch's Snare.

Nail successfully achieved the desired outcome through his exchange with Yuka. With unwavering focus, he harnessed his exchange power, causing the vase in his left hand to abruptly vanish. In an instant, the coveted branch separated from Céwiaretza materialized in his right hand. Nail had finally reaped the rewards of his persistent efforts, securing the essential component for the creation of the Witch's Snare.

As he held the branch, a profound sense of satisfaction and accomplishment enveloped Nail. Sensing the potent energy emanating from the object, he knew that he had taken a significant stride toward the second stage of the Witch's Snare. This moment, etched into his memories, marked a pivotal juncture shaping Nail's destiny.

With meticulous care, Nail safeguarded the branch as he advanced with unwavering determination in the construction of the Witch's Snare. The subsequent step demanded enchanting the branch with the element linked to the witch and crafting the corresponding intricate drawing. Armed with a fusion of his inner power and wisdom, Nail readied himself for the formidable task that lay ahead.

Embarking on his unique rituals, Nail positioned the branch thoughtfully and initiated the enchantment process. Through a profound state of meditation and unwavering focus, he endeavoured to attune his mind and body with the elemental essence of the witch. Guiding his instincts, he sensitively felt the energies surrounding him, ensuring precise and accurate enchantment through a harmonious alignment of his own energy with that of the witch.

As time elapsed, Nail's drawing ability flourished as he meticulously crafted the symbolic representation of the Witch's Snare on the ground. The merger of the branch with the associated elemental force established a connection that would effectively govern the power of Sögré. Each line and symbol materialized with precision, a testament to Nail's intense focus and magical prowess.

Upon the completion of the drawing, Nail scrutinized his work on the ground. The second stage of the Witch's Snare was now successfully concluded. Before him lay a formidable tool – a creation poised to confront Çarh and Deka, elevate his own power, and facilitate the attainment of the coveted necklace he sought.

Nail harboured strong conviction in employing the Witch's Snare as a means to secure the necklace. However, he remained cognizant of a profound truth – entrapping an intelligent Sögré, particularly one as astute as Deka, posed a formidable challenge.

Carefully executing his Witch's Snare plan with utmost discretion, Nail ensured that Deka remained oblivious to the impending threat, thereby maintaining his strategic advantage. Yet, an unforeseen event transpired recently, throwing a wrench into Nail's meticulously laid plans.

While in the guise of a fly and visiting Nail's shop, Çarh serendipitously stumbled upon the radiant drawing of the Witch's Snare on the floor. Bewildered by the sight, Çarh grappled with an attempt to comprehend the unfolding situation. Limited by his fly form, he sensed the gravity of the matter but couldn't fully grasp the details. Upon returning home and recounting the experience to Deka, the topic sparked keen interest in her.

Sûr

In the ensuing conversation, a pregnant pause hung in the air before Deka, with a calculated glance at Çarh, asked the pivotal question of whether he was prepared to learn the truth. As silence settled in, Çarh found himself echoing the question in his inner world, eagerly anticipating Deka's revelation. The weight of the unspoken truth loomed, and Çarh fixed his gaze on Deka, impatiently yearning to unravel the mystery. Simultaneously, Deka, sensing Çarh's curiosity, grappled with her own excitement, yearning to divulge the truth but grappling with where to begin. The silent exchange between them painted an atmosphere laden with anticipation and untold revelations.

Deka locked eyes with Çarh, her gaze penetrating into his. "What Nail drew is a Witch's Snare," she elucidated. "It's a tool he intends to use against us, possibly in the impending battle. This object holds significant power and has the ability to temporarily confine Sögré to a specific area. Nail's intention is to incapacitate us, so we must exercise caution."

A palpable sense of worry and doubt clouded Çarh's expression as he absorbed Deka's explanation. He pressed on, emphasizing the potential threat posed by the Witch's Snare and the need for vigilance in the face of Nail's strategic move.

As Çarh grappled with the weight of Deka's revelation, a myriad of questions flooded his mind, each seeking clarity on Nail's intentions and the workings of the Witch's Snare. Yearning for more information, he inquired, "So, how does the Witch's Snare work? Is there a way to render it ineffective?"

In response, Deka offered a thoughtful smile. "The working principle of the Witch's Snare is quite complex," she began. "However, its power is derived from the object used to create the drawing. If we can obtain that object — the branch severed from Céwiaretza – we have the means to render the Witch's Snare ineffective."

As Çarh absorbed Deka's explanation, a strategic spark ignited in his mind. Seeking confirmation, he inquired, "So, we need to seize that branch piece to render the Witch's Snare ineffective, is that correct?"

Deka nodded in affirmation. "Yes, you understood correctly. The branch is the energy source of the Witch's Snare. If we can seize it, we can neutralize the power of the Witch's Snare. However, we should be aware that it won't be easy. Nail may have taken significant measures to protect the Witch's Snare."

Deka emphasized the formidable challenge that lay ahead, cautioning Çarh about the potential measures Nail might have taken to safeguard the Witch's Snare. She stressed the importance of preparedness at every step and fixed her gaze on Çarh, speaking with utmost seriousness. "Our greatest weapon is actually you, Çarh! Your power and abilities will give us a significant advantage in this struggle."

Though Deka's words instilled a sense of fear within Çarh, they simultaneously rekindled his self-confidence. Her unwavering belief in him served as a potent motivator. Speaking with determination, Çarh acknowledged, "Yes, maybe I can truly make a difference in this battle. Despite Nail's precautions, we can render the Witch's Snare ineffective by using my power. But we must be cautious and act cleverly." The unfolding challenge demanded a delicate balance between acknowledging the risks and embracing the strength Çarh brought to the impending conflict.

Deka expressed her approval with a nod. "I know; I see the power and potential within you. I completely trust you in this struggle."

Sûr

After a brief pause, Deka took a deep breath and met Çarh's gaze with determination. "The truth is, Çarh," she continued, "If things don't go well on the path to seizing the Witch's Snare, we must consider all possibilities. Nail's magical power can be quite impressive, and he can be a cunning adversary. If things go awry, we must be prepared for the worst-case scenario." The gravity of the situation hung in the air, and Deka's candid acknowledgment underscored the need for careful consideration and strategic planning in the face of potential adversity.

Çarh's heart quickened, and a sense of curiosity propelled him to ask, "What is the worst-case scenario, Deka? What could we face?"

With a serious demeanour, Deka responded, "In the worst-case scenario, the Witch's Snare could trap either you or me. If it ensnares me, Nail gains possession of the necklace. But, if it traps you, he would likely attempt to sever Sûr from you, and in that unfortunate event, you will most likely die." The gravity of Deka's words hung heavily in the air, emphasizing the dire consequences that loomed in the event of the worst-case scenario.

Deka's words cast a chilling reality over their focus. Çarh, sensing the gravity of Deka's seriousness, shivered at the implications. Under the influence of the Witch's Snare, both of them would be exposed to great danger, and the depth of fear was reflected in Deka's expression.

Silently, Çarh met Deka's gaze, the weight of the impending risk settling heavily in their hearts. The words choked in his throat as he acknowledged, "So, depending on whom Nail traps, we will either lose your life or Sûr. This is a significant risk."

Deka's eyes held an unwavering determination. "Yes,

Çarh. It is a significant risk. However, our duty is to protect Sûr and the other innocents. If I get trapped by Nail, I want you to continue the fight and do everything to save Sûr. If you get trapped, I will do the same. In this struggle, sacrifices may be necessary."

Çarh, grappling with the weight of Deka's words, wondered about the nature of these sacrifices. A slight unease lingered in his eyes, driven by the desire to understand the risks they would be undertaking in this war. The impending battle seemed to demand not only physical strength but also an acceptance of the potential sacrifices that loomed on the horizon.

Deka, after taking a deep breath, responded, "Sacrifice may mean putting ourselves in danger, even risking our lives. While struggling against Nail's power, we might have to risk leaving our loved ones behind. We might need to jeopardize Sûr, our safety, or even our own existence to stand against Nail's malevolence. In this war, we might have to abandon our own interests and pursue a greater purpose."

Çarh listened thoughtfully to Deka's words, grappling with mixed emotions. The concept of sacrifice beckoned a path that demanded courage and selflessness, yet it also evoked feelings of fear and potential loss. Finally, he uttered, "So, we might risk our loved ones, even our lives, in this struggle." The gravity of their mission underscored the weighty decisions that lay ahead, challenging them to confront not only external threats but also internal dilemmas.

Deka's eyes remained resolute. "Yes, Çarh. In this struggle, we might lose ourselves and risk our most valuable assets. But remember, this war is for Sûr's future. If we withdraw, Nail's malevolence could spread further. Our sacrifice is necessary to ensure the safety of the innocents."

Despite Deka's words, Çarh sensed a lingering mystery. The determination in her eyes and the ambiguity in her narratives left him uneasy. A lingering suspicion crept in, making him believe that there was a move or plan that he wasn't aware of, adding another layer of complexity to the impending struggle.

With a blend of curiosity and concern, Çarh approached her. "Deka," he spoke seriously, "there's something you haven't told me clearly, isn't there? A move, a plan... I'm aware of it. Please, tell the truth plainly. What are you hiding from me?"

Deka hesitated momentarily, then took a deep breath. Determination and sorrow mingled in her eyes. "Çarh," she confessed in a quiet voice, "the reason I kept the truth hidden is because I wanted to protect you. In this war, you have a crucial role to play. But I thought that knowing the truth would put you in even greater danger." The weight of Deka's revelation hung in the air, underscoring the delicate balance between transparency and the preservation of Çarh's safety.

Mixed emotions played across Çarh's face. "Deka," he expressed with a hint of frustration, "if I carry a significant responsibility, I want to know. No matter what, I want to know the truth. I trust you; be honest with me."

Indecision flickered in Deka's eyes, but she couldn't resist the sincerity in Çarh's words. "Okay," she finally conceded, "I'll tell you. But know that learning this truth may expose you to greater danger." The air hung with a sense of impending revelation, as Deka prepared to disclose the hidden facets of their complex reality.

Çarh indicated his readiness to listen, waiting patiently for Deka to reveal the hidden truths. She took a deep breath and commenced, "As you know, your task is to carry Sûr.

Your fundamental duty is to safely carry the soul of Israfil within Sûr. However, individuals like Nail, who desire this power, can attack you, just as they did to the previous Sûr carrier, and take your Sûr. Some consider Sûr as a valuable source of power and a collectible item."

Çarh signalled for Deka to continue, his attention unwavering. After a momentary pause, Deka met Çarh's gaze with determination, her eyes reflecting confusion and uncertainty. "In such a situation, you can use your true power to protect yourself. The power we haven't told you about until now," she revealed, a noticeable tremor in her voice. As Çarh's eyes bore into hers with curiosity, Deka continued to speak, her words seemingly caught in her throat.

"Çarh, you are actually more than what you think," revealed Deka, her words carrying a weight that seemed to hold the air still. "You are not just born as a Sûr carrier. You are a part of Sûr. You carry the soul of Israfil within you."

Çarh recoiled in shock. "What do you mean?" he asked, his voice shaky and filled with bewilderment. "I am just a Sûr carrier, tasked with protecting Israfil's entrusted soul." The revelation stirred a whirlwind of emotions within Çarh, challenging the very essence of his understanding of self and purpose.

Deka continued with unwavering determination in her eyes. "Yes, you fulfil the role of a carrier, but there is a deeper meaning to you carrying Israfil's soul. You are the only person who can directly use the power of Sûr. Israfil's soul moves with you, strengthens with you."

Çarh was astonished. What did this mean? Was there another entity within him? Was Sûr alive and active within him? Complex thoughts swirled in his mind, and amidst the confusion, he felt the excitement of being aware of this potential power within him. The revelation opened a new chapter in Çarh's understanding of himself and the intricate role he played in the unfolding events.

Deka continued to unveil the truth in silence. "Here, Çarh, when you wish to make the ultimate sacrifice, you can release Israfil's soul by tearing Sûr apart yourself, merging with Israfil and breathing life into Sûr. This is the supreme sacrifice and reveals your greatest power. As Sûr rises within you, you become a part of Sûr. Israfil's soul merges with you, and with a breath heralding a new era, you spread your energy throughout the entire universe."

Facing Deka's words, Çarh experienced a mixture of fear and excitement. The prospect of such a profound sacrifice, of surrendering his own existence, stirred complex emotions within him. Yet, amidst the uncertainty, there was a promise of transformation and the announcement of great power. In the midst of these conflicting emotions, he noticed the deep belief in Deka's eyes and her supportive smile, adding a layer of assurance to the revelation.

Deka continued with a calm demeanour. "This journey may be challenging for you. Confronting the darkness within yourself, battling your fears will be necessary. But remember, you are the guardian of Sûr, the carrier of Israfil... This significant responsibility is an opportunity to reveal the power hidden within you. And believe me, this journey will take you to your true potential."

Understanding Çarh's curiosity, Deka replied sincerely, "When you breathe Sûr, Israfil's soul will spread freely and embrace the entire universe. It is a moment of transformation. With your power, you reveal its soul. The breath of Sûr signifies a rebirth with its energy. By affecting everything around you, it changes the balance and lays the foundation for a new order."

As Çarh contemplated Deka's words, his excitement swelled. The prospect of using the power of Sûr in such a profound way held the potential to instigate genuine change in the universe. However, he also had to grapple with the weight of responsibility that came with this extraordinary power. Balancing his own will with the presence of Israfil within him, navigating the path ahead required careful consideration.

Deka, attuned to Çarh's thoughts, stood ready to guide him. "When using the power of Sûr, you will feel the guidance of Israfil within you. Israfil will be your companion, inspiring you in the right direction. Continuing your inner journey is crucial to maintaining balance in your power. Trust yourself, and you can breathe Sûr at the right time by listening to your inner wisdom."

As Çarh grappled with the weight of the consequences of breathing Sûr, he asked with unease, "Will everyone die after I breathe Sûr?" The question echoed with fear and concern, reflecting both his personal apprehensions and a profound worry about the future of humanity.

Deka, recognizing Çarh's anxieties, responded calmly, "Breathing Sûr does not mean everyone will die. On the contrary, when Sûr is breathed, it affects the universe with a massive wave of energy. However, this effect is not so destructive as to cause everyone's death. Breathing Sûr signifies transformation and change. The old order gives way to a new one, but this change may have different outcomes for everyone." Deka's reassurance aimed to alleviate Çarh's concerns, emphasizing the nuanced and transformative nature of the impending change.

Çarh felt a measure of relief at Deka's explanation, though uncertainties still lingered within him. He sought further clarification, asking, "What about people during this process of change? How will they be affected?"

Deka, understanding Çarh's need for clarity, responded, "With the breath of Sûr, people will find the opportunity to explore their inner potentials more deeply. Change will allow some to gain new powers, others to further develop their abilities. The purpose of people's existence, their relationships, and thoughts will also undergo transformation. However, how this process will unfold and affect everyone cannot be precisely predicted."

Despite Çarh's eagerness to believe in Deka's explanations, a lingering doubt and fear persisted within him. The idea that everyone would perish after the breath of Sûr insidiously grew in his mind. What troubled him was the nagging suspicion that perhaps Deka was concealing the truth. Could she be lying to protect herself?

Caught in this internal turmoil, Çarh turned back to Deka and asked with a slightly trembling voice, "Deka, could it be true that everyone will die when Sûr is breathed? Are you telling me lies to keep me from being scared?" The tremor in his voice revealed the vulnerability beneath the surface, as he grappled with the uncertainty surrounding the potential consequences of his actions.

Deka, attempting to empathize with Çarh's concerns, wore a saddened expression. "Çarh, I don't want to lie to you. However, we must also accept the truth. Breathing Sûr is an event that will transform the universe, but it is not a power that will cause everyone's death. In this transformation process, people will encounter different outcomes; some will gain strength, some will change. Death signifies the end of the past and the old order."

Upon hearing Deka's sincere response, Çarh felt a slight

relief from his fear. Deka's trust and loyalty somewhat calmed his doubts. However, he still needed more information to fully understand the nature of the profound changes they were about to face.

Attempting to dispel his doubts and seek the truth, Çarh takes a step and summons the Elf. Responding to his call, the Elf appears promptly and approaches Çarh. With a mix of fear and curiosity still present in his eyes, Çarh turns to the Elf, signalling his readiness to inquire about the truth.

The Elf, approaching Çarh with a deep sigh, looks into his eyes with a compassionate expression. "Çarh, guiding you on your inner journey is my duty. Chasing after the truth requires courage, and I'm happy to assist you." The Elf's supportive words indicate his commitment to helping Çarh navigate the complexities of the impending events and uncover the truth that has eluded him.

While listening to the Elf's words, Çarh feels conflicts within his heart. Torn between trusting Deka on one side and embracing the Elf's wisdom on the other, he remains ensnared in a state of uncertainty. Despite this internal struggle, an insatiable curiosity propels him forward, intensifying his desire to unveil the truth.

As Çarh silently advances, the Elf joins him, standing by his side. Speaking in a gentle tone, the Elf asserts, "Facing the truth entails confronting fear and doubts, not avoiding them. I understand your reservations about breathing Sûr. However, it's crucial to remember that the truth is inherently complex, defying confinement to a singular answer. To uncover it, you must take courageous steps."

In an attempt to overcome his fear, Çarh cautiously questions the Elf, "What will happen when Sûr is breathed? Will everyone perish?"

Sûr

The Elf takes a deep breath and responds calmly, "Breathing Sûr induces a profound transformation in the universe. The destiny of all is shaped by this metamorphosis. Some gain strength, others undergo change, and some may cease to exist. Death, in this context, marks the conclusion of the old order and the commencement of something new. Yet, it's vital to understand that everyone's fate is influenced by their personal choices and inner strength."

The uncertainty and turmoil reflected in Çarh's eyes capture the Elf's attention. With profound insight, the Elf comprehends Çarh's concerns and responds sincerely, "Çarh, breathing Sûr is indeed a last resort, a choice intricately tied to your inner journey and sacrifice. As you unravel Sûr, you will meld with Israfil, unveiling the true power of Sûr. This transformation comes with great responsibility and change. Merging with Israfil means stepping into a new existence, becoming an integral part of the world from that moment onward."

The Elf's words alleviate the turmoil within Çarh, serving as a poignant reminder of his inner strength. Confronting the truth and making sacrifices demands courage, yet it is imperative for him to recognize that on this journey, he will unearth his uniqueness.

The Elf continues, "When you blow the Sûr, a new purpose and responsibility will unfold before you. The power of Israfil will be wielded by your hands, extending its influence through you to the world. Regardless of the journey's outcome, it is crucial to heed your inner truth. Remember, as the chosen bearer of the Sûr, you play a unique role in the universe.'

With his mind swirling with Deka's and the Elf's explanations, Çarh proceeds towards his room in a state of mental confusion. His thoughts resemble a storm, influenced by the weight of their words. However, upon entering his room and gazing into the mirror, he pauses for a moment.

The mirror locks eyes with the reflection, and Çarh gazes into his own eyes. The Sûr is reflected on his face, and in that moment, a profound understanding of his purpose dawns upon him. Establishing a connection with the power of the Sûr, the reflection in the mirror becomes a symbol of inner wisdom, guiding him.

Confusion in his mind gives way to clarity, and a sense of inner peace envelops Çarh. Instead of vocalizing his thoughts, a quiet wisdom takes over. Accepting the journey offered by the Sûr, he succumbs to a deep slumber.

While Çarh peacefully sleeps, Nail's men lurk in every corner, silent and vigilant. Driven by determination, Nail's ambitious followers move swiftly, their target set on Deka and Çarh. In Nail's ruthless gaze, capturing Deka takes precedence. Once she is in their clutches, their plan is to seize the necklace and then apprehend Çarh. Beyond acquiring the Sûr, Nail aims to safeguard himself against the potential activation of its power.

As Nail's operatives navigate with silent steps, they cloak themselves in shadows, patiently awaiting the opportune moment. Their eyes gleam from within the darkness as they relentlessly pursue their targets. Nail's orders are explicit, and their resolve to fulfil the mission is unwavering. Upon capturing Deka, Nail's ambitions are poised to soar even higher, fuelled by the dream of possessing the coveted power within the necklace.

Nail's ultimate target, however, is Çarh. Beyond carrying the Sûr, Çarh possesses the rare ability to integrate the soul of Israfil within himself. Nail is willing to risk everything to obtain the power of the Sûr, aiming to exert complete control over it by capturing Çarh.

Nail steadfastly regards the Witch's Snare as the ultimate weapon, embracing blind faith in its capabilities. He believes this mystical object grants the ability to overcome and control any obstacle. Unbeknownst to him, as he advances his plans, Çarh and Deka are aware of the presence of the Witch's Snare. This unawareness becomes an advantage for Nail, who prefers to keep his rivals in the dark about his true power. With sincere conviction, he believes that his meticulously crafted plan will unfold flawlessly.

Nail continues his calculated progress with cunning intrigues and manipulations, intending to wield his dark power to incapacitate Çarh and Deka. His strategy revolves around defeating them using the formidable power of the Witch's Snare. However, Nail's blind faith and clandestine plans may unwittingly set the stage for his own downfall.

Nail's intense focus on his devious machinations blinds him to the possibility that Çarh and Deka could uncover the weaknesses of the Witch's Snare through their innate powers and intelligence. The strength of their resolve and determination are variables Nail failed to account for. His overreliance on the Witch's Snare might have obscured his judgment, turning it into a potential vulnerability.

Nail, fuelled by cunning and ambition, decides to set a trap by constructing a paradox to lure Deka. In his eyes, he believes he has identified a vulnerability in Deka's mental and spiritual framework. Viewing paradoxes as a potent tool, he plans to use them to attract and captivate Deka. Nail's strategy involves creating chaos, ensnaring her in a puzzle that she must solve.

If Nail's plan were to succeed, Deka would be drawn

into the gravitational field of the paradox. While she is immersed in unravelling this intricate puzzle, Nail would seize the opportunity to capture and control her. As Deka navigates a complex labyrinth within her own mental world, Nail would swiftly move in, pouncing on her and taking control.

However, Nail's true aim went beyond merely capturing Deka; he sought to incapacitate Çarh by using Deka as a tool and ultimately seize the Sûr. His dark plans were designed to elevate him to a position of power, fulfilling his desire for the coveted strength.

With cunning and intrigue, Nail successfully crafted a paradox, drawing Deka toward him. The paradox introduced contradiction into reality, sowing chaos and confusion within Deka's mental labyrinth. Fuelled by a strong desire and curiosity, Deka advanced toward the scene, driven to unravel the complexity before her.

Meanwhile, Çarh remained in a deep sleep, untouched by the intrigues of Nail and the confusion that enveloped Deka. Oblivious to the machinations and turmoil unfolding, he traversed the depths of dreams and the subconscious, unaware of the significant task awaiting him in the future.

As Deka hastened toward the unfolding complexity, an inner sense warned her that this paradox wasn't a natural occurrence. Remaining open-minded, she carefully surveyed her surroundings, as her intuition signalled an impending danger. She recognized the need for caution against Nail's intrigues.

At that very moment, unexpectedly, Nail's men approached in silence and discreetly sprinkled powdered sage on Deka's face. Sage, renowned as a deterrent, temporarily nullified magic. With her hands bound, Deka found herself unable to harness her powers. Under the influence of sage, her mind blurred, and coherent thinking eluded her.

Nail's men craftily ensnared Deka in a dire situation, successfully executing their plan to capture her. In this moment of helplessness, she was rendered powerless, limited, and vulnerable.

With silent steps, Nail approached Deka, a triumphant smile adorning his face. The ambitious gleam in his eyes radiated the confidence of having gained superiority over her. Held powerless and helpless by the men, Deka sensed Nail drawing one step closer to his goal.

"I finally got you," Nail declared with a victorious tone. "Now, it's time for Çarh. After capturing him, the Sûr will be mine, and the power of Israfil will be under my control."

With these words, Nail explicitly asserted his dominance and expressed his fervent desire to capture Çarh. To him, this marked the final stage of the game, an opportunity to showcase the winner. Nail believed that his plan was unfolding flawlessly, and he harboured absolute confidence that nothing could thwart him.

When Çarh reluctantly opened his eyes, still in a drowsy state, an instinctive concern enveloped him as he looked around for Deka. Her absence created a sense of worry in his heart. Sensing something amiss, he picked up his phone to call her, but unexpectedly, Nail's voice echoed through the phone.

"Nail, what have you done to Deka? Where are you keeping her?" Çarh asked with growing anxiety.

Nail's voice carried a mysterious tone. "If you want to save your girlfriend, come to the shop," Nail said enigmatically.

Çarh found himself in a state of bewilderment. A complex mix of emotions churned within him – worry, anger, and simultaneously, a burning desire to rescue Deka, along with a hint of fear. The thought of succumbing to Nail's threat was unsettling, yet he couldn't bear the uncertainty about the safety of his loved one.

In a desperate attempt to handle the situation, Çarh wanted to summon the Elf, believing that with the Elf's help, he could confront Nail. However, the Elf remained unresponsive to the call, adding to Çarh's unsettled state.

After contemplating for a while, Çarh made his decision and set out on the path to Nail's shop. A flicker of hope burned in his heart; perhaps he could rescue Deka and thwart Nail's treacherous plan. However, an undercurrent of worry and uncertainty troubled him.

When Çarh arrived at Nail's shop, they faced each other with determined expressions. A victorious smile adorned Nail's face, having ensnared Deka in the Witch's Snare. Çarh's heart began to pound rapidly, the desire to protect his loved ones intertwining with his efforts to rescue them.

In a corner of the shop, he noticed another Witch's Snare. His eyes suddenly widened with keen alertness, realizing that this mysterious object posed a threat to him as well.

Çarh locked eyes with the Witch's Snare and decided to keep his distance. He needed to be prepared against Nail, as he was reluctant to take any action before rescuing Deka. Gathering his courage, he stepped toward Nail, awakening the warrior spirit within him.

Facing Nail with unwavering determination, Çarh spoke, "Nail, I remember. I remember what you did to the previous Sûr carriers – how you weakened them and tore their Sûrs apart. But this time, you won't be able to do the same."

Çarh assumed a stance that mirrored his belief in his inner power and his defiance against the fate of the previous carriers. Noticing sparks in Nail's eyes, Çarh gathered his courage.

"I carry the Sûr, and I will do everything in my power to fulfil this duty. I will fight against you to protect my loved ones, facing any danger that comes my way," Çarh continued with unwavering determination.

Interrupting Çarh, Nail spoke confidently, "My boy, you are still very young and just a teigretexen, not even a true Sögré. Don't talk to me about power. Now, I will tell you what will happen. I will take Deka's necklace, and you will tear the Sûr and give it to me. Do we understand each other?"

Faced with this proposal, Çarh stood thoughtfully. He had to make a choice among the options presented to him. Despite Nail's dismissive words, Çarh did not waver in his belief in his inner strength and responsibility. After a moment of contemplation, he responded with unwavering determination.

"Nail, perhaps I'm not a true Sögré, but I am aware of the power within me," he declared. "I will never give you Deka's necklace, and I won't tear the Sûr either. I won't yield to your demands. I will fight against you, demonstrating my strength and determination."

In response to Çarh's resolute declaration, Nail, with a frustrated expression, turned to his men and ordered, "Attack Çarh!" His men immediately sprang into action, and a moment of silence gave way to a grand magical battle.

Çarh harnessed the strength within and resisted Nail's men. The young teigretexen, acting with conviction, countered them by using his spells to render them ineffective. In the enchanted atmosphere where magical energies converged, sparkling explosions rising to the ceiling mesmerized everyone.

Meanwhile, Nail watched from the sidelines, grinding

his teeth in frustration at the unexpected resistance he encountered. His plan had failed, and his confidence in his own power was shaken. Çarh's determination and resilience proved to be an unanticipated obstacle for Nail.

Çarh found himself fighting against numerous enemies simultaneously. Though he hadn't yet utilized his power of soul transformation, he continued defending himself with a combination of defensive and offensive spells against his adversaries.

In the magical battlefield where the air crackled with energy, Çarh, employing sharp and effective spells, sought to neutralize his opponents. Creating protective shields woven from powerful energy flows, he deflected enemy attacks while simultaneously retaliating with offensive spells.

However, Çarh's primary goal amidst the chaos of the battle was to reach Deka. Carefully planning his steps, he navigated through the tumult, scanning her with his eyes at every turn, attempting to move through the enemies and reach her.

Beyond rescuing Deka, Çarh sought an opportunity to disable the Witch's Snare. Amidst the noise and explosions of the battle, Çarh surveyed the battlefield, searching for the branch that connected to the Witch's Snare. Contemplating its possible location, he examined every detail of his surroundings.

While defending against his adversaries with his spells, Çarh focused attentively on the surrounding objects and the environment. With each passing second, he moved with the hope of discovering the piece on which the Witch's Snare was drawn.

When Çarh noticed the branch tucked into Nail's belt amid the intensity of the conflict, he momentarily froze in astonishment. Swiftly shifting his eyes towards Nail, he grasped the plan and moved into action with a sigh.

In the midst of the chaotic battlefield, Çarh hastened his steps towards Nail, approaching carefully, and successfully obtained the branch. This small but crucial fragment would play a pivotal role in nullifying the effect of the Witch's Snare. Nail, in disbelief, asked, "Did you know?" Çarh confidently responded, indicating that he was one step ahead, "Nail, we're always one step ahead of you."

Nail immediately took action, positioning himself behind Deka and trapping her. Threatening Çarh, he demanded the immediate surrender of the Sûr. Sporting a dark smile, he issued a threat to kill Deka.

Faced with Nail's threatening words, Çarh felt a surge of anger and concern. Deka's safety hung in the balance, and Nail intended to take the Sûr along with her. Taking a deep breath to gather his powers, Çarh responded calmly, "We have no deal, Nail. If you dare to harm Deka, you should consider the consequences."

Meanwhile, Deka fought to free herself from Nail's tight grip. A momentary glance at Çarh reassured her, feeling his courage and belief. Her trust and support created a glimmer of hope within her.

As Çarh continued his argument with Nail, an unknown danger approached. Suddenly, Nail's men silently closed in behind Çarh, seizing him. After a moment of surprise, Çarh unleashed the power within him – a manifestation of what is known as the wave of soul transformation for Çarh.

The magic emanating from Çarh's body envelops the shop, affecting everyone inside. Nail's men undergo an abrupt soul swap with other beings.

However, Deka and Nail, being inside the Witch's

Snare, remain unaffected by this powerful spell. While Deka looks around in astonishment, she observes the effects of Çarh's soul transformation wave. Nail, realizing his plan has unravelled, turns toward Çarh with an angry glare.

Challenging Çarh, Nail speaks in a ruthless tone, asserting that Çarh has no other choice and emphasizing that Deka's fate lies in his hands. Nail trades the branch in his hand for a knife, tightly holding it against Deka's throat, creating a tense moment for readers. Addressing Çarh, Nail demands that he either give him what he wants or face the girl's death.

Faced with the immediate threat in front of him, Çarh gathers the power within. Confronted with Nail's offer, Çarh faces a difficult choice: Will he accept to give what is asked, or will he risk Deka's life?

Caught in indecision, Çarh notices the meaning in Deka's eyes. Using her gaze, Deka indicates approval of something. This moment sparks a glimmer of hope within Çarh.

Stepping towards Nail, Çarh displays a sign of determination. The approval given by Deka empowers Çarh with strength and courage. Filled with unwavering determination, Çarh moves to rescue Deka and put an end to Nail's malevolence.

As Çarh becomes acutely attuned to the potent force resonating within him, an unwavering certainty floods his senses. Acting with resolute determination, he proceeds to extricate the Sûr from his head, a decisive action that he instinctively recognizes as the righteous path, not only for himself but also for Deka. The process of severing the Sûr unfolds with a profound significance, akin to the delicate unfurling of an ancient tapestry, each thread woven with destiny.

Sûr

As the Sûr is unbound, Israfil's soul emerges, a radiant manifestation akin to a celestial beam of light gracefully commencing a mystical dance in the surrounding air. The ethereal display captivates Nail, Deka, and Çarh, who stand transfixed, entranced by the enchanting choreography of Israfil's liberated spirit. It is as if the very essence of Israfil is orchestrating a ballet of transcendence, each movement imbued with an otherworldly power that transcends the physical realm.

In this mesmerizing dance, the intertwined souls of Nail, Deka, and Çarh are afforded a profound glimpse into the captivating allure and formidable strength residing within Israfil's soul, now harmoniously fused with Çarh's being. The significance of this transformative moment reverberates, echoing the sublime convergence of fate, magic, and the indomitable will to shape one's destiny.

As Israfil's soul merges with Çarh, an overwhelming surge of relief and tranquillity washes over him, like a gentle tide soothing the tumult within. The once turbulent sea of inner turmoil and uncertainty now recedes, making way for the crystal-clear waters of clarity and resolute determination. In this harmonious fusion, Çarh finds solace, as if the chaotic whispers of doubt and conflict have been silenced by the serene melody of Israfil's essence.

The union of their spirits brings forth a profound transformation within Çarh. It's as if a storm-ridden sky has given way to a tranquil dawn, casting aside the shadows of uncertainty. Now, a serene understanding envelops him, and the path ahead unfolds with unmistakable clarity. In the quiet sanctuary of this newfound equilibrium, Çarh perceives with unwavering certainty what was once shrouded in ambiguity. The union with Israfil's soul becomes the beacon illuminating his purpose, guiding him towards a destiny now illuminated by the radiant light of assurance.

Çarh, his heart now unburdened by the weight of unsaid emotions, turns towards Deka, and with unabashed sincerity, he opens his soul, expressing the depth of his affection. "I love you," he declares, the words carrying the weight of honesty and vulnerability. In that moment, the air seems to shimmer with the sincerity of his confession.

Deka, attuned to the authenticity in Çarh's voice and the sincerity etched across his features, receives this declaration with a knowing understanding. Her response is not in words but in the gentle curvature of her lips, forming a loving smile that transcends language. It is a silent acknowledgment that speaks volumes, affirming the reciprocity of their emotions.

As Çarh breathes life into the Sûr, a formidable surge of energy emanates from him, coalescing into a colossal wave that pulsates with raw power. This immense energy creates a radiant spectacle, transforming the night sky into a luminous canvas painted with the ethereal hues of the unleashed force. The surrounding objects, touched by the resonance of this cosmic power, quiver and sway in response, as if acknowledging the profound energy coursing through the very fabric of existence.

The heavens themselves seem to bow to the majesty of this unleashed energy, as the atmosphere becomes a living tapestry of vibrant colours and undulating waves. The dancing beams of light in the air, intertwined with the surging energy, craft a mesmerizing ballet that transcends the boundaries of the tangible world. It is a visual symphony, where each note is a manifestation of the unleashed power, orchestrating a celestial dance that captivates all who witness its splendour.

In this transcendent moment, Çarh is not just a conduit for raw energy, but a living manifestation of his own potential.

Sûr

The overwhelming sense of power and might coursing through him liberates him from the constraints of his former self. It is as if the very essence of his being has ascended, breaking free from the shackles of limitations.

Yet, this revealed power is not solely confined to the physical realm. It serves as a manifestation of Çarh's inner fortitude, courage, and resolute determination. The harmonious union with Israfil's soul unlocks not only physical prowess but also taps into the depths of Çarh's character. It represents a harmonization with the natural flow of the universe, aligning his essence with the cosmic forces that govern existence. In this transcendence, Çarh becomes a living testament to the profound interplay between personal strength and the vast, cosmic energies that shape the fabric of reality.

Across the globe, the resounding echoes of Sûr being blown evoke a collective sense of awe among those fortunate enough to hear it. For those acquainted with the profound significance of this sound, an immediate understanding of what lies ahead stirs within them, accompanied by a deep-seated excitement. The blowing of Sûr serves as a symbolic proclamation, signifying the conclusion of one era and the dawning of another.

Sages, witches, wizards, mediums, and supernatural beings, attuned to the mystical vibrations of the universe, lend their ears to this celestial melody. In the resonant notes of Sûr, they discern crucial clues about the unfolding future, perceiving it as a cosmic awakening. The wisdom ingrained in these individuals' whispers that a universal transformation, long prophesied and enshrined in legends, is now unfurling.

This pivotal moment, foretold in prophecies, now manifests before the eyes of both humans and otherworldly beings alike. The vibrations unleashed by the blowing of Sûr ripple through the world's energy fields, guiding souls through a profound transformation process. Those familiar with the sound converge from diverse corners of the world, forming a collective gathering where knowledge is exchanged. Belief systems, traditions, and teachings intermingle, enriched with new insights and interpretations.

Amidst this cosmic symphony, a palpable sense of hopeful anticipation for the future takes root. People, ignited by an innate desire to explore new potentials and align with the cosmic current, embark on a journey of self-discovery. The blowing of Sûr becomes a catalyst for a higher frequency in the world's rotation, and those attuned to this sound find themselves accompanying the universal melody. Standing on the precipice of great transformation, they recognize that the doors of a new era, swung wide open by the ethereal notes of Sûr, beckon them towards a future where change is not only inevitable but embraced with open hearts and enlightened spirits.

CHAPTER 20
THE CYCLE

Upon opening his eyes, Çarh found himself immersed in a world that had shed its familiar trappings, leaving behind a canvas of unfamiliarity. The once vibrant brilliance that had momentarily blinded him was replaced by a profound silence, embracing the landscape in tranquillity. Emerging in the midst of this newfound reality was the silhouette of a serene tree, its presence casting a serene calmness over the surroundings.

In awe, Çarh took in the sweeping panorama that surrounded him – an expansive plain unfolding amidst lush greens, trees adorned with vibrant blossoms, and a gentle breeze whispering through the air. The authenticity of this scene was undeniable, yet comprehending the nature of his location and the intricacies of this transformative shift demanded the passage of time for full revelation. As Çarh stood amidst this altered reality, the tableau of his surroundings hinted at a fresh beginning, a new era for humankind waiting to unfurl its secrets in the hushed stillness of the unknown.

Gradually emerging from the shelter of the tree, Çarh embarked on an exploration of this unfamiliar realm. Each step was cushioned by the softness of the grass beneath his feet, leading him into the captivating embrace of a sky painted in hues of blue. Nature unfolded its enchanting beauty around him, revealing a thriving landscape that beckoned him further.

The air, infused with an undeniable sense of peace, wrapped around Çarh like a comforting shroud, immersing him in a profound tranquillity. As he ventured deeper into this serene environment, the sights and sounds of the thriving nature heightened his senses. The symphony of rustling leaves, the sweet fragrance of blossoms, and the gentle caress of the breeze formed an immersive experience, creating an ethereal haven where time seemed to stand still. In this tranquil haven, Çarh found himself captivated by the harmonious dance of the elements, each moment unfolding with a quiet grace.

Empowered by the force within him and guided by the spirit of Israfil, Çarh sensed the inception of a transformative journey. This world, a masterpiece of beauty and tranquillity, marked the threshold of a new era of consciousness. Recognizing that profound mysteries awaited unravelling in the vast expanse of the universe, Çarh understood the imperative for humanity to unite in harmony and love. Within the serene backdrop of this tranquil world, Çarh's evolution unfolded, intertwined with a greater cosmic purpose.

As Çarh continued his contemplative walk, he delved into profound reflections, acknowledging the pressing need for people to unite in exploring the concealed secrets of the universe. The journey illuminated his realization that a profound understanding, unity, and solidarity were indispensable. Each individual, he discerned, had to tap into their latent potential and harmonize with the grand order of the cosmos.

Taking respite from the warmth beneath the shade of a tree, Çarh gazed towards the expansive cosmos. A surge of power and love coursed within him, and in this new world, he stood poised to take strides that would propel humanity into a profound transformation. His aspiration crystallized into a commitment to become a guiding force, steering people towards a shared journey of unity and love.

This uncharted realm marked the genesis of a journey that infused Çarh with hope and inspiration. He committed himself to unravelling the profound meaning of his existence within this enchanting environment, pledging to unveil the veiled secrets concealed deep within the vast expanse of the universe. His purpose crystallized into a clear mission: to forge connections among people and actively contribute to the restoration of cosmic balance.

Simultaneously, amidst the awe-inspiring beauty of this new world, Çarh grappled with a profound question: was this reality or merely a figment of his imagination, a dream, or an illusion? The uncertainty lingered, casting doubt on the authenticity of his surroundings. Yet, the emotions and experiences coursing through him were undeniably genuine. The last recollection etched in his memory was Israfil merging with his being and the resonating echoes of the Sûr being blown. Çarh, in an effort to grasp the reality of his existence, concentrated his mind, attempting to summon the memories – the moment Israfil's spirit entered, the ethereal notes of the Sûr, and the surrounding beam of light. However, the recollections were obscured, lost in a nebulous haze. Whether propelled into a new dimension by the power of the Sûr or existing in a tangible reality, the transformation within Çarh and the profound sense of peace that enveloped him suggested that this wasn't just a dream. It was an awakening, a tangible evolution that transcended the boundaries of mere illusion.

Çarh found himself delicately navigating the intricate realm between dream and reality. It occurred to him that, perhaps, alongside Israfil's soul, he had transcended to a different dimension and undergone a rebirth in this unfamiliar world. Yet, even if this were an elaborate dream, the emotions and experiences coursing through him remained palpably real. It seemed as though the universe was presenting him with a magical encounter, exceeding the boundaries of human comprehension.

Inhaling deeply, Çarh made a conscious decision to dissolve the distinctions between reality and dream. Whether this world existed in a tangible sense or merely as a construct of his subconscious, he recognized that taking proactive steps to explore its mysteries was imperative. Even if it were a dream, Çarh resolved to seize the opportunity, leveraging the power within him to progress toward unlocking the secrets of the universe.

Amidst a tapestry of complex emotions, Çarh continued to navigate the uncharted territories of his being in this surreal realm, where the boundaries between reality and dream blurred seamlessly. This transformative journey, straddling the realms of adventure and inner metamorphosis, was only just commencing. As Çarh delved deeper into the enigmatic landscapes of this newfound world, he embraced the ambiguity, poised at the intersection of reality and reverie, ready to unravel the profound mysteries that awaited him.

Beneath the unforgiving sun, Çarh cast a careful gaze upon the tree, its branches weaving shadows amidst the scintillating light. With a brief mental vibration, he discerned the identity of the tree—it was an apple tree. The fruits dangled enticingly before him, a spectacle of vibrant reds that instantly stirred the hunger within him, audibly protesting in the rumbling of his stomach.

The alluring scent of the apples wafted through the air with the gentle breeze, instigating a subtle conflict within Çarh. On one front, there was the visual temptation of these captivating fruits, while on the other, a deep-seated hunger and the vivid imagination of their splendid taste. The apples, resplendent in their beauty and freshness, presented Çarh with an inner struggle as he wrestled with the desire to resist devouring them.

After a prolonged contemplation, Çarh mustered the strength to exercise self-control. Achieving a delicate equilibrium between consciousness and desire, he felt a sense of triumph in that moment. Despite the dazzling allure of the apples, Çarh chose a path of restraint. He recognized that observing the fruits and nurturing his inner transformation through the utilization of his inner power held greater significance than indulging in their immediate consumption.

Despite the persistent desire for the apples, Çarh chose to exercise restraint, taking a deliberate step back to sit in the comforting shade of the tree. Battling the persistent pangs of hunger, he summoned his inner strength, transcending the immediate allure of the fruits, and redirected his focus towards a deeper understanding. Determined to nourish his inner world, Çarh decided to invest time in observation and introspection, recognizing this as a pivotal moment to discern his true needs and aspirations in this new world – a genuine victory marking the onset of profound inner transformation.

Seated in silent solitude with his contemplations, Çarh, shielding his eyes from the scorching heat, scrutinized the surroundings with care. Amidst the shifting shadows, gently swaying with the light breeze, he noticed peculiar shapes taking form in the sky – silhouettes resembling flying creatures. This revelation intrigued him, as he realised he had never encountered such species before.

Intrigued, Çarh followed the shadows, embarking on a journey of observation. The creatures, gracefully navigating the air, captured his attention with their elegant movements. The twists of their wings, the reptilian contours of their bodies, and the vibrant hues they displayed underscored the enchanting diversity of nature. It dawned on Çarh that these beings might originate from an unexplored corner of the universe, potentially representing a previously undiscovered species.

However, the enigmatic creatures that had captured Çarh's attention held a significance far beyond his initial observations. These beings were not contemporary wonders but remnants of a time long past, having faced extinction thousands of years ago. As Çarh's gaze followed the graceful movements of these creatures, he found himself embarking on a journey through the annals of evolutionary processes. Their existence served as a poignant reminder of the once-abundant richness of nature, and simultaneously, it instilled within Çarh a deeper reverence for the intricate tapestry of the environment surrounding humanity.

Fixating his eyes on these mysterious beings, Çarh allowed his imagination to traverse the corridors of time. Propelled back thousands of years, he stepped into an era where nature reigned supreme, and human development had not yet taken root. In the sky, the shadows of colossal creatures traversing the ancient forests seemed to sway like spectral dancers. Çarh pondered the true nature of these shadows, recognizing them as intricate threads woven into the cosmic tapestry of life. These species, evolving over generations only to vanish with the passage of time, symbolized the perpetual transformation inherent in the natural world.

This profound discovery prompted Çarh to reflect on humanity's intricate relationship with nature. Overflowing with admiration for the beauty and fragility of the natural world, he contemplated the implications of past species extinctions caused by human actions. In this moment, Çarh grappled with the understanding that the disruption of the natural balance, brought about by human activities, had led to the extinction of countless species in the past — a sobering realization that heightened his sense of responsibility toward preserving the delicate equilibrium of the environment.

Despite Çarh's attempts to blink his eyes and return to the familiar reality of the waking world, the dream persisted, cocooning him in an extraordinary experience. While logic dictated that it was merely a dream, the vividness of the moment left him suspended in a state of introspection, acknowledging the undeniable reality of his sensations and perceptions.

Within the dream, Çarh found himself on a journey that transcended the confines of time, delving into the depths of the past. This surreal experience, challenging the limits of human understanding, brought to his awareness the tenuous boundary between reality and the realms of imagination. The dream, with its enigmatic narrative, hinted at the possibility that dreams might serve as conduits, opening mysterious doors to deeper levels of human consciousness.

A growing conviction settled within Çarh — that this dream held messages meant specifically for him. Perhaps the events of the past, as unveiled in his dream, were guiding pathways shaping the future. The shadows of ancient beings served as poignant reminders of the imperative changes needed in humanity's relationship with nature.

As these contemplations swirled through Çarh's mind, a presence drew near from a distance. With each advancing step, the silhouette crystallized, revealing the figure of a woman. To Çarh's astonishment, the woman bore a strikingly familiar face – it was Deka.

Çarh's gaze fixated on the abrupt transformation in Deka's appearance, her sudden and unadorned presence raising profound questions about her existence. Amidst the hushed silence, an excited query escaped Çarh's lips, "Deka, where are we? What unfolded after the Sûr was blown?"

In response, Deka paused briefly before speaking with sincerity, "Çarh," she began, "With the resonance of the Sûr, the entirety of Earth was reset. The echoes of the past paved the way for a fresh start. You and I, together, will shape this new existence."

Deka's revelation sent waves of chaos through Çarh's mind. The narrative she presented transcended the boundaries of his understanding, introducing a reality that seemed almost inconceivable. How could the world be wiped clean? Were they the sole survivors in this new existence? The amalgamation of hope and concern rendered this new reality a complex tapestry.

In a state of astonishment, Çarh locked eyes with Deka. Her reassuring gaze and sincere words became a source of encouragement. The warmth and understanding emanating from Deka fortified Çarh, granting him the resilience to stride forward into this uncharted beginning, hand in hand with her.

Even though the imprints and recollections of the past had been wiped clean, Çarh now found himself burdened with the responsibility of shaping the course of the future. His thoughts wrestled in contradiction, navigating through a tumultuous sea of emotional fluctuations. In these moments of uncertainty, Deka's presence and elucidations served as a guiding beacon.

Deka continued, "In this reset world, we will embark on the journey of building a new life together – a life that unfolds before us as a blank canvas. Drawing wisdom from the mistakes of the past, our mission is to forge a society that reveres both nature and humanity. We shall strive to live in symbiotic harmony with the environment, emerging as a beacon of hope for the future of humanity."

As Çarh absorbed Deka's words, a myriad of questions welled up within him. Would he willingly embrace this new beginning, forsaking the echoes of the past? Despite the uncertainties shrouding the path ahead, he understood the imperative of mustering his courage and advancing hand in hand with Deka. Perhaps, within this reset world, lay the opportunity to rectify the errors of humanity and construct a more sustainable and enlightened future.

With a burgeoning sense of enthusiasm ignited by Deka's vision, Çarh fixed his gaze upon her. Beyond the transgressions of the past and the harm inflicted upon nature, this fresh start held the promise of hope. Together, they would join forces to unravel the intricacies of nature and stand as guardians, protecting its inherent value. The blank canvas of this reset world beckoned, inviting them to paint a narrative of redemption and renewal.

In the wake of Deka's explanations about the world's reset following the blowing of the Sûr, Çarh found his mind entangled in a web of internal questioning and lingering doubts. Accepting this truth proved to be a formidable challenge, and he voiced his uncertainties, asking, "Did I blow the Sûr, and then only you and I remained, with everyone else gone?"

In response to Çarh's searching gaze, Deka maintained a serene smile. She took a moment to acknowledge the complexity of emotions coursing within him before responding, "Çarh, we find ourselves in an unprecedented event without a clear understanding of how the world was reset. The Sûr was blown, erasing the traces of the past, and together, we embarked on a new beginning. Yes, as far as we know, only you and I remain – others have... disappeared."

As Deka's words permeated Çarh's consciousness, a tentative acceptance began to replace his lingering doubts. Embracing this new reality, teeming with unknowns and uncertainties, seemed to be their only viable option. There was no turning back now, and rather than dwelling on understanding the past, they stood at the threshold of an opportunity to explore and shape this unfamiliar world.

With an understanding gaze directed at Çarh, Deka approached him, reaching out to hold his hand. Feeling the warmth and reassurance in Deka's touch, Çarh sensed a flicker of clarity amidst the lingering uncertainties. The weight of the past had been lifted, replaced by the potential of an uncharted future.

Deka continued, her voice a steady anchor in the sea of uncertainty, "Our journey ahead may be filled with events that elude complete understanding, Çarh. However, in this moment, we stand at the threshold of a new beginning. Together, we have the power to shape the destiny of this world, to explore its mysteries, and to forge a path forward."

With a newfound resolve, Çarh looked into Deka's eyes. The unspoken understanding between them transcended the need for exhaustive explanations. In this reset world, they held the responsibility to navigate the unknown and build a future grounded in harmony and respect for the environment.

As they faced the horizon of this unexplored world, hand in hand, Çarh and Deka embraced the promise of the unknown, ready to unfold the chapters of a story that transcended time and resonated with the echoes of the Sûr. The world around them, born anew, awaited their touch, their decisions, and their shared commitment to crafting a narrative of redemption and renewal. Together, they embarked on a journey into the mysteries of this reset world, where every step forward carried the weight of limitless possibilities.

In the gentle embrace of this unexplored horizon, Deka turned to Çarh with a playful smile and asked,

"By the way, you didn't eat any apple, right?"

Çarh chuckled, admitting he hadn't, and Deka replied, "At least!" They shared a knowing smile, their hearts filled with the promise of a shared journey in a world reborn.

Murat Karagoz

Endnotes

[i] Tö'guarro: It means to be reborn in Heikwounnéls. It is a spell for witches to regain their powers.

[ii] Sögré: It means witch in Heikwounnéls.

[iii] Céwiaretza: It means the centre of magic in Heikwounnéls. It is also the name of the tree of life that controls magic. Its location is in the cold land.

[iv] Israfil, also spelled as Israfel, is an archangel in Islamic tradition. In Islamic belief, Israfil is responsible for blowing the trumpet to announce the Day of Judgment, signalling the end of the world. He is one of the four archangels in Islam, alongside Jibril (Gabriel), Mikail (Michael), and Azrael. Israfil's role in Islamic eschatology involves blowing the trumpet, also known as the Sûr, to herald the resurrection of the dead and the beginning of the Day of Judgment. The Quran makes a reference to this event in various verses. While there is limited detailed information about Israfil in Islamic scriptures, his significance lies in his role as a key figure in the apocalyptic events that mark the culmination of human history in Islamic belief.

[v] Long name for Elf. Elves (séenger) are divided into two types. Vital Elves (wöviaséenger) and Fate Elves (högreiséenger). Halte, the Elf's name, is one of the elves who usually rule the endings, known as the Last Elves (napréséenger).

[vi] Long name for Mab. Witches gain magical powers according to the day they were born. For this reason, witches are named according to the day of their birth and the element to which they were born. Mab, witch of 8 July (Tiaxöpra de Sreimtai), bound by water (il cuae), descendant of Pémadruiren.

[vii] Teigretexen: It means a backup witch. A backup witch is a person designated in case the full witch fails to fulfil her duties.

[viii] Heikwounnéls: A term referring to a language reportedly developed among witches in the 1600s. Initially designed to maintain the secrecy of spells, it is now used as the daily communication language among witches. Additionally, Kapalitza serves as the official language of the Ministry of Magic.

Murat Karagoz

---

^{ix} Neirkwöpia: It is the word used by witches to greet each other.

^x Buenuta: It means earth in Heikwounnéls.

^{xi} Tömté: It means a reflection which is a doppelganger of a Sögré that looks exactly like itself in Heikwounnéls.

^{xii} Duete: It means magic in Heikwounnéls.

^{xiii} Sögrétza: It means Coven refers to a group of witches who gather for ritualistic and magical purposes. The term is commonly used in the context of modern witchcraft and Wiccan practices. The size of a coven can vary, and its members may follow a specific tradition or set of beliefs within the broader umbrella of witchcraft. The concept of a coven has historical roots in medieval and early modern witchcraft trials, where it was often associated with accusations of secret gatherings and magical activities. Sögrétzas are affiliated with the ministry of witches known as Kapalitza.

^{xiv} Gate of the Shawl: In the Ottoman Empire, when the Sultan wanted to leave the Imperial Harem in disguise, he used the Horse Ramp, also known as the Great Embarkation. To leave the palace and mingle with his subjects, the Sultan would dress as a dervish or a merchant, leave through at the lower end of the Horse Ramp is the Gate of the Shawl, and ride down to the city. According to palace records, the sultans who used the ramp most frequently for this purpose were Murad IV, Ibrahim, Mustafa III, and Mahmud II.

^{xv} Harem: It refers to the private quarters of the sultan, where the women of the imperial family, including wives, concubines, female relatives, and servants, resided. The harem was a secluded and highly guarded area within the imperial palace, such as the Topkapi Palace in Istanbul. The Ottoman harem had its own administrative structure, and women within the harem played various roles, including managing household affairs, educating princes and princesses, and engaging in cultural and artistic activities.

^{xvi} Sultan Selim II: He was, also known as Selim II, the Sultan of the Ottoman Empire from 1566 to 1574. He was the son of Sultan Suleiman the Magnificent and Hurrem Sultan (also known as Roxelana). Selim II ascended to the throne after the death of his father in 1566.

[xvii] Sultan Murad IV: He was, also known as Murad IV, the Sultan of the Ottoman Empire from 1623 to 1640. He was born in 1612 and ascended to the throne at the age of 11 after the death of his father, Sultan Ahmed I. Given his young age at the time of his accession, his mother, Kösem Sultan, served as the regent until he came of age.

[xviii] Sultan Mehmed IV: He was, also known as Mehmed the Hunter, the Sultan of the Ottoman Empire from 1648 to 1687. He ascended to the throne at the age of seven following the deposition of his father, Sultan Ibrahim I, in 1648.

[xix] Ryöschaett: Born as a reaction to the Witch Hunts in medieval Europe during the 1500s, this ideology was developed by the leader of the time, Ryöscha Heikwounnestes. The ideology can be succinctly expressed as follows: Decisions made based on false prejudices not only result in the act of destruction by those seeking to eliminate realities within society but also lead to the perpetrators overlooking the damages inflicted on society; thus, these individuals cannot escape living with the pain caused by both destruction and the resulting harm to society.

[xx] Kapalitza: It is the name of the place where individuals accused of being witches were imprisoned in the 1500s. After Ryöscha Heikwounnestes' resistance, Kapalitza became a central location for the Sögré community to control magic and protect the Sögré. Over time, similar centres were established in many cities. Kapalitza is at the top of this entire system, and all controls are executed from there. Elves govern Kapalitza.